Bobby White

Bobby White

*Her Fight Against High Seas,
Drugs, and Kidnapping*

A Novel

Theodore L. Davis

iUniverse, Inc.
New York Bloomington

BOBBY WHITE
Her Fight Against High Seas, Drugs, and Kidnapping

iUniverse books may be ordered through booksellers or by contacting:

iUniverse
1663 Liberty Drive
Bloomington, IN 47403
www.iuniverse.com
1-800-Authors (1-800-288-4677)

ISBN: 978-1-4401-4961-0 (sc)
ISBN: 978-1-4401-4963-4 (dj)
ISBN: 978-1-4401-4962-7 (ebk)

Printed in the United States of America
iUniverse rev. date: 07/14/2009

For Lydia, Heidi and Andrea

About the Author

T. L. Davis sailed as a boy on Sebago Lake in Maine; it was the beginning of a lifelong passion with sailing. He has been published in a number of nautical magazines including the *Ocean Navigator* and *Living Aboard*. Ted is a full time artist: **www.schoonerridgeart.com**.

Preface

This novel is based on a true story. The story appeared, as a news item, in the *Boston Globe* back in the early 60's. It was so compelling, so horrific, it remained in my mind all these years. With the help of the Brunswick Writers Group and my friends listed below I am able to bring this story to you. All names and places have been changed and are not related to the true story in any form.

The writing of this book would not have been possible without the help of Janet K. Albright, an award-winning creative writer, and Jack Paquette, the author of *A Boy's Journey Through the Great Depression*, *Blowpipes*, and *A History of Owens-Illinois, Inc.*

Chapter One

October 1970

Daddy's coming to get me; I know it. I just know it. Boy, I wish I had some water. The calm sea lapped against the bright yellow, inflatable life raft. The high-level cirrocumulus clouds indicated unsettled weather ahead. *I hear something, if I could lift my head. Don't see anything. Maybe it's a helicopter, can't see anything.* The child collapsed back down on the floor of the dinghy. *Brad, don't put so much wood on the fire, you're burning my legs. Mom, Brad's burning my legs. Where's my father? He should be here by now. Water, I need some water. Mom, Brad is burning my legs. Tell him to stop making the fire so hot. That noise again. Can't lift my head . . . can't lift it. Dreaming, must be dreaming. Need something to cover my legs. Wish I had something to cover my legs they're burning up in this sun. I wish a boat would hurry up and find me. Daddy, Daddy.*

Aboard the *Argo Merchant* Manny had his 7X50 binoculars pointed off the port bow. "Hey, Pedro, do you see something out there?"

"Where, Man?" Pedro had the galley duty that day on the tramp steamer *Argo Merchant,* a small freighter with her best years behind her. The crew did not have the affection for the *Argo*

Merchant normally acquired by professional seamen. Constant breakdowns under way called for an innovative captain, a jack-of-all-trades, someone who could also return the ship to port. Captain Boucher was that type of man - somehow he always managed to get his ship back to port. This day the *Argo Merchant* was on her return run from Barbados, headed for St. Vincent.

"Over there, you banana. Here, take a look with these," Manny said as he handed Pedro his binoculars.

"All I see is water, Man. Hey, you want coffee?" Pedro adjusted his dark blue baseball cap, the one with the white "NY" letters on front. He had been a Yankees fan ever since his cousin caught a fly ball at Yankee Stadium.

"Gimme those glasses. Christ, if you hadn't dropped these suckers they wouldn't be giving off a double image." Manny's three-day stubble was turning gray in spots. He wore his dirty, captain-style hat backwards as he looked through his binoculars. Manny had the morning watch, filling in as third mate. The captain had confidence in Manny for he was conscientious in his work. The company would not pay for a third mate, so the captain improvised. He picked the brightest among the crew to stand watch.

"Hey, I'd swear there's something out there, maybe a raft." Manny banged his binoculars with his hand. The lens would not line up for a single image. "You think I should call the captain?"

"You better not call the captain, Man, he doesn't like coming up here for nothing." Pedro never stood quite straight; he preferred a forward lean. Pedro wore his shirtsleeves rolled up, showing off numerous tattoos. His light blue work shirt and bellbottom dungarees were the uniform of the working seaman.

"Maybe I should take her off autopilot, ease her over there, and have a closer look." Manny continued looking through his

7X50's as he adjusted each lens. The bridge of the *Argo Merchant* had fixed windows foreword, with little breeze coming in the two doors port and starboard. Standing watch on the bridge was not a comfortable experience. The first and second mate scheduled their watches for after the sun went down.

"You crazy, Man, that would really make the captain bullshit. Hey, you want coffee or not?" Pedro adjusted his baseball cap again.

"Yeah, you're right, Pedro, it's probably just a piece of driftwood, but it looks kind of yellow."

"Christ, you're seeing things. No one would be out here on a raft, Man, too many sharks," Pedro said.

"I don't know, Pedro, I think I should call the captain," Manny said as he held his glasses on the object.

"Yeah, you go ahead, Man, I think I'll just hang around, and watch the captain rip you up." Pedro had a big grin on his face.

"Captain, this is Manny on the bridge. I think maybe there's a raft or a small boat off to our port." His nervous voice cracked.

"Yeah, okay, Manny, I'll be there in a minute."

Again the child heard the sound of engines. She tried to look up, but her head would not lift. *Must be dreaming again, I can't tell if I'm dreaming or if it's real. Sounds like a ship. Maybe they'll give me water and then leave? Go back to their boat and tell the captain that it's just a kid that wants some water. Suppose they don't have any water?*

The captain came into the wheelhouse, gave a few coughs and fished in his shirt pocket for a cigarette. His lighter worked on the first try. The captain had a look around, then said, "Okay,

Manny, where's this thing you're looking at?" Manny pointed about three points off the port bow.

"Hand me my glasses, will you." Captain Boucher had been on the water most of his fifty-one years. He had served on a number of ships, from sailboats to oil tankers. Boucher earned his master's license at the age of thirty-one. He had a promising career, until he lost a ship.

Captain Boucher brought his 7X50's into focus on the object in question. A scowl came to his forehead. He lowered the binoculars, and then wiped the lenses with his handkerchief. For some time he was not sure what he was looking at. The captain had a faint smell of Jack Daniels on him. He needed a shave. "Manny, I have no idea what it is, but if it is a lifeboat and someone's in it? We better take a closer look. Pedro, stop adjusting your hat, I'm not going to bite you." Pedro adjusted his cap quite often when he was nervous.

"Okay, Manny, take her off auto and head over there. We got a few extra hours. Docking time is not till ten tomorrow. A closer look won't hurt I guess," the captain said as Manny set a new course toward the object. Small breezes flicked across the water, changing the color just enough to play hide and seek with whatever they were headed for. The captain kept his binoculars focused. He wore a clean white shirt with dark blue pants. The crew believed his fetish for a clean white shirt each day came from his naval academy days. He had a full stock of dark hair that would have given him a younger look if it were not for his wrinkles. The captain had a curt manner that kept the crew on their toes.

"It could be a rowboat that broke loose in that hurricane. Maybe just some old dinghy that got washed off the shore," Manny said. He was making an attempt to soften up the captain if it turned out to be nothing. The object got bigger; the color was yellow.

Captain Boucher moved out of the wheelhouse onto the port wing of the bridge to get a better look. "I think I see something in the raft, Manny," the captain said. Manny had handed the wheel to Pedro and followed the captain. "Here, take my glasses; I think yours are ready for the deep six," the captain said.

"Well, I'll be damned, you think he's dead? I don't see any movement," Manny said as he held the captain's binoculars on the object.

Mom, tell Brad not to make the fire so hot. He's burning my legs. Mommy, I need some water. Can I have a drink of water, pleeeeease? Mommy, can't you hear me? I want some water. I've got to have some waaateeer. The child slipped into unconsciousness.

Chapter Two

Maintenance on the *Argo Merchant* was kept to a minimum due to the lack of a full crew. The rust spots on her deck and bulkheads got larger each day. The crew referred to her as the "Old Rust Bucket."

"Manny, go down on deck and get a couple of guys, lower the Avon. Power over there and take a closer look. If the person's dead bring him back in the dinghy. We'll hoist the whole thing on board," the captain said as he ordered Pedro to cut the power. It would take about a mile before the freighter lost headway.

"Aye, Captain," said Manny as he headed down the ladder. Three men lowered the hard-bottom inflatable after the ship slowed down to a near stop. They scrambled down the ladder and jumped in wearing their bright orange life jackets. Manny hit the starter and the big outboard came to life. She kicked up a rooster tail as the bow of the Avon lifted and headed for the dinghy.

"Ease off on the power; we don't want to swamp it," one of the crew cautioned as they approached. They circled the dinghy once to see if it had a name. Coming up alongside slowly, one reached out and held onto the rubber raft. Inside the inflatable the men found a young child who was either asleep or dead.

No one wanted to be the first to touch the child. Finally the limp body was transferred to the hard-bottom boat. They looked the raft over for any signs of identification. They found nothing inside or out: no articles, water bottle or a hint as to where the raft came from. The seamen decided to let the air out of it, and let it sink.

The captain and Pedro stood on the bridge with mouths open as the unconscious body was lifted onto the small freighter. "Jesus Christ, what the hell is that kid doing out here?" In his thirty years on the water Captain Boucher had never encountered a castaway. He waited until the Avon was back on board, then said, "Pedro, take the helm, I'm going down on deck."

"What's the heading, Skipper?" Pedro asked.

"Go back to the original heading," the captain shouted over his shoulder as he made his way down the ladder. The men carried the body up to the second deck of the superstructure. "Take it easy, guys," Boucher cautioned. The *Argo Merchant* had two decks above the main deck. The second deck had four small cabins and two larger ones. The cabins were for the paying passengers. On this trip only the smaller cabins had been occupied. Now one of the larger cabins was being used as a temporary sickbay. On the upper deck level of the freighter was the bridge, the navigation room, and two cabins. The larger of the two was the captain's quarters, and the smaller room belonged to Mr. Jacques, the first mate.

"On the bunk, that's it," the captain gave close supervision. "Manny, get up to Mr. Jacques's cabin, tell him to get his ass down here. He knows some first aid, maybe he can help," the captain said.

"I think you'll need more than first aid, Captain," Manny said in all seriousness.

"Don't be a smart-ass, Manny. I think Jacques would make a good nurse. Well get going, don't stand there looking at the poor kid." The captain was not comfortable around sick people. As long as the child was breathing, he would turn the responsibility over to his first mate.

"Mr. Jacques. . . Mr. Jacques," Manny called as he knocked on the cabin door. "The captain wants you down in one of the passenger cabins right away."

"What the hell does he want now? Can't a guy get some sleep around here?" Gerry said as he pulled himself up from his bunk.

"We found a kid on a raft, half alive," Manny said, standing in the doorway. "Captain thinks you'd make a good nurse."

"What, somebody on a raft?" Jacques questioned.

"Yeah, don't think the kid's going to last till we get to port. He's in pretty bad shape," Manny said.

"Jesus Christ, what the hell is he doing out here on a raft?" Gerry was not slept out, and felt a little grumpy. He pulled his pants on, grabbed a shirt, looked in the mirror and said, "Shit."

As Gerry Jacques entered the cabin he saw the captain and two crew members looking down at the bunk. That's strange, he thought, why aren't they doing something?

"Where the hell have you been, Gerry, sleeping again?" the captain asked.

"Ah, come on, Captain, you know I've been on watch all night. Give me a break." Gerry's uncombed hair and wrinkled shirt gave him the appearance of being half awake.

"Look, Gerry, we plucked this kid off a life raft about ten minutes ago, looks in pretty tough shape. I'll radio ahead for an ambulance. If we can keep the kid alive until we get to port then we're off the hook. I don't want anybody dying on my ship, too much paperwork," the captain said.

"Sure, Captain, I'll try, but if the kid should croak before we get there, don't blame me. How's his vital signs?" The captain and two seamen moved back to give Mr. Jacques some room. The castaway looked half dead, and was badly sunburned on the face, arms, and legs. The lips were cracked, the face swollen, hair matted.

"That's for you to find out. I'll be up on the bridge if you need me. Gerry, do the best you can, okay?" Captain Boucher put his hand on Gerry's shoulder.

"Aye, Captain," Gerard Jacques said as the captain made for the door. Mr. Jacques had been sailing with Captain Boucher for three years now. They made a good team. Jacques had worked his way up the ladder, starting as an able-body seaman ten years ago. When he signed onto the *Argo Merchant* the captain took a liking to him, and loaned him the books required to take his tests for a first-mate rating. Gerry Jacques had trouble with celestial navigation, and felt he'd never get it. He was never good at math, but the captain showed him a few tricks, and one day it dawned on him. Mr. Jacques had a light complexion, thinning blond hair and blue eyes. He stood five feet eleven, with a strong build, and generally was in a good mood. He was the captain's right-hand man, and was looking forward to being captain of his own ship someday.

"Gotta get some water into the kid, but being unconscious, I don't know, he'll possibly drown if I just pour the water down his mouth." Gerry turned to one of the deckhands. "Al, go down to the galley, have the cook get you a clean squirt bottle with some fresh water in it. I'm going to see if I can squirt water into his mouth."

Al returned from the galley in a few minutes. "Cookie says he ain't got no clean squirt bottle."

"Oh, Christ, here, you stay with the kid. I'll go down and get one." As Gerry left the cabin the new passenger groaned. Gerry heard it, stopped in his tracks, and hollered back, "Keep talking, I'll be right back." When Gerry returned the survivor was mumbling.

"It's okay, kid, I'm just going to squirt a little water in your mouth, there, how's that?" One eye opened, then closed. Out came the tongue. Gerry squirted some more. "Get me a glass of water, quick. I think he's coming around." Gerry squirted more water into the mouth.

The child mumbled a few words. Gerry was unable to make them out. He noted the red legs, and then asked a few questions. The casualty was too weak to respond.

Manny came into the cabin to check on the new passenger. "Hi, Mr. Jacques, how's it going? Is the kid gonna make it?"

"Touch and go right now, Manny," Gerry replied. "Mumbled a few words, but I couldn't make them out. Would you go down to the galley, and get a bucket of ice, and a towel. I'm going to try to cool the legs down a bit," Jacques said.

"Okay, Mr. Jacques, but I wouldn't want to be in your shoes if this kid shits the bed."

Chapter Three

On the island of St. Vincent, Chief Inspector Dupree started his day with a visit to the governor's office. The governor had asked the inspector to drop by his office as soon as possible. On his way over to the governor's office the inspector thought he would have a look at his town. It was Friday morning in Kingstown, and driving by the bustling market he could smell the fresh vegetables, fruits, meats, and fish. The market was not yet full of shoppers. He drove past the department store on Bay Street, the duty-free shops and the liquor store. Kingstown is located in the southwestern part of the island on a mile-long swath of land hugging Kingstown Bay. Behind the town the inspector looked up at the green hills and ridges. The city is full of old-world charm, with its cobblestone streets. The twelve-block section is easily walked and perfect for browsing.

"Ah, Inspector Dupree, my dear friend, come in, come in. Have a seat. No, don't sit down. I have some business to discuss with you, but not here. Let's take a walk in the park," the governor said. He was a good-natured fellow when things were going his way.   His excess weight was more pronounced by his short stature. The governor always seemed to wear the same wrinkled seersucker suit along with his panama hat. He puffed as they walked along Victoria Park. Inspector Dupree thought his walk was more of a waddle.

Across from the park is the Catholic cathedral, St. Mary's. Built in 1823, it displays an amazing mixture of Moorish, Romanesque, and Georgian styles. The dark, volcanic-sand bricks are all twisted together and reminded the inspector of St Mark's Basilica. Then, on the other hand, St Mark's was beautiful when compared to this monstrosity.

"Inspector, I am pleased that you stopped by, for I have some troubling news. It seems that two men are here from the States, from one of those organizations that's always looking for trouble."

"Governor, I believe you must be speaking of the CIA, FBI, or perhaps the DEA," the inspector said.

"Yes, yes, that's the people, the two of them, down here asking questions about drugs. I don't like people coming to my island asking a lot of questions," the governor said. It was a bright, clear day with a slight ocean breeze, just right for a walk in the park. Pigeons followed the pair looking for a handout.

"I know, we're keeping an eye on them, Governor. They got off the plane yesterday," the inspector said. He was enjoying the day as he walked straight up, shoulders back, head high. He often thought of getting a riding crop to go along with his World War I style uniform. Inspector Dupree was almost good-looking. His receding hair line was graying at the temples, it gave the impression of someone in his late forties. He was very proud of the uniform that he had made by his favorite tailor.

"Yesterday? Are you watching them close? What do they want? Why haven't they come to my office?" The governor patted his face with his handkerchief.

"Not to be alarmed, Governor, they will come to your office

or mine today, I'm sure," Dupree replied, making an effort to calm the governor down. "Perhaps they have heard rumors."

"Rumors? Rumors? What rumors?" the governor asked.

"Rumors about drugs going through our island," the inspector said. He bought two ice creams as the governor headed for a park bench.

"Drug traffic . . . drug traffic. Now, I know we have some boys on the waterfront that may be involved in something, but drug traffic? No, no, not on my island," the governor said.

"Now, Governor, they do give a lot of money for your war chest. Also, I have heard that the people who rent them dockage and warehouse space are not complaining. Also, they have been very generous to the police department. We haven't asked a lot of questions." The inspector licked the sides of his ice cream cone to keep it from running down onto his hand.

"Alright, a few things are unloaded, repackaged, and shipped to somewhere. So what's the harm? Who gives these people from up north the right to come here, to my island, asking a lot of questions? I'd say it's up to you, Chief Inspector, to take care of this business." Melted ice cream dripped down onto the governor's shirt.

"If they are here on official business they must report to your office or mine," the inspector said as he sat down beside the governor. He took out his handkerchief and offered it to the governor. "There, ice cream on your shirt, sir."

"Please get me some water, my good fellow, we shall talk a little more," the governor said. He used the inspector's handkerchief to wipe his brow, then his shirt.

The inspector returned with a small bottle of water from the pushcart vendor. "Now, Governor, these men are not going to leave the island unless it appears that they have done their job. If they should happen to disappear, a dozen more agents would be down here to take their place."

"Do you have a plan, Inspector?" the governor asked.

"I shall have a talk with our importers. Perhaps they can come up with something. I am sure a satisfactory solution to this little problem can be found," the inspector said.

"I hope you're right, Inspector. We don't need people coming down here poking their noses in our business," the governor said.

"Not to worry, Governor," the inspector reassured. "The problem shall be taken care of in short order." *I wish I had some idea how to resolve the problem- must find a way.*

"Ah, my dear Inspector, you are my man. I have no doubt that you shall take care of things as always. Please, you and your lovely wife must come by some evening for dinner. Keep me informed of the progress you are making on this matter. We don't want this thing to get out of hand," the governor said.

"I will, Governor. I'll keep you posted," the inspector said.

The governor patted his head again. "If these people are down here just fishing that's one thing. If it's more than that the whole operation must be shut down. Do you understand me, Inspector?"

"Yes, Governor, it will be taken care of. Now if you will excuse me I must get back to the office. It's been a pleasure talking with you; please not to worry. The men from the States will be gone in a week or two, rest assured." Dupree stood, gave a slight bow, and said "Adieu, Governor."

The inspector's next stop was the Water Front Café which the importers were known to frequent. The Water Front Café was near the waterfront, or as near as one would care to be considering the hurricanes that hit the area every now and then.

The café was noted for its large breakfast servings of home-fried potatoes and eggs with squid and ketchup. The place did little to no business after the lunch hour. The building showed its age, the need of repairs was evident.

"Good morning, Carlos, or is it afternoon already? I'll have a cup of coffee, no menu, please. Tell me, is your boss here?" the inspector asked.

"Yeah, the owner is here, but he's no boss. I'm the boss. I run this place pretty good, no?" Carlos asked. He was serious about his work, and had an outgoing personality when around people of his own kind. It was hard to tell his age for his looks never changed over the years. His build was on the thin side compared with the owner of the café. The local joke was that the restaurant was referred to as Laurel and Hardy's. The café was a local hangout, a bit run-down at the heels, but not out of place in this section of town.

"Of course you do, Carlos, and you make great coffee. Look, go out back . . . tell that fat slob the inspector would like to see him?" Dupree sat down at one of the empty tables. Joseph Biello, the café's owner, was an American/Italian who came to the island eight or ten years ago and never left.

"Ah, Joseph," the inspector said. "How's it going? Come over here, sit down, have some of your fine coffee." The large man squeezed from behind the counter, and sat down with the inspector. Biello was pushing three hundred pounds on a five foot seven frame. Maybe not three hundred pounds, but he certainly looked like it. It was an effort for him to get from behind the bar.

"Never drink that mouth wash. Now, what the hell did I

do wrong this time? I know this is not a social call. What's the problem, my girls getting too fat for you?"

"No, Joseph, your girls are just fine. Nevertheless, you're correct, this is not a social call. I would like you to set up an appointment for me with the Kaiser."

"The Kaiser!" Joseph shouted with a surprised look.

"That's correct, my friend, the Kaiser," the inspector said.

"Hey, I don't talk to the Kaiser. Nobody talks to the Kaiser. Nobody I know of has even seen the Kaiser. What the hell do you want with the Kaiser?" Joseph signaled Carlos for a drink.

"Look, I know you have connections. I want you to set up a meeting with the Kaiser. I want to meet him here in your parking lot, in the later part of the evening. Say about ten o'clock. Now, you let the Kaiser pick the date and get back to me; here's my card. Call me at the office, don't leave a message. Speak directly to me, no one else, do you understand?" Dupree looked straight into Joseph's eyes to make his point.

"Okay, okay, I'll get you the appointment. What's in it for me?"

"Tell you what, you get me the appointment and I'll let you stay in business for another year. It won't be easy. I've had complaints from the Department of Health, the vice squad, even complaints about the bad food. I've also heard that some of your girls are doing drugs," the inspector said.

"Okay, Inspector, I get the point. You'll hear from me tomorrow. Don't forget to pay for the coffee on your way out." Joseph struggled to get up from the chair. He pulled himself behind the counter.

Carlos, cleaning the counter, watched the inspector leave. He called to Joseph, "That was the chief inspector. What the hell's he's doing down here? Slumming?" Joseph came out from the kitchen. "In case you haven't noticed, Carlos, I have some

20

important connections in this town. I got friends upstairs. How else do you think I keep the girls working?" Joseph said.

"I hear he owns a big house up on the hill. Yeah, and he's got servants, and a chauffeur that drives that big black car of his. Boy, some guys have it made. Someday I'm gonna get me a car like that," Carlos said.

"Yeah, yeah, what you gonna do, Carlos, rob a bank or something? Besides, I don't think he got all that stuff by being a cop. Christ, Carlos, cops don't make that kind of money," Joseph said.

"What you talking about? You think he's crooked or something? That guy never did nothing wrong in his life. Shit, he evens pays for his own coffee," Carlos said.

"Dream on, Carlos. I don't know where he gets his dough, but I know that cops don't make that kind of money."

Chapter Four

"Daddy, Daddy, I'm over here," the child called out. "Over here, I'm over here."

Manny had returned with the bucket of ice. Jacques wrapped the ice in a towel and applied it to the child's legs. Gerry Jacques stood over the youngster shaking his head. "Christ, I wish I could do more. I've cooled down his legs and squirted water in his mouth. There must be more I can do. Manny, go up on the bridge and ask the captain for the medical book. Maybe there is something in that book that can help me," Jacques said.

"Yeah sure, Mr. Jacques, right away," Manny said as he left the cabin in a hurry.

"Here, have some more water." Gerry squirted water into the child's mouth. He was relieved to hear the captain approach. "Oh hi, Captain, thanks for the medical book," Jacques said as he reached for the book.

"Yeah, I thought I'd see how the kid's doing. Any improvement?" Captain Boucher asked as he pushed his captain's hat back on his head.

BOBBY WHITE

"I'd say a little better, he's in and out of consciousness and talking a lot," Jacques said.

"Well, what's he saying?" the captain asked.

"Ah, mostly calling for his father. Maybe this book can help me. The problem, as I see it, is dehydration. I'd like to get more water into him, but I have no idea how to do it. I don't want to drown the kid," Jacques said.

"Well keep up the good work, Gerry, I'll check back later on. He looks better now than when we first brought him in. If you get tired use one of these bunks. I don't want the kid left alone. If you need anything have one of the crew bring it to you," Captain Boucher said.

"Aye, Captain, you got it. I'll be here until we reach port. Have a good evening." Gerry opened the book. "Let's see, dehydration, dehydration, where the hell is dehydration?" Gerry mumbled as he thumbed through the thick medical book. "Where the hell is dehydration? No wonder doctors spend a lifetime in school. They're trying to figure out how to read this damn book. Ah, here it is, dehydration." Gerry ran his finger down the page. "A lack of water causes dehydration. Shit, I know that. Let's see, they're talking about needles, and intravenous injection. Is there anything I can do now without needles?" Jacques questioned.

Al stopped by on his way to the galley to have a look at the patient. "How the hell can I get water into him without needles or intravenous injection?" Jacques asked. "They're talking here about some kind of fluid?"

"Hey, you're the doctor, not me. If I were you I would figure out something. The captain won't be too pleased if this kid doesn't make it to the hospital," Al said.

"Yeah, you're right, Al. That's why I'm reading this fucking book," Gerry said as he squirted water into the kid's mouth.

Hours later, Gerry awoke after having fallen asleep on a nearby bunk. He checked his watch: four in the morning. His next instinct was to get some coffee, but first he had to check on the kid.

"His legs have cooled down. His breathing is good and the pulse is getting better. I think he's going to make it. One tough kid I'd say. Now for some coffee."

Down in the galley the stale coffee smelled terrible. The coffee must have been made yesterday. Gerry dumped it down the sink. He then hunted for the filters. With a fresh cup of coffee Gerry climbed the ladder to the bridge where Al, the second mate, had the watch.

"Good morning, Al, how's it going?"

"Nothing happening up here, man, just water, water, and more water. A ship passed us about two hours ago. I gave her a holler on the VHF, but no comeback. I don't think anyone was on watch. Man, those big ships running without a watch on the bridge is crazy," Al said.

"Yeah, you're right, Al, there should be a law against it. As a matter of fact there is a law against it. Look at it this way, when you're up here in the middle of the night, everyone sleeps much better. I know I do," Jacques said.

"You're full of shit, Mister Jacques. Is that why you're up here at four in the morning?"

"As a matter of fact, Al, I'm up here to wake up a little. I've been up with that shipwrecked kid most of the night," Jacques said.

"How's he doing, man?" Al asked.

"He's doing much better now. I think he's going to make it. I just hope he hangs on till we get him to the hospital. Talk to you later."

When Gerry walked into sickbay he was startled to see the child awake. "Good morning, how ya doing?" the first mate asked.

"Where am I?"

"You are on a ship headed for St. Vincent," Jacques replied, pulling his chair up closer.

"Where's my father?" the survivor asked.

"We found you on a rubber dinghy yesterday. You were alone." Jacques sipped his coffee.

"My father is coming to get me. Does he know I'm here? Is he here on this ship?" Jacques's patient asked.

"No, not here yet, but I am sure he's coming." Jacques figured that a little white lie wouldn't hurt at this time. "How about a drink of water, or some soup?" he asked.

"I'm very thirsty, awful thirsty."

Jacques looked at the child's chapped lips. He held the glass up to the child's mouth. The castaway sipped, until his eyes closed. He was asleep again. Jacques removed the towel from under his chin, set the glass down, and scurried to the captain's cabin.

"Captain Boucher, Captain Boucher," Jacques said as he knocked on the captain's door.

"Yeah, I'm awake, what the hell is it," the captain said.

"The boy; he woke up, talked to me. He had a drink of water," Jacques said.

"Well, that's good news, Gerry. What's his name?" Boucher asked.

"Ah . . . his name?" Jacques questioned.

"Yeah, goddammit, what's the kid's name?"

"You're not going to believe this, but I forgot to ask," Jacques replied, looking down at the floor.

"Well Christ, Gerry, go down and ask him. I need this info for my log," Boucher said.

"Aye, Captain, but I can't ask him right now. He went back to sleep."

"Okay, Gerry, you stay with him, and when he awakes again, for God's sake get all the facts." The captain finished dressing, and reached for his sextant. The light was breaking on a cloudless day; the ship was back on schedule. They were due in port that morning so Mr. Jacques felt the urgency to get the information the captain wanted. Jacques made a detour on his return trip to the improvised sickbay.

"Hi, Tim, you got the galley duty this morning?" Jacques asked.

"Yeah, alcoholic cook got drunk again last night, asked me to fill in. Said he owed me one. Boy, some day I'm going to collect on all the ones he owes me." Tim was a man about forty-five, thin and round-shouldered. Jacques wondered if he ever changed his undershirt. The cigarette hanging out of his mouth looked permanent.

"Yeah, you do that, Tim. In the meantime, how about some eggs over easy? Oh, and some of that ham. Would you heat up some soup for the kid? If he comes around again, I would like to see if I can get some soup into him," Jacques said.

"Coming right up, Mister Jacques," Tim said.

The wind was picking up as Jacques made his way back to sickbay. The ship had a little roll to her. The waves were beginning to build. Jacques found something to read as he settled in for the day. He did not want to awaken his patient if he could help it. When the boy moved, Jacques dropped his book and leaned forward in his chair. The boy opened his eyes again, and Jacques offered him some water.

"What's your name?"

"Could I have another drink, please?" the child whispered, in a voice so weak that Gerry had to lean close.

"Yeah, sure, do you have a name? Could you tell me your name?" Jacques asked.

"Bobby."

"Bobby. That's a nice name. Here, open up, Bobby. Do you have a last name?"

"White, Bobby White," the patient replied.

"Here, take another sip. Would you like some soup? Here, take some soup. Did your ship go down in a storm, Bobby?" Jacques asked.

"Sailboat, I was on a sailboat and a hurricane came," Bobby said.

"But that storm was a week ago. You've been on that raft for a week?"

"I guess so. I'm not sure," Bobby said.

"How about another taste of soup, Bobby?" Jacques reached for the soup as Bobby made an attempt to sit up.

"Here, Bobby, don't get up. Open wide, that's a big boy."

"I'm not a boy. I'm a girl," Bobby said.

"Oh sorry, I thought, you know, 'Bobby'. I thought you were a boy," Jacques said.

"My name is Roberta, but everyone calls me Bobby."

"Here, Bobby, take some more soup." Jacques held the spoon up to Bobby's lips.

Before the soup was half gone, Bobby was asleep again. Gerry Jacques did not have much from her, a name and that was it. "Maybe her boat went down in the storm, and she had been the only one to get aboard the dinghy. Damn, I wish I had gotten the name of her boat. Maybe she'll wake up again in a few minutes. I can't go to the skipper with just her name. Christ, he's going to want to know the boat size. Who was on the boat? The destination and God knows what else. Come on, Bobby, wake up before the captain gets here," Jacques pleaded.

An hour later Bobby opened her eyes. "Is my father here yet?" she asked.

"Ah . . . no, Bobby, not yet, but we expect him soon. What was the name of your sailboat, Bobby?" Jacques asked.

"I don't know," Bobby said.

"Do you remember where you were sailing to?"

"No."

"And you were with your mother and father?" Jacques asked.

"I guess so, I don't remember," Bobby said in almost a whisper.

"What island were you sailing to, Bobby?" Gerry Jacques was pushing for all he could get.

"I don't remember," Bobby replied.

"And where is your sailboat now?" Gerry leaned closer.

"I don't know," Bobby said, her eyes starting to fill.

"Okay, okay, don't cry, it's going to be all right. Here, take some more soup." Gerry held the spoon up to her mouth again.

"Hey, he's awake. That's good news, Gerry," Captain Boucher said as he entered the cabin. He took off his hat and pulled up a chair beside Gerry. Bobby looked frightened. "What's your name, boy?" the captain asked.

"Her name is Bobby, Captain, she's a girl," Jacques injected.

"A girl, a girl," a wide-eyed captain said.

"Right, Captain, her name is Roberta, she goes by the name of Bobby."

"Bobby? That's it, just Bobby?" the captain asked.

"No." Bobby said, her voice being a little stronger.

"Her name is Bobby White, Captain." Gerry said.

The captain leaned forward in his chair. "What ship you from, Bobby?"

"She doesn't know her ship," Jacques said.

"Let her do the talking, Gerry," the captain ordered. When he moved forward in his chair Bobby started to cry. Because this made the captain uncomfortable he put his hat back on and got up from his chair. He then put his hand on Jacques's shoulder, "Okay, Gerry, I'll stay out of it. Just get me all the info, and bring it up to the bridge."

"Aye, Captain," Jacques said as he removed the captain's chair and placed it back by the other bunk.

It was seven in the morning when the *Argo Merchant* picked up the harbor pilot outside of Kingstown, St. Vincent. By the time the tugs eased the freighter into her berth, the ship's clock struck ten. Two men carried Bobby on a stretcher down the gangplank and into the waiting ambulance. Gerry Jacques thought it would be best that he stay with Bobby until she was checked into the hospital. He was expecting a bright, shiny ambulance with lots of lights. The vehicle was not bright; it needed a wash, and a little loving care.

"Hey, guys, this girl's very sick, she's not up to one of your wild rides to the hospital. Just take it easy, okay?" Jacques asked.

"Hey, mon, we always take it easy. On this island no one's in a hurry," the ambulance diver smiled. The driver's co-worker must have been along for the ride, for he was not interested in the patient.

"Thanks, guys. I'll be in back with the girl, so nice and easy, okay?"

"You got it, Captain," the driver said.

"Here, take my hand, Bobby, we're going to the hospital where they'll take good care of you. When your father shows up, I'll tell him where you are," Jacques said.   Bobby managed a half smile.

Chapter Five

Word of the shipwrecked girl reached Chief Inspector Dupree late that morning, about the time he was having his third cup of coffee. Inspector Dupree ran a tight ship with the help of Sheri, his indispensable office manager. She was a good-looking woman in her late twenties who ran the office with the help of two police officers that were ready for retirement. Sheri always dressed conservatively, with her long, dark hair tied back and up. The inspector always treated Sheri with the upmost respect. He often wondered if there was a wild side to this prim and proper feline. Never was there any indication of this, but still he could not help but wonder.

"Sheri, my first stop after lunch will be the hospital; I'm going to see where the shipwrecked girl came from. I haven't heard of any ship going down in that hurricane," the inspector said.

"Would you like me to check with the Coast Guard?" Sheri asked.

"Good idea, and also you could check with the Coast Guard in Miami." Sheri smiled at the inspector. The inspector and his driver, Sergeant Tanquay, walked out the back door of the old granite building. The Central Police Station was severely damaged by fire on October 26, 1866. Rebuilt in 1875 as a building for the militia, it was also used for ordnance, and as a battery. The parking area in the rear was large enough for several police cars. As the two entered the police car, the inspector said, "To the hospital, Sergeant, I've got to check on a castaway."

"Right you are, Inspector," the sergeant said as he drove the car out onto the street. Sergeant Tanquay was the inspector's official driver when it came to police business. Dupree's big, black limo was the family car, and his wife's primary transportation. He kept it out of sight as much as possible. Dupree had been looking for a chauffeur/bodyguard for the limo for some time. He felt it prudent that his wife be protected whenever she left the villa.

Dupree entered the hospital in good humor. "Good afternoon, nurse. I'm Inspector Dupree," he said as he removed his hat, stood tall and gave the nurse a slight bow.

"We know who you are, Inspector," the nurse said as her eyes sparkled. "I bet you're here to see the young girl that was brought in this morning." Several nurses gathered around the inspector.

Must be the uniform, Dupree thought, smoothing his jacket. "You are absolutely correct, my lovely. May I have her room number?"

"Sorry, doctor's orders, no visitors allowed today. The doctor wants her to have another day of rest before having visitors," the nurse said. She smiled as she reached for the ringing phone.

"See you tomorrow then, my lovely." Dupree clicked his heels and gave another slight bow. He loved playing the part of chief inspector. His favorite movie was *Casablanca*. He watched it several times a year, and knew every line.

Inspector Dupree's next stop was the waterfront where the *Argo Merchant* was docked. He wanted to have a chat with the captain. Sergeant Tanquay pulled up in front of the gangway; the inspector stepped out. Asking the driver to wait for him in the car, the inspector smoothed his jacket and started up the ramp.

"Hey, Manny, look who's coming up the gangway," Pedro said.

"Looks like the police, Pedro, you're in trouble now. I told ya not to put that weed in the cake mix," Manny said with a big grin on his face. Both Manny and Pedro had the boring task of scraping rust spots, and then applying a rust-protective base paint. This was an endless job so why hurry.

"Good morning, gentlemen, I'm Inspector Dupree of the St.Vincent Police Department. May I speak with your captain?" the inspector asked.

"Sure enough, Inspector, he's up on the bridge, follow me." Manny turned and climbed the ladder with the inspector right behind him. Dupree was having trouble keeping up. When they reached the bridge, the inspector was out of breath. As they entered the bridge the captain was huddled over his book work.

"What is it, Manny?" Captain Boucher asked as he looked up.

"Captain, the police are here. I think you're in trouble with the law."

"Thanks, Manny, now go below and keep painting. Good morning, officer, I'm Captain Boucher, what can I do for you?"

"Good morning, Captain, I'm Inspector Dupree of the St. Vincent Police Department. I'm looking into the matter of the young girl you picked up at sea." The inspector looked around the bridge, for this was a first for him.

"Well, Inspector, I can't tell you much. We found her floating in a rubber dinghy about here," the captain said as he pointed to a spot on the chart.

"And when was that, Captain?" the inspector asked.

"Yesterday, about ten in the morning. Manny, the seaman that brought you up here, spotted her first. He then called me to the bridge. We couldn't tell much from the distance, so I headed over to take a closer look. We were a little ahead of schedule so I figured why not take a closer look. Much to my surprise, we found this girl in the dinghy," the captain said.

"Did she give you any information, Captain?" asked Dupree.

"Yeah, she came around enough to give us her name. Also that she had been on a sailboat, sailing to somewhere," the captain said as he shrugged his shoulders.

"Hmm, interesting. Captain, did she give you the name of the sailboat?"

"Afraid not, Inspector, she gave us her name, Bobby White, and that's all I have."

"That's strange, I have no report of a sailboat going down in these parts, but then she could have been drifting for a week. Maybe her boat went down in the hurricane. Did the dinghy have a name on it?" the inspector asked.

"Nope, no name, Inspector, my boys checked it out, found nothing, so they let the air out of it," the captain said.

"Well, good enough, I'll get over to the Coast Guard and see if they got anything on a boat going down. Pleasure meeting you, Captain," Dupree said as he clicked his heels and nodded his head. As headed down the ladder, the thought crossed his mind that the ship needed a little sprucing up.

Two well-dressed men were waiting for Inspector Dupree when he returned to his office later that afternoon. The men introduced themselves as George Greenier and Mike Doyle. Said they worked for the CIA, and then asked the inspector if they could speak to him in his office. Dupree's office was decorated in the style of the late thirties. His desk was dark, stained oak, as were the two chairs in front of the desk. The oak book cabinets that once were bright yellow had turned dull over the years. Large windows behind his desk brightened the room. On the walls were pictures of past inspectors, police sergeants and several mayors. In front of the inspector's desk was a faded oriental rug. The inspector was comfortable with his office and refused all attempts to redecorate.

"Have a seat, gentlemen. What brings you to our island? Certainly it's not the sun and sand, not in those fine suits," Dupree said. Behind his polite exterior lurked a deep suspicion.

"That's correct, Inspector, we are here on business. I would like to get right to the point." Doyle, the older of the two men, seemed to be the one in charge.

"But, of course, you Americans are always in a hurry. No beating around the bush, get right to the point. That is what I like about you people: work, work, and more work," Dupree said.

"Well it's not as bad as that, Inspector. We do relax once in a while, after the job is done," Doyle replied with a grin.

The inspector surmised that Doyle was the hardnosed one. Greenier, who was younger, and more intense, appeared to be taking it all in. Mike Doyle fit well into what one would expect from a federal agent. A man in his early forties, short haircut, no extra weight on his body, dark suit and brown shoes. The bulge under his suit coat was obvious. George Greenier, in his late twenties, seemed to be imitating Doyle's dress and manner. His business suit gave the impression of being off the same rack as Doyle's. But Greenier did not lack the fashion style of his boss - he wore black shoes.

"May I see your credentials, gentlemen?" Both men laid their IDs and passports on the inspector's desk. One would think that the cameras were rolling, for Dupree took his time scrutinizing each document. "Your papers seem to be in order, gentlemen. What can I do for you?"

"Inspector Dupree, we've been sent down here to confirm rumors that have been circulating for some time now. We have heard, from a reliable source, that drugs are being channeled through your island," Doyle said. He wore his uncompromising detective face.

"Drugs . . . drugs on my island?" Dupree questioned.

"That's right, Inspector, these rumors have been flying around now for some time. My government has asked me to check it out," Doyle said.

"I see. Your government has asked, and what did our government say?" the inspector asked.

"This has all been arranged on the highest of diplomatic levels. Your prime minister, Sir James Mitchell, has agreed to this investigation," Doyle said. He was now acting cocky, as if he were the man in charge.

"I have no doubt of what you say, gentlemen, but until such time as I have confirmation, I must ask you not to conduct your investigation. Do I make myself clear?" Dupree asked.

"Inspector Dupree, my orders are to start immediately. If you have a problem with that, go see the prime minister," Doyle said.

"Fine, gentlemen, I shall see the prime minister. In the meantime you shall be our guests. I am sure you will find our jail quite comfortable," Dupree said.

Dupree reached for the intercom. "Sheri, would you be so kind to send in Sergeant Tanquay."

When the sergeant walked into his office the inspector said, "Ah, Sergeant, would you please escort our guests to the more comfortable units out back?" Sergeant Tanguay was well aware of the meaning of the inspector's reference.

"Gentlemen," Tanquay said as he opened the door and motioned with a sweep of the hand.

"What's the meaning of this?" Doyle asked.

"Just follow the sergeant, and do as you're told, or I shall have to use force," Dupree said, tapping his pencil on the desktop. Over the years the inspector had developed a look, a facial expression that made people move.

The two agents jumped to their feet, unable to speak for a moment. "You can't arrest us, we're federal agents. We're here on official business. Get your hands off me. I'll have your ass for this." Sergeant Tanquay left the room, and returned with three fellow officers. This persuaded the two agents that they had little option. The sergeant led the agents to clean but antiquated cells.

When Sergeant Tanquay returned to the inspector's office Dupree asked the sergeant to close the door behind him and said, "Sergeant, I have an appointment this evening, and I'll need you to drive my limo."

"Fine, Inspector, what time shall I pick you up?" Tanquay asked.

"This is related to an investigation I'm working on, it's strictly confidential. Do you understand?" Dupree asked.

"Certainly, Inspector," the sergeant said.

"Make it about nine thirty this evening, Sergeant, at my home. We won't be working long, only a couple of hours," Dupree said.

"Whatever it takes, Inspector, you know I never complain when it comes to overtime." Sergeant Tanguay had been on the force for eleven years. He was in his middle thirties, strong looks, intelligent. He loved his occupation and dedicated his life to police work. He was married but his wife was never seen in public with the sergeant. No one questioned him on this matter. At the annual softball game he always had an excuse for her absence. Some people in the department believed that the sergeant had his eye on the inspector's job.

As he sat alone in his office the inspector's mind was on the meeting. The words, 'no one I know has ever seen the Kaiser,' rang in his ears. *Backup should not be necessary, but then, one never knows.* The inspector sat at his desk. He kept tapping his pencil, deep in thought.

Chapter Six

The fifty-foot schooner *Vagus* was on a starboard tack, with a good southwest wind blowing at twelve knots. The schooner was heading south. On board were the White family: Jason, his wife Helen, called "Tess," and their two children, Brad and his younger sister, Bobby. They were enjoying an adventure of a lifetime. The only other member of the crew was Captain Mark Borman. The captain worked his schooner out of Boothbay Harbor, Maine, during the summer months. At the end of the summer season he sailed his boat south to the Windward Islands, in the Lesser Antilles, for winter chartering. This year he thought he would try his luck in Barbados. The White family was his pay/work crew. Jason, a dentist from Camden, Maine, was taking his first family vacation since starting his practice some years before. He and his family had boarded the charter boat in Bermuda for the second leg of Captain Borman's fall passage.

It was eleven o'clock in the morning. Jason and Tess were standing watch together. This was their third day out after leaving Bermuda. The family had fallen into the daily routine quickly. They were enjoying the sailing vacation of a lifetime.

"What a great day for sailing. This is just the kind of vacation

I've been dreaming about. It doesn't get any better than this," Jason remarked to Tess as they sat in the cockpit.

"Just a lovely vacation, Jay, we've had some great weather. I only hope it stays this way," Tess replied as she looked up at the fair-weather clouds.

"I wouldn't worry about the weather, sweetheart. The reports are fine for another couple of weeks as far as the weatherman can tell. What are the kids up to?" Jason asked.

"They are both forward on the deck catching up on some school reading," Tess said as she stood up to check on them.

"What's for lunch? I'm starved. This salt air sure gives a guy an appetite. I could eat a whale," Jason said as he checked his course. He made a small adjustment to the self-steering system.

"You're eating the poor captain out of his stores. Perhaps you should slow down, honey." Tess was stretched out on the port side of the cockpit with a book.

"Oh, I don't think so. The captain has done a good job in stocking his boat. That water-maker is a fine piece of equipment. Sure makes a lot of water," Jason said.

"Yes, a nice gadget as long as it keeps working," Tess said with a wrinkle on her forehead.

"The captain has made this cruise a number of times. He knows what it takes for a comfortable trip." Jason was captivated by the self-steering system and the straight track the schooner was keeping. "What say you hop down below and make us a few sandwiches," Jason asked.

"Okay, keep an eye on the kids." Tess made for the main hatch. She waved to Bobby, who happened to look up at that moment.

Down below Tess moved into the galley. She was starting to make lunch when the door to the captain's aft cabin opened.

Mark Borman entered the galley. The passage from Borman's aft quarters to the main cabin was through the galley. Sharing this area of the schooner was the mechanical room in the center of the boat, and on the starboard side, the head for the aft stateroom. The captain pushed past Tess in the tight quarters, holding onto Tess's hips as he squeezed by.

"You have a nice ass. Is that why they call you Tush?" Mark said with a grin.

"It's Tess and please, Captain, keep your hands to yourself. This is not the Love Boat." Tess's kitchen knife came down hard on the cutting board.

"Hey, sorry, I was out of line. No, really, I'm sorry. I lost my head, but you do have a cute ass," Borman said with a grin.

"Captain, perhaps you should go on deck, check the weather or something. I've got lunch to make." Tess was not as firm as she would have liked to have been. She had indicated to Jason, the other day, that she felt something was strange about the captain.

"You got it, Tess." Borman came on deck, joining Jason in the cockpit. Jay was smaller than the captain. Borman was six feet one and a little over two hundred pounds. He was in good physical condition for a man in his early fifties. Jason, on the other hand, was younger and smaller. He was about five-feet-ten tall, on the thin side.

"How's she going, Jason, she holding course?" Borman asked while checking the compass.

"Holding just fine, Skipper," Jason replied.

"Well, keep your eyes open. Let me know if anything changes." The captain looked around. He checked the set of the sails, the clouds, and the kids up forward.

"Tess is down below making us some lunch," Jason offered.

"Well, that's fine. Ask Tess to bring my lunch to my cabin.

I'm catching up on some paperwork," Borman said. "Keep up the good work."

"Aye, Captain," was Jason's nautical reply. Borman ducked his head and descended the ladder.

A few minutes later Tess came up from below with a stack of sandwiches. She called forward to Brad and Bobby, "Lunch time kids, come and get it." Brad and Bobby closed their books. They made their way aft to the cockpit, no need for a second call.

"Oh, Tess, Mark would like his lunch in his cabin," Jason called out, passing on the captain's request.

"Oh no, not me, I'm not his stewardess. Maybe he should wait on himself. After all, we're paying for this trip," Tess said, still smarting from the encounter in the galley.

"It's just a sandwich, Tess. He is not asking for much," Jason said.

"Well, you can bring his sandwich down then, if you think it's not much."

Jason reached for a sandwich. "Bobby, take the captain's lunch down to his cabin for me, will ya? Thanks. Oh, and bring up something to drink while you are down there." Jason could always count on Bobby, a bright girl with a lot of bounce, sand-colored hair, and azure eyes. Bobby was 12 years old. A good student who was not fond of the sea or sailing, she would have preferred to be back with her friends. She had missed the tryouts for the cheerleading squad, and also several band rehearsals. Her days were filled with writing to her friends, reading, and doing her schoolwork.

"What would you like to drink, Mom?" Bobby asked.

"Water is fine for me, Bobby," Tess replied.

"Fine for me too," said Jason, eating at the same time.

"I'll have a soda," Brad said in his sassy way.

"Get it yourself." Bobby was not about to wait on her brother.

Borman had been watching the weather faxes for some time. He did not like what he saw. A low-pressure area was forming off the coast of Africa. If it formed into a hurricane and headed his way, Mark and his schooner could be in trouble. He turned to the weather channel on his single sideband radio but found no mention of a hurricane. The forecast was for fair weather for the foreseeable future. Bobby knocked on the captain's door.

"Enter," Borman said without looking up.

"Your lunch, Captain Mark," Bobby said as she placed the plate down on the navigation table. She looked around at the captain's comfortable aft cabin. In the center of the cabin was a twin-size bed with built-in furniture on either side. On the starboard side, foreword, was the door to the head, and on the port side was the captain's navigation station. The door out of the aft cabin was port of center. Bobby started to back out.

"What's the hurry, Bobby? Sit down, I'll show you how this radio works," Borman said with a pleasant smile.

"Can't stay, I'm needed on deck." Bobby was picking up the salty language. She didn't want to miss out on the sandwiches, for Brad had a big appetite. Borman turned back to the weather fax machine. The paper came out in spurts. Borman watched the jerky motion closely.

This is not good. I don't like the looks of this at all. Borman shook his head.

Back on deck Tess asked Jason, "How much work did you agree to when you made your deal with Captain Borman?"

"Well, Mark said that we would not have that much work

to do. The winches are all power operated. He said that mostly we would be cooking and cleaning up after ourselves. Two meals a day and the lunches would be catch as catch can." Jason was enjoying his sandwich.

"That's it?" Tess asked.

"Well, he also mentioned that we would be standing regular watches along with him. He said that the three of us could stand four-hour watches each with eight hours off." Jay was being as forthright as the captain had been, not sugar coating it or understating the agreement. "The captain also said that most of the money we paid him would go for food and maintenance. He's not interested in making money on this passage. He just wants to get his boat down south." Jason stood up and looked around, scanning the horizon.

"Mommy, when are we going to get there?" Bobby asked.

"I'm not sure, Bobby, it's a six-day trip and we are about halfway there. Perhaps you should ask the captain," Tess replied.

"I don't understand that stuff. He points to a spot on the map, then talks of wind, currents, and stuff. I just want to know if we are making any progress."

"Chart, Bobby. It's a chart, not a map," Brad corrected.

"Okay, so he points to a chart, what's the difference?" Bobby asked.

Down below in the aft cabin Borman now heard weather information that worried him. After fine-tuning his single sideband radio to the weather channel, Bermuda came in clear. *Not good, not good at all. That low depression off the coast of Africa is moving west. Shit.*

In the main cabin the evening meal was being cleaned up. Dishes had been washed and were drying in the wood rack. Jason was going over the school assignments with Brad. Life on the schooner had taken on a regime that the family had fallen into with ease. Brad was asking his father how the watch schedule worked. A three-man crew can take a four-hour watch with eight hours off.

"Four-hour shifts aren't bad. The captain takes the most difficult watch, midnight to four in the morning," Jason said.

"Your watch starts at four in the morning, and then mom takes over at eight, right?" Brad said.

"That's right; she has been up for an hour or so and has made breakfast for the crew. Her watch is from eight till noon; she has a lot of company."

"I wish I could take a watch once in a while," Brad said as he turned the pages of one of his school books.

"I know you would like to stand regular watches, but for now you're a sub. Subs are important if someone wants a break, or gets sick or something like that."

"Yeah, I know, Dad." Brad was 14 years old and a freshman in high school. He liked baseball, played Little League. He was a successful pitcher. His team was the Red Sox, and hated the Yankees. "How come Captain Mark never takes his second watch?" Brad asked.

"Well, Brad, he sleeps all morning; in the afternoon when it's time for his watch he's busy with navigation and things. I'd rather he's doing his navigating. I don't mind filling in for him. Look at it this way, Brad, it gives you a chance to steer the schooner."

"How come Captain Mark takes the watch that's in the middle of the night?" Brad asked.

"Well, the captain told me that he likes to be on deck with just his boat, the wind and the stars. He also likes to shoot the stars when the dawn breaks, something about seeing the stars and the horizon at the same time," Jason said.

"Wow, I bet it's nice sailing a boat in the middle of the night. When I have my own boat, that's what I'm going to do, sail all night long."

"That's great, Brad, but for now all you have to do is your homework. Now let's get to it."

"Okay, Dad, tomorrow Captain Mark is going to show me how his radios work, and how he knows where we are on the ocean."

The following forenoon Brad knocked on the captain's door. He poked his head in half way and asked if the captain had time to show him his radios.

"Yeah sure, Brad, come on in. I was just listening to the BBC, catching up on world news," Borman said.

"Wow, these radios are super." Brad's eyes opened wide.

"Yeah, well, they do the trick, I guess."

"What does this radio do?" Brad pointed to the SSB that was fastened to the wall.

"That's my single sideband radio; also called a shortwave radio. It gives me my contact with the outside world. I can tune in to stations that give me the exact GMT, weather reports, also political news."

"What's GMT, Captain Mark?"

"Oh, that's the Greenwich Mean Time. You know, the time at the meridian, in Greenwich, England."

"Don't you mean Greenwich Meridian Time?"

"Yeah, that would be the logical conclusion. You see time varies, sometimes the world speeds up and then it slows down.

To have the same time, all the time, they have a mean time. You could call it the average time, got it?"

"I suppose so," Brad replied. "What does the other one do?" he asked.

"That's my ship to ship, or ship to shore radio, known as VHF. This radio has a limited range of twenty to twenty-five miles."

"I know what VHF is, very high frequency, right?" Brad said.

"You got it, kid," Borman said as he played with the knobs.

"That's not very far when you're on the ocean, is it, Captain?"

"No, but I use it for contacting other ships to confirm my position. It's a double check on my navigation. Also I can check the local time and date. Getting the date wrong really screws up the navigator. It throws all your calculations out the porthole." The captain liked talking about his equipment. Brad was taking it all in.

"That's cool, Captain Mark. Can you talk to people all over the world?" Brad asked.

"Well, yeah, if the weather conditions are right. I use Morse code, this little gadget right here. If the conditions are right my signal will bounce off the sky, and sometimes land in China or even further."

"Is it hard to learn Morse code, Captain Mark?" Brad asked.

"Not that hard, once you get the hang of it. If someone really wants to learn it, then I'm sure he can. A lot like talking in another language," Borman said.

"I'm going to own a boat someday. I'm going to sail all over the world, so I guess I'm going to have to learn all this stuff," Brad said with confidence.

"So you're going to be a sailor, huh?" Borman asked.

"Yep, just like you, Captain Mark."

Bobby was having her lunch in the cockpit and asking her mother once again, "Mom, when are we going to get there?" The cockpit on a fifty-foot schooner is large and comfortable. Forward and in the center of the cockpit is the main hatch. Just inside the hatch is the ladder down to the main cabin. Benches line the cockpit port and starboard. The benches had cushions with back rests. Aft in the cockpit is another large bench running from side to side, or athwart. In front of this bench was a large, mahogany steering wheel. The wheel was the captain's pride and joy. He had found it at a nautical junk store in Newport, Rhode Island. It replaced a smaller wheel of the same vintage.

"In two or three days if we don't get becalmed. Depends on the weather and how hard the wind blows," Tess answered.

"But, Mom, you say that every time I ask. We must be making some progress," Bobby whined.

"Tell you what, Bobby, I'll ask your father to check with the captain right after lunch."

"Okay, Mom. I think the captain likes you."

"Don't be silly, Bobby. I think the captain just likes women," Tess smiled.

"Is that why you're not going into the captain's cabin?" Bobby asked.

"I wouldn't want to be alone with him, if that's what you mean."

Chapter Seven

The inspector's black limo pulled into the parking lot of the Water Front Café. His right-hand man, Sergeant Tanquay, was at the wheel. Both men were out of uniform.

When Sergeant Tanquay shut off the engine Dupree felt the stillness. It was unnerving. As he sat in the back of his car his stomach growled. He hoped that Tanquay did not hear it. He wondered what the Kaiser looked liked, and would he be friendly. Or would he be course, businesslike and ill-mannered. The inspector hoped he would be businesslike and well-mannered. After what seemed like an hour, but was really only ten minutes, the rear door opened, and in stepped the man known as the Kaiser.

"Good evening, Inspector, it's a pleasure meeting you," the stranger said, holding out his hand. Dupree ordered the sergeant to drive up the New Sandy Bay road toward Georgetown. The inspector had not yet acknowledged his guest.

"Well, Inspector, to what do I owe the pleasure of your company?"

The inspector held his finger to his lips. Dupree said something about enjoying a drive along the ocean road. The inspector did not address his guest by name. He said very little as the big, black limo made its way along the winding road. When the vehicle came to the lighthouse the inspector told the sergeant to pull over. To his guest he suggested taking a walk along the beach.

The two men got out of the car, and headed toward a starlit beach. A fresh breeze lapped small waves onto the shore. The beaches on the windward side of the island are not recommended for swimming due to the breakers that crash furiously, after their long journey across the Atlantic. The long beach with its black sand made for a picturesque setting, which was lost on the Kaiser.

"Inspector, I'm a busy man with little time for joy riding, or romantic walks on the beach. So what's on your mind?" the Kaiser said pleasantly.

"Sir, we have two men down here from the States asking a lot of questions about your business." The inspector took a deep breath, noted the gulls hunting for food. The moon was slipping behind a cloud.

"I see, Inspector, and you want me to take care of these two men, right?" The Kaiser was a heavyset man with a shaved head. He was of average height, although seemed taller due to the fact that he stood ramrod straight. He looked a lot like a German general in civilian clothing.

"No, no, my good man, I wish it were that simple. These men are federal agents who must return to Washington, stating that their mission was accomplished. If they don't return in good health a dozen more just like them will be here doing more than just asking questions." The inspector watched the eyes, face and body language of the Kaiser.

"So what do you suggest, Inspector?" the Kaiser asked.

"We need someone to give them, someone who's believable as the head man, someone to take the fall. Do you have such a man?" the inspector said. The Kaiser did not answer for some time. He walked down the beach with his head down, deep in thought, with the inspector by his side. When the inspector started to say something the Kaiser held up his hand. A signal that, Dupree felt, the Kaiser was thinking and did not want to be interrupted. After what seemed like a long period the Kaiser came out of his trance.

"I believe you are right, Inspector, nevertheless finding the right man will not be easy. Not only must the man be believable as the head of the operation, he must also be dead when he turns himself in. You see, Inspector, 'dead men tell no tales'," the Kaiser said.

"I agree, Herr Kaiser, but how does a dead man turn himself in? Also the whole operation must be shut down for a while," the inspector said as he watched the Kaiser's eyes, waiting for his reaction.

"This will cost people a lot of money. People are not happy when they're losing money. Are you prepared to take the heat from these people?" the Kaiser asked.

"Herr Kaiser, I do not like the idea of shutting the operation down. No one here on the island will like the idea; however, I don't see we have much of a choice. If we don't shut down voluntarily, it will be shut down for us."

"You have a good point, Inspector. This requires some thought. How does a dead man turn himself in, and then convince the authorities that he's the head of a drug-export business?" the Kaiser asked, shaking his head.

"We must meet again, and soon," Dupree said. "The governor wants these men off his island as quickly as possible. Give me a call when you have something."

"I'll need your number," the Kaiser replied.

"On second thought, it's not safe for you to call me. I'll have to call you. We may have a leak somewhere. Rumors of your import/export business have reached all the way to Washington," the inspector said. Into the inspector's mind came the face of Mike Doyle saying that rumors have been circulating around Washington for some time.

"Yes, furthermore the leak could be right in your office," the Kaiser added with a frown. "Here, Inspector, my card. Use the phone number listed here. Dial the last four numbers backward. That, my friend, will get you to my private phone."

Dupree reached for the card. "Thank you, Herr Kaiser."

"Call me tomorrow evening, say about eight. I should have something for you by that time. Now, get me back to the city, this place is depressing," the Kaiser said as he headed for the limo.

Sergeant Tanquay drove up to the front entrance of the inspector's villa. Dupree said goodnight and thanked the sergeant. Tanquay then parked the car in the garage and mounted his Vespa. The cool night air in his face brought a smile to Sergeant Tanquay as he bent the Vespa around a turn. He pretended he was on a Harley.

Once inside his home the inspector removed his jacket and loosened his tie. He walked in his study, and settled down into the big leather chair with a worried look. *How did rumors of drug trafficking reach all the way to Washington, D.C.? Who would be spreading such rumors, and for what reason? Someone must feel that they are not getting their share of the business. I think I'll have a taste of brandy, and then see if I can get some sleep. This business is giving me gray hairs.*

Chapter Eight

"Mommy, Mommy, come look," Bobby said from the bow of the schooner. She was watching the dolphins ride the bow wave of the boat. "Mommy, dolphins, hurry. Oh, they're beautiful. Look at them swim, right in front of the boat, they must be a family." Tess and Bobby enjoyed watching the dolphins and the sea birds. This was a good indication that land was not that far away.

Brad was back in the cockpit talking with his father. He loved sailing, and was enjoying the trip. "Dad, how do you know when to reduce sail? Captain Mark can just come up here and tell us to take down this sail, or put up that sail, or do this, or do that. Like, how does he know what the schooner needs?" Brad asked.

"You see that instrument over there? Well that tells the angle of heel of the boat. If the boat is heeling too much then you reduce sail. If the wind has slacked off some and the boat is not heeling enough, then you add sail," Jason said as he checked the horizon.

"Wow, you sure know a lot about sailing, Dad. Did you have a boat when you were a kid?"

"Well yes, I did, as a matter of fact. I had a small boat known as a day-sailer. My father belonged to a yacht club. They had races for the kids every weekend during the summer. What a lot of fun. I even won a race or two," Jason said.

"How come we don't belong to a yacht club? Boy, that would be super, sailing around Penobscot Bay," Brad said.

"To tell the truth, Brad, I have been intending to get a sailboat, now that the business is well established."

"You are? You really are? What kind of a sailboat. How big, as big as this boat?" Brad asked.

"Slow down, Brad, I said that I was thinking about it, and no, not a boat as big as this one. I was thinking about something in the thirty to thirty-five-foot range, perhaps an older boat. Something we could work on. You know, a fixer upper," Jason said.

"Oh, that would be super, Dad. Wow, that would be great. Our own boat and then we could join a yacht club, right?" Brad said.

"Now keep this to yourself, Brad. I haven't mentioned it to your mother yet. I think she has an inkling what with all the sailing books and magazines I buy."

"Dad, could I handle the wheel again?" Brad asked.

"Sure, here, let me take her off the autopilot, now watch the compass. Don't let her get too far off course. That's it, just hold her steady. You're doing a good job. Hey, you're a natural sailor," Jason said.

In the aft cabin of his handsome schooner Borman had picked up the information he had been dreading. The low-pressure area had formed into a perfect circle. "God, I hope it's not a hurricane. Please, God, not a hurricane," the captain was perpetually talking to his radios.

A gentle southwest wind pushed puffy clouds across the sky. Tess had the morning watch, taking over from Jay. Jay was catching up on some small talk with his wife while he ate his breakfast. "Captain Mark tells me that Janis Joplin died," Jayson said.

"Who's Janis Joplin?" Tess asked.

"A rock star . . . did a lot of screaming. I understand she lived on the edge. Over-did the drug thing," Jayson said.

"That's a shame. By the way, did you ask the captain the date? Bobby wants to date her letters," Tess said while checking the horizon.

"Yeah, October 4, I think," Jayson replied.

"You think? Maybe you should ask him again," Tess said.

"No, I'm sure, October 4," Jason answered.

"How's your breakfast?" Tess asked.

"Very good, excellent as always, the salt air sure gives one an appetite," Jason said.

"What other news did the captain come up with?" Tess asked.

"Well, Nixon announced that he'll be pulling out 40,000 troops by Christmas," Jason said without looking up from his plate.

"That's good news. I always worry about those guys in Vietnam. Not a job I'd want," Tess said as she checked the compass. Her duty was to watch the compass and the horizon for other boats or ships. If there was a change in the wind speed or direction she was to call for help. Being on watch is mostly just that, keeping a watchful eye on all the indicators, then sounding the alert if anything changes. If the wind should pick up, heeling the boat excessively, the autopilot strains to keep the boat on course. This in turn uses excessive amounts of battery power. A balanced boat will use less current to run the autopilot. Captain Borman will run the diesel engine once or twice in a twenty-four hour period to top off the various batteries.

Borman was in his cabin keeping a close watch on the weather forecast. *Christ, this low-pressure area off the coast of Africa looks like a hurricane. The winds are moderate right now. Yeah, this is how those suckers start. By the time the storm moves across the Atlantic, the winds get faster and faster. The damn winds can build up to over 150 miles or more, a category five storm. Wouldn't that be just ducky? I hope this thing doesn't turn north, if it does it will put us right in the middle of it.*

Borman tracked the storm by plot positions he penciled in each hour. The weather fax spit out small-scale charts that covered all of the Atlantic. *If the weather people can get a handle on the direction this storm will take, maybe I'll be able to get this boat on the less dangerous side of the eye. I suppose I should keep the crew updated on this storm. It definitely could be heading our way. Just great, this is all I need, a goddamn hurricane. With a crew like this I may as well be on my own. On second thought, it's worse than being alone. Now I've got this family to look after.*

The weather channel was now focused on the developing storm, with updates every fifteen minutes. The weather fax showed a large low-pressure area moving west. Mark came up on deck to tell Jay that a hurricane might be headed their way. Jay was filling in for Borman's afternoon watch.

"Hi, Jay, how's she holding?" Borman asked.

"Holding well and sailing herself, staying the course. I hardly have to touch the wheel," Jason answered.

"Jay, I've got some news about the weather," Borman said as he looked at the set of the sails.

Jay turned to look at Mark and said, "What's up, Captain? Is this good weather going to hold until we get there?"

"Well, I'll tell ya, Jason, we may have a hurricane headed this way," Borman said as he fired up his Zippo. He took a long drag on his cigarette. Jason look stunned, frozen in place, mouth open.

"Hurricane . . . hurricane? The hurricane season is over. You said so yourself. What do you mean a hurricane? We can't have a hurricane now. Look at the sky, it's perfect," Jason said.

"Jason, old man, it's not for sure. She could be heading this way. I'm going to break out the sea anchor and attach it to one of my three-hundred-foot lines. Tell your family to secure all loose items below. I don't want anything flying around if the going gets rough."

"Yeah, sure, Captain, here, take the helm."

Down below, in the main cabin, Jason pulled his family together. He informed them of the impending storm. No one said a word at first, and then Bobby spoke up.

"Is it a bad hurricane? Are we in trouble? What are we supposed to do?" Bobby looked worried.

"The captain didn't say for sure that we'll get a hurricane. He just said that it's headed west, but if it turns north the way the last one did, then . . . ," Jason did not sound too convincing. "Look, guys, we have a very experienced captain. He knows how to handle his boat. I'm sure he has been through a lot of these storms before, so let's not panic. Let's just do what he tells us, and everything will be okay," Jay said, attempting to reassure his family.

Bobby was not convinced. Brad was thinking that the storm would be exciting, and Tess looked troubled. "Well, what does the captain say we should do?" Tess asked.

"The first thing we must do is to put everything away. The captain said he doesn't want to see things airborne if we do get hit with a storm. Put all the books away and all the pots and pans. Get everything under cover. Make sure that all doors and drawers are closed tight and locked. Get out the leeboards on all the bunks. I'll be back in a while," Jason said as he turned and climbed the ladder. The White family all started talking at once.

Up on deck nothing had changed. With clear blue skies and a steady southwest winds, things looked just fine. "Take over, will you, Jay? I'm going below to check on the storm." Jason took the wheel, gaving Borman a look as if to say, 'I hope you're kidding.'

Borman sat down at his navigational station. The small table had two radios secured to the bulkhead, one over the other. On the wall with the radios were the ship's clock, a barometer and a compass. On the navigation table were his charts, weather fax machine, plus other sundry materials for plotting and navigating. Borman's favorite navigation tool was his sextant, stored secured in a wooden box. Borman had a back-up sextant, one that he picked up in a pawn shop years ago. It was covered with a patina of green seating in a box lined with green felt when he found it. He sent it to Germany to have it refurbished by the manufacturer. When it was returned it was as good as new.

Back on deck, a few hours later, Jason looked at the sky with a cocked eyebrow. Off to the west thunderheads were forming. Jay turned on the autopilot and went below to inform Borman.

"Captain Mark, the storm is coming. The sky is black off to the west. You better come topside and have a look," Jason said, talking fast, trying to stay calm.

"Jason, I'll be up in a minute, hold your course," Borman said. He was listening to the weather station from Bermuda in addition to taking notes. Jason turned and hurried up the ladder. Back on deck, he checked the sky and did not like what he saw. The sky in the west was now black with flashes of lightning. The distant sound of thunder unnerved him.

"Okay, Jay, I'm here. Yeah, that's a storm all right. Go forward and ease the halyard on the main. I'm going to take in a reef. When this storm hits, we don't want a lot of sail up, so let's take a double reef," Borman said. Jay hooked himself up to the safety line and moved forward. Borman engaged the autopilot. He was right behind Jason. The two of them got the double reef in the mainsail, then headed for the foresail.

"Get up on the foremast and ease off on the halyard. I'm going to drop this sail completely!" Borman said with volume over the crashing of the sea.

"Good work, Jay. Now leave the club-footed jib as is, and take in the headsail all the way." Borman was all business as he prepared for the storm. "Well, Jason, the last fix I had she was about four hundred miles southeast by east. She seems to be following the same path as Donna did in September of 1960." Borman was not the type to understate the situation.

"Which way is southeast by east, Mark?" Jason yelled above the sea.

"That way, sailor," Borman pointed forward, off the port bow.

"But the storm is over there," Jason said, a trace of panic in his voice and a confused look on his face.

"Yep, that's a storm all right. You see, it's this way. That storm over there is just a thunderstorm, not the hurricane that I've been plotting," Borman said in a relaxed manner. "I've been through a number of thunderstorms. On the other hand, a hurricane, now that's another matter."

"Captain, you mean to tell me that there are two storms?" Jason raised his voice as the wind had picked up quite a bit.

"Yep, something like that," Borman said.

The thunderstorm hit hard: strong winds, steep waves, making a lot of noise. Tess, Brad and Bobby were down below, frightened. Jason and Borman were on deck holding the boat on a broad reach. Lightning flashed, thunder boomed, while the boat plowed ahead. Jason and Borman both had on their safety harnesses. They were tethered to the boat, wearing full foul-weather gear.

"What happens if one of the lighting bolts hits the boat?" Jason yelled at the captain.

"Not to worry, Jason me lad, we have a steel cable over the stern attached to the rigging. This line acts as a ground, the lightning should go right into the ocean," Borman said. The captain seemed a little too confident for Jay, who replied, "And what happens if the lightning does not go into the ocean?" Before Borman was able to answer, a cracking boom of thunder shook the boat, flashes of lightning everywhere. Jason headed for the rail. He said something about Europe. Green water washed over him as he crawled back to his seat next to the helm. Borman had a smile on his face as he looked at Jason.

Down below, Jason's family was in a panic. Bobby and Brad were each in a bunk. Tight fists grabbed the sides of their bunks. Tess was trying to hold onto her seat. A magazine, life jacket and other items were flying around the cabin. The job of tying all down had not been completed before the storm hit.

Tess moved to the main hatch. She yelled up, "Jason, are you okay? Is the boat okay?" No one answered; the storm was louder than Tess could holler. Back on deck the wind was howling, green water was filling the cockpit, draining out of the four large drainpipes. Water on the deck rushed aft and drained out the deck scuppers. There was a slight smile on Borman's lips. He was pleased with the way his boat was handling the storm. More thunder, sheets of rain, and lightning brightened a very dark afternoon.

Three hours after the storm hit, the worst of it seemed to be over. The thunder and lightning had moved off to the east. The heavy rain had slowed to a more comfortable downpour. The boat was holding her course, handling well.

"Go below, Jay, and see how your family is doing," Borman said without looking at him, his eyes focused on the sea, the set of the sails.

Life on board was returning to normal. Borman went back to his cabin. Tess and Bobby were cleaning up the mess below, while Brad and Jay were on watch.

"The seas are still awfully rough, Dad," Brad said as the schooner bounded along. The second reef had been shaken out of the mainsail, but the foresail was still down.

Borman poked his head out of the hatch to give Jay a new course to hold. "Jay, take a new heading, west by southwest."

"Captain, what the hell is that in degrees? You know this compass is in degrees." Jason was still a bit edgy from the storm, and tiring of Borman's nautical games.

"That would be about 236 degrees, call it 240, and hold that course. Got it?" Borman ducked back into his cabin mumbling to himself, *Landlubbers.*

Borman turned his attention to the upcoming storm. A well-formed circle of clouds was picking up speed. She was about halfway across the Atlantic, and heading for the Windward Islands. Mark plotted his dead reckoning position. He had not had a position fix since yesterday. He liked to plot his position by shooting the stars in the morning. This morning had been cloudy.

I hope this hurricane is not bending north. Reports from St. Vincent are not good. There could be a lot of damage to the Grenadines. If this sucker turns north we could be hit hard as it heads for Bermuda. We're three days' sail from Barbados, so let's hold this course and hope the storm keeps going west toward Jamaica.

Forward in the main cabin, Tess and Bobby were working at putting everything back in its place. "You were a brave girl during the storm. I was frightened out of my mind," Tess said.

"You were frightened? I thought I was going to die in my bunk. I was holding on so tight my hands got numb. I never want to go through that again; it was the pits," Bobby said.

"Just a few more days, Bobby, just hang in there," Tess said.

"I'll be glad when we're off this boat; I've had enough of Dad's adventure. Did you see how things were flying around?" Bobby waved her arms in the air. "I thought we were in a space-ship or something. I think Brad was scared too."

"I'm sure Brad was just as scared as the both of us were. We have a very good captain, he will have us off this boat just as soon as he can," said Tess reassuringly.

"And then can we fly straight back home?" Bobby asked.

"I don't see why not. Of course we must transfer at Miami, and then it's direct to Boston."

"I sure miss my friends." Bobby sat down with a dreamy look in her eyes.

"Well, you certainly will have a lot to tell them when you get back," Tess remarked. Bobby smiled at her mother.

Chapter Nine

Jason was on his second watch of the day from four in the afternoon to eight in the evening. The storm had passed. The light of the day had given way to a cloudy night. Brad and his father were in the cockpit talking about the storm.

"Boy, Dad, that was some storm, but I wasn't scared. Exciting at first, then I went to my bunk, and just hung on."

"I'll tell you, Brad, no fun up here on deck. The wind was howling, the waves were breaking on deck and I was seasick," Jason said.

"You were seasick, Dad?" Brad questioned.

"Well, just a bit. Pretty rough up here, no fun at all," Jason replied.

"Well, to tell the truth, I was a little seasick myself, but I just hung onto the bunk, and closed my eyes," Brad said.

"Brad, I got some bad news."

"What's that, Dad?"

"Keep this to yourself, got it?"

"Sure Dad, not a word to anyone, what's the secret?" Brad asked.

"The captain told me that the real storm will be coming in a day or two."

"What do you mean the real storm?" Brad asked.

"Keep your voice down. The captain said that the storm we just went through was not the hurricane but a thunderstorm. The hurricane may be still headed this way."

"Oh no, you mean we've got to go through another storm?"

"It looks that way, Brad. We're about three days' sail away from Barbados. If the storm turns north we'll be right in the middle of it. What we have to do is hope and pray the storm keeps going west," Jason said.

"Will that help us, Dad? I mean, if it keeps going west, will it miss us?"

"Uh-huh, that's what Captain Mark tells me," Jason said.

"Boy, I hope the storm keeps going west, Dad," Brad said.

A few stars were peeking through the clouds. Borman had his sextant out, trying to shoot three stars for a fix.

"How does he know which star to look for?" Brad asked in a whisper.

"I'm not sure, Brad, but he must have a book that tells him which stars will give him the best fix," Jay said, playing the part of the seasoned sailor. Tess was down in the galley getting supper ready. The odors were wafting up through the main hatch. Mark had completed his sights and had gone below to work out the boat's position.

"Dad, what if he gets it wrong? Would we be lost at sea?" Brad asked.

"No, Brad, the captain keeps a dead-reckoning position on the chart. That is, he has a mark on the chart where we were. To that he adds his speed and direction each hour or so. This will give him a good idea where we are now. And that is confirmed after he works out his sights," Jason said.

"It sounds awfully complicated for me. I just hope he knows what he's doing."

"Don't worry, Brad, he'll get us there okay. Captain Mark makes this trip every fall," Jason said.

The winds had died by evening; the schooner was becalmed. Borman sat down with Jay and Brad in the cockpit. "Jason, my friend, it looks like the best thing for us to do is just sit tight. If we turn the iron sail on and power until the wind picks up, we could be at Barbados just at the wrong time. If this storm turns north, the way the experts are predicting, it's best not to be near land. If we are in Bridgetown Harbor and a boat breaks loose, it will have a domino effect. All it takes is one big boat dragging her anchor. It could wipe out a bunch of other boats that are holding their ground," the captain said.

"How far are we from Barbados and Bridgetown Harbor, Captain?" Jay asked.

"About two and a half days, which means we have plenty of sea room if we stay where we are," Borman said.

"Well, Captain, you know best. I don't mind a few extra days at sea. However, I'm not sure about the ladies, so it's best not to say anything. Let's just sit here and see how this thing plays out," Jason said.

"You know, Jay, I envy you," the captain said.

"You envy me, with this beautiful boat? You're free as a breeze, with not a care in the world, and you envy me? That's rich," Jason said with a smile.

"Seriously, Jay, you have a beautiful wife, two nice kids, no worry about money. You know I had a beautiful wife once," Borman said.

"What happened, Captain?" Jason asked.

"Oh, that was years ago. You know how kids are. They think

the world owes them a living. I thought that all I had to do was sit back and watch the money roll in. She got tired of supporting me and left. It was my fault. She sure was beautiful. I still carry her picture," Borman said.

"You still carry her picture after all these years? How long ago was it, twenty – thirty years?" Jason asked.

"Yeah, thirty years ago, I still think of her. I think of what might have been. The family we could have had. Well, I screwed up. That's life. I'm going to take a little rest before my watch. If I should doze off just bang on the door," Borman said as he got up.

"Good enough, Captain. Brad, it's about time you hit the bunk too."

"Aw, do I have to?" Brad liked being with the men, talking shop.

"Get below, sailor, and hit the sack. That's an order," Jason said.

"Aye, aye, Captain," Brad replied with a mock salute.

In his aft cabin Borman sat down at his navigation station. Thoughts of his first wife led to thoughts of his second wife. Mark thought back four years to the time he purchased his schooner and the convenient way he came by the money.

"Mark, darling, let's go for a drive. It's a lovely day, too good a day to sit around the house." Judy, Borman's second wife, was ten years his junior, and always on the go.

"Yeah, sure, a drive in the country will do us good. What say we explore some of the back roads; take some roads we've never been on before?" Mark said. He was on dry land and hating it. He had come ashore, three years before, broke, after losing his boat along with all his possessions. A shore job would not pay him the money he needed to replace his boat. He would have to scrimp and save for ten years before he would be able to buy the boat he wanted. The fastest way to money, he figured, would be to marry money. Borman's second wife, as it turned out, did not have the money he was led to believe, Judy, on the other hand, was under the impression that Captain Mark Borman had the money. Now his problem was how to get the boat he was dreaming of. He had been following the boat market for some time. He had spoken to a few brokers. His long list of dream boats was now down to three and he was ready to act. All he needed was the money.

"There's a map out in the car. I'll go out and have a look at it while you get dressed," Borman said as he headed for the door.

"Okay, darling, I'll be out in a few minutes." Judy would dress up if she were going to the local dump; high heels and makeup, were always a must when leaving the house.

"Take your time," he called back over his shoulder. Borman was looking for a road he had been on a few weeks ago, a small backcountry road with little to no traffic. The road he was trying to find went over a small river. *Where the hell was I that day? Ah, here it is. Here's the river and the bridge.*

"All set, darling, I'm ready to go. Did you find what you were looking for?" Judy asked as she came bouncing out of the house.

"Yeah, I sure did, Judy. I found just the road for a beautiful country drive. Hop in," Mark said. Judy turned the car radio to her favorite station as they drove out of town and into the Maine countryside. As they passed farms and fields she put her seat back and relaxed, a contented smile on her face. She didn't notice Mark's grim look as he continually scanned his surroundings. *It's a shame that Judy is not a boat person. Too bad she hates the sea, sailing, foul-weather gear and the beautiful smell of a foul bilge.*

Now where's that bridge? It should be coming up any moment. Mark spoke the last two sentences aloud as they drove along.

"What bridge, honey?" Judy asked. She had the visor down and was touching up her makeup in the mirror.

"This bridge, sweetheart!" With that statement Borman yanked the wheel to the right. As the car started down the embankment, Borman opened his door and rolled out. The car continued down into the river. In a few minutes it was gone. Borman stood at the edge of the water watching the bubbles. He held his handkerchief to his left elbow that quickly turned red. An automobile had been some distance behind Borman. When the driver saw Borman go off the road, he stopped. A young man came running down the embankment.

"Christ, mister, you okay? I saw your car go off the road, you okay?"

"Yeah, I'm fine. Would you stop at the next house and call the police? I don't feel right about leaving," Borman said.

"Sure, mister, sure thing. Your arm is bleeding pretty bad, mister. Do you want an ambulance too?"

Borman convinced the boy that if he would just call the police all would be fine.

He went back to watching the bubbles and thinking of the insurance money. It would be more than enough for the boat he wanted. A faint smile crossed his face.

"Look, Officer, I must have dozed off for a second, about here, where the car went off the road. When the car hit the gravel, my wife screamed."

"Then what happened?" the officer asked.

"I slammed on the breaks but the car kept going," Borman said.

"Kept going? What happened to your brakes?" the officer asked.

"I don't know. It must have been the gravel. The car just skidded on the gravel," Borman explained.

"Okay, so then what happened?" the officer asked.

"I opened my door and rolled out of the car. The car careened down the embankment into the river. My poor wife never had a chance. I ran after the car, but I was too late. The car was already in the water, and I'm not a swimmer," Borman said in his convincing manner.

"How long did it take for the car to sink?" the officer inquired.

"The windows were open, so she filled right away. Sank in a few minutes, I looked down and saw nothing but bubbles. I should've jumped in the water after her. Maybe I could have done something to save her." Borman, with a few bruises, and a trickle of blood running down his left forearm, stood staring at the water. "The car sank fast, nothing but bubbles, nothing but bubbles. I wish I could have done something." The officer was sympathetic.

The schooner had been becalmed now for almost twenty-four hours. The big storm had moved a lot closer. Borman had been keeping a close track on this fast-moving storm. The wind speeds were in excess of a hundred and ten miles per hour. *Christ, it never rains but it pours. Let's see, with its present rate of speed we should start feeling the wind any time now. God, the center of this storm will be hitting Barbados tomorrow. Well, it's too late now to get on the west side of the storm.* Borman poured himself a couple of fingers of scotch. He then went forward to the galley for some ice cubes. *Riding this storm out on the sea anchor will be better than in the harbor at Barbados. The boats in that harbor are gonna get slammed. Well there's nothing we can do but secure all equipment and sails, hope for the best. Christ, I wish I had a real crew with me. If money weren't so tight I would've hired an able-bodied seaman for this cruise. Well too late for wishing now. Shit!*

Chapter Ten

Into the Water Front Café walked a thin man. It was generally known that Jesus was somehow connected to the Kaiser. This mysterious person was avoided by most. He was not a pleasant man to look at. The type of person that kept no company as far as anyone could tell.

He greeted Carlos, and then asked for the big man. Jesus took a seat in the corner of the restaurant and waited. Joseph Biello squeezed from behind the counter and sat down with Jesus.

"What's up, Joseph?" Jesus asked.

"Something's up, but first did ya bring the snowflakes? My girls don't work without the snow," Joseph said.

"What do you mean 'something's up'?" Jesus asked again, his eyes darting. He was always in a hurry, never saying more than was necessary. His trademark was the toothpick. It never left his mouth.

"First, we do business, then we talk," Joseph said as he wiped the sweat off his face with his oversize handkerchief.

"Here, take this, gimme the bills." Jesus handed Joseph a small package.

"What the hell is this? You shortin' me again, you son of a bitch." Joseph was as strong as a linebacker. Jesus, on the other hand, was no more than 130 pounds in wet clothes. A thin-faced person with boney hands, Jesus had developed a nasty look to offset his small stature. Most people stayed clear of him based on rumors of his quick temper and long knife.

"Hey, that's the right count. I don't package this stuff. That's done by the Kaiser and his packers back at the warehouse," Jesus said.

"Yeah, yeah, but it feels short. It looks short. I'll weigh it myself, later," Joseph said as he stuffed the package in his pocket.

"Yeah, you weigh the stuff. Now, tell me what you smell," Jesus snarled.

"It's probably nothing, but the chief inspector was here the other day asking me to set up a meet with the Kaiser. Now, that's not a big deal except for the fact that there are a couple of dudes down here from the States asking some dumb questions. They look like DEA men to me," Joseph said.

"Those fucking narco jerks. I'd like to blow them into little pieces. What kind of questions are they asking?" Jesus asked while chomping on a toothpick.

"That's for you to find out, my man. I'm in the restaurant business, not the info business," Joseph said.

"You can call it the restaurant business but most people I know call it the pimping business." Jesus grinned, amused at his own humor.

"Get the fuck out of here. I've got to weigh this shit." Joseph squeezed back behind the counter as Jesus left with a worried look on his face.

The inspector drove down to the warehouse on the waterfront, the one that was being used by the drug importers. He wanted to take a look at the operation. See what was available for a giveaway, if need be. He parked his car on the side of the building, had a look around. The waterfront warehouses were one-story buildings made of brick. The brick had come to the island as ballast many years ago. He decided to go inside. The warehouse was large, empty, and dark. The inspector paused for a moment. He thought he heard something. Seeing nothing, he walked slowly, waiting for his eyes to adjust to the murky interior. Again he thought he heard something. Now he was feeling uncomfortable. He could feel his heart picking up speed. He unsnapped the cover on his revolver. Again, hearing a noise, he turned around quickly and three feet away from his face was the thin man, Jesus. The inspector was startled; he tried not to let it show.

"And who might you be," the inspector asked with as much composure as he could muster. Jesus' dark eyes penetrated through the darkness. The toothpick stuck out of the corner of his mouth.

"Johnny DeJesus, better known as just plain Jesus, what's your problem?"

"Nothing serious, just a minor building violation," the inspector said.

"Now they're sending a cop down here to do the work of a building inspector? This island's going to the crapper." Jesus was not the type of person that one would care to meet in a dark, empty warehouse, even if you were the police chief.

"I've had a complaint about the sprinkler system. I was told it's inoperative. What can you tell me about the sprinkler system?" This was a terrible excuse for being in the warehouse but the inspector was caught off guard. Jesus' nasty expression was now visible as the inspector's eyes adjusted to the lack of light. He kept his right hand close to his gun.

"Hey, what do I know about sprinkler systems? Why don't you talk to the owner?" Jesus said.

"And who might that be?" the inspector asked.

"Whoever pays the taxes on this fucking building," Jesus said.

"Thank you for your help, my good man. I shall contact the owner. Good day," Dupree said as he walked toward the door. He reached for his automobile door with a shaking hand. He slammed the police car in first and squealed the tires as he left. Dupree was upset with himself for the lack of composure under pressure. For some time he has been feeling the need for a long vacation.

At the appointed time Inspector Dupree made his phone call to the Kaiser. The Kaiser said that he had given this problem considerable thought, and he had come up with a plan. He asked for a meeting later tonight. They both agreed to meet at the same beach. The inspector heard the phone click. He looked forward to hearing the Kaiser's plan.

That evening the inspector arrived before the Kaiser. This time Dupree was alone. He could not afford arousing the suspicion of his driver, Sergeant Tanquay. Clouds made of a dark night at the beach. As the inspector waited in his car, he went over a number of possibilities, but none of them seemed realistic. *How can a dead man turn himself in, and then convince the CIA men that he heads up a drug operation? Well, if the Kaiser has the answer to this problem I'd certainly be impressed.*

The Kaiser arrived twenty minutes late. By this time the inspector was walking the beach. He thought he might as well enjoy the ocean, or as much as he could see while he waited. When the Kaiser caught up to Dupree, he was halfway down the beach. The Kaiser apologized for being late. He could be a man of charm and grace when required. This night his disposition was pleasant. The Kaiser asked as to the inspector's health, his wife, and then presented his plan. Unfortunately he put forth a risky plan, risky for the inspector, that is. Dupree was boxed in; he had to agree. He nodded his head as he listened to the details. The inspector listened intently and asked a number of questions. That feeling was back in his stomach, the feeling that he was getting too old for this kind of work. The feeling that he would like to end this second income, after all, he had enough money. Well, enough to live comfortably on this island anyway.

The inspector sat in his car after the Kaiser left. He was going over the plan again and again. Dupree was starting to feel miserable about the fact his part of the plan required his personal involvement. *This is a precarious plan at best. Hopefully I won't get a bullet in the head. Christ, I wish I were ten years younger. Look at my hands; they're shaking. If I had the guts I would shut the whole operation down, and kick the Kaiser off the island.* This thought had been going through the inspector's mind several times a day. He knew that he and the governor were too deeply involved. Bringing down a powerful man such as the Kaiser would also bring himself down, maybe even six feet under.

Dupree's mind was racing as he drove home. He was not about to give up his home, his family, and his position. *No not now, not when I've worked so hard to get here. I've got to go along with the Kaiser and hope for the best. Damn. My leather chair, some good music, and a little brandy should calm me down.*

Chapter Eleven

"This storm will be here some time tomorrow. The winds have already started to pick up. Let's get ready for it, guys," Borman said to Jason and Brad. He had his captain's hat on, squared away, barking orders at his crew while his feet were planted behind the spoke wheel. He was in his glory as the schooner bounded along. "Now she's picking up her skirt!" Borman shouted to the wind.

"Jason, take Brad forward, lower the foresail and secure it to the boom. Get a line out of the lazarette and tie her down good. When you're done with that, take another reef in the main." His hat was pulled down tight, jaw set, shoulder-length, dirty-blond hair flying in the wind. He was wearing his old pea coat, the one his father had worn while he was taking Liberty ships across the Atlantic during the big one, World War II. When the seas start flying over the rail, Borman would change to his foul-weather gear. "Come on, you guys, get that sail secured. When you're done with that, wrap a line around the headsail. I don't want that damn thing flying loose when this storm hits. The club footed jib is okay for now."

Jay and Brad went forward to work on the foresail. Brad turned to his father and said, "Hey, Dad, this guy is ordering us around like a football coach. I thought we were the guests on this boat."

"Hang in there, Brad, we're only two days or so away from port, so for now we'd better do as he tells us. We've got no choice if we want to survive this storm. We've got to put our trust in him. He's a good captain; he'll get us through okay," Jason said. He and Brad had secured the foresail, and now were warping a line around the big head sail. The problem was they couldn't get the line high enough. The seas were starting to build, the deck was moving up and down, green water was starting to come over the bow.

"Get that goddamn line up there, higher. Get the kid up on your shoulders and secure that sail. Do it now, before things start getting rough," Borman shouted. Jason pushed Brad up the forestay with one hand, with the other hung onto the stay. The headsail was furled around the stay. The new rig had been installed in Maine just before the start of the summer season.

Brad was hanging on with one arm, pushing the line up the stay with the other. He tied the line and then tried to wrap it around the sail. Instead the line wrapped around Jay's body and Brad's arm and legs. The whole thing was a mess. Borman engaged the autopilot, made his way forward.

"You guys are making a fucking mess up here. Get out of the way!" Borman began to unwrap the male half of the White family. Jason held on while being washed by waves breaking over the bow. An extra-large wave came over the bow and washed Jason aft. Brad came sliding down the stay, banging Borman on the head. Borman gave out a yell as Brad somersaulted over him and ended up on his father. Borman barked at Jason, "Get aft and grab that wheel, we're off course. I'll finish up here."

Jason made his way back to the wheel, fighting to stay on

his feet. Dripping with water, he grabbed the wheel, released the autopilot, and got the big schooner back on course.

Borman, having completed the work forward, pushed Jason away from the wheel and resumed his position. "You guys get below and get your foul-weather gear on, these seas are building faster than I expected," Borman said as he made a course correction.

Down below Jay and Brad found Tess and Bobby with their life jackets on, packing an emergency bag. "Dad, we're packing this bag in case we have to abandon ship," Bobby said in a high state of excitement, moving fast, speaking in a high, squeaky voice.

"Now take it easy, Bobby. Things are going to be just fine. Already we have lashed the foresail, reduced the mainsail and lashed the headsail. Captain Mark knows just what to do. It may get a little rough down here, but just hold on. This is a strong boat, nothing to worry about," Jason said.

Borman called down the main hatch, "Get up here, you guys, I need that storm jib up in a hurry." Jason and Brad scrambled to get their foul-weather gear on and rushed up the ladder. "Get the storm jib out of the starboard locker and hank it on the jib stay. You know, the stay that carries the club footed jib. Shake a leg, you guys, we don't have all day," the captain growled.

Jason and Brad had been working to get the boat ready for the storm the better part of the morning and were just about worn out. Working hard on a moving deck is rough on experienced seamen, but on this crew exhausting. Brad was falling down every other step. Part of the problem was that his legs were forever getting tangled around his safety line that was attached to the jack stay. The storm jib had been located and the two of them were making their way forward with the sail. Borman was watching their progress, wishing he had a couple of seamen on deck.

"Get that sail hanked on and bring the sheets back to the wench. No, not two sheets on one wench, you lubbers. And don't foul the shrouds. Keep the sheets clear, Christ." Borman shouted.

With work on the storm jib completed, the jib drawing, the boat was balanced. The man and boy dragged themselves panting back to the cockpit. It was a brutal morning for Jason White and his son.

The seas were building; the wind had increased to forty knots. The schooner was working under a triple-reefed mainsail and a storm jib. "If the wind gets higher, we'll drop the main and secure it to the boom. After that, the storm jib will be dropped and I'll cast off the sea anchor." Borman was contemplating his next move but did not believe his crew was up to the task. Both Jason and Brad had the onset of seasickness. Jay gave out a loud burp, while Brad yawned. Next it was Brad's turn to burp while Jay yawned.

"Jason, take the wheel. I'm going forward to get the sea anchor ready. Might be needed sooner than expected, and stay away from those big breakers while I'm up on deck," Borman barked.

Down below Tess and Bobby had secured everything they could possibly think of. Bobby was not feeling well, and had taken to her bunk. Tess was putting on a brave face for the sake of the family, but she would have given anything to be back on dry land - any dry land.

"Mom, have you ever been in a hurricane before?" Bobby asked.

"A few, Bobby, but in Maine we only would get the tail end of the storms."

"Do you think this boat is strong enough for a hurricane?" Bobby asked.

"Of course it is, honey. This schooner can take anything that old storm can give. Captain Mark, Dad and Brad have done a good job getting the boat ready, so don't worry about a thing," Tess said.

"Yeah sure, Mom, 'not to worry about a thing', I wish I could believe that," Bobby said.

"If we do get into trouble, we can contact the Coast Guard. They'll send a plane out here in no time. We have two dinghies that can hold everybody. I'm sure things will be fine. Don't worry," Tess reassured.

"Okay, Mom, but if you don't mind, I think I will worry just a bit," Bobby said.

The motion in the main cabin is best endured by lying down. The up and down, along with the forward motion, confuses the balancing mechanism within the inner ear. This confusion causes seasickness, for it feels a lot like being in an elevator that drops fast, leaving your stomach on the top floor. The last person to be overcome by seasickness is the helmsman, because his eyes are on the horizon, a point of reference that keeps the balancing mechanism somewhat satisfied. But there are some people who never get seasick, such as Captain Mark Borman.

Down the main hatch came two bodies, looking like cats that had fallen into the toilet bowl. They stumbled into the main cabin, headed for their bunks. They laid there with foul-weather gear still on and sea boots dripping water.

Tess made her way over to Jason. "Do you want something to eat, dear?"

"Not right now, sweetheart, my stomach is a little upset," Jason replied.

"How about you, Brad, would you like something to eat?" Tess asked.

"No thanks, Mom, I don't feel so good either," Brad said.

Borman had been at the wheel the better part of the day. With the winds blowing a steady forty-five knots and gusting up to fifty-five, it was time to take down sail and set the sea anchor. Mark gave a yell from above the main hatch: "All hands on deck. Get up here, you deck apes, it's time to take down all sail." Everyone heard 'all hands on deck'; the rest of it was blown away by the heavy winds. Jay and Brad pulled themselves from their bunks and headed up the ladder.

"What the hell does he want this time," Jason said to the ladder, as he and Brad willed their bodies up on deck.

"Brad, you take the wheel. Your father and I are going to take down all sail. Now look, hold the boat up as close to the wind as you can. On second thought . . ., Jay, you take the wheel and hold her up tight to the wind. I've got the power on, so when the sails come down she'll lose speed and she'll want to fall off. Give her power and keep the bow into the waves. If she falls off we could get into the trough of the waves and get rolled. Don't let her get in the trough. You got that, Jay?" Borman asked. Jason nodded his head while Brad was over at the rail feeding the fish with his seasick stomach. "Now look, Jay, when I throw the sea anchor overboard, throw the engine in reverse, and give her plenty of revs. We don't want the boat to run over our line and get tangled in the screw, okay? You got it?" Borman asked.

Jason got a sick feeling in his stomach and replied, "Look,

Captain, you better stay at the wheel. Brad and I will take down the sails."

"Yeah, I guess you're right. Remember, one hand for the ship and one hand for yourself. If you or your son go overboard don't except me to be coming back for you. Now get up there and secure those sails," the captain yelled above the storm.

Down below, the motion was rough, the air stale. Both Tess and Bobby had taken to their bunks in the main cabin. As the wind howled, the boat crashed through the seas. The rigging screamed like a bad opera. The mother and daughter were in appalling shape, frightened and seasick. The main cabin had two bunks on either side of the dining room table. When a meal was served the two leafs of the table were brought up, and the crew sat on the bunks to eat. Two more bunks, port and starboard, where higher up. Leeboards helped keep the crew in their bunks. The schooner had a foreword cabin with two bunks, a private head, built in furniture such as drawers and closet. This cabin was used by Jason and Tess in normal crusing conditions. Up on deck, the crew had managed to release the main halyard. The sail was halfway down, dancing the jig, out of control. "Get that goddamn sail down, quick." Borman hollered at full volume. The wind did not carry his voice more than a few yards. Jason and Brad were clawing at the sail, pulling on the reef lines, trying to stay upright. The safety lines kept the pair from going overboard, but were very difficult to work with. Green water coming over the deck, coupled with the strong winds, made for very little progress. A job that would take no more than ten minutes turned into a half hour of gargantuan effort. After what seemed like hours the main sail was secured, and the man and boy headed forward to take down the storm sail. This time, even with the violent movement of the deck, the sail came down, was removed from the stay, and stored.

"I've got the sea anchor, Dad. Here, you can throw it overboard," Brad said.

"I've got it, Brad, signal Mark that I'm about to throw it overboard. I'll pay out the rode and cleat it off. You get back to the cockpit." Jason heaved the sea anchor overboard. The schooner lost its forward motion. Jason counted the marks on the rode, 100, 150, 200, 250, 275 feet; he then wrapped the rode around the cleat in a figure eight and headed back to the cockpit.

Jason and Brad were exhausted. Borman had a grin on his face as he said, "What's the matter, boys? A bit worn out, are you? Well, get used to it, a lot more of the same is coming before this storm is over."

The big schooner settled on her sea anchor, pushed back by the wind and the waves. The violent motion of beating into the heavy seas was gone. With everything secured on deck, the crew retired to the main cabin. "What's for supper, Tess?" Borman asked with a grin. Tess replied with a groan from her bunk. "Well I guess I'll just grab some sea biscuits and retire to my cabin. Call me if anything comes up."

Tess sat bolt upright in her bunk, and shouted at the captain, "Who's taking care of the boat? Nobody's on deck! What's going to happen?"

"Nothing is going to happen. The boat will take care of herself so long as the sea anchor holds." Borman was still grinning as he pushed his hat back on his head.

Tess flopped back into her bunk. "This is just great. The boat will take care of herself. I hope he's right."

"She seems to be riding better," Jason said in a weak voice.

The noise outside was deafening. Inside the water was sloshing over the cabin sole. Water was leaking into the boat from small areas that had opened up from the twisting and racking of the hull. Old leaks that had been caulked reopened and new ones appeared. "Dad, there's water in the boat. Look, it's over the floor. Do something, Dad!" Bobby said, shaking and crying.

"It's okay, Bobby, I'll just turn the pump on." Jason was up and headed for the pump switch in the mechanical room. He threw the switch, and the water level began to recede.

Borman was up the ladder poking his head out of the hatch every fifteen minutes, checking the horizon. His crew was in their bunks, holding on tight, having a fitful night. The cabin, being closed up against the sea, had the foul smell of seasick stomachs. A box of teabags had emptied itself on the cabin floor. It was turning the bilge water a dark brown as it found its way over the floorboards. Every now and then a groan could be heard from one or more of the White family.

At four o'clock in the morning, Borman shook Jason and informed him that it was his turn to keep watch. "Make yourself some tea or coffee and check the horizon every ten or fifteen minutes. You got that?" Borman asked.

"Yeah sure, Captain, I'm awake. How is the schooner holding up?" Jason asked.

"We're fine as long as the sea anchor holds. But if that line wears through at the chock, all hell will break loose," Borman replied.

"Can't you put a double line on it or something?" Jason asked.

"Wish I could, but it's too rough out there to do anything," Borman said as he retired to his cabin.

Jason poked his head through the hatch. He was frightened by the violence of the storm. The waves were higher than the main mast of the schooner and they were breaking over the boat. The decks were no sooner cleared of one wave than the next one came rushing right behind it. The wind was screeching through the rigging. The rigging in turn vibrated, shook and shuddered. The whole scene was one of nature gone mad. Jason, unable to see more than a few yards beyond the schooner, pulled the hatch closed and retreated to the main cabin. The foul air, dampness and violent motion of the main cabin was heaven compared to the storm outside.

As dawn broke, Jay poked his head out of the main hatch as instructed by Captain Borman. The situation had not changed. Again Jason pulled the hatch closed, then made his way down the ladder to the galley. As he lit the stove to warm up some old coffee, the boat's motion changed, and, with a roar, Jay was airborne to the opposite side of the cabin. He landed on his face with Brad, Bobby, and Tess tumbling down of top of him. The cabin that had started to show light of the day was now dark. Water was pouring in through the main hatch where a slat had been left off for ventilation. The family's screaming and crying was louder than the storm outside as they tried to disentangle themselves. The boat began to turn to the upright position as the water stopped flowing in through the hatch. The schooner settled in the trough of the waves.

Tess screamed when she saw that Jason's face was covered with blood. Jason had broken his nose and was bleeding profusely. The water in the cabin was over a foot deep. It was mixed with coffee, tea, blood and other sundry items, including the effluvium from the overturned buckets that were used by the seasick crew.

The captain came stumbling out of his cabin, announcing to no one in particular that the sea anchor had let go. Pulling on his foul-weather gear, he headed up the ladder, out into the storm.

To his horror, he realized the engine would not start. Water had entered the engine room, and shorted the batteries. Borman made his way to the sail locker and pulled out the first sail he touched. After fishing around, he found a long line and tied it to the sail. This makeshift drogue, or sea anchor, was heaved overboard with its line secured to the deck. This brought the schooner out of the trough of the waves and set the schooner stern-first to the storm. "Ah, Christ," he yelled, "that won't do it. She needs another. I hate using my good sail for this, but it beats being rolled again." He tied a three-hundred-foot line to a second sail, heaved it over the stern. He tied the line off to a deck cleat. "Now that's more like it; she's settled down to a more reasonable speed."

Waves were breaking over the stern. A major weak point were the slats that covered the entrance of the main hatch. These slats were not designed to take breaking waves head-on. The other problem was that the cockpit did not have time to drain before the next wave hit.

If I had a crew, I would've attached this jury rig to the bow, but with a dentist and a boy for a crew, the stern will have to do. Back in the cabin, Borman told Jason to keep watch while he got some sleep. With two black eyes, a crooked nose and toilet paper stuffed in each nostril, Jay nodded his head.

"Honey, you'd better lie down, I'll go on watch," Tess said while getting her foul-weather gear on and looking for her sou'wester.

"Okay, but don't go on deck, just stick your head out of the hatch, okay? Have a look around," Jason said.

"What am I looking for, Jay?" Tess asked.

"Just other boats or ships, there's no land around for hundreds of miles."

"Here, Jay, take these aspirin before you lie down and make

sure your leeboard is up." Tess made her way up the ladder, poked her head out into the storm. She was frightened by what she encountered. Huge waves, howling wind, a cockpit full of green water, visibility down to near zero. "Oh my God. Oh my God. If I ever survive this storm, I'll never go sailing again in my life," Tess said as she retreated to the main cabin. The deep water over the cabin floor alarmed her. "Captain Mark!" Tess yelled as she opened the aft cabin door.

"Now what's the problem? Christ," Borman said.

"The water is over the floorboards." Tess yelled in panic.

"Well, turn the pump on. Damn it," Borman yelled.

"The pump is on. Damn it." Tess shouted back.

"Ah, the drain must be plugged. I'll have a look at it." Mark made his way to where the bilge pump was located. He removed the floorboards. "Jesus Christ, there're teabags covering the drain. No wonder there's water in the cabin. I thought I told you guys to secure everything down below before this storm hit," Borman said.

"Captain, we're guests on your stinking boat. We're not seasoned sailors, and we are doing the best we can. Just shut your big mouth and unplug the drain." Tess was reaching down for all she had. A large grin crossed Borman's face.

"You're a feisty bitch, now aren't you? Let's say we get together for some shore leave when this little cruise is over," Borman said as he cleared out the intake of the bilge pump.

"I'll shore leave you with a bottle over the head if you don't start acting like the captain you should be." Tess was fighting back like a bear with cubs. She had an injured husband, two sick kids and a crazy captain. She was at her wits' end. The captain stood up as the water started draining out. He gave Tess a smile and returned to his cabin. Tess sat down and cried.

By the middle of the day the boat was riding better. The waves and winds were still high but not as bad as during the previous night. Tess had fallen asleep along with the other members of her family. Borman was keeping watch and felt that the worst of the storm was over. *If my makeshift drogue holds, we should be able to set sail again by tomorrow morning. One more night on the sea anchor won't hurt. It'll give my crew a chance to rest.* Borman was in the galley making his lunch. He shook his head as he looked at the White family, each one in a bunk, sound asleep. *I suppose I should go up on deck and check to see if the boat has sustained any damage. Well, I'll have my lunch first, and then get my foul-weather gear on.*

Borman climbed out of the hatch, snapped on his safety line. With the wind at his back he made his way forward. The main sail was still secured to the boom. Borman put his head down and continued forward. Foresail had worked its way loose. *I wish those jerks would learn some knots.* Borman retied the line and hung on to the mast. He looked around to see if anything else needed his attention. *Waves are still high. The wind must be blowing forty to fifty knots. Let's check the anemometer.* The one encouraging note was that the boat was riding up one wave and down the other. Borman made his way to the stern to check his makeshift sea anchor. She seemed to be holding fine. *Now if I only had someone to stand watch while I try to figure out where the hell we are.*

Chapter Twelve

Sergeant Tanquay drove over to the area southeast of town, known as the Villa. It is a popular tourist destination with many hotels and bars. In the lounge of the third hotel that the sergeant tried were two men at the far end of the bar. This was one of those bars that gave you the feeling that you could get drunk in. It had the caress of the island yet it also felt like home. It felt like a bar on Fifth Avenue that you could drop into after a hard day's work. The two men were in deep conversation. Tanquay had to look twice, for at first he did not recognize the men. Doyle was the first to see the sergeant coming. He gave Tanquay a cool reception. "Tell your boss to start packing his bags. He's not long for this island when we get through with him," Doyle said.

"I can understand your displeasure with my boss, gentlemen," Sergeant Tanquay said politely. "However, he asked me to find you, to tell you that he would like to see you both immediately. I believe it is about the drug business," Tanquay said.

Doyle threw his drink down his throat, and slapped Greenier on the back. "Let's go, George. Thanks, Sergeant, we're ready, your car out front? "

As the sergeant and the two men from up north walked into the inspector's office, Dupree stood behind his large desk. "Gentlemen, come in, have a seat," Dupree said, in a friendly manner, as he motioned Doyle and Greenier to the oak chairs. "Thank you, Sergeant, for finding these men so quickly. That'll be all for today." Sergeant Tanquay nodded his head, and closed the door behind him. "Gentlemen, I have some good news. I've heard, from a reliable source, that there could be some drugs coming in by boat this evening. Now I don't have the precise time, although I do know the area where the boat will be docking."

Doyle looked at the inspector with one eyebrow raised. "How come, all of a sudden, you're hearing about drug shipments?"

"Agent Doyle, I was very skeptical about your story of drug trafficking on my island. Then I gave it some thought. I came to realize that your government wouldn't be sending you here just to lie on the sand at their expense," Dupree said as he rolled a cigar between his fingers.

"You can say that again, Inspector." Doyle said. "Want a light?"

"No thanks, I don't smoke. Last night I went to the waterfront," Dupree said as Doyle interrupted.

"And some poor soul just happened to come along and volunteer all this excellent information," Doyle said.

"Agent Doyle, I can't reveal my sources; however, they do know what's going on around the waterfront. The information I get is generally reliable," the inspector said.

"Well, come on, Inspector, spell it out. What's the game plan? Are we going after this boatload of drugs or what?" Doyle asked.

"Precisely why I have invited you here. I am planning a

stakeout of the area. I feel it is important that you gentlemen be there, as observers, of course," Dupree said.

"Now you're talking, Inspector, let's get to it." Doyle was on his feet and ready to go. With his right hand he reached across his chest and under his suit jacket. He felt for his sweetheart, his pet, nine-millimeter, thirteen-round persuader.

Dupree walked the site of the stakeout with Doyle and Greenier to find the right spot. The inspector wanted to be close enough to the water to see any boat movement, yet be out of sight. The site of the boat landing had been prearranged with the Kaiser.

Inspector Dupree wondered if he had the nerve to follow through with the plan. He was able to present a calm exterior by thinking of his overstuffed chair, classical music and his brandy.

Sergeant Tanquay, the fourth member of the group, was parking the car farther away. The inspector's information was that he could expect a delivery before midnight. A high-powered launch would pick up the merchandise from a freighter anchored in the harbor. It would then be delivered to the packers in the warehouse. The night was damp, foggy, with a light rain. Dupree picked an area between two rundown buildings that gave an excellent view of the dock where the suspect launch would be landing.

Doyle was skeptical about finding a boatload of drugs. He asked the inspector how sure he was about this delivery. He was suspicious of the inspector, and very doubtful that he would be intercepting a boatload of dope this soon into his investigation.

Chief Inspector Dupree informed Doyle that he was not given a printed schedule, but that his sources were generally reliable. The inspector was wearing his old trench coat with the collar turned up against the light rain.

"You can call me Mike, Inspector. No need to be so formal on this isle of paradise," Doyle said.

"Mike it is," Dupree replied.

"And what is your name, Inspector?" Doyle asked.

"You may call me Inspector Dupree. That's what my wife calls me," the inspector said as he broke a faint smile. Greenier doubled over with laughter.

"Be quiet, my friends," Dupree said as he lifted his binoculars. "I hear a motor."

"That's a powerful boat," Greenier remarked.

"Yes, powerful indeed," the inspector said as he focused his binoculars in the direction of the purr of an engine. Out of the dark came a slick mahogany speedster with two men onboard. They powered up to the float and tied the fenders to the cleats on the small deck. A gangway from the pier led down to the float. Surrounding the float on the sides and back were numerous dinghies from the pleasure boats moored in the harbor.

"Stay here in the shadows, my friends. Sergeant, make sure that the three of you are out of sight. I'll walk up to them; they should know who I am. If I see that they're carrying the cargo we're interested in, I'll blow my whistle," Dupree said.

"If you blow your whistle, they might blow your head off," Doyle said.

"Good point. I'll hold my flashlight behind my back. I'll give you a flash if I see what we're looking for. If they're just joy riding, which is not likely, I'll not flash my light," the inspector said. Doyle agreed to this plan, nodded his head. Greenier was dancing up and down.

"What the hell is wrong with you?" Doyle whispered.

"I gotta piss," Greenier answered.

"Too late, the boat is at the dock," Doyle whispered.

As the men tied up the boat, the inspector made his way down the gangway, onto the float. He had slipped his gun out of its holster. He kept it out of sight in his trench-coat pocket. Both men in the boat were surprised to see him.

"Out boating this rainy night, gentlemen?" Dupree asked.

"Yeah, what's it to you," Jesus said from behind the helm.

"I see you're carrying some merchandise," the inspector said.

"What's your problem? Hasn't the Kaiser taken care of you this month?" Jesus asked.

"I don't see how that is any of your business," Dupree said. With that remark the inspector pulled his pistol from his pocket and fired directly at Jesus' head. Another shot to the head of the second man rang out. The inspector jumped on board to check his marksmanship. Both bullets had hit their mark. *Damn, what a mess. God, I hate this kind of work.* Dupree was putting his gun back in the holster as Doyle and Greenier came running down the gangway and onto the float.

"What the hell's going on?" yelled Doyle.

"They went for their guns. I asked what was in the boxes, and they went for their guns," the weak-kneed inspector said. He hoped that his uncontrollable shaking would not be noticed in the dark.

Greenier looked at the two dead men and said, "Jesus Christ."

"No, the other one is not Christ," the dry-mouthed Dupree said.

"What the hell did you shoot them for? I don't see any guns," Doyle asked, as the two agents poked around the boat with their flashlights.

"What a pity. I was sure they were going for their guns," the inspector said.

"Let's have a look at the contents of these boxes. George, see if you can find a pry bar, a screwdriver, anything," said Doyle. He wrestled the top crate into position as Greenier returned with a pry bar.

"Here, try this, Mike," Greenier said.

Doyle pried opened the wood box, pulled out a plastic bag. He cut it open with his penknife. "Your information was right on, Inspector, my congratulations."

"Thank you, Mike," said Dupree as he gave Doyle a slight nod. "Now, I must call for some help. Let's not touch anything until the lab boys get here. Also, I'll need photos of this mess. Sergeant, go back to the patrol car, call headquarters, tell them what we need."

"I'd feel a lot better, Inspector, if these guys had guns." Doyle looked down at the two dead men, and then at the inspector.

"It's a good thing for me that they didn't have guns." The inspector wiped his brow with his handkerchief. He was relieved that the night's business was over. Both Doyle and Greenier stood looking down at the bodies, shaking their heads.

Chapter Thirteen

Though menacing seas were still rough with large waves and swells, the worst of the storm was over. The winds had come down a good deal. The interior of the schooner was a terrible mess. A major effort would be required to get the cabin back to a livable condition. The White family was recovering from seasickness. They were making some attempt at cleaning up the main cabin. Jason, as the head of the family, was putting up a good front. He had a large bandage on his nose, and two black eyes. His children had fared somewhat better. Bobby had a lump on her head, and Brad thought he had cracked some ribs. Tess came through the storm physically unscathed, but her mind would need about two weeks on dry land to recover. She swore she would never go sailing again.

Captain Mark Borman had retired to his cabin and broken open a new bottle of single-malt Scotch. The reason for the celebration was his survival. He was well aware that it could have gone either way. He slumped down in his chair and poured about two inches into a glass he had filled with ice cubes on his way through the galley. It was time for Borman's second watch of the day; however, Jason was filling in as usual.

Borman was seated at his small navigation station, going over the books. *These books are foul, Mark old boy. You've been avoiding the obvious. Your chartering business is going down the head. You're one helluva sailor, Old Salt, but as a businessman you're bilge water. Your bank account has been going downhill for the last four years. It's almost bottomed out. Something needs to be done Mark, my friend.* Borman failed to admit the obvious. His personality was not conducive to building the public relations needed for a following, or even a recommendation from former guests. He felt that the people on vacation wanted to be pampered, waited on, that they were fat, lazy landlubbers. A recurring thought was that the women needed a good screwing, and that the men should be dumped overboard.

That's just my opinion. All who agree raise your hand; I've got my hand up. How about the rest of you guys? Mr. Sextant, what do you think? Hey you, Mr. VHF, have you got your hand up? I can't see them. You guys are a bunch of wimps. How about another drink? Borman, with an empty glass, moved out into the galley for some more ice cubes. He checked out his crew. The White family was a sorry mess; they looked as bad as the mess they were trying to pick up.

Borman slammed the books closed and poured a second drink onto the fresh ice cubes. He then slumped back into his chair. *What to do? What to do?*

"What would you like to do?" The little voice in the back of his head asked.

Let's see, a nice little shack on top of a hill, overlooking the sea, and maybe a swimming pool. Yeah, that would be nice, and on an island somewhere in the Caribbean. Somewhere with little to no taxes to pay, and while I'm at it, a beautiful bitch. Let's see, someone with long black hair and big boobs. Oh, and let's not forget the fishing boat, something in the thirty-foot range. Doesn't have to be fancy, just a good fishing boat, one that can take a running sea.

"Well, Mark ol'boy, how do we get from here to there?" Borman's little voice was at it again.

As the afternoon turned into evening, and the dent in the bottle of Scotch became larger, Borman formulated a plan.

Let's see, I could scuttle the schooner and collect the insurance. Great idea! I could say that the boat went down in the storm. Hey, that sounds like an excellent idea.

"But you're forgetting one thing, Mark, the White family," Borman's inner voice reminded him.

Oh yeah, the White family, let's see, the White family. Most unfortunate, lost at sea, went down with the boat, I guess. Ha, ha, yeah, went down with the boat I guess. Well that's the breaks. Some people win and others lose. Mark started to laugh at this idea, and the more he thought about it, the more he laughed. *Lost at sea, what a shame, such a nice family.* Borman, now deep in thought, was starting to round out his plan for living the good life. *Look at the money I could collect, and who could challenge my word? No one, that's who. I could collect enough money for that nice grass hut, with the swimming pool atop the hill, yeah, overlooking the sea. Now, let's see. How do we get rid of the jerks on board?*

Jay was on his second watch of the day, 4:00 to 8:00 p.m. when Borman came up for some fresh air. Borman made the rounds, checking the set of the sails. He was, at the same time, making a note of the location of each member of the family. Tess, Brad and Bobby were down below, cleaning up the main cabin. The main hatch was open. Borman replaced the hatch boards. Jay thought that was a little strange because the top board was normally not in place, for it allowed extra air into the cabin. Jay noted that Borman had a strong smell of booze about him, and his motion was less than steady.

Borman poked around in the lazarette, where he found the item he was looking for, an old cast-iron belaying pin, used for doing in energetic fish. One whop on the head and the fish was forever still. Borman tucked the pin under his belt and covered it with his shirt.

"How's it going, Jay? How's the nose?" Borman asked.

"It's extremely painful, but look on the bright side, we're here. We survived," Jason said.

"Yeah, we made it, didn't we?" And with that comment Borman lifted his belaying pin and with full force brought it down inches from Jay's head. The deck was still lively from the rough seas. With all the booze in him the captain was not that steady. He had missed his mark. Jay fell over the wheel and then to the deck, rolled over and got to his feet. Shocked and surprised by Borman's behavior, he dodged the second swing of Mark's weapon.

The wheel turned as the boat came up into the wind. The crew below wondered about the strange motion of the boat, then forgot about it. Jason let out a groan as Borman's weapon landed on his forearm. He backed away. Borman was after him. The unsteady deck made both men stumble and fall. Jason was up first, looking around for a weapon, couldn't find one. He moved behind the main mast, using it as a temporary shield. The boom swung wildly, and Borman saw it a second before it knocked him to the deck, stunning him. Jay sprang from behind the mast, landing on Mark. He grabbed for the belaying pin. The captain, being the larger of the two men, rolled over on top of Jason. With the roll of the deck Jay was able to get out from underneath. He grabbed his assailant by the throat with one hand, and reached for the belaying pin with the other. He got a hold of Mark's waist. Borman was able to free his arm from Jason's grip. He swung his heavy pin, catching Jay beside the head. Jay rolled over groaning. As the boat heeled, Borman gave Jay a hard shove that sent him overboard. The breaking waves covered the sound of the splash. Borman returned to the wheel with a grin on his face.

That bastard put up a pretty good fight for a small guy.

Down below, with the cabin looking better, the subject of food came up. "Bobby, would you go up and ask your father if he would like something to eat?"

"Sure, Mom, what are his choices?"

"We got Spam and beans, beans with Spam, hash and eggs, Spam and eggs and so on."

"Okay, Mom, I've got it." Bobby slid the hatch open, saw the captain at the wheel. "Captain Mark, is my father up here?" Bobby asked.

"Nope, haven't seen him," Borman replied.

Bobby slid the hatch closed and returned to the main cabin. "He's not up there, Mom," Bobby reported without question.

"Not up there. What do you mean 'not up there'? Of course he is up there; he's on watch," Tess said.

"Captain Mark is on watch and he said that he has not seen Dad."

Tess got a sick feeling. Her mouth dropped open, her legs felt weak. "What's the matter, Mom? You don't look so good." Bobby asked.

"Bobby, would you check the forward cabin? Brad, would you please take a look in the captain's cabin?" Tess knew that Jay was on watch, and that he never came below.

"Not forward, Mom, I'm sure he's on deck and that the captain is just playing tricks," Bobby said.

"I'm sure you're right, Bobby. He's up on deck. The captain has a bad sense of humor," Tess replied weakly.

"Not in the captain's cabin, Mom. I wonder where he is?" Brad asked, returning from the aft cabin.

"Brad, would you go up on deck and find your father?" Tess said with a fragile voice.

"Sure, Mom." Brad slid back the hatch, hopped over the hatch boards. Borman was at the wheel, whistling. Brad stayed clear of Mark, hooked up his safety line and moved forward onto the deck. The deck was moving up and down. It was obvious to Brad that no one would be on deck this dark night. After checking both port and starboard sides it was very clear that his father was not there. Brad unhooked his safety line and hopped over the hatch boards.

The captain engaged the autopilot, removed the hatch boards, and took a firm grip on his belaying pin. He started down the ladder. Bobby and Brad stood in front of their mother at the far end of the main cabin, each one shaking with fear. Mark approached the family without a word; the belaying pin said everything. Tess looked around for something to protect her family, a pair of scissors, anything. Pots, pans and knives were at the other end of the main cabin, in the galley. Tess could not take her eyes off the sinister look in Borman's eyes.

Brad made a lunge at the captain. The belaying pin came down upon Brad's head. Brad fell to the floor unconscious, blood rushing from a large scalp wound. Both Tess and Bobby screamed and threw themselves on Brad. Tess was next to feel the belaying pin as she covered her son's body.

"Shut your fucking mouth, bitch, you're hurting my ears,"

Borman yelled as he came down hard on her head. Blood splattered onto the captain's clothing. "Ah shit, look what you've done to my good pants," he said.

Jay woke up coughing, choking, spitting out blood. Water washed over him. For a moment he did not know where he was. In the distance he saw the schooner heading away. He remembered losing the struggle with Borman. "You son-of-a-bitch. Hurt my family and I will haunt you the rest of your life. You son-of-a-bitch! Tess, Brad, Bobby," he screamed, then lost consciousness and sank beneath the waves.

Bobby, sensing her turn was next, pushed past the captain while he was looking at the blood on his pants. The young girl was up the ladder and out on deck before the captain knew she was missing. Bobby ran for the dinghy; it was secured to the main cabin in an upside-down position. It was a solid wood dinghy, much too heavy for Bobby even if it had not been tied down. In a panic, she ran forward to the emergency life raft that was folded in a plastic box. Just as she opened the box, she heard Mark on deck. He had just banged the hatch open and saw Bobby forward. Bobby, shaking beyond control, reached for the bright red ring on the inflatable dinghy. She was unable to pull it. She watched Mark coming up the deck with horror in her face.

"Relax, kid. I'm not going to hurt you, nay, not you. I wouldn't have hit your brother either if he hadn't come at me like that." Mark reached for the red ring on the emergency dinghy. Bobby jumped back. The dinghy inflated with a tremendous force.

"Look, kid, I'm going to put you in the dinghy and then I'm going below to get your mother and brother, okay?" Borman said. Bobby tried to speak, but words would not come out. Mark picked up the raft, eased it over the side. He held onto the painter, walked the dinghy to the stern and tied it off. "Okay, kid, into the dinghy before I change my mind." Bobby got into the raft stumbling and crying. Mark started for the main hatch, but then he stopped. He turned around and untied the painter. The raft was free.

"Mommy," Bobby screamed. The dinghy carried her away from the schooner as the high winds and heavy seas tossed the inflated rubber raft. The twelve-year-old hung on with numbed fists. Her throat grew dry, her voice barely audible. When she awoke in the morning the schooner was gone. She was alone.

Chapter Fourteen

Borman stumbled down the ladder into the main cabin. He looked at the bodies on the cabin sole. He thought about bringing them topside and pushing them overboard. *Why bother? I'll just pull the plug in the morning and my friends will go down with the boat. Now I need some sack time. Tomorrow I'll set sail in my little cat-rig dinghy. Must think up a good story about why I was sole survivor. What's for supper? I'm starved.*

The following morning Borman poked around the galley, filling his survival sack. He could not resist the impulse to take his sextant with him. *A shipwrecked sailor with a sextant, how would that look?* he reflected. *But then who will question me or check my belongings. The natives won't ask or care what's in the box. Oh hell, take it, I'll think of something when the time comes.* Borman packed several cans of sardines, bread, peanut butter, jelly and three quarts of water. In a duffel bag he stuffed his foul-weather gear, and a large umbrella to protect him from the sun. *May as well be comfortable.*

Cloudy skies and calmer seas greeted Borman as he pulled away from the sinking schooner. He delayed raising the sail to watch the love of his life go down. *It's just a boat,* he told himself, yet the pain of seeing his home of the last four years go below the waves was heart-wrenching. *It's just a boat, just a boat. I'll get another one, even prettier. Think of the money she'll bring, get a grip old salt, it's just a boat.*

The course he had plotted would take him to the nearest island. His heading was west-southwest. This heading would take him to the islands of Tobago Cays, forty nautical miles away.

Let's see, two knots per hour and about fifty miles away. Twenty-five hours give or take an hour or so. I'll dump my food and water at the first sight of land. The natives won't ask a lot of questions. Borman was now in a good mood for things had gone just about as he planned. He began to sing:

"I'm off on the morning train, across the ranging main.

I'm off to my love with a boxing glove ten thousand miles away.

So blow ye winds high-ho, a sailing we shall go.

We'll live no more on England's shore, so let the music play."

The little dinghy had a center board that gave the boat good directional stability. The cat-rig sail moved the dinghy along at a reasonable speed for something that size. Borman had a small pocket-size compass that was left behind by a guest a few years ago. It was the type of compass used by hikers. The boat was cramped for a man of Borman's size. His long legs were the problem; he could not get comfortable. Late in the evening he trimmed the sail and fiddled with the rudder, trying to get the dinghy to hold a course. She was just too small to sail by herself. Borman resigned himself to holding the rudder all night long. Going without sleep would give him more of a look of a ship wreaked sailor.

The middle of the next day Borman sighted land. He realized that the island he was headed for was just about where it should be. He thought about putting his food and water into a bag, and with a weight, sending it to the bottom, when he was closer to shore. He spotted a native fishing boat headed his way, then hurried to get food and water into a bag, and overboard quickly. A quarter of an hour later the sailboat was upon him.

"Ahoy, Sailorman. . .Sailorman, what you doing out here in that small boat, man?" The thirty-foot wooden fishing boat lowered its patched, dirty mainsail and came alongside of Borman's dinghy. Two men in the sailboat were native fishermen. The boat was the low maintenance type with its white paint peeling off the sides. She had two sails, the gaff rig main sail, and a fore sail or jib. Both sails had patches over their patches, hand sown, not fit for cleaning the bilge, Borman reflected.

"Hey, man, you don't look so good. You've been sailing long time?" Both fishermen were shaking their heads. Borman slumped over the tiller, putting on a good show.

He lifted his head and croaked, "Water, need some water."

"Sure, mon, here, take this bottle. We can tow you ashore, mon." Borman reached for the bottle of water. It did not look as if it were fit to drink. He thought he saw small things swimming around in the not-so-clear water. He filled his mouth full, and then pretended to vomit over the starboard side. Borman handed his rescuers a line that was tied off the stern of their boat. The main sail was raised to half the mast height. A full mainsail would move their boat too fast for the small dinghy, and swamp it.

When they reached the shore the village people gathered around the shipwrecked sailor. They pulled his dinghy up onto the beach. The two fishermen half carried Borman off the boat. With his head down and an arm around each of the fishermen,

Borman walked as if he was in pain. When they arrived at one of the larger huts, they laid him down on one of the bunks. Borman smiled at his new friends and thanked them. His nurse, a middle-aged woman with a bunch of kids, could not do enough for Borman.

"Hi, I'm Mark, you have a nice place here. What's your name?" Borman asked.

"You're a sick man, Mark. You lose your ship?" the woman asked.

"Yeah, lost it in the hurricane; gotta phone? I should report it to the Coast Guard."

"There's a phone on Mayreau Island, I know that, mister. Maybe on one of the other islands, but not here, not this island, that's for sure."

"What's the name of this island?" Borman knew he was on one of the islands in the group called Tobago Cays. The major islands in the Tobago Cays are Palm Island, Petit Rameau, Petit Tabac, Petit Bateau, and Jamesby.

"Oh, this island is called Jamesby. Everyone calls me Matte," the woman said. The kids were fascinated by the sailor. They ran for whatever he desired. Borman enjoyed being waited on and made sure his recovery was slow. He had a comfortable bed with decent food and clean water. *Not a bad life*, he thought. The down side was that there were no electricity, no phone, and the radio needed new batteries. Borman liked the place, for it was comfortable in a primitive way.

After a week of playing sick, Borman was getting restless. "Hey, Matte, how often does the steamer come to this island?" Borman asked.

"When you feel better, you take the mail boat to the big island north of here, okay?" Matte said.

"Yeah, that's right, I'll catch the mail boat," Borman said.

"No mail boat comes to this island. The mail boat comes to Mayreau, but not to this little island. I don't think it comes to any island in Tobago."

"What's the name of the big island north of here?" Borman asked.

"That island is St. Vincent, many hours away."

"How many hours away?" Borman asked.

"Oh that take you half day by mail boat," Matte replied.

"Good, that's the island I'm going to. When did you say the steamer gets here?" Borman asked.

"That boat comes to Mayreau two times a week. Never comes to this little island," Matte laughed and laughed some more at the thought of the large boat coming to their little island.

"What day will it come next, Matte?" Borman's watch, the one with all the hands on it, had stopped running after the struggle with Jason.

"Today is Sunday. You got plenty time. That boat comes Tuesday and Friday," Matte said.

Borman told Matte that he would be down on the beach and to call him when it was time to eat. The brilliant white sand and dazzling, and luminous blues of the water gave Borman the feeling that he did not have to go further than this. His favorite pastime was lying on the beach, and adding up the insurance money he hoped to collect. Jamesby is the smallest island in the group. On the eastern side of the island it has one of the best beaches of all the Tobago Cays. Palm trees come almost down to the sea, giving shade to the sun-baked sand. *With a few modern conveniences, life on this island could be comfortable. Not bad, not bad,* Borman thought. But then he's mind turned to a good bottle of Scotch, and women.

Chapter Fifteen

The following day, Doyle and Greenier were in Inspector Dupree's office, going over the events of the previous night. The conclusion was that the two men who died were definitely in the drug business. Doyle was still uneasy about the inspector shooting two unarmed men. When he wrote his report, he intended to show that the two dead men were not armed and that the inspector acted without cause.

"Inspector, I am making out my report and I would like it to agree with your report as much as possible." Doyle and Greenier were seated in front of the inspector's desk. Doyle had his black notebook on his knee. Greenier had a larger notebook and was writing continuously. Doyle looked over, noted the scribble, and shook his head.

"Certainly, it is always good to have our reports agree," the inspector said as he sat in full uniform. He looked at his hat on the rack, then his watch. He was thinking that he did not need an interrogation by people from up north.

"You said you shot the two men because they were going for their guns, although no guns were found," Doyle said.

"Correct, no guns. Nevertheless, my friends, remember that it was dark. These people shoot first and never ask questions afterward. Also, I was aware of the price on my head. These same people blew up my car a while back, almost killed my wife. It could very well have been yours truly in that car, no?" Dupree used his hands to simulate the explosion of the car.

"Yeah, you're right about that. What made you think that they were going for guns?" Doyle asked.

"Gentlemen, when I told them to put their hands up, they both put their hands down. Naturally I assumed that their guns were down in the darkness. I wasn't taking any chances. I feel sorry for the poor men's wives, if they were married, but for those men, no, I feel nothing," the inspector said. "Those waterfront rats were dangerous drug dealers and for that they die. We do not allow such people on our island." Dupree then put his head down and started moving papers around. "Now, gentlemen, if you have no more questions, I have a truckload of paperwork to catch up on."

"Oh sure, Inspector, I guess we're all set here. You were a brave man last night. I don't believe that I would have gone down on that dock alone. In fact, I would have wanted more than George here for backup." Greenier opened his mouth to speak, but Doyle spoke first, as both men stood up. "Inspector, pleasure meeting you. Next time we come to your island, don't be throwing us in jail," Doyle said with a grin.

The inspector stood up and shook hands with both agents. "My pleasure, gentlemen, and please, if you are here again on assignment come to my office first. Understood?" Dupree asked.

"You got it, Inspector." With a slight smile and a wave, the two agents were out the door.

Dupree called after them as they walked down the hall toward the front door. "Mike, George, remember, if you are down here on business, you must come to my office first."

"Right you are, Inspector. You'll be the first to know." Doyle half turned around as he spoke and waved goodbye.

When the inspector arrived home that evening he was greeted at the door by Ute, the family cook. Ute, a German immigrant, was a little above average height. She had gray-green eyes, auburn hair and sported a soft golden tan. She was in her early thirties, a good-looking woman, by any man's standard. "Inspector . . . Inspector, are you all right? We read about you in the papers this morning."

"Yes, I'm fine. What's all the fuss?" the inspector asked.

"You never said a word about it at breakfast this morning. You never talk about your police work," Ute said.

"Really nothing," Dupree said as he removed his hat and jacket.

"Nothing? The paper said you shot two men. You call that nothing?" Ute questioned. She had been with the Duprees for a couple of years now, ever since the car bombing. The cook at that time also filled in as the chauffeur. A misunderstanding led to the unfortunate event and the cook/chauffeur lost his life. The inspector always felt that a person called Jesus was involved, but he was unable to connect anyone to the crime. At the dinner table, Madam Dupree was upset at what she read in the paper. "Chief Inspector, I know you are a hands-on person, but last night was just too much. You have the whole police force working for you. Let them do the dangerous work. You are too valuable a person to be playing with guns. Running around at night with God knows what kind of ruffians. Promise me that you'll let the younger men do this kind of work. You must have young, unmarried men that have no family to look after," Madam Dupree said.

"You are absolutely right, my darling. I'm far too old for such things," the inspector said as he reached for the wine carafe. "And we do have several young men on the force who are gaining in experience each day."

"Thank you, Inspector, I knew you would understand."

It was not until eleven the following morning when Dupree was able to break away from the office. The inspector did not feel right about driving a police car himself. He felt the dignity of his office called for him to be chauffeured. Sergeant Tanquay drew the duty this day. His first stop was the hospital to check on the person found on the raft. "Good morning, Inspector. Are you here about the girl found at sea?" the nurse asked with a smile as she looked up from her desk.

"Good morning, Nurse, yes, I am. Will the doctor permit me to see her now?" Dupree asked as he stood erect, with his hat under his left arm.

"She's on the second floor, room 204. Her name is Bobby White," the nurse said before answering a ringing phone. The inspector bounced up the stairs, trying to prove to himself that being close to fifty was not a handicap. He walked down the hall in his military fashion, and found room 204. Dupree knocked with a light touch and spoke softly.

"Hello, anyone home?" Dupree asked. Bobby did not answer, but looked frightened, for she had never seen this type of uniform before. "Good morning, young lady. I am Inspector Dupree. Welcome to our island. The nurse tells me your name is Bobby White."

"Yes," answered Bobby softly as she stood by the window.

"That's a nice name. Is Bobby short for Roberta?" Dupree asked.

"Uh-huh," Bobby said.

"Well then, Bobby, do you remember being picked up by a ship and being taken here to this hospital?" the inspector asked.

"Yes." Bobby was bewildered, frightened, and not talkative.

"And can you tell me how you happened to be on a raft in the middle of the ocean?" Dupree asked.

"No," Bobby answered.

"Maybe your boat sank?" Dupree suggested.

"I don't know." Bobby's eyes began to fill.

"That's okay, Bobby, it will come to you. In a few days, you'll feel better and you'll remember everything," Dupree said.

"I hope so," Bobby said as tears rolled down her cheeks.

"I'll be back tomorrow with flowers. Do you like flowers?" Dupree asked.

"Yes," Bobby said.

The inspector picked up his hat, which he had laid on the nightstand. "Fine, then I'll be back tomorrow. Now you get plenty of rest; things will work out just fine. Bye for now." The inspector gave a slight smile, tucked his hat under his left arm, and nodded his head.

That evening the inspector and Madam Dupree were having their evening meal. Dinner was a formal affair, while breakfast and lunch were consumed on the run or in Ute's kitchen. Madam Dupree took great pleasure in this formal repast. Madam Dupree always dressed elegantly and was involved with a number of charitable organizations. Her favorites were the library, the museum, and the hospital. Flowers were always the centerpiece of the table. Ute's meals were enviably enjoyable.

"I stopped by the hospital today, met the girl they found on the dinghy," the inspector said as he filled his plate.

"Oh, how is she doing?" Madam asked.

"Recovering very nicely, I'm told. She will be released in a couple of days," the inspector said. He was enjoying his dish of seafood salad: shrimp, conch, and whelk.

"Whom will they release her to, dear?" Madam Dupree asked.

"That's the problem. You see, we have no information on her. She has temporarily lost her memory," the inspector replied.

"The poor thing, where will she go? What will become of her?" A troubled look came over Madam Dupree.

"Perhaps we could have her here for awhile. We have room and with a little love and care, I'm sure she will regain her memory quickly," the inspector said.

"But, of course, darling, for a little while anyway. But what happens if she does not recover her memory? We would have to find a home for her, and that would not be easy on this island," Madam said, looking concerned.

"I'm sure we could find a permanent home for her, if need be. But for now she could stay in the guest bedroom." Ute entered the dining room with a pot of coffee. The inspector smiled and thanked her.

"Darling, I must defer to your judgment on this one. If you think it's the right thing to do, then fine," Madam Dupree said.

"It's settled then," the inspector said. "I'll inform the hospital that she will be released in my custody."

Madam Dupree smiled.

Chapter Sixteen

Borman said goodbye to all his new friends at the foot of the gangway. There were Matte and her five children, and Matte's sister Carleno. Carleno brought along two of her older children to look after Matte's younger ones. Matte's uncle came along, for he was the owner of the boat. His boat was an oversized rowboat, homemade, of wood. The outboard motor was one that he had salvaged years ago. Half the male population on the island tried their hand at making the motor run. This ritual has continued through the years. The motor is now considered communal property.

Borman said goodbye, with hugs and kisses all around. He then climbed the gangway and waved before entering the ship. He waved again from the rail of the main deck. Ten smiling people waved back, several skinny dogs adding their barks. Borman went to the purser's office to made arrangements for passage. "Here, sign right here," the purser said. He had a drawn face, dour personality. He was dressed in a shirt two sizes too large. His suspenders cut into his shoulders. "This is the amount of your passage, and these are other charges. You get one free meal, more than that and you must pay extra. We expect prompt payment," the purser said.

"Don't worry, you'll get your money just as soon as I hear from my bank. I always pay my debts," Borman said. *Here is a guy that really does not like his job,* Borman thought. *Similar to all bookkeepers, he wants to be the boss, but knows that will never happen.* Mark Borman was in an upbeat mood. The grim-faced purser was not about to get him down. He signed the paper, received his copy, and then asked, "Where will I find the captain?"

"On the bridge, I guess, but I wouldn't bother him now. We're on a tight schedule," the purser said. Borman looked at the purser and winked. He then headed for the bridge. The purser gave him a dirty look and returned to his ledger. Borman found the captain on the bridge, wiping his hands.

"Good morning, Captain. I'm Mark Borman, shipwrecked sailor. You know, you look familiar," Borman said.

"Yeah, well, I've got one of those faces," the captain said.

"I know you from somewhere, Newport, maybe? Newport, Rhode Island. That's it. We had a few drinks together, on the waterfront, a couple of years ago."

"Yeah, could be, uh ... uh," the captain replied.

"Borman, Mark Borman."

"Hi, Mark, I'm Paul Chivas. Newport, huh? I've spent some time there," the captain said.

"We met at a bar, can't think of the name," Borman said.

"Yeah, I've been known to have a drink or two. We could have had a drink together. You say you've been shipwrecked?" the captain said. He must have been working in the bowels of the machine room; his shirt and hands were covered with grease.

"Yup, that's right. My fifty-foot schooner went down in the hurricane with all hands, 'cept me," Borman said.

"How is it you didn't go down with the boat?" Chivas said. The captain didn't look up from cleaning his hands.

"I was up on deck checking how the sea anchor was holding. All of a sudden she let go. I rushed back to the cockpit to start the engine, but wasn't quick enough. The boat got into the trough of the waves. We got rolled," Borman said.

"Sounds to me you were extremely lucky. Did you have a life jacket on?" the captain asked.

"Nope, the dinghy broke away, wasn't far off when I came up for air," Borman said.

"How long did it take you to reach shore?" Chivas asked.

"Three days, no food, no water, fortunately, no more storms," Borman watched the captain's eyes.

"You were one lucky son-of-a-bitch," the captain said. He finished cleaning his hands.

"Right, Captain, very lucky, however that's life on the sea. Some people win and others . . .," Borman shrugged his shoulders.

"What was the name of your boat, Mark?" Chivas asked.

"*Vagus,* one of the prettiest schooners you'll ever see," Borman said.

"*Vagus*, huh, that's strange, I haven't heard of any schooner going down in that hurricane," the captain said with a quizzical look on his face.

"That's because I haven't reported it yet. I've been on Jamesby Island for almost a week, in bad shape. I whacked my ribs on something when I went overboard," Borman grabbed his left side, making a face as if it had happened yesterday.

"A phone call would have done it," Chivas said, as he looked Borman straight in the eye.

"If they had a phone on that island, I'd have reported it," Borman said as his eye twitched.

"Yeah, I've seen those villages. All they have are dogs and chickens." The captain reached for a cigarette in his shirt pocket.

"See that group of people headed up the road? They nursed me back to health. Nice people, going back to their island now. Nice people," Borman said as he continued to watch Captain Chivas' eyes.

"So you couldn't get the word out? Never contacted the Coast Guard? Couldn't send a runner to an island with a phone? No one looked for survivors?" Chivas asked.

"Nope, those people never heard of a phone. Maybe I should have sent someone to the next island. My ribs . . . my broken ribs, I wasn't thinking straight." Borman was starting to feel uncomfortable.

"Well you'd better report it as soon as you get to St. Vincent," Captain Chivas warned.

"Sure, will do, Captain." Mark figured he'd better change the subject. "I understand all the good bars on the waterfront in Newport are gone. Tourists taken over, I've heard."

"That's right, Mark. Tourists are taking over everywhere. It's hard to get away from 'em." Captain Chivas moved to the wing of the bridge to see how the unloading was going, and Borman followed. "Well, if you will excuse me, I've got to get this tub unloaded and back to St. Vincent," the captain said as he wiped his shirt with the rag.

"Yeah sure, Captain, I'll just find a deck chair in the shade somewhere and stay out of the way. Been having engine problems?" Borman asked. The captain grunted and then yelled at a couple of seamen on the deck below. Borman took the hint and left.

Captain Chivas turned to look at Borman as he departed. The look on the captain's face was one of suspicion.

Chapter Seventeen

Inspector Dupree and his wife entered the hospital and were greeted by the head nurse near the reception desk. "Good morning, Nurse Gagne," the inspector said in a pleasant tone.

"Good morning, Inspector Dupree," Miss Gagne responded with a smile.

"I would like you to meet my wife, Madam Dupree," the inspector said.

"Good morning, Madam. I'm pleased to meet you. You're quite a celebrity on this island," Nurse Gagne said.

"Oh, how's that?" Madam Dupree asked.

"All the work you do. Helping the kids in the hospital, fund raising, and all the committees you're on."

"I've been thinking of cutting back," Madam said.

"I hope it's not your hospital work you'll be cutting back on," the nurse said.

"Oh no, not the hospital, I rather enjoy working here," Madam Dupree said with a smile.

"Bobby White is ready to be released, Inspector," the nurse said as she looked down at her clipboard. "She's doing much better, she's up and around and eating well. The doctor tells me that she'll make a quick recovery."

"I have made arrangements to have her released to my custody," the inspector said as he tried to look at the nurse's clipboard.

"Yes, it's noted here, go right up. It was a pleasure meeting you, Madam Dupree." The nurse rushed off down the corridor when she saw a doctor she wanted to talk with.

"Hi, Bobby, I'm Madam Dupree, the inspector's wife. We have come to take you home with us." Bobby was at the window when the Duprees walked in. Madam Dupree extended her hand with a smile. "You can stay for as long as you like."

"I'd rather find my mother and father and go to my own home," Bobby said in a soft voice.

Madam Dupree gave Bobby a box wrapped in white with a bright red ribbon. "And where is your home, Bobby?" the inspector asked.

"I don't know," Bobby said, as her eyes filled.

"Don't bother with that now, Bobby. Open your present and see what the inspector has bought you." Madam Dupree sat on the bed. Bobby sat on the chair next to her and pulled on the ribbon. Bobby smiled when she saw the items in the box.

"Thank you, Inspector, thank you, Madam, there're very nice." Bobby held up a tank top and shorts. Madam Dupree was concerned about the size.

"We can always take them back if they don't fit, Bobby. When you're ready, take your things and come with us. In a few days you'll remember where your home is. Then you can call your mother and father," Madam Dupree said.

"Will I remember my phone number too?" Bobby asked.

"Certainly, everything will come back to you. The doctor said it may take a couple of days." Madam had her fingers crossed on that white lie. "Then your parents will come and pick you up, no?" Madam Dupree said warmly. Bobby grabbed her brown paper bag with a toothbrush and a few odds and ends she'd received at the hospital. Madam Dupree put her arm around the child as they walked to the elevator.

In the living room of the stucco house halfway up the hill, the inspector said, "Bobby, I want you to make yourself at home. Madam Dupree will take very good care of you. I must return to my office. If I'm away too long, the whole island will turn to crime." The inspector smiled, gave her a little bow and left.

"Come, Bobby, let me show you our home. I know that you are going to love it here. Your room has a beautiful view of the ocean."

"How long will I be staying?" Bobby asked.

"For as long as you please, Bobby. The inspector is looking for your father and mother. I know he will find them for you," Madam Dupree said.

"This is a beautiful house, Madam, but how will the inspector know what my father looks like? I can't remember myself. I am trying to think what he looks like. I can hear his voice but his face . . . uh . . .," Bobby said.

"What about your mother? Can you describe her?" Madam asked.

"Well, almost. She is tall with light-colored hair and a soft voice," Bobby said thoughtfully.

"And what about your brothers and sisters?" asked Madam Dupree.

"I don't know." Bobby began to cry. She sat down on a small rocker and covered her face with both hands.

"Don't cry, Bobby." Madam knelt down beside her and put

her arm around the girl's shoulder. "Tomorrow, we'll go shopping for some nice clothes and new shoes. We'll have lots of fun and soon you will be in your own home," Madam said. Whenever Madam Dupree was depressed, she would go shopping to cheer herself up. She was hoping it would work for Bobby.

Bobby slept fitfully her first night in the Dupree villa. She felt welcomed although deeply distressed by her loss of memory. From her room as she could look out to sea, she had a strange feeling. The sea attracted her yet frightened her. Images of high winds and rough seas made knots in her stomach.

"Breakfast is ready," Madam Dupree called up the stairwell. Bobby followed her to the kitchen. "You met Ute yesterday. She's from Germany," Madam Dupree said.

"Hi, Bobby, do you like your eggs hard, or soft?" Ute asked.

"Hard, I guess. I'm not sure," Bobby replied.

"This morning we are going to get you a dress, shoes, stockings and maybe a hat. Do you wear hats, Bobby?" Madam asked.

"I guess so. Do the other kids here wear hats?" Bobby asked.

"Well perhaps hats are for dress-up. You'll need a dress for special places," Madam Dupree added.

"Bobby, I have asked Madam Dupree if she would pick up a few things for me at the market," Ute said pleasantly. "Maybe you can help her with the shopping?"

"Sure, Ute, but I don't know if I can be of any help. I don't know much about shopping," Bobby answered.

"You'll do just fine, Bobby. It's a short list," Ute said.

After breakfast the two rode off to town in the family sedan with Murphy at the wheel. The family chauffeur was Murphy's cover; his primary job was bodyguard for Madam Dupree.

Murphy had recently been hired by the inspector to look after his wife. A retired policeman from up north, he had arrived on the island about six months ago. He was looking for a little part-time work, nothing too strenuous or exciting. Murphy had come to the island for peace and quiet but found that he was getting bored. He wanted something to keep him busy. The inspector hired him after checking out his story with the chief of police in Stamford, Connecticut. Murphy was a little below average height, wide, and powerful. Thinning on top, gray hair showed at the temples. He carried a little more weight than he liked, thought about going on a diet someday. Twenty years of police work had taught him to be suspicious. He had started his career in Brooklyn, got a transfer to the Big Apple for the excitement. After eight years of married life his wife wanted to move to the country. Stamford was country enough for Murphy. NYC was getting on his nerves. He figured he had been lucky so far. Lucky to still be alive, he transferred to Stamford where the pace better suited his middle age.

"Oh Bobby, look there in the window, look at that dress. Don't you think that dress would look just wonderful on you? Would you like to try it on?" The dress was off-white with light blue trim. It ended below the knees of the mannequin.

"I don't know, Madam. I don't know about wearing a dress." Bobby was wearing her new outfit, the tank top and shorts.

"Well, let's go in. Maybe you will see something you'll like." Madam Dupree enjoyed shopping. Next stop was Edwin D. Layne & Sons Ltd. on Bay and Middle Streets. Layne was a sizable department store where you could find everything from clothing to hardware.

The two hours of shopping flew by. Soon the three of them were having lunch. Murphy was relieved to be able to set the bundles down. The party sat at a little table in the open-air courtyard of the restaurant. The fourth chair was stacked high with boxes and bags. Bobby was quiet about her new outfits. Thoughts of her family, the sea, the dinghy, were foremost in her mind. She wondered where her mother and father were, and why they had left her alone on the dinghy.

"What did you buy, Bobby?" Murphy asked.

"Oh, I got a new pair of sneakers, and two pair of shorts, and a couple of blouses. Oh, and a dress. I look funny in a dress."

"I don't believe you'd look funny in anything, Bobby. I bet you look like a perfect lady." Murphy would rather be drinking a beer, but Madam Dupree had ordered a bottle of chilled wine. A tall, thin glass of white wine in front of Murphy looked a little out of place.

The next day, the Duprees, taking advantage of the inspector's free day, had Ute pack them a lunch. The three headed for a beach on the west side of the island. Richmond Beach is at the end of the road near one of the highest peaks on the island. Richmond Peak tops out at 3,523 feet above sea level. Inspector Dupree drove his other car on such occasions, a four wheel drive, mud-covered jeep. Madam Dupree sat next to the inspector, and Bobby bounced along in the back seat holding on with delight. Madam Dupree believes that the inspector considers the mud a badge of honor. She gave up long ago asking him to clean the jeep up.

After parking the car high above, a little hike down to the beach was required.

"Here, Bobby, let me adjust your rucksack. There we are, is that comfortable for you?" the inspector asked.

"That's fine, Inspector. I can smell the lunch Ute made for us," Bobby said.

"Madam, how's your pack, too much for you to carry?" the inspector asked.

"Oh no, Inspector, it's fine, let's head for the beach," Madam Dupree said.

The trio made their way down the trail to the gold-colored sand. It was a perfect day for the beach; white, puffy clouds, the sea a bright blue. This out-of-the-way beach was a favorite of theirs because they shared it only with the birds at this time of the year. Aside from the backpacks that carried personal items such as beach towels, cameras, and suntan lotion, the Duprees always tugged along their little red wagon. The red wagon was for the big stuff such as the shade tent, hibachi, cooler, briquettes and other assorted items.

"Here's a good spot, Inspector. Can we put the tent up right here?" Bobby asked. She was beginning to feel comfortable with Madam and Inspector Dupree. The inspector sat in his little beach chair under the shade tent reading the daily paper. Bobby and Madam Dupree, in a playful mood, ran down to the water.

"Madam Dee, this is a beautiful beach. I love it here but I'm worried about my family. I wonder if they know where I am?" Bobby said.

"The inspector is working on it. I'm sure he'll come up with something in a few days. He checked with the Coast Guard to see if any ships sank in the hurricane. Also he's looked at the missing-person reports. Don't worry, he'll find your parents. He's very good at his job," Madam Dupree said.

"Are there any sharks around here?" Bobby asked.

"No, not here, only on the other side of the island, where the reefs are," Madam answered.

"Does the inspector swim? Will he come in the water with us?" Bobby asked.

"Oh he swims, sometimes, but mostly he just loves to sit on the beach and read his paper," Madam said.

"Do you see something out there?" Bobby said, pointing to what could be black dorsal fins. "I thought I saw something moving."

Chapter Eighteen

"Yeah, that's right, mail the money to the Western Union, in Kingstown. Password? Let's see. Right, I'll need a password. Kram, that's Mark backwards." Borman was standing in a phone booth making his first call to his bank back in Boothbay Harbor, Maine. He was without funds with the exception of a few hundred dollars he had in his wallet when he left his schooner. Borman needed cash to open a bank account. "Yeah, St. Vincent, in the Caribbean, Western Union, and do it now. Thanks for the help, I appreciate it." His second call was to his insurance agent. "You got it, Stanley? I lost the whole thing, the boat and all the passengers. I was lucky I didn't go down with them. It was a hurricane, you moron. Christ! You must know what a hurricane is, don't you?"

Borman's phone booth was just outside a gin mill called Barney's. Barney's was on the waterfront southeast of Kingstown, in the area known as Villa. This is where you'll find many of the island's hotels, restaurants and bars, also a few boutiques and an antique store. Villa Beach and Indian Bay are two white-sand beaches divided by a small, hilly projection.

"Look, send me cash now and we'll work out the details later. Yes, cash. I'm standing here with sand in my pockets, and that's it. My bank is sending some money. It's only enough for a week or so. Wire the money to my bank here on St. Vincent. I'll be opening an account when my money comes from my bank. I'll call you with the account number. Take down this number, it's a bar on the waterfront called Barney's."

When Mark finished his phone call, he felt that Stanley had the picture and that money would be coming. In the meantime he'll run up a tab at Barney's.

"You see, Governor, this fellow Jesus was caught with the goods. They were right in his boat when he pulled up to the dock. Obviously these people were the importers. And then, when they both went for their guns, I was left without a choice. I fired first, very lucky for me," the inspector said. He was holding another meeting with the governor in Victoria Park. He was explaining the reason the two agents from up north left the island so soon. He did not mind playing the part of the hero for he knew it would be relayed to the prime minister.

"Well, you certainly were a brave man, my good fellow. I know Mr. Mitchell and I are very pleased you were able to clear things up in such a short time. I'm sure you'll be getting a letter of commendation from the prime minister."

"A letter of commendation is fine, Governor. Perhaps a raise in pay would be in order?" The inspector knew it would snow in St. Vincent before he'd get a raise.

"I'm afraid a raise is not possible, my dear Inspector. We work for the love of the island, not for monetary gain. I'm sure you understand."

"Yes indeed, Governor, as they say, 'money's not everything', although it does help pay the bills," Dupree said with a faint smile.

"Let's talk about our problem, Inspector. Now, I would like

you to get things under control. I will not have people coming here, to my island, asking a lot of questions. U.S. agents should never be here." The governor, dressed in his wrinkled suit, was fanning his face with his sweat-stained hat. "If we get any more of these investigations, we must shut the whole operation down permanently, do I make myself clear?" The governor, seated on the park bench with a flushed face, was particularly concerned.

"If there's a leak somewhere, I'll find it, Governor."

"You must have a talk with your people to see how rumors of drug trafficking reached all the way to Washington." The governor wiped his brow.

"I'll find it, Governor," Dupree said. His mind raced down the list of possible culprits.

"If there is a leak in the operation somewhere, it must be plugged. Do you understand, Inspector? It must be plugged." When it came to business the governor was as tough as donkey meat.

"Governor, your point is well taken. Rest assured I will find the perpetrator. Now I must take my leave, lots of work today." The inspector clicked his heels and gave a slight bow. The inspector always dressed in his tailored uniform. Very seldom did he remove his jacket or loosen his tie. The weather could be steaming hot but the inspector, at all times, looked cool.

"Yes, good day, Inspector, and remember if this leak is not found our boat will sink." There was no mistaking the tone of the governor's voice.

Back at the office Inspector Dupree spoke to Sheri: "Would you be so kind as to get Chief Urquhart, of Stamford, Connecticut, on the line."

Sheri dialed long distance. "Your call is ready, Inspector. I'll transfer it to your office."

"Good day, Chief Urquhart. I have one of your former police officers working for me. Yes, the man we spoke of several weeks ago. Yes, Chief, he's working out just fine. According to his resume he retired from the force in February of this year, is that correct? Would you repeat that please? He retired in 1968? Are you sure of that date? June of 1968. There seems to be a discrepancy here. This resume indicates that Mr. Murphy retired in February of this year. Can you think of any reason there's two missing years on his resume?" The inspector was not pleased with this apparent discrepancy. "Do your records show if Mr. Murphy transferred to another government organization such as the FBI or the CIA, perhaps the Drug Enforcement Agency? No information after he left the force, huh? Well, if anything comes up give me a call? Here, take down my number, call me collect. Thank you, Chief Urquhart, and if the winters get too cold for you up north please come down to our island. You'll be very welcomed here. Good day, sir."

Two years missing from Murphy's resume . . . two years. Why would Murphy be covering up two years? I hope he didn't transfer to some federal agency. I hope he is not playing the undercover thing. For that would be a shame. No, no, I must not even consider such an evil plot, but then, stranger things have happened. The inspector headed for the Water Front Café.

"Inspector, welcome to my humble café." Joseph sat in the far corner of the restaurant. "Have some coffee."

"Cream, no sugar," the inspector said as he sat down at Joseph's table.

"Carlos, coffee for the inspector," Joseph said. He then

lowered his voice. "I see in the papers that you shot my good friend, Jesus. What the hell did you do that for? Now where am I supposed to get my stuff?" The place was empty with the exception of Carlos behind the counter.

"If Jesus was your friend, you've been keeping very poor company. Now what's this stuff you're talking about?"

"Nothing, Inspector, nothing at all. Jesus was one of my best customers."

"Look, Joseph, I need some information. Now if you want to stay in business you'll get me the info I'm looking for," the inspector said in a low, firm voice.

"Oh Christ, Inspector, I don't know nothing. Nobody tells me nothing, and I don't ask. Just mind my own business, keep my nose to the grindstone, so to speak."

"You've never worked a day in your life. Now, come up with the information I'm looking for, and I won't close you down. Got it?"

"Come on, Inspector, I'm just a humble shopkeeper."

"You call taking numbers and the girls upstairs being humble? If you were humble you'd be out back cleaning that grimy kitchen."

"Okay, okay, what ya looking for?" Joseph asked.

"For some strange reason, we've had federal agents down here from the States asking questions about dope. Now, I'd like to know who is spreading such nasty rumors."

"It's like I said, Inspector, I don't ask questions and nobody volunteers nothing." Joseph had the pleading look of innocence on his face.

"Look, I'm not playing games here, and don't give me that innocent look. It'll be in your best interest to give me any bits of information that happen your way. I know you got your fat ears tuned to what's going on the waterfront."

"Sometimes I hear things," Joseph said in a low voice.

"It wouldn't surprise me if you had every table in the joint wired for sound."

"Yeah, yeah, wired for sound, that's far out."

"If I don't hear from you, this place is history. Your girls upstairs will be on workmen's comp. I'll shut you down faster than you can say shit. Do I make myself clear?" The inspector gave Joseph a glaring look.

"Alright, alright, you're the boss. I'll be in touch the minute I hear something. Now, I've got work to do. By the way, don't forget to pay for the coffee on your way out."

The inspector was alone on the beach where he was once again meeting with the Kaiser. He was thinking of changing their meeting place to Fort Charlotte on Berkshire Hill. The fort was named after King George III's wife. It was built in 1806, 600 feet above the bay. When the fort was active it supported 600 troops and 34 guns. Dupree felt that it attracted too many tourists, not a safe place to meet. He paced the beach with head down. The dark clouds of the day had not moved out, making for a dark night. It had been raining, off and on, most of the day.

"Herr Kaiser, the governor seems to think that those two agents were here on a tip. I must ask . . ., do you have a disgruntled employee? Maybe someone whose toes have been stepped on without you realizing it," the inspector said.

"Inspector, it is very wise of you to be suspicious. That is a good quality for a man in your position. I'm also very suspicious, especially of the men working for me. My boys understand if someone would say the wrong thing, he's a dead man."

"Does it work?" Dupree asked.

"The money's good, that's why the men work hard, they keep

their mouths shut. We haven't buried anyone for some time now. With the exception of the two men, who happened to be in the wrong place when you solved the problem of the drug ring."

"Most unfortunate, a nasty bit of business. It turns my stomach when I think about it," Dupree said.

"I hope there's not a new problem. I cannot afford to lose any more men or merchandise. I'd say that you take a hard look at the people working for you. I've heard that you have a new chauffeur, an ex-police officer, I believe," the Kaiser said as he turned toward the inspector, lifted one eyebrow.

"Yes, an ex-police officer by the name of Murphy," Dupree said.

"Aren't you taking a chance hiring a cop? Are you positive he's retired?" the Kaiser questioned.

"I'm looking into his background, every day of it. If he's the problem, I'll know about it, and take care of it."

"While you're at it, Inspector, check out the other people working for you. Jealousy and greed can corrupt a man's soul, screw up his thinking."

"You're so right, Herr Kaiser, some people never know when they are well off. The person causing this problem will beg for death before I am through with him. Now let's get out of this rain."

Back home that evening the inspector poured two fingers of brandy into his snifter, put on the headphones, and sat down in his overstuffed leather chair, contemplating the problem at hand. *There's a solution to this problem. I must put my mind to it. I must somehow set a trap, not only for Murphy, but for anyone in my office who thinks they know something. If there is a leak on my end, I'll find it. I hope it's not one of my boys.* When the brandy was gone and the music was over, our inspector was fast asleep.

Chapter Nineteen

Sheri answered the phone. The voice on the other end was deep and raspy. "Hello, let me speak to Inspector Dupree. I have an important message for him."

"I'm sorry, but the inspector is not in. You may leave the message with me. I'm the inspector's secretary." Sheri wrote the message down with much difficulty, asking for each word to be spelled. "What language is this, German?"

"Yes, it's German, keep it to yourself. I wouldn't want the wrong person getting their hands on this piece of information," the voice said.

"Don't worry, sir, the message will be delivered by one of our most trusted men. Except . . . I'm sorry, sir, the inspector does not speak German. How is he to read this message?" Sheri asked.

"The inspector is a clever man. Just see that he gets the message." Sheri assured the caller that the inspector would get the message as soon as possible.

"Oh, Sergeant Tanquay, are you on your way to meet the inspector?" Sheri asked.

"Yeah, he asked me to meet down on the waterfront. I'm headed there now."

"I just received this message for him. Would you please give it to the inspector?   I was told it's important and confidential. See that he gets the message right away. I was told that it's urgent."

"Oh sure, Sheri, no problem," the sergeant said as he headed out the back door to his patrol car. He looked at the folded piece of paper on the seat next to him. The sergeant read the message the best he could, then drove off to meet the inspector. The note read: *Verschiffung soll am Freitag abend am landeplatz ankommen.* (Translation: Shipment next Friday night at the landing strip.)

"Hello, let me speak to Inspector Dupree. I have an important message for him."

"The inspector is not here at the present. This is his wife. May I take the message? I'll see that your message is delivered promptly," Madam Dupree said to the person on the other end of the phone.

"Okay, but I must warn you that the message is in German, and it should be delivered right away, very important," the voice said.

Madam Dupree was puzzled. *Why would the message would be in the German language?* Madam Dupree thought. She wrote the message down word for word and asked to have each word spelled. She hung up the phone and headed for the kitchen.

"Good morning, Murphy, I see you are having some of Ute's famous coffee."

"Good morning, Madam. Yes, Ute's coffee is the best on the island. No, it's better than that, it is the best in the world."

"I have a message for the inspector and the caller said it was important. Would you find him and deliver this message as soon as possible?"

"Certainly, Madam, I'll call his office, Sheri always knows where he is." As Murphy pulled out of the driveway and headed down the road, he glanced at the note. The note read: *Verschiffung naechsten Donnerstag abend im hafenviertel.* (Translation: Shipment next Thursday night at the waterfront.)

The inspector had set his trap. He went over the plan in his head a number of times. *I hope I haven't left out any important details. Now if we have unwelcome visitors on the island in a few days I will know that one of my two closest employees cannot be trusted. If the people in the fancy suits don't show, then my suspicions must turn in other directions.* The inspector was walking the waterfront not far from the spot where that nasty bit of business had taken place a few nights previous. *Neither Sergeant Tanquay nor Murphy speak German, so if they simply deliver the message, there is no harm done. On the other hand, should one of them take the trouble to have the message translated, and if strangers do show up at either place, I have the man I'm looking for.* Dupree's solitary walk brought him to the area where his friend kept his powerboat.

I really hope that neither man is guilty of betrayal. I've worked with Sergeant Tanquay many years; he's always been a good cop, a trusted man. On the other hand, he could be looking for my job. I've heard rumors. Dupree walked out on the float, eyeing his friend's boat. *One never knows about people. Maybe he thinks that my job is glamorous. Little does he know of the things I have to do, just to maintain a decent standard of living. It's enough to turn one's hair gray. And then there's Murphy, the two missing years on his resume.* The powerboat was buttoned up tight. *He is such a good bodyguard and chauffeur. I would hate to lose him. On the other*

*hand, I'm disturbed to think what would happen if either man has
stabbed me in the back.*

At home on Tuesday evening the inspector sat in his study,
relaxing in his favorite leather chair. He thought about the events
of the past week. *Here I am, setting a trap for two men who work
very close with me. How is it I can be so suspicious? This job is doing
me in. I'm getting to the point where I don't trust anyone.*

The inspector thought he'd play something light on his stereo.
He reached for the LP of Die Zauberflote. *Well, I've not heard of
any strange men in town, nope, nothing, not a word. No fancy suits,
nothing from my boys out at the airport.* Reaching over to adjust
the volume he thought, *If the agents from up north were coming,
they would be here by now. Only two days to go before the supposed
shipment to the waterfront, and three days to go for the simulated
shipment at the airport.*

The inspector closed his eyes. *I feel like such a louse having
doubts about my men. Tomorrow I'll check out the hotel where the
Americans stay. If the agents were coming, that's the place that they
would be.* Before the first side of the record was over the inspector
was fast asleep.

The following morning the inspector was having his breakfast
in the kitchen, and making small talk with Ute. Madam and
Bobby were sleeping late. "Ute, how is Bobby getting along? Is
she adjusting?" Dupree asked.

"It's hard to tell, Inspector. If I had known her before she lost
her memory…"

"Yes, I see. I've tried every source I can think of. No missing-
person reports, no ships going down in that last hurricane,
nothing. It's all very strange."

"I'm sure she'll remember; she just needs some time," Ute said.

"Let's hope so, Ute. Well, I'm off for another day of hard work at the office. Oh, have Madam Dupree call me if there is a problem with Bobby. We should keep a close eye on her."

Late in the afternoon the inspector was able to break away from the station. He drove out to the strip, or Villa, as the natives call it. He drove a police car the few miles out of town on the southernmost tip of the island. He thought he would try the hotel where Mike Doyle and George Greenier stayed the last time they were on the island. He wanted to make certain that people like Doyle or Greenier had not slipped by unnoticed. The first place to check would be the lounge, being close to cocktail time. As he walked into the lounge, he froze in place. Sitting at the far end of the bar were Doyle and Greenier. The agents were in shorts and sport shirts, sipping those tall, fruity drinks the tourists like.

"Well, if it is not my old friends, Mike and George. Welcome back to our island. Are you here on business or pleasure?" The inspector was chagrined to see them, although he kept his tone cordial.

"We are here on pleasure, Inspector. We were so impressed with your island we thought we would come back for a short vacation. You did mention that we would be welcomed anytime," Doyle said with a half smile.

"Yes, of course you're welcome. And just to show you how pleased I am to see you, I would like to invite you both to my home for dinner tomorrow night. My wife would like to meet your wives. She has heard much about you two."

"Love to accept, Inspector, however, tomorrow night is out of the question; we have a previous engagement," Doyle said as he bent down to his straw.

"A previous engagement, well then, how about Friday night?" the inspector was now toying with them.

"Yes, Friday night. Ah . . . ah, George, are we free Friday night?" Doyle looked to his partner for a way out.

"Nope, not Friday night, Mike. We have tickets to the theater, remember?" Greenier replied.

"But, gentlemen, we don't have a theater on this island. Perhaps you have tickets to the movies." The inspector in full uniform, standing tall and straight, enjoyed playing his part. He loved the old war movies where his uniform was the style of the times.

"Oh yes, it's the movies. George, what the hell is wrong with you?" Doyle asked.

"Well, gentlemen, enjoy yourselves, whatever it is that you are here for. And please stop by my office if you are here on official business. You know that we must keep track of such goings-on. We can't have people coming here from foreign counties and doing police business on their own. You know that, don't you, Mike?" the inspector asked.

"Yeah sure, Inspector, we'll be in touch if we ever decide to do any police business, won't we, George?" Greenier was sipping his drink and almost choked on that line.

Driving home that evening the inspector was upset at finding the two agents back on the island. *That's it then, one of my most trusted men has stabbed me in the back. If the agents show up at the waterfront tomorrow night, Murphy is the culprit. On the other hand if they show up at the landing strip on Friday night Sergeant T. is my man. Now, why did those two say they were busy both nights? I hope Murphy and Tanquay are not working in tandem. That would really shake my trust in humanity, my two closest men working against me. No, that could not be, not the two of them together, heaven forbid.*

At home the Duprees' evening meal was a special time. Bobby, as a new member of the family, sat at the middle of the table. The meal was served in the dining room, with the centerpiece of fresh flowers. "I have important business to take care of tomorrow evening, Madam, and maybe the following night as well," the inspector said.

"What's this all about, dear? Don't tell me that those two agents from the States are back here again," Madam Dupree asked.

"They are, and dressed as tourists. They could be on vacation, but I have my doubts. I may be working late into the night."

"Oh, Inspector," Madam Dupree exclaimed. "Must you work tomorrow evening?"

"I hope not, however one can never tell, such is the police business," Dupree said.

"There's a wonderful movie playing; I thought the three of us could go." The Duprees did not have much of a social life outside of the family. The inspector preferred it that way.

"Say yes, Inspector, it would be great fun." Bobby was starting to feel relaxed with the Duprees. "Oh please, Inspector, pretty please?"

"I hate to turn you down, ladies. If I am not available for the next two evenings, bad things could come to this house. And, I might add, the people in it."

"Oh, Inspector, you have been reading too many mystery novels. This island is a paradise with a lot of beautiful people on it. How could anything be so important?" Madam Dupree questioned.

"Right you are, Madam, this island is a paradise and the only way to keep it that way is to stop things before they happen," the inspector said.

Bobby spoke up, "I don't think there are any gangsters here on St. Vincent, are there?"

"What I'll be doing tomorrow night is nipping things in the bud, so to speak, and that's my job. For the next two evenings, I will be nipping things in the bud."

"Okay, Inspector, promise you'll take us to the movies the first night you have off." Bobby had become very fond of the inspector.

"I promise, Bobby, perhaps it'll be as soon as Saturday night."

"Oh, that would be super." Bobby asked to be excused. She went upstairs to listen to her kind of music.

On Thursday evening Inspector Dupree settled down in the cabin of his friend's cruiser. He went over his plan several times. *Let's see, the high-speed launch will come into the dock at about ten. There'll be three or four men on board with a case of beer. It must look like a party.*

A launch similar to the one used last week has been chartered for this show. *The two agents from up north will be lying in wait. They'll recognize the boat.* The inspector was anxious about this operation for he was having a hard time believing that Murphy was an undercover agent. *Those two missing years on his resume make me nervous. After all he's a cop, or was a cop.*

His friend's boat was several slips away from the action, hidden by a larger cruiser. Dupree was dressed in his garage clean-up clothing. Most people would not recognize him out of uniform. *Nine-thirty. My friend keeps a very neat ship. I wonder where the brandy is? Brandy, brandy, ah, here it is. Not a brand I care for. Oh well, beggars can't be choosers, as the old saying goes. Sure is a dark night.* Dupree had moved up to the flying bridge. *Hmm, nice binoculars, good sharp image, no one in sight yet. I'll just keep quiet and enjoy my drink.*

Ten minutes after the hour, the launch powered up to the dock. The crew seemed to be enjoying themselves. *If I didn't know better, I'd say these people are having a party,* Dupree thought as the launch bumped the dock rather hard. One man jumped onto the dock and tied off the bowline. The stern of the launch drifted away from the dock.

"Get that stern tied off," someone shouted. One of the crew, with a line in his hand, jumped for the dock and missed.

"Man overboard," another person shouted. The whole process was a comedy of errors. After a fashion, things were under control. The night was very quiet after the motor was turned off. Dupree turned the binoculars in the direction where he thought the agents would be waiting.

I'll give them some time to unload their things and make their way home. If Mike and George are lying in wait, I need to give them plenty of time.

A half hour had elapsed since the men left the speedboat. All was quiet on the waterfront. Dupree sucked in a lungful of air, and let out a sigh of relief. *That's it then, no agents.*

On the drive home Dupree thought about the nonevent of the evening. *Well, my friend Murphy is off the hook. Nevertheless he still has the two missing years on his resume that must be explained. I'll just have to ask him directly. If he has a good explanation, I'm sure he will not mind telling me. I must thank my friend for the use of his boat and the brandy. Maybe I should buy a boat someday. Someday, yeah someday.*

Dupree arrived at his office the following morning bright and early. "Good morning, Sheri, you're looking lovely this morning."

"Good morning, Inspector, you're looking well-rested yourself," Sheri said.

"Thank you. As a matter of fact I did sleep rather well last night. Look, would you get ahold of Murphy and ask him to meet me for lunch at the Cobblestone Inn, about one this afternoon?"

"Isn't that the rooftop restaurant on Upper Bay Street?" Sheri asked.

"Yes, I'd like Murphy to feel at home. I understand that the food there is well prepared."

"I wouldn't know, Inspector, I've never eaten there. I don't know any cosmopolitan people."

"Well if it was not a business meeting, Sheri, I would invite you along," Dupree said with a smile.

"Oh, Inspector, you have your reputation to regard. Your wife would be more appropriate," Sheri said.

"Sheri, you are so right," the inspector replied with a broad grin. "We must not start rumors. The island is small and people do talk." The inspector winked at her as he left.

The rooftop restaurant had an excellent view of the bay. Meals were served under large sun umbrellas. The inspector sat under one of the umbrellas, sipping a martini with a twist of lemon, and absentmindedly staring out at the ocean. Murphy was about ten minutes late. When the inspector spotted him he said; "Hi,

Murphy, come have a seat. I understand the food here is very good. Have you eaten here before?"

"Afraid not, Inspector, I'm a man of simple tastes. Now, what the hell is this all about? I have the feeling that you have something up your sleeve." Murphy, always direct and to the point, was not noted for his diplomacy.

"Well, let's order you a drink, and then we'll talk about it."

"Fine with me, I'll have a beer." The waiter, dressed in a white jacket, with a white tea towel over his left arm, acknowledged the order.

"Murphy, during a routine check into your background, Sheri informs me that she found two years missing from your resume. I'm sure there's a simple explanation."

"So that's what this is all about. My God, for a moment I thought something was wrong," Murphy said.

"Very embarrassing for me, Murphy, I hope you understand. You see we are forever having people coming here from God knows where, looking for trouble. It's my job to keep trouble off the island."

"Inspector, I assure you that I am nothing more than a retired cop looking for his isle of paradise. The two missing years are something I prefer not to talk about."

"My friend, you must take me into your confidence. Whatever you say will go no further than this table."

"I'd rather not talk about it," Murphy said with his head down, looking into his beer.

"It's important that you account for the missing years. If I am satisfied, you shall hear no more about it," Dupree said.

"Okay, Inspector, I'll take your word on that. You see, I took early retirement because I had a nervous breakdown. I spent two years in the country getting well; a long, hard journey. The good news is that I am fine now. That's the reason I am not going back to police work. Now, if you would like to check my story, I'll give you a phone number, gimme your pen," Murphy fumbled around for a piece of paper. "This number is the country estate that nursed me back to health," Murphy said as he scratched the number down.

"Enough said, my good man, let's just enjoy our lunch. You have my word, you shall never hear about this conversation again."

"Fair enough, Inspector, I'll drink to that." Murphy lifted his glass with a grin.

Inspector Dupree arrived early at the landing strip on Friday evening. He sought out his hiding spot. He wanted to be close to the action, but well hidden. He assumed that the plane would be landing against the wind, at the other end of the field. He brought along field glasses so as to bring faces up close. His attire was right out of *Field & Stream.* Camouflage jacket and hat, with dark pants, the one exception was the lack of face paint. The Kaiser informed the inspector that the field would be lit with the headlights from several autos. The excuse for the night landing would be that the pilot was practicing his night flying for an upgrade in his pilot's license, something about an instrument rating.

The boys from the speed launch were right on schedule, lining up their cars. At approximately ten thirty the inspector heard the plane. He saw its landing lights. The plane made several passes over the field. *He must be a good pilot; a night landing of this sort's not easy,* thought the inspector. The pilot made a bouncing landing on the makeshift landing strip. It was a light plane with an overhead wing. There was room for two people, the pilot and a passenger behind him. The wheels were fixed in place with fat tires for landing in grass-covered fields. The plane came to a stop more or less where the inspector had guessed. When the engine was shut off, the night was quiet. The car lights went out one by one until darkness settled in.

Another wasted evening, the inspector moaned. *Now I wish I had gone to the movies with Bobby and Madam.* Loud voices came from the far end of the landing strip. Two cars came speeding up the field, headlights bouncing up and down. Both cars came to a sliding stop, as two men jumped out of each car. Guns drawn, the men were yelling as they came running toward the plane. The pilot climbed down from the plane with his hands in the air. Dupree watched while shaking his head. "Sergeant Tanquay. . . Sergeant Tanquay, how could he have been so stupid?"

"Hold it right there, mister, on the ground, hands behind your back!" Agent Doyle was leading the attack with his partner right behind him. Dupree did not recognize the other two men. As it turned out, they were also agents.

"George, check the plane while I get the cuffs on this guy," Doyle commanded, enjoying his role as the tough cop.

"Nothing here, Mike," Greenier shouted.

"Look in the back section where they keep the luggage." The thought of no drugs on the plane never crossed Doyle's mind.

"Nothing in back, Mike," Greenier shouted again. All the while the pilot, lying face-down on the ground, did not say a word.

"George, take the men and search the area. I'll check the plane again," Doyle said as he moved toward the plane. "George, wait, over here," Doyle said as he motioned Greenier to come closer. "What the hell is going on? I know drugs are here somewhere.

Look at the men at the other end of the field. They're not making a run for it. Something doesn't add up."

"Beats me, Mike, maybe we've been set up," Greenier said.

"I think you're right, George, I bet the inspector had a hand in this," Doyle replied.

"Yeah and when he hears about our midnight party at the airstrip he'll be a raging bull," Greenier said.

The next morning the four agents were locked up in the two cells in the back of the police station. They had been roused out of their beds in the wee hours of the morning and placed under arrest. The inspector, enjoying his coffee, was talking to his secretary and office manager. "Please forgive me, Sheri, for putting you through all this paperwork. I had no idea that these men were down here on assignment. When I spoke to them the other day, they assured me that they were here on vacation. Now, here they are, down here on our island, causing all sorts of trouble. I am sure the prime minister will be calling the governor and the governor will be calling me."

"Then what, Inspector?" Sheri asked.

"Then, I will have to release my charges, except in the meantime I'll take a stroll in the park," Dupree said.

"But, Inspector, aren't you going to be here when the governor calls?"

"My Sheri, I don't think so. I shall be taking a stroll in the park. I asked these people to please come to my office if they were down here on official business. They completely ignored my request," Dupree said.

"Inspector!" Sheri exclaimed. "How could they?"

"A few hours in our comfortable little cells out back won't hurt. I wish I could make it a few days. Although we wouldn't want to be the cause of an international flare-up, now would we?" the inspector said with a twinkle in his eye.

Dupree was in a good mood when he returned home that afternoon, for the leak has been plugged. The fact that his ship would not be sinking was a great relief. The governor would be pleased. The agents were released later that day. The four men signed an agreement stating that they would never again conduct police work on the island without first obtaining permission from the Chief Inspector. Doyle and Greenier, along with the other two agents, were upset upon leaving the police station. All four agreed that they would somehow extract their revenge on Chief Inspector Dupree.

Saturday was a day off for the inspector. His greatest pleasures were reading history books and listening to classical music. Bobby came bouncing into the study.

"You're home, Inspector, oh good. Can we go to the movies tonight? Please, Inspector, can we?" Bobby asked.

"I don't see why not, my young lady. Yes, why not. It should be lots of fun, just the three of us." The inspector's good mood radiated throughout the house.

"Oh super, I'll go tell Madam Dee. She'll be thrilled. I just know she'll be thrilled." Bobby ran through the kitchen and into the garden to give Madam Dupree the good news.

Later that evening, after the movies, the trio walked down Bay Street. They turned into a restaurant. As they sat at a small table having coffee and ice cream, the conversation was about the agents from up north. The inspector related how the agents could not believe that they were back in his jail again. "And I told them that the phones were down, that they would not be released until we had permission from the governor."

"I didn't know your phones were out of order today," Madam Dupree remarked.

"When the phone would ring, Sheri would pick it up and pretend that she couldn't hear." Bobby and Madam could not stop laughing.

"Then what happened?" Bobby asked.

"Well, they wanted to know how long it would take to get the phones fixed. I told them that the people on this island do not move that fast. It may take a couple of days."

Bobby stopped laughing long enough to ask, "Are they still in jail?"

"No, I'm afraid not. The governor called and left a message with Sheri. Said he could appreciate my position, but he felt it best to release the men."

"Well I hope that will teach them a lesson," Madam Dupree added. "Those people have some nerve."

Chapter Twenty

"Okay, Bobby, hiking it is. I'll tell Ute to pack us a lunch and the inspector can get the car," Madam Dupree said. "Let's climb Mount La Soufriere. Are you up to climbing a mountain, Bobby?"

"Sure. Is it a high mountain?" Bobby asked.

"High enough for me," the inspector joined in.

"It's a volcano, but don't worry, it's not active now," Madam added.

"Are you sure it's not active?" Bobby asked as she wrinkled her forehead.

"Nothing to worry about, you have my personal guarantee," the inspector said with a smile. "The last time it erupted was back in 1902, that was sixty eight years ago."

"Do you remember when it happened?" Bobby asked.

"Contrary to popular opinion, I'm not that old, young lady."

"We could drive up the Leeward Highway to the Botanic Gardens. They have every flower and tree that grows in the Caribbean. They even have a breadfruit tree that is over fifty feet high. It is said that Captain Bligh brought it to the island back in 1765, or somewhere around there," Madam Dupree said.

"I'd think climbing a mountain would be more fun." Bobby added.

The inspector drove his mud-covered jeep along the narrow, scenic road up the west side of the island, headed for Rabacca Day River. They passed Georgetown, once the center of the sugar industry. They then turned inland through the Orange Hill banana plantation. Madam Dupree, who was never fond of the open-air jeep, rode in front. Bobby, with a smile on her face, bounced along in the back seat. Rabacca Day River was once a hot river of lava. The well-marked trails lead to the crater of La Soufriere at 4,048 feet. It is a six-hour round trip for the fit and healthy. The view of the crater is well worth the effort.

Bobby, feeling better, began to sing:

> "It's a long way to tickle Mary
> It's a long ways to go."

"Bobby, where did you learn that? Those are not the right words," Madam Dupree said.

"But, Madam, that's the way the kids at school sing it," Bobby said.

"Not an appropriate song for a young lady," Madam scolded. At that moment the inspector picked up the tune:

> "It's a long way to tickle Mary
> It's a long ways to go."

"Inspector, you're corrupting this child," Madam Dupree protested. Bobby then joined in with the inspector:

> "It's a long way to tickle Mary,
> The sweetest girl I know.
> Goodbye, my Piccadilly,
> So long Harold Square.
> It's a long, long way to tickle Mary,
> But my heart's right there."

The cloudless sky and low humidity pushed the hikers up the mountain. The two-hour hike brought them through the bamboo groves, a tropical rainforest, and then a barren landscape of scrub-like vegetation. Bobby was first, Madam Dupree behind her, farther back, the inspector, huffing and puffing. Before the final trudge up a rocky lava field, Madam Dupree said, "I'm winded, we've climbed high enough. Let's break for lunch, after that we'll head back down." She sat down on the side of the trail, removed her red neckerchief and wiped her forehead.

"Yes, let's take a break. Aren't you getting tired, Bobby?" the inspector inquired.

"Aren't we climbing to the top, Inspector? We can make it to the top, can't we?" Bobby questioned.

"I'm sure we could if we got an early start. First I must spend a couple of weeks in the gym, working out. However, for today, I think not. Both Madam and I are tuckered out," the inspector said.

The three found a spot with a panoramic view of the ocean. Bobby devoured her first sandwich. She slowed down on her second. Bobby's melancholy had been lifting in recent days.

"Bobby's appetite is improving." Madam noted, speaking to the inspector.

"Look at that bird, it's beautiful. Look Madam Dee!" Bobby said.

"I see it, oh, it's gone. That was an Amazon parrot, our national bird. I didn't think we'd see one today; it's endangered," Madam Dupree said.

"My mother liked birds. Are there snakes around here? I hate snakes," Bobby said.

"We have a few, but they're harmless. Do you remember anything else about your mother?" Madam asked.

"No!" Bobby looked down, pulled on a blade of grass as a tear came to her eye.

"The big ones wrap themselves around trees," the inspector said, noting Bobby's dejection when questioned about her mother.

"What are they called?" Bobby asked.

"Congo snakes. They won't bother you if you don't bother them. Just stick to the trail and keep out of the rainforest," the inspector replied.

"No way will I be going into the rainforest, no way," Bobby said.

"Look, Bobby, down there, see that banana estate?"

"Where?" Bobby asked.

"Over there. They grow oranges, too," Madam said. She was on her feet, putting on her backpack. "Bananas are our most important export. They bring money to our island, and help pay the inspector's salary."

"Is that true, inspector, they pay you in bananas?"

The inspector was not listening. He looked at Bobby with the oddest expression. Madam Dupree smiled, trying hard not to laugh. "No, Bobby, they pay him in cash."

On the way down the mountain they had more time to enjoy the songbirds, and the view of the ocean. The ocean breeze pushed the fragrance of the aromatic rainforest up the mountain.

Madam spoke of the sad and shocking news of the death of Sergeant Tanquay as they passed the banana plantation on their way home. "It was only a few days ago that I was talking to the Sergeant. I can't believe he's gone," Madam Dupree said.

"Yes, poor Sergeant Tanquay, he should never have gone fishing in that old wooden boat," the inspector said with an innocent look.

"I must have flowers sent right away," Madam Dupree said. She shook her head in disbelief. "Do you know what the funeral arrangements are?"

"No, not yet, I'll make a phone call just as soon as we get back. The accident is under investigation," the inspector said.

"I certainly hope so," Madam Dupree said.

Bobby ran into the kitchen to tell Ute about the Amazon parrot. "She was beautiful. You should have seen her colors," Bobby said with excitement.

"What are you talking about, Bobby?" Ute asked

"A bird, a beautiful bird," Bobby said.

"Are you sure it was a female?" Ute asked.

"I guess so, and we saw the rainforest, and the banana plantation. They grow oranges there too," Bobby said.

"Sounds like you had a very exciting day," Ute said.

"So exciting I'd like to go back tomorrow, but the inspector said he needed to go to the gym first," Bobby said.

After parking the jeep in the garage the Duprees walked toward the side entrance that led to Ute's kitchen. "Poor Sergeant Tanquay," the inspector said. "I have always told him that some day that old wooden boat would sink beneath him. Now he is gone. What a shame. What a pity."

"But I didn't think the sergeant's boat was that old. He certainly was a charming person, with his whole life ahead of him." Madam Dupree said.

The inspector made no response. He always felt that a person who leaked information should never go fishing in a leaky boat.

Chapter Twenty-one

Madam Dupree, Bobby and Murphy went to town early for the best pick of food in the open marketplace. On Friday and Saturdays the market is particularly well stocked. People come in from the outlying neighborhoods to the Central Market, on Upper Bay Street, to sell their wares. In the bustling market one will find a superb selection of fresh vegetables, fruits, meats, and fish. The people are colorful and full of good cheer. It's always a fun time shopping at the market.

"Oh, Madam Dee, look at this fruit. Can we have some?" Bobby asked.

"Why not, and let's not forget the conch. What other items has Ute on her shopping list?" Madam Dupree asked. She moved into the shade of a tree to read her list. "She has here shrimp and whelk for tomorrow's dinner, along with callaloo soup," Madam Dupree said.

"Callaloo soup? What's that?" Bobby said, making a face.

"It's very good the way Ute makes it," Murphy injected.

"Doesn't sound good; I hope I like it," Bobby said.

The early shoppers were picking over the fruit and vegetables. The market was not as crowded as it would be in an hour or so. Murphy walked a few paces behind Madam Dupree and

Bobby, carrying their bundles. He looked around for anyone he considered suspicious. Murphy had the habit of running different scenarios through his mind. What if this happened, or what if that happened.

"Ute wants bread, black bread," Bobby said.

"Let's get the bread last," Madam said as she squeezed a melon. "It won't get flattened by the heavy vegetables in the bag."

"I heard Ute say she wanted . . . ," Bobby stopped midsentence, unable to speak.

"What is it, Bobby? What's the matter?" Madam Dupree asked.

Bobby's mouth was open, moving, but no sound was coming out. She stammered and pointed. Her face was flushed. People stopped what they were doing, and stared at Bobby. Someone said, "What's wrong with that child?"

Bobby pointed to a man four stalls away. Murphy set his bundles down and came to Bobby's side. "What is it, Bobby? What's the matter?

Madam Dupree put her arm around Bobby. "Who are you pointing at, Bobby?"

The man Bobby was pointing at stared wide-eyed for a moment, then dropped his bundles and ran. Murphy spotted the man, and started after him. The man was fast, he bumped people out of his way. He knocked over a display of fruit as he turned the corner. Murphy's short legs pumped up and down; however, he was unable to keep up. When Murphy turned the corner, the man was nowhere in sight. He ran another half a block, then gave up.

Bobby found her voice, and screamed long and loud. Murphy returned out of breath, looking very puzzled.

"Whoever he was, he got away, Madam," Murphy said.

"Who was it, Bobby?" asked Madam Dupree. "What did you see?"

"That man, he's from our boat," Bobby stammered.

"The sailboat you were on?" Madam asked.

"Yes, yes. It was the Capt . . .," Bobby said crying, shaking, and trying to talk.

"What captain, Bobby?" Murphy asked.

"Capt . . . Capt . . . Captain Mark," Bobby cried out.

"Who is Captain Mark?" Madam Dupree asked.

"Captain Mark. I think he killed everybody," Bobby said.

"You mean everyone on the boat?" Murphy asked.

"Yes, I think he killed . . .," Bobby said with difficulty. Murphy and Madam Dupree led Bobby to a park bench nearby. Bobby, crying uncontrollably, sat between Madam Dupree and Murphy, who were trying to make sense of what she was saying.

"Did he kill your parents?" Murphy asked. Bobby nodded her head.

"And your brother, and sister too?" Madam asked.

"I don't have a sister." Bobby blew her nose with Murphy's handkerchief.

"Oh my God, Murphy, we've got to get back to the house and call the inspector. That man, whoever he is, may try to get off the island before the police can talk to him," Madam Dupree said.

As Murphy drove the limo Madam Dupree stayed with Bobby in the back seat. Bobby tried to tell her story. It came out in pieces, a bit here, more there. Madam Dupree was patient but puzzled.

"He came down the ladder with a club in his hand," Bobby said.

"And did he try to kill you?" Madam Dupree asked.

"No, he hit my brother on the head and then he hit my mother, and I . . . I . . . I ran up on deck," Bobby said as she tried to tell her story.

"But how did you escape? Where could you go?" Madam Dupree asked.

"I . . . I tried to pull the cord on the emergency life raft, but I couldn't. Captain Mark came up behind me," Bobby said as she blew her nose again.

"Did Captain Mark put you in the life raft?" Murphy asked.

"Yes, he said that if I got in he would go below and get my mommy and Brad," Bobby said, wiping her tears.

"Then your family was okay? They were down in the cabin?" Madam Dupree asked.

"I don't know. He started to go below, then stopped. He turned around and untied me. He waved and hollered, 'You'll see your family up in heaven, kid'." Bobby held her hands to her face and sobbed.

Murphy had his head half turned around, trying to hear and drive at the same time. Madam held Bobby close to her and tried to comfort her as best she could.

When Bobby was able to speak again she said, "It was dark and the waves were big."

"You poor thing, did you have water or food?" Madam asked.

"No, he didn't give me anything. And then a wave hit and the raft rolled over," Bobby said.

"You and the raft rolled over?" Murphy asked.

"Yes, I just hung on until a little later another big wave hit the raft again and turned it up the right way," Bobby said.

"But how did you get back into the dinghy with all those

waves and wind?" Madam Dupree asked. She could not believe what she was hearing.

When Murphy reached the villa he turned into the drive. "Come, Bobby, I'm calling our doctor. He'll give you something to calm you down," Madam Dupree said. She then asked Ute to sit with Bobby while she called the doctor. After her call to the doctor, Madam Dupree called the inspector. "Inspector, I should have called you first. I'm not thinking straight. Come home, please. It's Bobby. You won't believe the story she just told me. She recognized a man in the market, said he killed her parents."

"Killed her parents?" the inspector repeated.

"Yes. She called him Captain Mark. The captain of the sailboat she was on."

"I'm on my way. Put first put Murphy on the phone," the inspector said. "Murphy, did you get a good look at this guy? Could you identify him in a lineup?" Dupree asked.

"I wouldn't say I got a good look, but I think I could identify him. I chased him for a while, he must be in good shape. I couldn't catch him," Murphy said.

"Okay, I'm on my way. Don't leave the house until I get there," the inspector said.

Acting Sergeant Courtois, the inspector's new driver, drove through the city traffic, and up the hill to the villa, passing all others on the road. When the inspector entered the house, his wife was waiting for him. "Inspector, I've put her to bed. The doctor said he'd be here in an hour or so," Madam Dupree said.

"You said she saw a man at the market and her memory came back?" the inspector asked as he removed his coat and hat.

"It certainly seems that way. I wanted to give her one of my pills to calm her down; I thought it best to wait for the doctor.

She would like to talk to you. Her story is chilling, horrific," Madam Dupree said.

When the inspector entered the bedroom, Bobby tried to smile. "Bobby, my little darling, what happened today? Who did you see?" Dupree asked.

Bobby started crying as the inspector held her hand. When Bobby was able to talk her story came out a little at a time. The part about Bermuda and sailing in fair weather was not hard to tell. "My mother thought the captain was kind of weird," Bobby said as she wiped tears from her cheeks.

"Then what happened?" Dupree pulled his chair closer to the bed.

"During the hurricane the boat went upside down and my father broke his nose."

"Did anyone else get hurt?" the inspector asked.

Bobby nodded her head. "My brother hit his ribs. He said he thought they were broken, and I got a bang on the head." Bobby had difficulties with the end of the story. The inspector was patient and asked a number of questions. In the end, Bobby was able to put it all together for the inspector. "Are you sure the person you saw was Captain Mark? You're positive it was he? Not someone who just looked like him?" Dupree asked.

"It was Captain Mark. I know it, I know it." Bobby said.

"Okay, Bobby, we'll find this man. Then you can have a good look at him. Excuse me while I make some phone calls," Dupree said. He left the room, and almost bumped into his wife, who was carrying a cup of weak tea to Bobby.

"Inspector, I'm so upset. Do you really think that this man killed her family?" Madam Dupree asked.

"It's hard to tell right now. If we can bring him in for questioning . . .," the inspector shrugged his shoulders. "Sit with her awhile, I have some calls to make," Dupree said as he gave his wife a hug.

"Governor, Dupree here, I'm delaying all flights off the island. We may have a killer on the loose," the inspector said.

"We can't be delaying flights. Good God, man, think of the tourists. They have connections to make. How long do you intend to do this?" the governor asked.

"For several hours, maybe into the evening, I plan to alert all the marinas, and no freighters are scheduled to leave today. I'll have a sketch made," Dupree said.

"Well, get this thing over with quickly. This island is not your playground," the governor said, in a not-so-pleasant way.

"Thank you, Governor. I'll call you later with all the details." The inspector hung up the phone, then hurried out to the patrol car. "Sergeant, there may be a killer on the loose. Get back to the station, and put everyone in the department on alert. Send a man to each marina. Have them look for anyone who is acting suspiciously. Look for anyone getting ready for a long trip, or anyone who seems to be in a hurry. We do not want this killer getting off the island. Then find the sketch artist, get her up here as quickly as possible. I'll be waiting here for her," the inspector said.

Sergeant Courtois squealed his tires as he left the inspector's house, lights flashing, French-style horn blaring, weeeehorrrr, weeeehorrrr. Dupree returned to the house and went into the kitchen. "Any fresh coffee, Ute?"

"I was just about to make some. Do you have a minute?" Ute asked.

"Ute, I have just heard the most incredible story from Bobby. I don't have time to tell you about it. I've got to get it all down on paper while it's fresh in my mind," Dupree said.

"Madam Dupree has told me a little of what happened. I have difficulty believing it. The poor kid." Ute said.

"We must assume she's telling the truth. I'd like you to help make Bobby as comfortable as possible. The doctor will be here shortly. I'm waiting for the sketch artist. We need to know what this person looks like. Do you know where Murphy is?"

"I believe he went to the station, said something about helping to find the man Bobby was pointing at. He's extremely upset about letting the man get away," Ute said.

"If he calls in, tell him I want him here guarding the house. We don't want this guy slipping back here and eliminating the only witness against him."

Chapter Twenty-two

In the short time that Borman had been on St. Vincent, he had made himself comfortable. With the insurance money he paid off the mortgage on his schooner, purchased a house with a swimming pool, and found a girlfriend. The house was high on a hill overlooking the bay. He had also put a down payment on a powerboat for his charter fishing business. At his favorite watering hole, Barney's, he met the girl he had fantasized about, Jeannette Thibeault. She had long, dark hair, sultry eyes, and a life- style that was similar to her boobs: no visible means of support.

His surprise encounter in the market put Mark Borman in a panic. He was throwing clothing at the travel bag on the bed when his girlfriend appeared at the bedroom door. "Why are you packing? Where you going, honey?" Jeannette asked.

"Don't bother me now, sweetheart; I'm in one helluva hurry." Borman's eyes lit up. "Say, how would you like to go on a trip, just the two of us? I've got some unfinished business in the States, needs my immediate attention, very important."

"The States? I love to travel. You sure you want me to go with you?" Jeannette asked.

Mark Borman assumed the police would be looking for a

single guy. "I thought we could take my boat to a jetport on one of the larger islands."

"Sure, honey, but why bother with your boat when we can just take a plane from here to a larger island?" Jeannette said.

"Don't be asking questions. Just pack your bags, and let's get going," Borman said. His clothes were hitting the bed, sliding off onto the floor.

"How long we going for, honey?" Jeannette asked.

"Not long, two or three weeks. You'll love it there. Shake a leg now, boat's leaving," Borman said. Jeannette smiled as she rushed to her closet.

When the sergeant dropped the artist off at the villa, the inspector led her to Bobby's room. "Bobby, this is Carmen. She is going to make a sketch of Captain Mark. Do you think you can give Carmen a good description?" the inspector asked. Bobby, red-eyed, nodded her head.

"Hi, Bobby," Carmen said as Bobby gave a small wave with her right hand. Carmen was a working mother who had experience working with children. She was a fine portrait artist who sold her paintings in the market on weekends. Her gentle manner helped place Bobby at ease.

"Carmen, there's a killer who may get off this island if we don't have a good sketch of him," Dupree said.

"I'll do my best, Inspector."

"Give me a call as soon as you're finished. I'll send Sergeant Courtois up here for you and the sketch, okay?" the inspector said. The outward calm exterior presented by Dupree belied his inner tension.

"Certainly, Inspector, you realize that this may take a few hours," Carmen said.

"Fine, Carmen, except time is important." The inspector moved a chair and small table next to the bed. Carmen opened her art bag, removed her sketchpad and pencil. She smiled at Bobby. "Bobby, I've got some pictures of head shapes. Would you say his head is shaped like this?" Carmen asked, as she held up a card.

"The doctor will be here shortly, Bobby. Be a brave girl, help Carmen all you can. We'll catch this man. He won't get very far," the inspector said.

"I know you'll catch him. I just know you will," Bobby said. She then looked at Carmen, shook her head.

"Madam and Ute will be here with you. I'll be back just as soon as I can," the inspector said, then hurried out the door.

Dupree drove himself back to the police station in his jeep. He parked in the back of the building and entered through the dented steel door of the old granite building. The wood steps were worn from years of service. The inspector took them two at a time. He hurried through the dimly lit hallway that held the pictures of past inspectors, governors, and various police officers. Sheri held the office by the main entrance. The sliding glass window was always opened.

"Sheri, how did Sergeant Courtois make out getting the men posted? Are the planes at the airport delayed? Are the men at the marinas?" Dupree asked.

"Inspector, I was hoping you'd show up. It wasn't easy finding enough men for all the work you ordered. The governor is not going to like paying for all this overtime," Sheri said with wide eyes.

"I know. The governor is tightfisted. Where is Courtois?" the inspector asked.

"He's at the airport. A flight was ready for take-off. He stopped it and went on board," Sheri said.

"But how does he know who he's looking for?" the inspector asked.

"You know the Sergeant; he has a nose like a bloodhound," Sheri answered.

"I'm expecting a call from Carmen when her sketch is finished. Would you let me know as soon as she calls? Right now I need to smooth the governor's feathers," the inspector said as he headed for his office.

With his girlfriend in his pickup, Borman drove down to the Hemingway Marina, where he kept his boat. "Let's get these bags on board, sweetheart. I've got to top my tanks off at the fuel dock. Get on board, I'll pass you the luggage," Borman said. They had agreed before leaving the house that they would travel light. One travel bag and one handbag each would do it.

The Hemingway Marina had been upgraded with new floating concrete slips. Another pier had been added along with new slips to handle the demand.

"Look, Mark, there's a police officer coming down the dock," Jeannette said.

Borman looked up, sweat forming on his forehead. "No time for socializing now. Cast off the bow line, I'll get the stern line." He powered over to the fuel dock as the officer headed back to the marina office. The dock boy grabbed the line, tied it off, and began filling the two fuel tanks. The minutes ticked by. "Can't you pump gas any faster than that? Christ." Borman said. In the cabin he sat down at the navigation table and made some measurements. "Let's see, the boat burns about seven gallons per hour at a cruising speed of twelve knots."

"Is that the island we're going to, honey?" Jeannette asked.

"Don't know yet, gotta figure the fuel," Borman said. He then bent over the chart table and drew some lines.

Sergeant Courtois and Murphy showed up at the marina just as Mark's boat left the harbor. Officer Terence Pratt had drawn the marina duty. "Hi, Terry, this is Murphy, retired from the force up north. Anything going on down here, any boats making a getaway?" Sergeant Courtois asked.

"Hi, Murphy, nope, no action here, nothing suspicious going on so far. Just one boat left about ten minutes ago. The dock boy said they were going fishing."

"And who might that be?" Murphy asked the question before the sergeant could.

"Just some guy, and his girlfriend. Looked like they were going out fishing for a couple of days. He has a thirty-foot cabin cruiser, sort of a trawler type, good-looking boat," Officer Pratt said.

"Notice anything out of line? Were they in a hurry or taking their time?" Murphy asked.

"Kind of a hurry," the officer replied. Murphy was looking out over the harbor, trying to see the trawler. The sergeant was taking notes. "I thought it strange that the girl was wearing heels," Officer Pratt said.

Murphy's head spun around. "What, heels to go fishing? What the hell kind of an outfit is that to go fishing." Murphy's face flushed.

"How long have they been gone?" the sergeant demanded in a strong voice.

"Ten minutes or so, they couldn't have gotten far." Officer Pratt was embarrassed.

"That's our man, Sergeant," Murphy said with excitement.

Courtois closed his notebook. "Did you get a look at the girl? Was she from around here? Was she a local girl?" the sergeant asked.

"No, no one I recognized," Officer Pratt said. He shrugged his shoulders.

"Where's the phone? The inspector must know about this," Murphy said as he grabbed for the office door.

The launch, with three police officers, headed out of the harbor at a high rate of speed. The waves created by the launch disturbed a number of sailors living aboard their boats in the harbor. "Jerks," shouted one sailor as he waved his fist. People who live on their boats get a little upset when a powerboat makes a wake. It could set the boat rocking and upset glasses, dishes, or perhaps a cooking pot.

At the breakwater the launch turned north with spray breaking over the bow. The officers huddled in the cuddy cabin in an effort to stay dry. After an hour of pounding, the officers were ready to turn back. The skipper was enjoying the chase as long as the police department was paying him by the hour.

When Murphy and Courtois arrived back at the station, the inspector called a meeting. The meeting consisted of six men including Courtois and Murphy. They sat around the table in the lunchroom, a room scheduled to be painted next week. The pea-green walls were a deterrent to anyone's appetite. The brown color of the wood wainscot was affectionately called shit brindle.

"Gentlemen, first I have copies of Carmen's sketch. I'm told it's a very good likeness." Dupree handed out the sketches reproduced in black and white. The original was on tan construction paper sketched in charcoal. "If this department had a big budget, we'd have a high-speed patrol boat or perhaps a helicopter to go chasing after this guy." The smell of stale coffee permeated the room. "But since we don't have such fancy equipment, we must use the next best thing, our heads," Dupree said.

In a low voice someone said, "That leaves Pratt out." Chuckles went around the table.

"Hold it down, gentlemen. I want you to put yourself in Borman's shoes. You have a boat with maybe 100 gallons of fuel. We have no idea how much food is on board. Now let's go around the table and come up with all the different ways that he could escape us. First you, Sergeant," Dupree said.

"Well, if I were Borman, I would seriously consider my options," Courtois said.

"Yes, yes, we know that, now get on with it." Dupree said as he looked at the officers who were off duty. They were relaxed with their jackets off, ties loose.

"I would turn around in the middle of the night and head back to the harbor. I would then, very quietly, pull up alongside the freighter that's in the harbor. I would climb aboard and find a place to stow away," Courtois said.

"But, Sergeant, you are forgetting about the powerboat, also the fact that another freighter may come in the harbor tonight." The inspector was looking for holes in the sergeant's escape plan.

"I would have my friend take the boat around the island. Then at a distance from shore, open the seacock. Then she could row ashore in the dinghy." The sergeant had a grin on his face, for he believed he found the answer.

"Very good, Sergeant, but Borman would need a girlfriend competent with powerboats. It's a good idea, worthy of consideration. Murphy, your turn," the inspector said.

"I'd head for an island with an airport, a big airport, one with jets, lots of people. I'd melt into the crowd," Murphy said.

"Good thinking, Murphy, I've called every police chief within a hundred-mile radius. Also I've sent out sketches of this Mark character by charter plane to every island.

He could slip by, however that would be taking a big chance. Now what, gentlemen?" the inspector asked. The officers looked at one another. A few averted their eyes, hoping not to be called upon. Officer Joe Paquette raised his hand.

"Officer Paquette, you have an idea?" the inspector asked.

"Yes, Inspector, if this guy has 100 gallons of fuel he could travel some distance, north or south."

"That's right, Joe, what's your point?" Dupree said.

"Well, I was thinking that he could refuel and keep going. As long as the weather held, that is." Joe Paquette was one of the younger officers, in his middle twenties, very serious about police work.

"You have a good point. We have also been in touch with all Coast Guard units. We asked them to keep an eye out for the type of boat this man has."

Sergeant Courtois's eyes sparkled as he said, "He could loop around this island and head south. There's a bunch of islands south of here. He could hide out on one of them." St. Vincent has thirty-two sister islands, most of them uninhabited.

"That would be very unlikely. Sooner or later someone would give him away, or his boat would give him away. The next best thing would be to go to some uninhabited island. The problem is that it would be difficult to survive; finding food and water wouldn't be easy," the inspector said. He took off his jacket and loosened his tie. "Gentlemen, one plan we have not considered is for this culprit to go to a large island that has a small airport where he could charter a small plane. The small plane could then take Borman to a jetport outside the 100-mile radius. He would need an airport that's not heard of Mark Borman," the inspector said.

"I think you've hit the nail on the head, Inspector," Murphy said. He was looking at the inspector, nodding his head in approval.

"Sergeant Courtois, you'll be responsible for keeping a close eye on the freighter. Camp out on the *Star of Oma* itself if need be. Get to know all the places where one could hide. Hope no other freighter will come into the harbor. Murphy and I will take a small plane to Barbados. This is just a hunch but we must pick some island. I'm picking an island on the outer limits of his fuel range."

"We'll need some luck on this one, Inspector," Murphy observed.

"Any more questions, gentlemen? Good, let's get started. Murphy, pack a bag. Pick me up at seven. We're catching a chartered flight to Barbados. Sergeant, take the launch out to the freighter," the inspector said.

"Right you are, Inspector." Courtois gave a half salute, not quite a military salute.

"Murphy, I'll have Joe here take over your bodyguard duties. I wouldn't want this guy to double back and harm our only witness. Go out to the house now, have a look at all the locks, the alarm system, nightlights, everything, and find a dog." The inspector was very concerned for his wife and Bobby. He wanted them well protected.

"A dog? Where the hell am I going to find a dog?" Murphy was not a dog person.

"Start with the animal rescue league. They always have dogs

there. If you can't find one there, go to a pet shop. And get a big dog, one with a lot of teeth."

"A dog with lots of teeth? I thought all dogs had lots of teeth," Murphy said.

Chapter Twenty-three

The inspector was up early, having coffee in the kitchen. He was going through the motions of reading the morning paper, but his mind was on Mark Borman. He wondered if flying to Barbados was the right choice. What other island would he pick if he were Borman? What would be the best way to slip through the clutches of law enforcement? These thoughts had been running through the inspector's head all night long. Madam Dupree was not an early riser. Bobby was also sleeping late. The family doctor had arrived after Carmen left. Whatever sleeping potion he gave Bobby, it led to a peaceful night. The doctor informed Madam Dupree that if Bobby was not showing improvement in a few days he wanted to be called. The inspector's wife asked a lot of questions, and the doctor reminded her that he was not a psychologist. They both knew that the island did not have a resident psychologist, and there was not one on St. Lucia that they were aware of.

"Pardon me, Inspector, Mr. Murphy has just pulled into the drive," Ute said. Her spotless kitchen had a view of the garage and some of the driveway.

"Thanks, Ute. I'm going to say good-bye to Madam Dupree.

Tell Murphy that I'll be there in a minute. Wish us luck in catching this character," the inspector said.

"Auf wiedersehen, Inspector, I know you'll catch him," Ute said.

The inspector came out of the house carrying a light overnight bag. He looked up at the fair-weather clouds and felt that it was a good day for flying. Throwing his bag in the backseat, he sat up front with Murphy. "To the airport, James," the inspector said with a smile as he buckled himself in. Murphy headed down the hill toward the city, and then southeast to the E. T. Joshua Airport. There has been talk of expanding the airport into a jetport. A larger airport would bring in more tourists, with more tourist dollars. Others seem to think that it would change the character of the island. They argue that the type of tourists they want for their island are the ones that take the trouble to change to a smaller plane to get here. Inspector Dupree has not taken either side, waiting instead to see which way the wind blows.

"Inspector, there're a number of small airports a lot closer than Barbados. Why did you choose Barbados?" Murphy asked.

"You're right, Murphy, quite a few airports. Borman must realize that we would have them blocked off. Also, I checked with the marina to see how much fuel Borman purchased. It was not a lot of fuel; he was topping his tanks off," Dupree said.

"What does that mean?" Murphy said, shrugging his shoulders.

"If you were in a hurry would you take the time to top off your tanks? I don't think so, not if you were going to make a short trip to the next island," the inspector said. Dupree removed his hat.

"I see what you mean, Inspector. You know, you'd make a good detective," Murphy said.

"Well, thank you, Murphy. Coming from someone who was in the business, I take that as a compliment." The inspector turned on the radio. He removed Murphy's tape and inserted one by Telemann. Leaning back against the headrest, he tried to put himself in Borman's position.

When they reached the only airport on the island, Murphy now realized how small it was. Murphy drove past the hangar with the sign, *E. T. Joshua Airport*. He dropped off Dupree at the charter-plane office while he parked the limo. The inspector had completed the paperwork by the time Murphy walked into the office. It was in a small hangar used for repairing light planes. The smell of paint lingered in the air.

"What's that smell, Inspector?" Murphy asked.

"Oh, that's paint they use on canvas-covered planes. Meet Skip Johnson, our pilot. His plane is over there, the red one." Skip Johnson, a man in his early sixties, had a narrow face and gray, thinning hair. He wore the standard dark glasses and colorful shirt that seemed to be a uniform of the island hoppers.

"Pleasure meeting you, Murphy, are you a detective working with our famous inspector?" Johnson asked.

"Well yeah, in a way. My main occupation is being retired," Murphy replied.

"Good for you. Someday I hope to retire. Let's get your bags on board," Johnson said. He grabbed his baseball cap and started out the door toward the single-engine plane. He walked with a long stride, a man who enjoyed going to work.

"This plane looks a lot like an old Stinson Reliant," Murphy noted. It had an overhead wing, wheel covers, and seating for four. "Hey, this is quite a plane. It looks brand new. I bet she's fun to fly," Murphy said, checking the plane over.

"She's a beauty all right. I've been restoring her for the last seven years. Spent every cent I could get my hands on and then some. You have any idea how long it takes to get parts from the States? There's customs and yards of red tape. I was lucky it only took seven years," Johnson said.

"She sure is a beauty," Murphy said as he ran his fingers over the paint job.

"I'm ready for takeoff, Inspector, if you are." Skip Johnson's eyes sparkled when he spoke of his plane.

"We're all set, Skip," the inspector said as he fastened himself in. Murphy was seated behind the pilot.

"Okay, gentlemen, y'all buckled up? Put your headphones on. These phones will enable us to talk to each other and save our eardrums from a lot of noise." Skip kicked over the big radial engine, and let her warm up for a few minutes. He taxied over to the waiting area, tested his rudder, elevators, flaps, aileron and trim tabs. He followed a plastic-covered checklist, acting on each item as his finger touched it.

He radioed the tower and received clearance for takeoff. "Hold on, gentlemen, here we go," and with that Skip gave the plane full throttle. The restored flying machine headed down the runway with a roar. Halfway down the black asphalt the plane started to lift off. The engine was working hard as they climbed to 4,000 feet.

"What a gorgeous view," Murphy noted, looking out the window.

"How long will it take for us to get there?" Dupree asked Johnson, checking his watch.

"Well the island is 105 miles away, and we are traveling at about 120 miles an hour. The weatherman tells me there's a ten-mile-an-hour head wind. I figure we'll be there in about an hour of flying time, more or less," Johnson said. He checked his LORAN.

"Borman left the dock about two in the afternoon, and depending on how fast he pushes his boat, it should take him ten to twelve hours." The inspector turned to look at Murphy as he spoke.

"Is the airport open all night long?" Murphy asked.

Dupree shook his head. "Nope, the airport doesn't open until eight in the morning. The landing strip is at the other end of the island, up near Hope. Borman will have to catch a cab," the inspector said.

"But he'll have an hour's jump on us," Murphy observed.

"I talked to the police chief before leaving the office last night. He assured me that no chartered planes will leave that airport or the main airport before we arrive," Dupree said.

"Thanks for the info, Inspector. I felt guilty about sleeping last night knowing this guy is on the run. I forget that life on the islands is a bit slower than up north."

Skip Johnson had been quiet for some time. Upon close inspection the inspector noted that he was sweating. "Inspector, take the wheel for a minute, I don't feel so good," the pilot said as he loosened his tie. He removed his beat-up hat and wiped the sweat off his face.

"Take the wheel? I can't fly this thing. What'll I do with the wheel?" Dupree said, grabbing the wheel stiff-armed.

"Just hold her steady as she goes. Keep the wings level with the horizon. I – I – I've got a chest pain," Skip Johnson said. He slumped forward onto the wheel and passed out. The plane started into a nosedive, the noise level increasing to a howl.

"Pull back on the wheel. Pull back on the wheel," Murphy hollered.

"I can't, he's on the other wheel," the inspector screamed, hysterically.

"Okay, okay, take it easy; I've got him. Now you can pull back, slowly," Murphy said.

"Christ, Murphy, wake him up. He's the only pilot we've got," Dupree said as his death grip on the wheel turned his knuckles white. Beads of sweat formed on his forehead.

"Hold on, Inspector. You fly the plane, I'll attend Skip. Skip. . . Skip, wake up!" Murphy patted the pilot's cheek lightly.

"Murphy, what am I supposed to do here? Christ, I can't fly a plane," Dupree said.

"Just keep the wings level with the horizon and don't touch anything. I'll drag Skip back here." Murphy got his big arms around the pilot, pulled him out of his seat.

"What good is that going to do, Murphy? You know how to fly this thing?"

"I know something about flying, Inspector," Murphy replied, presenting a calm exterior.

"Well get your ass up here and do something before this thing goes into another nose dive," the inspector said. Sweat was now starting to drip from the inspector's forehead. Murphy buckled Skip into the other rear seat. He climbed into the left front seat, put on the headphones, took over the controls from the inspector. He checked all the instruments, and was relieved to find that nothing was out of place. Everything looked normal: the oil pressure, the RPMs, the wind speed, and manifold pressure.

"Look over here, Inspector. This is the LORAN; it tells us how to get to the airport. We have plenty of fuel. We don't have to worry about the landing gear. The wheels are already down," Murphy said.

"That's just fine, Murphy, but do you know how to land a

plane?" Dupree asked. He had his handkerchief out, wiping his face.

"I figure we will just radio the tower, they'll talk us down," Murphy said.

"Great idea, Murphy, except that landing strip has no tower; just a couple of hangars and an office. It's not an airport in the true sense of the word," Dupree said.

"No tower . . . huh? Look at the bright side. If it's as small as you say, then there will be little to no traffic to interfere with our landing," Murphy said. He was busy checking out the instrument panel and the cockpit layout. He wanted to be familiar with every knob, handle and gauge.

"You're right, as well as no ambulance to take us to the hospital, if we survive," Dupree said.

"Things aren't that bad, Inspector. I'll get her down, one way or the other," Murphy reassured.

"It's the 'other' that bothers me." When it came to facing the drug smugglers, doing what had to be done, Dupree was cool as a New York cab driver weaving through traffic. High up in a small plane with no pilot, he was out of his element, a bit panicky and trying not to show it.

"This LORAN is a beautiful instrument. It shows that we are headed right for the airport. It's not that far away. Look, Inspector, up ahead, there's the island. When we get to the airport, I'll do a fly around and have a look at things before going in," Murphy said. He had the look of a pilot; Dupree allowed himself to think that he was a pilot. Murphy circled the plane over the airport from a high altitude. He picked up the landing lights, the wind direction, noted the lack of traffic. He headed the plane away from the airport. "You see those lights down there, Inspector?" Murphy said, pointing to the landing lights. Dupree nodded his head. "I'm going to get about three miles away and then use them for my glide path," Murphy said.

"Whatever you say, Murphy, I hope you're right," the inspector replied.

"Well, we'll make a turn here, cut the speed down. I'm going to guess at the landing speed. I would say a plane like this should land around 80 to 90 miles an hour," Murphy said.

"Is there a book of instructions here somewhere? You know, something that tells how to fly this thing, maybe in the glove compartment?" Dupree's hands pulled and jabbed at everything nearby.

"I doubt it. Skip's been flying a long time. I don't think he ever used a book," Murphy said with a grin.

"I can't believe this is happening to me," Dupree said as he wiped his face again.

"If we go too slow the plane won't fly, on the other hand if we go too fast we'll overshoot the runway or blow a tire," Murphy said with a tight grip on the wheel.

"God be with us, my friend. Maybe I should close my eyes and hope for the best," the inspector said. Murphy slowed the plane down to 90 miles per hour, lowered the flaps and lined up the lights. As the land got closer and closer he cut the speed more. At 90 mph and then 85 mph, the plane was still too high over the runway. Murphy hit the throttle. The roar of the engine startled the inspector, who bolted upright in his seat and yelled: "What's going on? What's happening?" He grabbed his left leg to stop it from trembling.

"We're going around, Inspector. We're too high over the runway. I'm concerned that we could run out of asphalt. This time I will try to get a little lower," Murphy said.

"God, I hope you know what you're doing." the inspector said.

"Yeah, me too, Inspector," Murphy said. His second approach was a little lower. He had cut the plane's speed down to 80 miles an hour. Now, as the runway began he had the plane about 20 feet off the ground. The ground came up to meet the plane. Neither man said a thing as the plane touched the asphalt halfway down the runway. Murphy pushed the throttle forward to cut the engine. He then pulled the nose up slightly; the plane settled down. He applied the brakes; the plane came to a halt.

The inspector didn't move or say a word. Murphy kissed the wheel. "What a beautiful plane, and so easy to handle. Hey, Inspector, we've got to get an ambulance for Skip. Is that the office over there?" Murphy pointed to a small building at the edge of the field. The inspector nodded his head, as Murphy started out of the door. "You look after Skip. I'll be back in a minute," Murphy said as he broke into a jog.

Chapter Twenty-four

Mark Borman and his girlfriend arrived at the airport in a cab. It was about the same time as the ambulance for Skip Johnson. Dust kicked up as the driver came to a halt. Mark tumbled out of the taxi coughing. He paid the cab driver, grabbed his bags and headed for the office. Jeannette stumbled with her high heels on the uneven gravel road. She struggled with her heavy luggage. The hair on her forehead matted from perspiration. Borman barged through the door and walked up to the counter. He spoke to the man sitting at the desk, who was in his late twenties, on the thin side. He wore flight boots, and a tropical print shirt. Teardrop sunglasses sat on his desk. Other items on the desk were his phone, a stack of papers, and a stuffed parrot. The rest of the office consisted of shelves loaded down with motor parts and accessories.

"Hey, I need a hop over to Grenada, gotta catch a jet to the States," Borman said.

"The name's Charlie, mister. What I've got for you right now is nothing. Not until this afternoon," Charlie said, looking up from his paperwork.

"Look, Charlie, my flight to the States leaves this afternoon.

Don't you have anything that can fly me there right now?" Borman asked.

"Sorry, mister, if you're in a hurry, the main airport has planes going to the States all the time," Charlie answered.

Borman shook his head. "Wrong airlines, wrong connections. I need to get to Grenada," Borman said as Jeannette walked into the office looking worn out.

"Wish I could help you, fella, but my only plane for hire won't be back till this afternoon, that's it, sorry," Charlie said.

Borman banged his fist on the counter. "Christ! Look Charlie, there's a hundred bucks in it for you if you get me that flight now." Borman pulled out his wallet, and started counting out the cash.

"Sorry, pal, I just don't have a thing right now," Charlie repeated.

"Can't you call somebody? I'd make it worth his while," Borman said.

"Pilots are not the problem. We're short of planes," Charlie said without looking up. "We've got three planes and two of them are down for repairs."

Borman banged his fist down on the counter again, "Shit! Okay, where can I get some breakfast around here?"

Charlie got up from his desk and walked over to the counter. "Sure, across the street. The building looks a lot worse than the food."

"Yeah, yeah, any port in a storm I guess. Look, I'll be waiting for my ride across the street. Here's fifty bucks as a down payment. Don't sell my hired plane to anyone else, got it?" Borman said.

"Right you are, mister. It's your flight just as soon as she comes in. Your bags will be safe with us." Charlie held the gate open as Borman placed their bags behind the counter.

Theodore L. Davis

Borman slowed down his pace as the two of them walked over to the restaurant toward the aroma of coffee and bacon. Before entering the restaurant Borman stopped and looked around. He checked both sides of the restaurant, turned and looked back at the airport. He then had a look at all of the surrounding area.

"What'd looking for, honey?" Jeannette asked.

"Just checking the place out, that's all," Borman said as he opened the door. Jeannette entered the restaurant, Borman followed. They sat down at a table. Paint was lifting from the walls and ceiling. The curtains hung unevenly in the windows. The table rocked, chairs ready to collapse. "Just my luck; we gotta hang around here until this afternoon. What the hell are we going to do for three or four hours?" Borman asked.

"We could take a walk, honey. I've got some flats in my bag," Jeannette suggested.

Borman looked around. "I'm starved, where the hell is the waitress?"

The inspector and Murphy were at the plane, looking over the shoulders of the ambulance crew. Skip Johnson had regained consciousness and was insisting he was all right. The paramedics had him strapped to a gurney and were getting ready to lift him into the ambulance. Dupree leaned over Johnson while he lay on the stretcher. "Skip, you're going to the hospital for a check-up. That's it, just a check-up. Your plane will be fine right here. These guys will take good care of her. Don't worry."

"I feel fine, just got a little dizzy up there, that's all. That plane's my life. I don't feel right leaving her alone," Skip said with a worried look.

Dupree smiled, nodded his head. "Don't worry about a thing,

184

your plane will be fine right here. I'll make sure that they give her extra care and affection."

The men wearing white coats pushed the gurney into the ambulance. They moved to the cab and the ambulance pulled away. The two men headed for the office, both thinking how lucky they were to be on solid ground. The inspector patted Murphy on the back. "You did one helluva job bringing that plane in. How long have you been flying?" the inspector asked.

"I hate to tell you this, Inspector, but I don't fly. Never been up in a small plane in my life, before this," Murphy said with a smile.

"What? Who the hell you trying to kid?" the inspector said as his jaw dropped a foot.

"That's right, Inspector. Years ago I thought about taking flying lessons. I bought a book, *How to Fly*, but never got around to taking any lessons," Murphy said.

"That's it? You read a book on flying and that makes you a pilot?" Dupree said.

"No, I'm not a pilot. I was thinking of becoming a pilot. I studied the book. That's all." The inspector could not believe what he was hearing.

"Well, it's a good thing you bought that book, otherwise we wouldn't be here now," the inspector said.

Murphy began to laugh. "That's right, Inspector, perhaps you'd like to borrow the book?"

"No . . . no thanks, Murphy. Flying and the inspector just don't get along." Unfortunately the inspector's job called for some island hopping. The most expedient way of traveling between islands was by chartered plane. "I'll keep my feet on the ground, thanks, and take a boat." The inspector could not stop shaking his head as the duo headed for the office. Charlie looked up from his paperwork when they entered. "Good morning, I'm Chief Inspector Dupree, from St. Vincent. This is my partner Mr. Murphy," the inspector said. Dupree pulled out his copy of Carmen's sketch of Mark Borman. Charlie got up from his desk and walked over to the counter.

"I'm Charlie, pleased to meet ya. How's the guy in the ambulance?" Charlie asked. He shook hands with the inspector and Murphy.

"He's going to be all right, just got a little dizzy up there. We're looking for a man that looks something like this. We have reason to believe that he may be headed this way," the inspector said. Charlie took a long look at the sketch.

"A guy was in here just a few minutes ago that looked something like that. He's waiting for a charter to Grenada. Said he had to catch a flight to the States. Inspector Dupree . . . Inspector Dupree." Charlie's eyes lit up. "Oh, I almost forgot. I got a call from the police this morning. The chief told me not to charter out any planes until you arrived. Well it doesn't matter cause I won't have a plane until this afternoon," Charlie said.

"Where is he now?" Dupree asked, unable to stand still. "The man we are after is wanted for murder."

"Murder, wow . . . murder, he's across the street in the restaurant," Charlie said as his eyes widened. "He's with a woman; they left their luggage here."

"Good, if we miss him, and he comes back here, stall him. Misplace his bags or something. We're headed over to the restaurant now. He could be armed and dangerous, be careful," the inspector said. Dupree and Murphy hurried out the door.

"Thanks, guys." Charlie walked over to the water cooler. "How the hell can I be careful with a murderer, and at the same time tell him that I just lost his luggage? Shit." Charlie grabbed a paper cup, drew some water. He then looked around for an escape route if the killer should return. "What do I have for a weapon?" As he thought about his situation, he became nervous. "A carburetor is not much of a weapon."

As Dupree and Murphy headed for the restaurant, the inspector was planning his next move. "Look, Murphy, I'm going in the front door, then up to the counter. You go in the back door through the kitchen. When I see you're in position, I'll go up to this guy and ask for his identification," Dupree said.

"Okay, Inspector, be careful. If he's our man, I'll recognize him and I'll nod my head. Now don't be a hero. If he grabs you, drop to the floor, so I can get off a clean shot," Murphy said with a frown.

"Sounds like you have been through this before, Murphy." The conversation dropped off as they approached the building. The inspector motioned to Murphy to get around the back, counted to thirty, then opened the door after climbing four steps of the front porch. Borman and his friend were the only customers in the place. Mark Borman looked up at Dupree as he walked in. The inspector was in full uniform; Borman knew who he was. The fugitive lowered his head, whispered something to Jeannette. Dupree waited for Murphy to get into place. He walked over to the table. Borman, who was sitting with his back to the rear of the restaurant, did not see Murphy. Dupree looked over at Murphy to see if he was nodding his head. Murphy shrugged, able to see only Borman's back.

"Good morning, sir. May I trouble you for some identification?" Dupree stood ramrod straight, an imposing figure.

"Yeah, sure, but my papers are in my bags over at the airport," Borman said.

"Put your hands on the table, and don't move," Dupree commanded. He drew his gun out in a double tenth of a second. He motioned for Murphy to come forward. Murphy moved from the back of the restaurant, holding his gun on the suspect with both hands.

"That's him, Inspector, that's our guy. Get the cuffs on him," Murphy said. Borman didn't have a chance to react; the game was up, and he knew it.

"Place one hand behind your back," Dupree commanded as he got a cuff on. "Now the other hand," the inspector said. When both cuffs were on, a look of relief came over his face.

"What's your name, young lady?" Dupree asked.

"Jeannette Thibeault. I'm from St. Vincent," Jeannette answered.

"How long have you known this guy?" the inspector asked.

"Oh, I've known Mark for a long time, a couple of months. What's the problem, officer? We haven't done anything. I paid the parking tickets," Jeannette said with wide eyes, her mouth half open.

"Murphy, get on the phone, and get a cab out here. This guy is going for a boat ride," Dupree said.

"A boat ride?" Murphy questioned. "What's wrong with waiting for Skip to get out of the hospital? He's going our way, isn't he?"

"Very funny, Murphy," the inspector said as he moved to a table behind Borman and sat down. He removed his hat and picked up the menu.

Borman was shackled to a bench several cabin lengths away from his captors. The ship, *Star of Trinidad*, was one of the tramp steamers that made regular runs between the islands, delivering freight and passengers. On the first deck of the superstructure were the galley and several dining rooms. The second deck housed the passengers, with three cabins on the starboard side and three on the port. On the top deck were the bridge, the navigation room, cabins for the captain and the first mate. Dupree and Murphy were on the cabin level, leaning on the rail. Dupree kept his eye on his prisoner while Murphy, with his elbows on the rail, looked out to sea.

Borman talked to Jeannette in a whisper. He was explaining to her why he was in handcuffs, and why he was being escorted to jail on her home island. "They've got me mixed up with someone else, that's all. They got a sketch of a guy, and they think I look like him," Borman said.

"But they knew your name, honey," Jeannette retorted.

"I'll get this all straightened out when we get back," Borman replied.

"Are we still going to the States?" Jeannette asked.

"Sure, sure, just as soon as I get these jerks off my back," Borman said as he lifted his head and looked into Jeannette's eyes. "Now look, I want you to go up to the house and get my log book. It's in the bottom draw of my bureau, in my bedroom. Take it down to Barney's and ask Jake, the owner, to put it in his safe. You got that? Don't let the police in the house unless they have a warrant. And don't let them make a mess. You know, tearing the place up," Borman said.

"Sure, honey. Are they going to keep you in jail long?" Jeannette asked.

"If they think they've got something on me, I'll post bond. I've got to get my boat back to St. Vincent. Who do you know at Barney's that can pilot a boat?"

"I know a few guys that are fishermen," Jeannette replied.

"Well, if I can't post bond, we'll have to make some

arrangement." Borman sat there thinking about his situation. *What the hell have they got? A kid's word against mine and that's it. I should've done her in when I had the chance.*

The inspector kept a close eye on Borman. "I'd like you to know, Murphy, that I felt comfortable having a man of your caliber working with me back at the restaurant. Perhaps you would like to join the force?" the inspector said.

"Oh, no, not me, Inspector, I'm retired, remember?" Murphy replied.

"Yes, my friend, nevertheless I could make you an interesting offer. You're still a young man, relatively speaking," Dupree said.

"I appreciate that, sir, but you see the scars are still there. I needed to get away from guns, crime, and the clientele that we deal with in our line of work," Murphy said.

"I understand," the inspector said as he looked at Borman talking to Jeannette.

"Here, on your beautiful island, I'm relaxed. It took me a couple of years to recoup from my nervous breakdown," Murphy said. He turned around and looked at the inspector. "St. Vincent is just what the doctor ordered. In fact, I would recommend it to all those burned-out flatfoots up north." Murphy turned back to the sea, looked at the horizon, then up at the fluffy, cauliflower cloud formations. "Inspector, perhaps you should take some flying lessons. It's very relaxing," Murphy said. The inspector laughed, drawing a malevolent look from their prisoner.

"I'm sure it is, Murphy, if you have nerves of steel. If you ever feel like getting back in the saddle, so to speak, talk to me," Dupree said.

"Fair enough, Inspector. In the meantime I'll take pleasure in being the chauffeur for your lovely lady and enjoying Ute's delicious coffee," Murphy said.

"Now that you mention it, you do seem to spend a lot of time in Ute's kitchen. Not that I mind, I think it's good for Ute. She seems a little lonely since she left her homeland," the inspector said.

"She is a lovely lady. If only I were ten years younger. Well, I'm sure she wouldn't be interested in an old, broken-down cop from the States." Murphy looked out over the sea, drew a deep breath, and brought his fist up under his chin.

Dupree turned his head toward Murphy. "Don't be so sure, why sell yourself short? It's been said that you're only as old as you feel. On second thought I wouldn't want you to take away the best cook we've ever had."

"Don't worry, Inspector, I really don't think that I'd stand a chance with Ute. Did you know that she was a lab technician back in Germany? She worked with blood doing some kind of testing," Murphy said.

"No. I never knew that, really, a lab technician, huh? Madam Dupree did her background check. She never mentioned Ute's work in Germany."

"She married young, it didn't work out," Murphy added.

"Well that just goes to show, we never know what kind of people are going to show up on St Vincent. It attracts all types," the inspector replied as he kept watch on his prisoner.

"As long as it's the beautiful type, I'd say you're in luck, Inspector."

"I'll tell you, Murphy, coming home to Ute's cooking each evening is a pleasure. Love her apple strudel," Dupree said.

"Apple strudel and fresh coffee, there's nothing like it. To change the subject for a moment, I wonder how Bobby will manage knowing that she has lost her family," Murphy said. His face showed concern.

"She lost her mother, her father, and her brother; the whole family, what a shame. I hope she'll pull through it okay," the inspector said.

Murphy turned around to face Borman. "Inspector, what'd ya think of those two with their heads together? They could be cooking something up," Murphy said.

"I wouldn't worry about Jeannette; she's one of the local girls. She hangs out at Barney's. I checked with the office this morning. She has a clean record," the inspector said.

"Look at those eyes, Inspector. He's a killer all right. I can feel it," Murphy spoke in almost a whisper.

"Let's not jump to conclusions, my friend. The jury will want more than his word against Bobby's," the inspector said in a low voice.

"Maybe we can sweat a confession out of him. I've got some friends up north that would make him confess," Murphy said with a grin.

"No, I don't think so; however, thanks for the offer. We've done our job. Now it's up to the lawyers."

The sun was going down. The breeze that had been light all afternoon was starting to pick up. The hum of the diesels dominated the quiet of the sea. Jeannette pulled her sweater over her shoulders. Borman stretched his legs out and leaned his head back on the rail. "Go find me a cigarette, will ya, sweetheart, and a match too? I've got some thinking to do. Do you know the Water Front Café?" Borman asked.

"Sure, sometimes I have lunch there," Jeannette replied.

"When we get back, go see the owner, his name is Joseph. Tell him I want to talk to him. You got that?" Borman asked.

"Joseph, at the Water Front, you want to see him. Okay, I'll tell 'em," Jeannette said.

Chapter Twenty-five

Late in the evening Murphy pulled the limo into the driveway of Dupree's home. Before leaving the office the inspector had called, alerting the household of the good news of Borman's capture. Madam Dupree, Bobby, and Ute awaited their return.

"You must come in, have a drink with me," the inspector said to Murphy. "We must celebrate our good fortune."

"Thank you," Murphy said as the corners of his mouth turned up. "I'm always ready for a drink. I was just thinking how a cold beer would hit the spot about now." The front door opened, the women came out to greet their intrepid travelers. Bobby was the first to reach Dupree.

"Inspector, Inspector," Bobby yelled as she ran up to him. Murphy looked on with a pleased smile. "I am so happy you're back." Bobby threw her arms around the inspector's waist.

Dupree, putting his arm around Bobby, said, "So am I, Bobby, it's been a long, hard day." Bobby stepped aside so Madam Dupree could greet her husband. Murphy turned away; it was times such as these that he missed his wife.

The Duprees, Murphy, along with Bobby, sat in the living room, all talking at the same time. Ute served drinks, and then she sat down near Murphy, joining the celebration. Bobby sat next to the inspector and asked, "How did you catch him, Inspector? Did he put up a wicked fight? Did he have a gun?"

"Slow down, Bobby, you talk so fast. I will try to answer all your questions. First, I must tell you, we almost didn't make it. If it wasn't for our chauffeur here I'm afraid I wouldn't be here to tell you the story." Dupree stopped for a moment to sip his drink.

"Oh don't stop now, Inspector, what happened?" Bobby asked as she squirmed in her seat.

"Well, you see, Bobby, we were flying along in the chartered plane. I was up front with the pilot, Murphy here was in back." Dupree described the gripping story of how Murphy piloted the plane to safety. When he related how Murphy had never been up in a small plane before in his life his listeners gasped.

Madam Dupree was the first to speak. "But, Mr. Murphy, if you had never been up in a small plane before how on earth did you know how to fly it?" Murphy explained how he had bought a book on flying once with the intent of taking lessons. He kept the group spellbound for quite a while.

Madam Dupree then asked, "Would you fly again in a small plane?"

"Oh sure, I'm still interested in taking up flying lessons someday," Murphy answered with a grin.

The party broke up somewhere after eleven when Madam Dupree noted that Bobby was getting sleepy. She walked Bobby upstairs to her room.

"Murphy, no need to call me tomorrow, you deserve a day off," the inspector said as the two walked toward the front door. "I want to thank you again for all your help today."

"Don't mention it, Inspector, pleased to be of some service. It felt just like the old times again."

"Well my offer still stands. Anytime you feel like getting back in action."

"Thank you, Inspector; I appreciate your confidence in me. Good night." Murphy shook hands with the inspector as he departed.

When Madam Dupree came down the stairs from Bobby's room, the inspector put his arm around her, led her into the study. "Madam, how's Bobby holding up? Is she going to be all right?"

"It's hard to tell right now," she answered. "Bobby is still under the doctor's care. She mentioned her grandparents today, although could not remember their name or phone number. I told her that you would track them down, and get her the phone number."

"That's a tall order, Madam. Does she remember the name of the city or town she's from?" Dupree asked.

"Camden, Maine. She lived in Camden."

"And are her grandparents living in Camden also?" The inspector sat down in his leather chair. Madam sat across from him on the sofa.

"She doesn't know, but it's a good place to start."

"Maybe the Town Office can help. I'll try the Town Office."

Madam Dupree sat back in the sofa. "The doctor returned again today. He spent a half hour talking to Bobby."

"What did he have to say?" the inspector asked.

"He told me to keep an eye on her. To keep her busy, give her some responsibility. Maybe some work around the house, and to call him if she becomes despondent or isolates herself."

"Well, he's a good doctor," Dupree replied. "I'm sure if he feels he can't handle the situation, he'll call in an expert."

Several days later Madam Dupree was talking to Bobby while they were having breakfast in the kitchen. The kitchen was larger than one would expect for a house of four bedrooms. It had a rather professional look, with an island stove surrounded by a countertop with five wood stools. The stools with high backs could rotate 360 degrees, much to Bobby's delight. "Today, Bobby, we are going to the island of Bequia. We are going to be tourists. How does that sound?"

"Tourists? How do we act like tourists?" Bobby asked.

"The island is an hour south of here," Madam Dupree explained. "We can go to the shops at Port Elizabeth and then perhaps to Princess Margaret Beach. It is one of the most beautiful of all the beaches."

"Oh that sounds super, Madam Dee. Will the inspector come with us?" Bobby asked.

"I'm sure he would if you ask him," Madam Dupree replied. "He does have the day off and what better place to go." Bobby walked into the study where the inspector was reading the morning paper. She held her hands together in front of her, twisting her fingers around one another. With her chin down Bobby asked quietly, "Inspector, Madam Dee and I are going to Bequia. Can you come with us?"

"Bequia, Bequia," the inspector exclaimed. "That sounds like a great idea. I love that island, especially the Anthneal's Museum down in Friendship Bay."

"Madam Dee said they have a nice beach," Bobby ventured.

"The beach there is one of my favorites," the inspector answered with enthusiasm.

"Oh great, Inspector, I'll ask Ute to pack us a lunch," Bobby said with a big smile.

"Not this time, Bobby. I think we'll have lunch at a restaurant."
Bobby ran out of the study, into the kitchen to Madam Dupree.

"Madam Dee, Madam Dee, the inspector is going with us."

"That's wonderful, Bobby. Get your backpack; don't forget
your bathing suit and a towel. I'll call the Bay Lines to see when
the boat is leaving. Bobby, don't forget your camera."

On the boat over to Bequia Island the Duprees with Bobby
sat on the upper deck in front of the pilothouse. A bright, sunny
day with little wind added to the pleasure of the boat trip. Madam
Dupree and Bobby wore floppy hats and sunglasses to protect
them from the sun. Up to this point Bobby had been in good
humor, enjoying the cruise. Slowly a dark cloud gathered over
her. Her head was down, hands between her knees. It appeared
to Madam Dupree that Bobby could be crying.

"What's the trouble, Bobby? Are you seasick? What's troubling
you?" Madam Dupree asked.

"Oh, Madam Dee, It's just... It's just," Bobby's voice faded to
a whisper.

"Yes, Bobby, what is it?" Madam Dupree leaned toward her,
put her hand on her shoulder.

"It's the water, the boat, my mother, my father." Bobby
began to cry.

"Oh, you poor thing," Madam said as she hugged Bobby.
The inspector was trying to think of what he could do to help.

Madam Dupree held Bobby tight, gave her the inspector's
handkerchief. "Oh, Bobby, we'll be off this old boat in a little
while." The inspector sat down beside Bobby, removed his
sunglasses, fumbled for words.

"I am sure your mother, father, and brother are very happy in
heaven. I know that devil, Borman, will be in hell. He'll be there

forever, and the sooner he gets there the better," the inspector said.

"Oh, Inspector, do you really think so? Do you really think there's a heaven?"

"Of course there's a heaven and that's where your family will be waiting for you," the inspector's voice was not at all stable.

Madam Dupree, with her arm around Bobby, rocked back and forth. "Yes, Bobby, God will take care of that evil man. He'll get just what's coming to him, I'm sure."

The inspector got up from the bench, walked around the deck. He got halfway down the starboard side when he stopped in his tracks. Two men, standing close together on the fantail, were dressed in a manner that brought suspicion. Dupree thought he had seen these men before. Years of police work brought a tingle to the back of his neck. "Where have I seen these guys before? They look familiar. I've seen them before, but where?" Dupree took a step back. One of the men looked in his direction. The inspector looked out to sea, turned, and headed back to the bow. When he got to an empty bench, he sat down with a deep frown on his forehead. He was positive that he knew the men, but where, under what circumstances? *They certainly were not tourists. What business would two characters like that have on Bequia?*

Chapter Twenty-six

Inspector Dupree and Bobby were in the back seat of the limo. Behind the wheel Murphy was the quintessential chauffeur. He wore his gray jacket and gray cap, the one with the patent leather visor. When they arrived in downtown Kingstown the inspector leaned forward, "Pull up here in front of the courthouse. Bobby and I are going to take a look at the courtroom."

"Right you are, Chief," acknowledged Murphy as he pulled into a no-parking zone. "I'll wait right here and if any of your boys want me to move, I'll just tell'em who I am."

"Please be nice to them, Murphy, after all this car is not marked," the inspector said.

"Not to worry, Inspector, I won't throw my weight around," Murphy replied in mock seriousness. The inspector and Bobby headed for the courthouse. She held his hand and looked up quizzically at the old building.

"Bobby, this is our courthouse," the inspector said as he gestured. "It's a little old, although the people are friendly." The court house was built of local stone in 1798. It is located on Bay and Bedford Streets, opposite the marketplace.

"It looks creepy to me," Bobby said with a frown.

"I'd like you to see the courtroom before the trial. Maybe

get to know some of the people that will be there," the inspector said as he pushed open the large, oak doors. Over the years dark water stains had etched the beautiful wood. Beyond them was the main hallway with its high ceilings and marble floors.

"I've never been in a courthouse before," Bobby said, "Will the judge be in the courtroom?"

"No, not unless a trial is going on," the inspector replied. As the two walked down the hallway their footsteps echoed, shoes creaked. A right turn and a few more steps brought them before a set of double doors covered with leather. The doors had porthole windows at eye level. Finding the courtroom empty, the inspector motioned for Bobby to enter. The room seemed large to Bobby when she looked up at the ceiling. The inspector, taking Bobby by the hand, walked past the rows of benches to the judge's bench. Bobby bent backward to look up at the high ceiling. Pointing to the bench she asked it that is where the judge sat. The inspector nodded his head and then pointed to the other side and told Bobby that is where the defendant and his counsel will be seating.

Bobby pointed to the jury box and asked who would be there. Dupree explained that it was for the jurors. He then pointed out where the prosecution would be sitting.

"You see, Bobby, what a nice courtroom we have?"

"Where will I be sitting?" Bobby asked.

"You'll be right in the front row, along with me and Murphy." Dupree pointed to the benches on the left side.

"And where will Captain Mark be?" Bobby said as she wrinkled her forehead.

"Oh, he'll be sitting at that table over there, with his attorney," Dupree said as he pointed to the table on the right.

"That's not very far away," Bobby said as her worried look deepened.

"Come, Bobby, I'll show you the room where the jury will be casting their votes, this way." The two walked past the jury box, through a door, into a smaller hallway. The inspector opened the first door on the right. Bobby walked in; saw the long table in the middle of the room. Pictures hung on both walls overlooking the table. At the end of the room large windows gave a view of the courtyard.

Bobby was examining the rows of pictures. "Inspector, most of the people on this island have French names, but they don't look French."

"Oh, the pictures, yes, lots of French names. You see the native people, called Caribs, were very hostile to all Europeans. They tended to find the British, who claimed the island, more objectionable than the French," the inspector said as he sat down in one of the chairs. "The Caribs allowed the French to establish the first European settlement here, in the early 1700s."

"What happened to the Caribs?" Bobby asked.

"That's a long and sad story, however, in brief: They were rounded up, shipped to other islands by the British. That's after the Brits had sent in their troops to reclaim the island," the inspector said.

"Were the Caribs dark like the people here?" Bobby had a puzzled look.

"No, I believe the Caribs were a bit lighter. Let's say a light brown. The dark people on this island were brought in from Africa to work the plantations as slaves. The judge's ancestors were slaves."

"Inspector, may I ask you something else?"

"Sure, Bobby, I'm batting one for one, so far," the inspector said.

"Ah, Inspector, do I have to come face-to-face with Captain Mark when I'm in the courtroom? He scares me half to death," Bobby asked.

"Murphy will be by your side all the time, Bobby, you have nothing to fear. We would never let Borman get close to you. You don't have to worry." The inspector's words were comforting.

After leaving the deliberation room the inspector and Bobby were walking down the hallway. Hurrying in the opposite direction was the lawyer Jack Farrington.

"Jack, Jack Farrington . . . hi, I understand that you are going to be the prosecutor for the Commonwealth on the upcoming trial of Mark Borman," the inspector said as he stopped the lawyer in his tracks. Jack was in his early forties, a little above average height and starting to put on weight.

"Good morning, Inspector, yes, I have heard rumors to that effect, although no official word yet. I've wanted to speak with you about this case, on the chance that I do get the green light." Jack had been practicing law for over ten years, and was well thought of by the small group of lawyers on St. Vincent. As a prosecutor, Jack had a very good record.

"Jack, this is Bobby White. I'm sure you have heard of her," the inspector said.

"Well, yes I have. It's a pleasure meeting you Bobby. I'm very sorry to hear what happened to your family." Jack set his heavy briefcase on the floor, extended his hand.

"Pleased to meet you, Mr. Jack," Bobby said while shaking his hand.

"The pleasure is mine, Bobby, and if I do get this case, I know that we will work very well together," Jack smiled.

"Well that's it then, Jack," the inspector said. "I'll have a talk with the governor; tell him that you're interested in the case. Winning a case like this would be a great help to your career. Who knows? It could even make you a local hero," the inspector said with a grin.

"Inspector, I've got to run, tight schedule today. Pleasure meeting you, Bobby, and take good care of the inspector. Inspector, you know where I am when you're ready to talk. Bye." Jack picked up his briefcase, rushed down the hall.

The inspector thought that Bobby had enough for one day. He suggested that they get back to Murphy and break for lunch. Perhaps a nice restaurant and maybe a filet mignon would make this a perfect day.

"Inspector, could we go to the park and have a hotdog? I love hotdogs," Bobby asked.

"Hotdogs . . . why certainly, Bobby," the inspector said as he pushed open the big oak doors. Bobby ran down the granite stairs to Murphy and the waiting limo.

"To the park, driver," the inspector said as he brought up the rear. "We're having hotdogs for lunch." Murphy smiled, nodded his head as he closed the rear door, and hurried around to the driver's side. Later the three of them sat on a park bench enjoying their lunch along with throwing crumbs to the pigeons.

"Inspector, do you think Captain Mark will be upset with me when I tell the jury that he killed my mother and father? I mean will he come after me, and try to kill me too?" Bobby's concern was obvious.

"No, no, Bobby. He may be upset at your testimony;

nevertheless he'll be under guard. There will be policemen in the courtroom and others outside. You won't have a thing to worry about, not a thing, Bobby," the inspector said as he bit into his hotdog.

"And I'll be there too, Bobby," Murphy joined in. "I'll be sitting right in the front row with you and the inspector. We won't let anyone get close to you."

"Inspector, do you suppose that I could have another hotdog, please?" The circle of pigeons was getting larger.

"You sure can, Bobby, and how about you, Murphy? This round's on me," the inspector said.

"Well, in that case, count in me. Also another soda, if you wouldn't mind?" Murphy replied.

The inspector returned with his hands full. He passed out the food and sat down. He bought an extra hotdog so Bobby did not have to give hers to the pigeons.

"Murphy, I get the feeling we're being watched," the inspector said in a low voice. Murphy, with his mouth half open, froze. He looked left and then right, stood up, turned a complete circle. He looked at the inspector and shrugged his shoulders. Dupree stood up and pointed to two men who were walking away. Murphy turned quickly in the direction he was pointing, but the walkway bent around large trees. Murphy got nothing but a quick glance. Dupree motioned for him to sit down and asked him to finish his lunch. "They'll show up again, Murphy, and next time we'll be ready for them."

Chapter Twenty-seven

"If I had the money I'd get rid of this joint and move back to the States. Put it on the market. Doubt that anyone would buy it." Joseph mumbled and went back to reading his paper. "Hey, Carlos, you been following this stuff in the papers about the young girl they found on a raft?" Joseph said without looking up.

"Yeah, man," Carlos replied from behind the counter. "That's kind of weird. She spotted the guy who killed her family. That inspector friend of yours caught him in Barbados."

"I was thinking, Carlos," Joseph said as he lowered his paper. "What d'ya suppose the government would pay for the return of that girl if she'd happen to disappear?" Joseph said.

The restaurant had no customers; Carlos, with his standard dirty apron, moved from behind the counter. "Hey man, they need that girl for the trial. She ain't gonna disappear," Carlos said, wondering what Joseph was getting at.

"Yeah, that's right, Carlos. That girl's needed for the trial, and if someone should happen to tuck her away, hmmmm. I bet they'd pay a pretty penny to get her back," Joseph said.

"I know that look on your face, Joseph. It always spells trouble," Carlos said as his left eye twitched.

"I understand she lives with the inspector and his wife. I bet they've become fond of her, wouldn't you think?" Joseph said as the electrons sparked in his head.

"So they've become fond of her, so what?" Carlos questioned.

"I happen to know that the inspector is loaded with dough," Joseph said as he pretended to read.

"Hey, man. If you're thinking what I think you're thinking, forget it. What you're thinking is against the law, waaay against the law. Not only that, the inspector is not a guy to fuck with," Carlos said as his left eye began to twitch again.

"Hey, Carlos, where's your sense of adventure? With your share of a million bucks, you could retire. Never work again a day in your life," Joseph said.

"What makes you think that they'd give a million bucks for that girl? Christ, they're not even related. Man, you come up with the craziest ideas," Carlos said as he sat back and shook his head.

"That's why you're the bottle washer, Carlos, and I'm the owner of this joint. I've got ideas and sometimes they're pretty good, like the one I have right now," Joseph said as he pulled the paper up in front of his face.

"Yeah, your ideas will get you twenty years," Carlos said, still shaking his head.

"Hey, you wanna get someplace, ya gotta take a chance once in a while." Joseph lowered his paper. He looked Carlos in the eye. A customer walked in, waved to Carlos and Joseph as he sat down at the counter. Carlos slipped behind the bar, served him coffee with rum. He returned to the table in the corner. Joseph, speaking in a low voice, said, "You'll never get nowhere if you don't take a chance."

"I'll take my chances playing the numbers," Carlos said.

"The way I got this figured they'll never know who we are. They'd never catch us in a hundred years," Joseph said.

"Hey, man, what's this we stuff?" Carlos said as he sat back, folded his arms. "I'm not buying into this shit until I know it's foolproof. I'm not sticking my neck out for one of your crazy ideas, no way, man," Carlos said.

"Well, Carlos, maybe I don't need you for this one," Joseph said as he lifted the paper over his face. "Who the hell wants to give away part of a million dollars when all I have to do is hire someone for a few thousand? No, Carlos, I won't need you for this gig. Get back to work, forget I mentioned it, okay?" Joseph went back to reading his paper.

"Hey, I didn't say I wasn't in," Carlos protested.

"Well it sure sounded that way to me," Joseph said as he looked over his reading glasses. "Look, I'm busy right now, so get back to work."

"Okay, okay, I'm in. I just hope that you got it figured right, that's all, man. I know you're pretty good at this stuff, but there's always a first time for screwing up. Ya hear me, Joseph?"

"Yeah . . . yeah . . . yeah," Joseph replied.

The following morning, Carlos waited for a lull. He was not satisfied with the reassurances given by Joseph. He knew that the inspector was not a man to trifle with. Unless Joseph had a foolproof scheme he would back out before it was too late. Joseph had just settled into his favorite table in the back corner of the restaurant, picked up the local paper. Carlos came from behind the counter.

"Hey, Joseph, I been thinking," Carlos said.

"Look, Carlos, I'll do the thinking, and I'm still working on it. When I have my plan in place, I'll let you in on it. I've got some details to work out. Just some minor stuff, but I don't like loose ends. Don't worry about it, okay?" Joseph said.

"Ya sure, Joseph, but you've got to have a pretty good plan if you are going to fool with the inspector. Ya know what I mean, man?" Carlos asked.

"The way I see it, Carlos, we're going to have to grab the kid when she's alone. Right now that chauffeur is with her wherever she goes. If that guy is with her all the time, perhaps a little distraction is in order." Joseph put down his paper, looked at Carlos. He spoke in low tones. "Perhaps we could find an old truck that just happens to pull out in front of that chauffeur, and wham. In the confusion, my hired guys could grab the kid. They could hide her in one of the empty warehouses on the waterfront. What d'ya think?" Joseph said as he warmed up to his idea.

"Sounds good so far, but you're the thinker. You're looking at the easy part. The hard part is the exchange, money for the girl. That's when the cops always get their man," Carlos said.

"Shit, Carlos, that's just in those dumb flicks you've been watching. The hard part is not to let anyone know that you have money. When someone comes into a lot of dough, the first thing they do is have a few too many at the local bar. They start bragging about how rich they are," Joseph said.

"So a guy can't buy his friends a few drinks?" Carlos asked.

"Look, dumb ass, as soon as someone starts flashing a lot of money around, the cops get wind of it. The best thing to do is not to drink and then slip out of town when things settle down. The crime is always the easy part. The hard part is having money and not spending it, or telling anyone that you have it. You know, Carlos, it's just like being broke, except you're a rich bum." Joseph picked up the paper again, but crime was on his mind.

"Christ, Joseph, what good is it to have money if you can't spend it. I mean, shit, man, if I come into some dough I'm going to buy me a big car, the bigger the better. One of those V8 jobs from the States," Carlos said. He was off in his dream world.

"Well, Carlos, to keep us out of the slammer, I'm going to keep your share for at least a year," Joseph said.

"What? You can't do that. That's crazy." Carlos's mouth dropped a foot.

"Yeah, I know it's crazy, but it's the only way to keep the cops away from our door. Keep the stuff buried, off the streets. That way, no one will be the wiser. Hell, one year without money is better than twenty years in the cooler, right, Carlos?"

"You're right there, Joseph, but if I know the inspector you'll get more than the slammer. He'll hang you by the balls, just for the fun of it," Carlos said with a worried look on his face.

"Look, doing the crime is the easy part. Getting away with it is the tough part. If we pull the gig off right we won't only spend a year or so without money, but at the end of that time we'll have to slip off the island," Joseph said.

"You mean we couldn't live here anymore? What kind of a deal is that? I don't want to live someplace else. I like this island."

"Okay, Carlos, you live here dirt poor in your broken-down house. Me? I'm going to Miami, live the good life, beautiful cars and fast women. I'll buy a nightclub and be a big shot. Now that's the life, all the booze and broads you want," Joseph said.

"Yeah, Joseph, you sure know how to live it up. I'm with you, man. I'm with you all the way," Carlos said with a big smile. "Christ, I can see us now." Carlos leaned his chair back on two legs. He hooked his thumbs under his armpits. "Yeah, I can see us now. A beautiful blonde for me, and a fat girl for you, ha-ha,"

Carlos said. With that remark Joseph rolled up his paper and whacked Carlos over the head in a playful mood.

The more Joseph thought about his get-rich scheme the more he liked it. He was able to think of nothing else. Day and night he went over his plan looking for the weak spots, the pitfalls, the land mines. After several days of intense scheming Joseph believed he had come up with the perfect plan. In the middle of the morning he sat with his coffee and local paper. A break in business brought Carlos over to his table. "Look, Carlos, get a hold of your uncle tonight. Have him find an old truck you can borrow. We need a truck that's unregistered. Something they can't trace," Joseph said.

"Yeah sure, Joseph, no problem," Carlos said as the two had their heads together in the far corner table of the Water Front Café. Carlos's stained gray/white apron was his trademark. "My uncle has a lot of old trucks in his junkyard, some of them even run." Carlos had trouble sitting still. The idea of coming into a lot of money caused him to be light-headed.

"Okay, go to a junkyard at the other end of the island and find some plates. And for Christ's sake, don't drive the truck around. Just make sure it runs good and then keep it hidden. Don't forget to wear gloves, don't leave any prints behind," Joseph said.

"No problem, man, I can keep it at the junkyard. My uncle never asks questions. He's a great guy," Carlos said.

Joseph leaned close to Carlos. "Now look, not a word to nobody about our business. I want ya to get it through that thick head, if you say a word to anybody, anyone at all, you're a dead man. You know that, don't you, Carlos?" Joseph had grabbed Carlos by the shirt, pulled him up close to his face. Joseph had given up brushing his teeth for Lent; the odor was enough to make Carlos faint.

"Yeah, yeah, sure, Joseph, not a word to no one. You know I don't talk about business. Not a word to no one. Not a word, I swear on my mother's grave," Carlos said.

"Okay, you just tell your uncle that you have some stuff to move," Joseph said as he released Carlos. "Now, sit still and I'll tell you what I got so far. You drive the truck in front of the inspector's car. This will be in the morning when his wife and the kid are going shopping. I'll hire a couple of guys to grab the kid and take her to the warehouse." Carlos listened intensely, mouth half opened, eyes focused on Joseph.

"Sounds good so far, man."

"Now here's the part I like. I know an island south of here. We'll get a small boat for the people with the money, one with a VHF radio." Joseph was warming up to the idea. The place was empty but he still talked in a hushed tone. "We'll have a small book on board that'll tell'em which channel to turn to, and we'll talk in code."

"Talk in code? How the hell ya gonna talk in code? Boy, Joseph, are you sure about this?" Carlos asked. Joseph explained how the code would work. "But, Joseph, what's going to stop these guys from shooting right back here and telling the inspector all about us?" Carlos looked worried and scratched his head. Two men came into the café, and sat at the counter. In a few minutes Carlos was back at Joseph's table.

"That's simple, my man," Joseph said, speaking with a large grin. "After they drop off the money and we give them the girl, they'll start back for St. Vincent. Hidden in the boat will be a few sticks of dynamite. I'll hook it up to a radio receiver. All I have to do is push a button and wham! The boat blows up. No one will ever see them again, ha, ha, ha," Joseph said, shaking all over with laughter.

"Hey that sounds pretty good, Joseph, ha, ha, ha, ha." Joseph's laughter was contagious and Carlos was laughing along with him. "Boy, Joseph, you sure know how to plan things. You're one smart mother," Carlos said.

"You're fucking right I'm smart, and don't you forget it. This gig is going to make us rich. You just do as you're told and keep your mouth shut. Everything will go down just like I say. You got it, Carlos?" Joseph asked.

The two men at the counter had finished their coffee. They dropped some coins on the counter, waved as they left. "There're other islands in the same area, they won't know which island, until we tell them. Look, Carlos, I don't have all the answers yet, but I am working on it. Gimme a few more days; gotta sleep on it. Gotta make sure it's foolproof. I'm not about to pass up a million bucks. Not when the pickings are this easy," Joseph said.

On the drive to work the following morning, the inspector put his paper down and spoke to Murphy. "Murphy, I get the feeling that I'm being followed. I noticed two men, not locals, on the boat over to Bequia, and again in the park when we were having lunch."

"Did you get a good look?" Murphy asked.

"Yeah, two of them, they look familiar, but I can't place them," the inspector said.

"The same two guys each time?" Murphy questioned.

"I think so. In the park, I just got a glance, not a real good look. I'd like you to spend some time on this. Rent a car and dress like the locals. Poke around, see what you can find out about these guys," Dupree said.

"Sure enough, boss, and when I tag them, what do you want me to do?" Murphy asked.

"Keep out of sight, and see what they're up to. Find out who they are, and where they're staying. Keep a low profile, don't scare them off," the inspector said.

"You got it, chief," Murphy said, as he scribbled some words in his little black book. Murphy liked the idea of protecting the inspector and his family. It gave him a sence of purpose, a new lease on life. Things were getting dull before he signed up with the inspector for what he thought would be an easy job.

Chapter Twenty-eight

"Hi, Murphy, you're right on time this morning," Ute said as she was cleaning vegetables for the evening meal. Ute's kitchen had the scent of freshness when she was not cooking. Murphy loved his little kaffeeklatsch with Ute each morning. He admired the bright sparkle to her eyes, always fresh dress, the whiff of pleasing aromas when she walked by. Murphy got a tingle just being near her.

"Hi, Ute, yeah, the more I try not to think about coffee the more I want it," Murphy said as he sat down on one of the bar stools at the island counter in Ute's kitchen.

"Do you drink a lot of coffee?" Ute asked.

"Not that much, maybe five or six cups a day. I'm trying to cut down. I hear that much coffee is not good for you," Murphy replied.

"Murph, what's with the new outfit? Are you trying to go local or something?" Ute asked as she poured two cups of coffee.

"Naw, the inspector wanted me to look into something. I have to look like a local. What d'ya think?" Murphy asked.

"Well yeah, you look local all right," Ute grinned. "As soon as you finish your coffee Madam Dupree wants you to drive her and Bobby to the market."

"Oh, I almost forgot, this is market day. I've got this other project on my mind, the work I'm doing for the inspector," Murphy said.

"Want to tell me about it?" Ute asked.

"Wish I could, Ute, but for now it's all hush-hush. Maybe later on when the item is complete," Murphy said.

Madam Dupree liked getting to the open market early on shopping day. Bobby was in the backseat with Madam Dupree. She was in charge of the shopping list. Murphy drove the family limo. For his chauffeur duties he was dressed in his gray outfit. He was becoming a quick change artist with all the different hats he was wearing.

"Do you have Ute's shopping list, Bobby?" Madam Dupree asked.

"Right here in my pocket, Madam Dee. Ute wants us to buy some fresh fish."

"What kind of fish?" Madam Dupree asked. Ute had suggested that the shopping list be given to Bobby in an effort to give her some responsibility.

"She wants whatever fish came in this morning. You know how fussy she is about the fish being fresh. Let's see, she wants a lot of vegetables, and of course the black bread. Oh, here is something that you can pick out," Bobby said.

"What's that, Bobby?" Madam Dupree asked.

"Wine. I don't think they'd sell me wine," Bobby said.

"Don't worry about the wine, I'll get it," Madam Dupree said. At that moment an old, beat-up truck pulled out of a side street. The truck was in front of the family limo. Murphy hit the brakes hard and turned the wheel, but it was too late. Along with the screeching of brakes, the loud crash was heard blocks away. Murphy's body hit the wheel hard. His head struck the windshield. He was knocked unconscious. His body lay against the wheel, the horn blowing nonstop. Madam Dupree was thrown forward, hitting her head on the dashboard. She was face down in the front seat, blood dripping on the carpet. Bobby, being smaller, hit the back of the front seat. Within an instant the back door of the limo was pulled opened. A man reached in, grabbed Bobby by the arm.

"You're coming with us, kid," a loud, rough voice said. With her head spinning, vision blurred, Bobby stumbled behind the man who had a tight grip on her arm.

"Help! Help! Help!" Bobby yelled.

"Shut up, you brat." With that Bobby was thrown into the backseat of a waiting automobile. The rough man had a strip of duct tape ready. He secured the tape over Bobby's mouth. A gray bag was slipped over her head. The car, driven by a second man, pulled into the street. No one in the car spoke. Each man seemed to know his job, acting without directions. The sedan had dark-tinted windows, blocking the view of any potential witness. The car moved out of the downtown district and then doubled back. They turned up one street and down another to make certain they were not being followed. The driver headed for the warehouse.

When they arrived at the warehouse Bobby could hear one of her abductors say, "Close the door, get the kid into the crate." Bobby felt her heart pounding as someone pulled her out of the car.

"Into the box, kid, you're going for a cruise to the enchanted island," the rough voice said.

"Mumm, mumm." Bobby was trying to tell them that she needed to go to the bathroom. Bang, bang, bang, the hammer nailed the crate closed. Bobby could hear the voices fade, the car being driven out of the warehouse. Her hands were tied in front of her. She was lying on her back. Her hood had been removed after she was placed in the box. The container was long enough, although narrow, with very little room for moving around. The slats on top of the box were slightly apart, giving the child plenty of air. As the quiet of the warehouse settled in Bobby realized that she had been kidnapped. Her frightened mood turned to despair. Bobby began to cry, afraid that the inspector would never find her.

As morning turned to afternoon, activity in the warehouse increased. Bobby heard men's voices, forklifts moving boxes, people coming and going. Finally it was her turn. As her crate was being moved, her body slammed from side to side. She tried to yell out for help, but the tape still covered her mouth. After a short ride on some sort of loading equipment her box was set down, and the machine moved on. Two men grabbed her box and stacked it high up atop other boxes. Her new location was dark.

I'm going to get out of this mess. Nobody is going to kidnap me. I'm going to find a way to escape. I'm a brave girl, everybody says so. I'll show them. I'll think of something. I'll show them. If only I could get out of this box, must wait until the workmen leave, maybe tonight. If I could get my knees up like this and push. Bobby heard a creak of a nail; she stopped pushing. *Oh no, better not make any noise right now. I'll just rest and wait for night. I don't know why anybody would want to kidnap me? I don't have money or anything.* Tears rolled down her face as she shut her eyes and tried to rest.

Bobby awoke in darkness. The diesel engines gave off a constant hum. She realized she was aboard a ship, rolling slightly from side to side. Pulling her knees up under her chin, she pushed as hard as she could. A nail creaked. The board seemed to move as she pushed with all her strength.

If I could only get this board loose. If only I could kick it out. Bobby pushed and pushed with her knees, and the board creaked again. *Wow, I'm getting it. Maybe a good kick will do it.* Bobby kicked as hard as she could. *Oh my toe. My toe; I hope I didn't break anything. Better not try that again. Boy that hurts.* Bobby relaxed, contemplated her next move. She pulled her knees up again and pushed hard; nothing, not a creak. Tears came to her eyes as she realized that getting the board loose would not be that easy.

After a rest Bobby tried again. This time the board moved a little. She pushed and pushed with her knees, and the board popped on one end.

That one's loose, now for the next. Oh, I wish I were stronger; this board won't budge. Bobby worked the board with little results. She was tired, thirsty and growing weak. She pulled her legs up again. Just one knee would fit on the narrow board. This time she heard the creak, faint at first. She pushed harder, and the creak got louder.

Oh, I've got it going, I think, it feels loose. I sure could use a drink. Rest, that's what I need, got to rest a little. If only Murphy were here, he'd tear this box apart with his bare hands. Bobby pulled her legs up under her chin once again, pushed with all her might. Creeeak went the nails. The board was loose, Bobby was out of breath. She relaxed her legs, closed her eyes, and said a little prayer. One last effort and she should be out of the box. Bobby tried again, this time with all her strength. The board moved a little, enough to give her encouragement. With renewed spirit she worked the board until, without realizing it, she had worked two boards loose. One more board and she would be free. After what seemed like hours of pushing on the third board, Bobby was able to work the board loose.

Wow. What a creepy place. I must be down in the bottom of the ship. After squeezing out of the box, Bobby climbed down over the other boxes. *If I could only find a hook or something sharp. Need to rub the rope against something. I'll try this box.* Bobby rubbed the rope against the edge of a wooden box. *It's not working, need something sharper. Oh look, a mirror over the sink. It's too high. If only I could break it.* Bobby pushed a box over near the sink. She thought that if she could get up on the sink, she could break the mirror by kicking it. Balancing herself by leaning her head on the wall, she gave the mirror a kick. Nothing happened. *My shoe is too soft, got to turn around, kick it with my heel.* Again she balanced herself by bracing her head against the bulkhead. The youngster gave it all she had with the heel of her shoe. The mirror broke, the glass crashed to the floor. Bobby jumped down from the sink and looked for a suitable piece of broken mirror. *Now, if I can just cut the rope. It's a good thing they tied my hands in front of me.* Bobby held the glass between her knees, rubbing the rope against the glass. *It's working; it's working. Oh boy, I'm getting free. I'm free. Oh boy, oh boy, I'm free. Now for this tape on my mouth, ohh, ohh, ouch, ouch, jeepers that hurts.* Bobby sucked in a lungfull of air, and did it again.

"Now to sneak up on the deck, maybe find out where the ship is going." Bobby was now able to talk to herself softly. She peeped out the door of her storage room and saw a flight of stairs. She sneaked up the stairs without a sound. The metal stairs led to more stairs, then more stairs, going up, up. "Boy this is a big ship." Bobby opened the door at the head of the stairs. Fresh salt air hit her face. "Wow, what a ship. Lights up there must be where the captain is. I'll bet the captain will help me. Or maybe he's one of the kidnappers. Why would a captain of a big ship like this want to kidnap a girl?" Bobby sneaked up to the bridge, peeked in one of the portholes. "There's no one in there. I don't see anybody. I wonder who's steering the ship? It must be on self-steering, or something."

Bobby opened the door to the bridge and walked in. She looked around at all the equipment. The room was full of things, so many things that she could not find what she was looking for. "There, that looks like it. Hope it's the right radio. I'll just give it a try."

"Coast Guard, Coast Guard. Over." Bobby listened for a reply. "Calling the Coast Guard. Over." *Nothing; must be the wrong channel. There're so many channels here, I don't know which one to try.* "Coast Guard, Coast Guard. It's me calling. Over."

"This is the St. Vincent Coast Guard. Please identify yourself. Over."

"Coast Guard, Coast Guard, it's me, Bobby White, I've been kidnapped, and, . . . and. . ."

"What is the name of your ship, Bobby? Over."

"Hello, Coast Guard, I don't know the name of the ship. They put me in a box and . . . and," Bobby began to cry.

"Calm down, young lady, tell me your position. Tell me where you are. Can you do that? Over."

"I don't know where I am. I'm on a big ship and there is no one here. I'm up where the captain should be, where the wheel is, and all that stuff, but no one is here."

"Okay, young lady, we copy that. Can you look at the compass, and tell us what your heading is? Over."

"Okay, Coast Guard, let's see, the compass points to 190. No wait, 195, it's moving back and forth a little. Mumm . . .,

mumm," Bobby was grabbed from behind; someone's big hand was over her mouth.

Her assailant released his grip and said, "Excuse me young lady, but what the hell are you doing?" He grabbed the mike out of Bobby's hand. "Hello, Coast Guard. This is the freighter, *Aucocisco*. We are headed south with general freight to the Grenadines. Over," the man said as he held Bobby by the arm.

"*Aucocisco*, we have just had a complaint from one of your passengers saying that she has been kidnapped. Over."

"Coast Guard, I have the girl here on the bridge, I'll get back to you in a few minutes. Just as soon as I find out what's going on. Over."

"Roger, *Aucocisco*, we copy that, over and out."

"Now, young lady, what the hell is this all about? And no tall stories now. I can tell a lie a mile away," the seaman said.

"I . . . I, I was kidnapped and stuffed in a box," Bobby said.

"Now, who would want to kidnap a nice little girl like you, and if you were stuffed in a box how come you are up here on the bridge?" the seaman asked.

"No, it's true, I swear. Come, I'll show you the box," Bobby said.

"Well, I can't leave the bridge, stay put; I'll call the captain, okay?" The seaman threw a switch on a box. "Ah, Captain, this is Mike on the bridge. I believe we have a stowaway. Can you come up here and check out her story? Thanks, Captain." Mike clicked off the intercom, looked at Bobby and said: "Now look, little girl, you stay right here and don't move. I'm going to call the Coast Guard. The captain will be up here in a few minutes to check out your story, okay?" the seaman said.

"Okay, mister, but I was kidnapped. I'm not fooling," Bobby said with determination.

"Coast Guard, this is the freighter *Aucocisco* calling. Over," the seaman said. Bobby was looking up at the man, who was tall, large, with a dark complexion. He was wearing Navy-type dungarees and had a stomach that hung over his belt. His dungarees had bellbottoms; he was wearing a light blue work shirt with a navy blue watch cap.

"This is the St. Vincent Coast Guard, go ahead *Aucocisco*. Over."

"Coast Guard, I have called the captain, he'll be up here in a minute to check out the girl's story. For now, she insists that she has been kidnapped, and that's all I've got. Over," the seaman said.

"Roger, *Aucocisco*, please have the captain call us when he has the information, over and out." The man hung up the VHF mike and turned to Bobby. "My name is Mike, what's your name?" Mike seemed to be a gentle man and Bobby did not feel frightened.

"I'm Bobby White, and I live on St. Vincent with Chief Inspector Dupree," Bobby said.

"Bobby White? Bobby White? I've read about you in the papers. Aren't you the girl that was on a schooner that went down in that last hurricane we had? Well I'll be, so you're that Bobby White?" Mike said.

"But, the schooner didn't go down in the hurricane; we made it through the hurricane . . .," at that moment the captain walked onto the bridge.

"Well, what have we here, a new passenger? What's your name, young lady?" the captain asked. The captain was also a large man. He had a round face that was covered with a white beard. He wore a white shirt with three gold strips on the shoulder boards, and no hat. The captain reached for one of the armchairs that faced the operations console. He sat down and looked at Bobby with a smile.

"I'm Bobby White, Captain, and I was kidnapped. I really was," Bobby said.

"I'm sure you were, young lady. Mike, that name sounds familiar. Where have I heard it before?" the captain asked.

Mike was scanning the horizon for lights. "Captain, she's the girl that was on that schooner that went down in the last hurricane we had. Also, there's a trial coming up for the captain of that schooner. The papers said that the guy may have killed her parents." Mike was checking the compass, looking at the revolutions of the engine, the speed through the water.

"The captain of the schooner killed your parents? Why would he do a thing like that?" the captain asked.

"The inspector said that it was greed. He said that some people can never get enough, that they always want more money. And that Captain Mark did not want to work for a living," Bobby said.

"Who is this inspector fellow? Is he a friend of yours?" The captain appeared not to believe the story of this newly found stowaway.

"He's Chief Inspector Dupree, the head of all the police on St. Vincent, and the best detective in the entire world. He captured Captain Mark on the island of Barbados, and he's my very best friend ever," Bobby said.

"Wow, he sounds like some kind of a guy. Mike, get the Coast Guard on the horn, and have them call Inspector Dupree. Find out if he is missing a little girl," the captain said.

Chapter Twenty-nine

The inspector received the news of the accident shortly after it happened. When he got to the scene the ambulance was already there. Two police cars parked on the north side of the accident blocked traffic. The ambulance and a third police car blocked traffic on the south side. Inspector Dupree jumped out of the police car and ran up to Murphy.

He looked over at the ambulance and saw his wife, with a bandage on her head, lying on a gurney. She was being lifted into the ambulance. Murphy refused the gurney. He held a bandage to his head and walked unsteadily. A paramedic helped him toward the ambulance.

"Murphy, Murphy, what happened? Just a minute," Dupree ran over to the ambulance. "Madam Dupree, oh my God, are you all right? Can you talk?" The inspector was frantic.

"Step aside, Inspector, we've got to get her to the hospital," said the paramedic.

"I'm okay, darling, just a bump on the head. It looks a lot worse than it is," Madam Dupree said as the gurney was being pushed into the ambulance. Dupree ran back to Murphy.

"Murphy, tell me what happened." the inspector asked.

"Well, sir, this old truck pulled out right in front of me from a side street. I hit the brakes, but I was too late, he was too close. I think it was deliberate and Bobby is missing," Murphy said.

"Missing? Missing? What do you mean, missing?" the inspector was losing his composure.

"What I mean, Inspector, is that we can't find her, she's not here. When I woke up she was gone. Madam Dupree was in the front seat; no one was in the backseat," Murphy said.

"Holy Christ, Murphy, I don't like the looks of this. Do you suppose that someone is trying to eliminate the only witness we have for the upcoming trial? Look, Murphy, you go with Madam Dupree to the hospital. I've got to get back to the office. Look, have your head checked while you're there, okay?" the inspector said. He was standing close to Murphy, helping him to stand upright.

"Sure, Inspector, I'll keep a close eye on Madam. You go get your girl back." Murphy pushed off the inspector, headed for the ambulance. Dupree returned to his office in a hurry. A number of suspects were rounded up, a few held for questioning. The inspector made several calls to the hospital. A busy day at the hospital made it difficult to get information. On his last call, much to his relief, he was told that Madam and Murphy had been released and were on their way home.

Inspector Dupree stayed at the office making phone calls, and interrogating the characters that were brought in. The afternoon turned into evening. He spoke with his wife. She assured him that she and Murphy were not seriously injured. The inspector wanted to be with his wife, although he felt that being at police headquarters working to find Bobby was paramount. He had dozed off at his desk when Officer Pratt, working the night shift at the booking desk, woke him up. A call had come in from the Coast Guard.

"Pardon me, Inspector, you have a call from the Coast Guard, I believe it is urgent."

"Chief Inspector Dupree here . . . Bobby White! You've located Bobby White?" The inspector stood up from his desk. "Know her? Hell yes, I know her. I've been looking all over this island for her. We have an all-points bulletin out." The inspector was without his jacket, sleeves rolled up, and no tie. His desk was a mess, two empty coffee cups sat among the unfiled papers. "Where is she? On the *Aucocisco*, out at sea? Headed for the outer islands? Good God." Dupree sat back down again. "Oh, this is good news. Is she okay? Was she hurt?" Dupree asked.

"As far as we know, she's alright. We talked to her by VHF, she sounded like she was okay. She insists that she was kidnapped," the Coast Guard replied.

"I'm sure she was kidnapped. She's not the type to take a boat ride just for the fun of it," Dupree said as he looked around for some water to splash on his face.

"Hang up, Inspector, I'll get the ship on the radio, then patch into your phone. Hopefully they are not out of range," the Coast Guard said.

"This is great news, Coast Guard. I'll hang up now, and wait for the patch." Five minutes later the call came through. Bobby was so excited that she forgot that she was talking over a radio. Two people cannot talk at the same time over a radio transmission. The conversation was difficult; nevertheless the inspector was able to determine that Bobby was alright, the kidnappers did not harm her, and that she was in good hands. He talked to the captain, found out the ship's next port of call, and the estimated docking time.

Dupree called home and broke the good news to his wife. "Yes, Madam, she is safe, I'll be headed for the airport at first light. I'll be at the dock when the ship ties up. We'll fly directly home, arriving sometime tomorrow afternoon. I'm having a guard placed on the house. You take care of yourself, my dear. Put Murphy on the line, please? Murphy, hi, you've heard the good news. I'm flying to Union Island first thing in the morning. I'm having Officer Pratt send a detail out to the house. I want a guard on my place twenty-four hours a day. You get a good night's rest. You can sleep in the guest bedroom."

"Thank you, Inspector, but I'm okay. I can make it home alright; don't you worry about me." Murphy said.

"Murphy, you're not going anywhere, do you hear me? Now I insist that you don't leave my house until I get back. Good night, my friend." The inspector hung up the phone, and headed for a cot in one of the empty jail cells. He was able to catch a few hours' sleep before heading for the airport in the morning.

The inspector walked into the hangar at eight in the morning, still sipping his to-go coffee. "Hi, Inspector, how's it going?" Skip Johnson asked as the inspector entered the small hangar.

"Hi, Skip, how's the old ticker?" the inspector said as he looked for the owner of the small plane-charter business. Johnson was the last person he wanted to see.

"Oh, I'm fine, just fine. As a matter of fact I'm flying again. Yep, back in the charter business. Looking for a flight?" Johnson asked.

"Oh no, not me, no, no, I'm just here on a little police business; nothing serious," the inspector said. He was a little nervous just thinking of flying with Johnson again.

"Good morning, Inspector, what can I do for you?" Sam

asked. Sam was the owner of the charter business. He was a short, round man with a sense of humor. They shook hands.

"Hi, Sam, I'm here on a little police business. May I speak to you privately?" the inspector asked.

"Certainly, Inspector, certainly, right this way," Sam said as he motioned the inspector to his office. "Have a seat, would you like a cigar?"

"No thanks, Sam, gave it up years ago," the inspector said.

"Well, Inspector, what is this all about?" Sam asked as he lit up his cigar and leaned back in his swivel chair.

"Sam, I need a flight to Union Island. Now look, I'm not flying with Skip Johnson, never again. You know what happened the last time I flew with that guy," the inspector said, wishing he smoked again so that he could have a cigarette.

"Sorry, Inspector, but Skip is the only pilot I have if you insist on leaving now." Sam took a puff on his cigar. The light bounced off his forehead, which ended back behind his ears.

"I've gotta fly out now, except I'm not flying with Skip. Skip's a nice guy and all that, but his heart. I don't want my life depending on that heart of his," Dupree said.

"Skip's a great pilot, one of the best," Sam said.

"Yeah, but if his ticker stops beating while we are up there, what the hell am I supposed to do?" the inspector said in a voice that was an octave higher than normal.

"Oh, don't fret, Inspector, Skip's okay. He only has one heart attack a year, and most times he's not flying when it happens. Now, you want the plane or not? I've got this cute waitress over at the diner waiting for me. You should see her," Sam said as he smiled.

"Come on, Sam, I don't have time to listen to your love life," the inspector said.

"She's six foot tall with not a piece of fat on her body, long, blonde hair down to here. The roots are a little dark, but what the hell. My nose comes up to her boobs," Sam said, leaning back in his swivel chair and blowing smoke rings. He was off in his own little dream world.

"Sam, listen to me, I need a plane now, moreover I am not flying with Skip. You got that? I'm not flying with that guy, now get me that plane." The inspector was up off his chair pounding his fist on the desk.

"Inspector," Skip Johnson hollered from the front office. "If you need a lift I'm available. My plane is ready to go on a moment's notice," Johnson said as he gave out a long series of coughs like someone who has been smoking for too many years.

"Christ, Sam, do something," the inspector pleaded, lowering his voice.

"I wish I could, Inspector, but Skip is all I've got right now. My other plane is down for its yearly checkup. Won't be flying for a couple of days. They got the engine pulled apart. If we had another chartering service on this island, I would certainly suggest you use it," Sam said.

"Okay, Sam, you win. Sign me up for Skip, heaven have mercy on my soul," the inspector said.

"Now you are talking like a true island-hopper," Sam said with a smile.

Grim-faced, Dupree handed Johnson his traveling bag as he came out of Sam's office. They headed for the little red plane that looked as pretty as ever. Johnson went through his preflight routine with the skill of a seasoned pilot. The take-off was without incident. As they reached cruising attitude, the inspector spoke to the pilot through his headpiece. "Skip, I have been meaning to ask you. How's your heart these days?"

"Oh hell, my heart is fine. The doctor tells me that I should go to the States for surgery, but I don't have time for that bullshit. You know, I could die on the operating table or something. Who the hell wants to go through that crap?" Johnson said.

"Don't you think that flying a plane with a bad ticker is a little dangerous?" Dupree asked, as he wiped the sweat from his forehead.

"Oh, the way I look at it, when it's my time to go, I'll go, that's all," Johnson said.

"Christ, Skip, if it's your time to go that's fine with me, but I don't fancy going along with you." The poor inspector was as white as the gloves of a drill sergeant on inspection day.

"Calm down, Inspector, I have these little pills right here in my pocket. If something should happen just pop one of them in my mouth, okay?" the pilot said as he grinned.

"Yeah, sure, Skip, I'll just pop a pill in your mouth, then fly the plane myself." The inspector was not a happy camper. Skip grabbed his heart, and gave out a groan.   "Skip, if this is your idea of a joke, it's not funny," Dupree said.

Bobby made her way to the bridge as the large freighter nudged up to the pier with the help of two tugboats. The people on the bridge were busy. Bobby had been advised to stay out of the way.

"So many people down there, I wish I could find the inspector," Bobby said as she moved along the rail on the dockside of the bridge. She was hoping, hoping to spot her friend. The ship's whistle blew as dock lines were heaved, and trucks began coming onto the dock. The gangplank was lowered, and a few passengers were making their way onto the dock when Bobby heard a siren. An old police car was barreling down the dirt road, being chased by a cloud of dust. "It's the inspector. It's him, I know it is, I just know it, it's him," Bobby shouted, jumping up and down. She ran inside the bridge house. "Captain . . . Captain, it's the inspector; he's coming. He's coming in a police car," Bobby shouted, jumping up and down.

"Calm down, girl, calm down. I've got a boat to dock, and a thousand other things to do. Just hold on, we'll bring the inspector to the bridge. He'll need to sign some release papers, and then we'll go home, okay?" The captain had a big smile on his face.

"Oh, I can't calm down, I'm too excited. The inspector is my very best friend ever," Bobby said. Bobby ran back to the rail and saw the inspector getting out of the police car. "I knew it, I knew it. I knew he'd come get me. Inspector . . . Inspector, I'm up here." Bobby hollered and waved from the bridge. The inspector looked up, waved back. It took some time for him to get to the bridge, and when he appeared, Bobby ran into his open arms. The inspector warpped his arms around her shoulders, kissed her on the cheek. Bobby hugged him back around his waist and said, "Boy, I'm glad to see you, Inspector."

"Hold on, Bobby, I've got to talk to the captain. You know there are laws against people stowing away. The captain may ask us to pay for passage, or maybe freight. How are you? You look in good health. Did the men hurt you?" Dupree was holding both of Bobby's hands.

"I'm fine now, Inspector, the only problem I had was getting out of that box. They nailed it shut, and they wouldn't let me go to the bathroom," Bobby said, talking fast.

"I want to hear all about it. We'll talk on the way home, but first I want to get the paperwork out of the way. Afterward I'll have a look at the box they nailed you in." The inspector told

Bobby not to move, then went into the bridge house looking for the captain.

"Thanks, Captain, for taking care of my girl, we were quite worried," the inspector said as they shook hands.

"My pleasure, Inspector, you have some girl there. You should be very proud of her," the captain said.

"She's been through a lot lately," the inspector said. Dupree signed the required papers, and had a good look at the shipping crate. Upon leaving the freighter the pair entered the backseat of the dusty police car. Dupree requested to be driven to the airport.

When the police car arrived at the airport Bobby jumped out and had a look around. "Inspector, is that red plane over there taking us back to St. Vincent?" Bobby asked.

"That's it, that's our plane, Bobby," Dupree said.

"Inspector, is that the red airplane that you and Murphy had flown in to Barbados?" Bobby asked, looking at Dupree as she squinted her eyes.

"Why yes, I believe it is," the inspector said as he tried to project an air of calm.

"And is the pilot the one who had the heart attack?" Bobby asked, cocking her head to one side as she faced the inspector.

"Yes, I believe it is, Bobby," the inspector's calm exterior did not fool Bobby.

"Do you suppose he is going to have another heart attack while he's flying us home?" Bobby asked.

"No, Bobby, no, no, not at all, he's much better now. And he tells me that he has these pills," the inspector said. He was not only trying to convince Bobby, but himself as well.

"Inspector, I don't think I want to fly in that plane. Do you think we could wait for a boat?" Bobby asked.

"I wish I had the time to wait for a boat. I'd like nothing more than to wait here for a boat, believe me. Do you know what would happen if the bad guys, on my island, found out that I wasn't there?" Dupree asked.

"They'd steal things?" Bobby replied.

"That's right, Bobby, or perhaps worse things would happen. I think we'll just have to take our chances with the old red plane," Dupree said.

"Sometimes I wish you weren't the inspector," Bobby said.

"So do I, Bobby, so do I," Dupree said.

On the flight back Skip Johnson was in a good humor. He talked continuously about the upcoming trial, the weather, and his airplane. The inspector thought he'd never shut up. Bobby sat very quiet, with her head down, and her fingers crossed.

Chapter Thirty

Murphy felt personally responsible for the accident, and the disappearance of Bobby. He had been working almost around the clock in an effort to track down the owner of the truck that had caused the accident. Three days into his extensive detective work he finally came up with some answers.

Taking the granite steps two at a time, Murphy was out of breath when he opened the door to the police station. Conscious of his heightened state of excitement, he stopped himself before entering the building. He attempted to slow his breathing, and straightened his shirt. Murphy walked slowly up to the sliding glass window. Sheri was on the phone. Excited as a child, Murphy stood on one foot and then the other. Patience were not one of his strong points; he felt like grabbing the phone out of her hand.

"Sorry, Murphy, that person was long-winded," Sheri smiled, disarming Murphy.

"Hi, Sheri, I'd like to speak with the inspector, if he's not too busy?" Murphy said.

"He's never too busy to talk to you, Murphy. Just a minute, I'll buzz him." Murphy and the inspector were always on the lookout to find Sheri a mate; so far they had been unsuccessful. They both teased Office Pratt about dating Sheri, but Pratt was much too bashful when he was near Sheri. Poor Officer Pratt received extended ribbing from all the officers. If they ran out of conversation, there was always Pratt. One officer suggested that he just walk up to her and say 'you wanna fuck'. This always brought a hearty laugh from all the policemen.

"Go right in, Murphy," Sheri said as she smiled. Murphy then knocked on the inspector's office door, and let himself in. Dupree was at his desk, head down, working.

"Hi, Inspector, I found the owner of that old truck," Murphy said. His excitement showed through his attempt to be composed. He moved quickly over the Oriental rug, then sat in one of the two chairs facing Dupree's desk.

"That's good news, Murphy. We know the plates were stolen from another vehicle, one that has been in the junkyard for years. Who owns the truck?" the inspector asked.

"Inspector, the truck belongs to Juan Fangio. We questioned Juan, he said that he had loaned the truck to his cousin," Murphy said.

"Come on, Murphy, don't drag this out. Who's the cousin?" the inspector asked impatiently, looking up from his paperwork. The inspector felt that Murphy was onto something.

"The cousin just happens to work for . . . you've got it, Joseph," Murphy said.

"Aha. The infamous owner of the Water Front Café," the inspector said with a scowl. Murphy was grinning from ear to ear. "I thought so. Joseph, I might have known. That lowdown rackerfrack . . . that weasel . . . that water rat," the inspector said as he slammed his fist down on his desk and rose from his chair.

"What the hell is a 'rackerfrack'?" Murphy asked, in amazement.

"I'll explain later. Right now, we've got to bring in Carlos for questioning. I certainly appreciate your work on this case. You've done an outstanding job. I thank you for your efforts, Murphy," the inspector said.

"My pleasure, Inspector," Murphy said, still grinning.

"Anything new on my shadow?" the inspector asked. "Or should I say shadows?"

"Your suspicions were correct. I didn't want to say anything until I was sure. I spotted the same two guys showing up wherever you happened to be," Murphy said. "I obtained your schedule from Sheri. I would try to be where you were heading before you got there. A number of times I spotted the same two characters. They seemed to be very interested in your daily routine."

"Well, keep an eye on them. I might bring them in for questioning. See if you can find out who they are and where they live. Let me know if they make contact with someone else. For now I would like you to go out to the house, keep an eye on things. You could do that by cleaning the rental car or something. Also, see if my wreck is repairable, or if it should be junked."

"Right you are, Chief, I'm starting to realize your need for a bodyguard. At first I thought you were being overly cautious. Now I realize that we do have some bad fish on this island."

Murphy drove the rented car back to the villa, parked in front of the garage. After getting out the hose, a bucket, and other paraphernalia, he began washing the car. Much to his delight he saw Ute coming his way from the house.

"Oh. Hi, Ute, beautiful morning," Murphy said. He was pleased to see Ute. Elated to see how the sun bounced off her ochre-colored hair, the contrast of her tanned body against her white dress. What a gorgeous woman, Murphy thought.

"Hi. Yes, a beautiful morning, Murph. Would you like some coffee? It's freshly made," Ute asked.

"That's very sweet of you, Ute. You know I can't refuse your coffee." Murphy dropped the hose, followed Ute into the kitchen.

"I understand the trial is starting tomorrow," Ute said. "Will you be with Bobby?"

"I'll be right in the front row with Bobby by my side. She is a very bright kid, although I'm afraid this trial has her a bit on edge. I hope she can pull it off. There's a lot of pressure on her, poor kid. She not only lost her family, but now she must tell her story in front of that Mark Borman character," Murphy said.

"She is a bit upset; nevertheless, she has a strong will. I know she'll do alright," Ute said as she cleaned the stovetop. Murphy watched as he sat on one of the stools at the island counter.

"Look, Ute, uh . . .," Murphy hesitated.

"Yes, Murphy, what is it?" Ute asked.

"Well, I've been thinking that, well maybe, uh . . . What I mean to say is. Now you don't have to say 'yes'," Murphy said as he stared down into his coffee mug.

"Yes, Murphy, what is it?" Ute asked again.

"Do you think that, maybe, you'd like to go the movies with me? It's okay if you have other things to do, I'd understand," Murphy said.

"Don't be silly. I'd love to go to the movies with you," Ute answered with a smile.

"You would? You really would? Hey that's great. I don't know why, I feel like a kid again," Murphy said as his face flushed.

"Murphy, you are the sweetest, kindest person I know. I'm sure any woman would be proud to go to the movies with you." Ute's simper gave a sparkle to her eyes. She returned to the sink.

"The Saturday night movie is supposed to be good, if you can believe the papers," Murphy said. He got up to add some coffee to his cup. Ute followed him back to the island counter.

"Saturday evening is fine; if the movie is a stinker, then we can just walk out, right?" Ute said.

"That's settled then, I'll pick you up at seven," Murphy said with a big smile.

The judge pounded his gavel to settle the court down. The spectators and press had packed the courtroom on the opening day of the trial. The story of the trial had been running in the papers for some time. The islanders had taken a keen interest in it. They found it difficult to believe that a captain would murder three people and then sink his own boat to cover up the crime. Many on the island did not believe Bobby's story.

Seated on the right side of the courtroom, facing the judge, was Jack Farrington and his associate, Phil Sealy. Jack had agreed to be the prosecuting attorney for the government. On the left were Mark Borman, and his defense attorney, Bill Spring. Bobby White sat in the front row with Murphy by her side. Inspector Dupree was unable to attend the first day of the trial due to the pressing business of the kidnapping of Bobby. Madam Dupree and Ute sat farther back in the courtroom. The judge called for opening statements.

Jack Farrington stood before his table for a moment, unbuttoned his jacket, walked slowly to the jury box. "Ladies and gentlemen of the jury, the accused, Mark Borman, seated before you in this courtroom is on trial for a repugnant crime. He is not on trial for a murder of a member of a family, but the whole family, save one." Jack placed his hands on his hips, leaned forward. "And that one person is here in this courtroom to tell you, in her own words, how Mark Borman committed this horrendous crime." A buzz went through the courtroom.

The judge tapped his gavel, nodded at Farrington, "You may proceed, counselor."

"The defense will point out that Bobby White lost her memory, and that she has no recollection of the events on her last night on the schooner *Vagus*." Borman nodded his head in agreement. A few coughs were heard from the spectators. "Yes, Bobby White lost her memory. She lost it after the horrible events of that dreadful night. The night after the hurricane had passed. She lost her memory for a short period of time, a period of time needed for her body and mind to heal and recover from the ordeal. In that period of time, she was taken in by our own Chief Inspector Dupree and his wife, Madam Dupree. Bobby White received the loving care she needed for her recovery and she did recover fully. On the day she met Mark Borman at the marketplace here on St. Vincent, ladies and gentlemen, the face of Mark Borman brought back all the horrors Bobby White suffered her last night on the schooner. First, the disappearance of her father while he was on deck with Borman, then Borman coming down the ladder with a club in his hand, the clubbing to death of her brother, Brad, the clubbing of her mother when she came to the aid of her son, and finally, Bobby White's escape from the schooner. When the whole story is presented to you, ladies and gentlemen, you will realize the ghastly ordeal this child went through. The details are so vivid, so horrible; you will understand that such a story could not be made up." Farrington thanked the jury and sat down. He patted his brow with his handkerchief. Then he took a drink of water, and whispered to his associate, "This is not going to be easy."

Coughing and other noises from the spectators brought a few

taps of the judge's gavel. He looked at the table for the defense, nodded his head.

"Ladies and gentlemen of the jury," Bill Spring said in a voice that could be heard by the entire courtroom. Bill Spring was an old hand at trying unpopular cases. Less than average height, somewhat overweight, and with hair cut very short. He had lost most of it when he was still a young man. Spring addressed the jury while trying to close the button on his jacket.

"Mark Borman, the able and capable captain you see seated here before you, has been accused of an unspeakable crime." Spring walked close to the jury box. "Captain Mark Borman, a seaman for over thirty years, a man of responsibility, a man of stature, is accused of a crime he did not commit." Bill Spring made eye contact with each juror as he moved along the box. "He attended the Massachusetts Maritime Academy, where he graduated with honors at the top of his class. Captain Borman worked hard over the years for his rating of captain." Bill Spring gave up on trying to button his jacket.

"His training began on merchant ships that took him all over the world. He started as third mate and worked his way up the ladder. He received his 100-ton license from the U.S. Coast Guard twenty years ago. Four years ago he bought his own charter boat. Captain Borman built a very successful chartering business." The jury, watching Spring's every movement, took in every word. Bill Spring stopped for a moment, walked over to his table, sipped from his glass of water. As he set his glass down he gave an encouraging glance at Borman.

Attorney Spring then turned and walked back toward the jury. "Now does it sound reasonable to you, ladies and gentlemen, that a man of his rank, his stature, a man of his responsibility, and skill, would commit the crime he has been accused of?" The defense attorney was now starting to warm up to the jury. He could see the questions in their minds, sensed their desire for understanding. "I will show the members of this jury that Captain Mark Borman did everything in his power to save the White family and his schooner. He launched the emergency lifeboat, and then helped the White family into that boat. The last he saw of them is when the wind and the waves carried the raft off the stern of his beloved schooner. A schooner that was filling so rapidly with water that little time was left for him to save his own life. I will show this jury that Captain Borman risked his life getting the White family off his boat safely. Time he needed to unlash and launch the hard dinghy. Time so short, so precious, that Captain Borman was unable to store food and water in his dinghy. Food and water he desperately needed for his survival. Food and water needed for the long and painful voyage to the island that he happened upon by chance." Bill Spring interrupted his opening remarks, and walked to the center of the courtroom.

Over at the prosecution desk Jack Farrington and his associate were taking notes. One would whisper in the other's ear, then return the whisper. Bill Spring was becoming more confident as he spoke.

"Captain Mark Borman, ladies and gentlemen, is a man of character, leadership, a man who placed his ship and the White family above his own personal safety." Spring spoke louder from the center of the courtroom. He then walked toward the jury box. "If the schooner's hard dinghy had been unavailable that stormy night, our captain would have gone down with his ship. The rubber lifeboat was full. It would not hold another person." Bill Spring paused for effect. The members of the jury looked at one another. "As this trial unfolds, as witnesses are brought forward to testify to the character of this captain, you will find, ladies and gentlemen, that this captain is not the fiendish person of a child's wild imagination.

One can hardly imagine the difficulties this child went through, losing her family when the dinghy overturned in rough seas, then climbing back into the dinghy and drifting for days without food or water. Dehydrated and sunburned, she was unconscious when found. I submit, ladies and gentlemen of the jury, that this child, Bobby White, was so traumatized by these events that she lost her memory and has no recollection of the events that happened the evening she last saw Captain Borman." Borman's lawyer then walked in front of the jury and said "Thank you."

A hush fell over the courtroom. Members of the jury looked at one another as the judge tapped his gavel to bring order to the court. Spring placed his hand on Borman's shoulder as he sat down. He then whispered in Borman's ear, "That kid doesn't stand a chance. I'll run her into the ground."

Chapter Thirty-one

Jack Farrington rose from his table to address the court. "Your Honor, the prosecution calls Roberta White to the stand." Bobby felt her stomach drop, her legs go weak. She froze in her seat.

"Come on, Bobby, be a brave girl. Go up there and tell your story," Murphy said as he held her hand. Bobby didn't move. "Come on, Bobby, you can do it. I know you can." Murphy rose up, still holding her hand, as Bobby held back. Murphy leaned down and whispered in Bobby's ear. "Bobby, go up there and tell your story. Show everyone that Captain Mark can't get away with what he did. You're a brave girl."

Bobby got up slowly, and under her breath repeated over and over, *I'm a brave girl. I'm a brave girl. I'm a brave girl.* The sergeant of arms led her to the stand. After being sworn in, Bobby sat down in the witness chair.

"Now Roberta," Jack Farrington began.

"It's Bobby, everyone calls me Bobby."

"Very well, Bobby it is. Would you please tell the court what happened that night when the schooner went down?" Farrington asked.

"I didn't see the schooner go down. I was miles away when

that happened," Bobby said in a strong voice, forcing herself to speak up as she had been rehearsed.

"Tell us what happened the night after the hurricane had passed," Farrington asked.

"My mother told me to go up on deck and ask my father what he'd like for supper." Bobby's voice was starting to tremble.

"Would you speak a little louder, Bobby, so the jury can hear your story?" Farrington asked.

"Captain Mark was at the wheel, he said that my father wasn't there, and that he hadn't seen my father," Bobby said.

"Then what happened, Bobby?" Farrington wanted Bobby to tell the story her own way.

"I went back down below, and told my mother that Daddy was not on deck. My mother looked sick and asked me to go and see if he was in the front cabin. Next she asked my brother to see if he's in the back cabin." Bobby was getting her strength back.

"And was your father in either cabin?" Farrington asked.

"No. He wasn't on the boat any longer," Bobby said as she started to cry.

"I know this is very hard for you, Bobby, do you want a glass of water?" The prosecution was hoping that Bobby would not break down completely.

"Yes, please." Bobby's hands shook as she lifted the glass of water to her mouth.

"When you and your mother found out that your father was no longer on the schooner, what happened after that?" Farrington asked.

"Captain Mark came down the ladder with a small club in his hand. My brother tried to push him away from my mother; that's when he hit him over the head." Bobby was shaking.

"It's okay, Bobby, you're doing just fine. Please go on," Farrington said.

"My mother ran to help Brad and that's when Captain Mark hit her on the head," Bobby said as she started to sob. Farrington asked the judge for a short recess.

"Recess granted. Court will resume in twenty minutes," the judge said as he banged his gavel.

During the break Bill Spring huddled close with his client. The two whispered back and forth while Spring scribbled notes to himself. The judge's chamber opened when the break was over. Judge Larry McLean walked to the bench with his robe, open in front, flowing behind him. Bobby White, red-eyed, holding a handkerchief, was back in the witness chair. She had regained her composure enough to continue.

"Now, Bobby, you were telling the court how Captain Mark first hit your brother on the head, and when your mother ran to his side he hit your mother on the head. At this time what were you doing?" Dead silence prevailed in the courtroom.

"I ran between the table and Captain Mark's legs, then I ran up the ladder." Bobby's pain, in telling her story, showed on her face.

"When you went up the ladder and out the main hatch was Captain Mark right behind you?" Farrington asked.

"No, I don't think so. I didn't look back," Bobby said.

"Now, you are on the deck of the schooner. What happened next?" Jack Farrington asked.

"I ran forward, up near the first mast, and then I saw the white box that the rubber dinghy was in. I heard Captain Mark holler for me. I looked back and he was just coming out of the hatch," Bobby said.

"Did he have his club at that time?" Farrington asked.

"I don't know. I was so scared that I reached into the box and tried to pull the red handle."

"Yes, go on, Bobby," encouraged Farrington.

"But I couldn't pull the handle; it wouldn't work," Bobby said.

"And what was Captain Mark doing at this time?" Farrington asked.

"He came up behind me, I ran further up front. He reached into the box and pulled the handle."

Jack Farrington walked over to the jury box and from there he asked, "Did the dinghy blow up?"

"Yes. Captain Mark put the dinghy over the side. He led it to the back of the boat, then tied it to something," Bobby said.

"Did the captain tell you to get in the dinghy?" Farrington asked.

"Yes he did, but I was afraid. He said he would go below and get my mother and brother if I got into the dinghy," Bobby said as she blew her nose.

"And did you get into the dinghy?" Farrington asked as he walked along the front of the jury box.

"Yes, because I wanted him to get my mother and brother," Bobby said as she wiped her tears.

"Now you are in the dinghy. It's bouncing around behind the schooner because the seas are still rough. Captain Mark promised to get your mother and brother. He said he would put them in the dinghy with you. Is that not correct?" Farrington asked as he moved over to the front of his desk.

"Objection, the prosecution is leading the witness," Bill Spring said as he jumped to his feet, waving his glasses at the judge.

"Objection overruled. The prosecution is summarizing the events. Go ahead with your questioning, counselor," Judge McLean nodded toward Farrington.

"Now, Bobby, is that what Captain Mark said he would do?" Farrington asked as he walked back to the jury box.

"Yes."

"And what did he do?" Farrington asked.

"He untied the line and let me loose. He said that my family was in heaven, and that I'll be seeing them soon." Bobby began to cry.

"Just a few more questions, Bobby, and then you can go, okay?" Bobby nodded her head. "Did all of this happen before the hurricane, or after the hurricane?"

"It happened after the hurricane. The wind was still blowing hard and the waves were big, but the hurricane had passed by, everyone said so," Bobby said.

Farrington walked back to the witness stand to ask his next question. "How did the schooner behave during the hurricane?"

"Like a roller coaster until Captain Mark took down the sails, and put out the storm anchor," Bobby said.

"Did the schooner calm down after that?" Farrington asked.

"Uh-huh . . . it was much better after that," Bobby said.

"Did the sea anchor break, Bobby?" Farrington asked.

"Yes." Bobby nodded her head. "In the middle of the night. The boat went upside down, then it came back up slowly. Captain Mark went up on deck and tied a bunch of stuff together. He made a new sea anchor." Bobby was doing better.

"He made a new sea anchor out of things that were up on deck? How did he do that?" Farrington asked.

"I don't know. I was down in the cabin helping my mother take care of my father. When the boat rolled over my father hit his nose and broke it. There was blood everywhere. The cabin was a mess; the water was over my boots. I was frightened," Bobby said.

"Yes, I can well imagine that you were very frightened. After the schooner rolled upright, and Captain Mark made a new sea anchor, did that help the motion of the boat?" Farrington asked as he approached the witness stand.

"The boat was okay after that," Bobby replied.

"Did anyone else get hurt when the boat rolled over?" Farrington asked as he walked over in front of the jury box.

"Uh-huh, my brother hurt his ribs. He went to his bunk crying, and I got whacked on the head." Bobby was now speaking up.

"You hit your head? Was it serious?" Farrington asked.

"Well, at first I saw stars, and then I was dizzy. I had a big lump on my head, but it didn't bleed," Bobby said as she pointed to a spot on her head.

"Tell us what went on in the cabin after Captain Mark made a second sea anchor."

"The boat wasn't rolling from side to side any more so we all started cleaning up the mess, and getting the water out of the cabin. Captain Mark got the pump going again, and I helped my mother with my father's bleeding nose. We got him to lie down. Later that day, after the hurricane had passed, that's when Captain Mark started drinking," Bobby said.

"How did you know he was drinking, Bobby?" Farrington asked.

"Cause the fridge was in the galley just outside his cabin. When he drank he would come out of his cabin to get ice," Bobby said.

"Did the captain drink frequently?" Farrington asked.

"No, but when he did he stunk of whiskey," Bobby said. The jury paid close attention as Bobby told her story.

"Now, Bobby, would you tell the court when Captain

Mark started drinking on this day, the day after the hurricane?" Farrington asked.

"I think he started drinking in the afternoon," Bobby replied.

"Was it late in the afternoon, or was it early in the afternoon, say right after lunch?"

"We didn't have lunch cause we were still seasick," Bobby answered.

"But the captain was not seasick and he started drinking right after lunch. Is that correct?"

"Objection, the prosecution is leading the witness," Bill Spring said, rising to his feet.

"Objection sustained. The prosecution will rephrase the question," Judge McLean said as he pointed the handle of his gavel at Farrington.

"Now, Bobby, would you please tell the court at what time in the afternoon the captain started drinking?"

"I'm not sure, but it was around the middle of the afternoon."

"Your Honor, that's all the questions I have for this witness at this time. I would like to reserve the right to recall her later, if need be," Farrington said.

"Permission granted. Counselor Spring, your witness," the judge said.

Bill Spring moved from his table, charged the witness stand, or so it seemed to Bobby. The defense attorney looked evil to her, perhaps due to his close association with Captain Borman. She started to shake again.

"That was a very interesting story, Roberta," Spring said in a sardonic manner.

"My name's Bobby."

"Do you mind if I call you Roberta?" Spring asked.

"Nobody calls me Roberta, I hate it," Bobby said.

"Well then, Bobby, will you tell the court when you lost your memory?" Spring asked.

"I don't know," Bobby answered.

"Well was it when the boat rolled over, and you hit your head so hard that you do not recall what happened the day after the storm?" Spring was onto something.

"Just a bump on the head, that's all." Bobby's legs were shaking, she tried to hide them.

"Did you lose your memory during the hurricane because of fright?" Spring's craftiness showed in his eyes.

"No, I lost my memory when I was on the dinghy," Bobby said with determination.

"So now you do know when you lost your memory. A few minutes ago you said you did not know when you lost your memory. Which is it, Bobby?" Spring asked.

"I lost it when I was on the dinghy," Bobby said.

"It seems to me that if you do not know when you lost your memory, you could have lost it during the hurricane when you banged your head. Is that not a fact, Bobby?" Spring said.

"No." Bobby became more assertive with her answers.

"Is it not a fact that you made up this story about Captain Mark, and the sinking of his beloved ship?" Spring walked in front of the jury as he asked the question.

"Not a ship. It was a schooner, and I don't know if Captain Mark sank it or not." Bobby found her footing and became more self-assured.

"Just what is a schooner, Bobby?" Spring said.

"A schooner is a two-mast sailboat with the shorter mast up front of the bigger mast." The spectators commenced to buzz. Judge McLean tapped his gavel.

Spring was taken aback for a moment. "Now, Bobby, would you please tell the court how many days you were on the raft?"

"I'm not sure, but I can find out," Bobby said.

"Tell me, Bobby, did you keep a calendar while you were on the raft?" Spring asked with that crafty look back in his eye.

"No," Bobby said.

"Did you have a watch with the date on the dial?" Spring asked.

"No," Bobby replied.

"Then how is it you will know how many days you drifted on the raft? It is my understanding that you were unconscious when the freighter found you." Spring was hoping that if Bobby were boxed in, she would start making things up.

"Objection, Your Honor, unless my learned colleague for the defense can show what this line of questioning has to do with the crime, I will ask the court to have these questions stricken from the record." Jack Farrington was on his feet, jacket open, hands on his hips.

"Your Honor," Spring replied in a brusque voice, "I intend to show that the witness lost her memory when struck on the head during the hurricane, and the alleged crime or crimes, by my client, are a figment of her imagination."

"Objection overruled. You may continue, counselor," the judge nodded toward Spring.

"Now, Bobby, you were unconscious when you were rescued. Is that not a fact?" Spring asked.

"Yes," Bobby replied.

"Then you have no idea how long you were on the raft, do you?" Spring said with a smug look.

"No, but I can find out," Bobby replied.

"And how will you do that, Bobby, if you were unconscious and could not count the days?" Spring asked.

"Captain Mark, he was always on the radio telling people our position, and about the hurricane and stuff. The hurricane came to us on a certain day, and the freighter picked me up on a certain day. The captain on the freighter keeps a book. You can count the days that way." Bobby's reply impressed the jury.

"Bobby, did you like Captain Mark before the hurricane, that is, while you were cruising in nice weather?" Spring asked.

"No," Bobby answered.

"So you never liked the captain even when things were going along just fine?" Spring was in Bobby's face.

"Something creepy about him, even my mother thought so," Bobby said. This brought a grin to Farrington's lips.

"And because you did not like the captain you decided to make up this story. Is that not a fact, Bobby?" Spring asked.

"No, I didn't make up any story," Bobby answered with determination.

Spring had enough. "Your Honor, that's all the questions I have for this witness."

Judge McLean leaned over the bench and in a pleasant voice said, "You may step down, Bobby." The judge checked the time, called for a recess. "Court will resume at one this afternoon." Bang, the gavel came down.

After the lunch break the inspector pushed his way into the front row of the courtroom. He sat down next to Bobby as she grabbed his arm. Dupree looked at Bobby and smiled back. Murphy leaned over and whispered, "I have some info on your shadows."

"Good work, Murphy, we'll talk later," the inspector said.

"All rise." Judge McLean sat down, the jury and spectators

followed. After a few strikes with his gavel the judge announced that court was in session. The prosecution had presented its case. Their witness had testified and the defense had cross-examined. It was now time for the defense to present its case. The whirling blades of the overhead fans were the only sound that could be heard in the quiet courtroom.

"If it pleases the court, the defense will call Jeannette Thibeault to the stand," Spring said. The spectators sitting in the front rows turned to watch Borman's girlfriend being escorted down the aisle. After being sworn in Spring asked his first question: "Miss Thibeault, how long have you known the defendant?"

The witness answered in a weak voice, "For a long time, ever since he's been on the island."

"Now, Miss Thibeault, I would like you to speak loud and clear so that the jury may hear every word," Spring said.

"For a long time, ever since Mark's been on the island," Jeannette repeated.

"That's just fine, and how long would that be?" Spring asked as he removed his glasses.

"I have known Mark for about three months now," the witness replied.

"And in that time have you ever known Captain Borman to have a violent temper?" Spring had positioned himself close to the jury so that the witness had to speak up.

"Oh no, my captain has never raised his voice to me or anyone. He has always been a perfect gentleman." Jeannette Thibeault was wearing a short skirt and a low-cut blouse. It was an outfit that was not unnoticed by the men on the jury.

"Captain Borman has always been a perfect gentleman. Did the captain ever mention that terrible night during the hurricane when he almost lost his life?" Spring asked as he walked along the jury box.

"Yes, he did tell me some things, but my captain doesn't talk much, he's more a man of action." That comment brought a chuckle from the men in the courtroom. "He said that he waved to the White family as they left his boat. As far as he knew they were safe somewhere." The witness had a Marilyn Monroe manner of speaking. She sat upright with her shoulders back, spoke with a lot of body movement. The men of the jury were captivated.

"Now, Miss Thibeault, Captain Borman testified he saw the White family leave his boat and you assumed that they reached land the same as he did. Is that not correct?" Spring asked.

"Objection, the question calls for an assumption on the part of the witness," Farrington said, rising from his table.

"Objection sustained. Mr. Spring, you know better than to ask a question like that," the judge admonished.

"Miss Thibeault, please tell the jury in your own words what you know about the night Captain Borman lost his ship," Spring asked.

"Well, Mark told me that it was a terrible storm, a hurricane. He said that the sea anchor broke, and the boat got sideways to the waves, and the waves rolled the boat over," Jeannette answered.

"I see. Then what happened? Can you speak up a little?" Spring asked.

"Well, he told me that he managed to inflate the emergency boat and get everyone in except himself. He said that there was not enough room for another person," Jeannette said.

"And why, Miss Thibeault, did he decide to abandon the ship and put the crew in the dinghy?" Spring had a short list of credible witnesses so was working this one as much as possible.

"Oh, that's easy, the boat was filling with water," the witness said with a smile.

"And just how much water was in the boat?" Spring asked.

"Objection, Your Honor, the witness was not at the scene. Her testimony would be hearsay." Farrington was again on his feet.

"Objection sustained," the judge said as he gave Spring a look that said 'watch yourself, buster'.

"Miss Thibeault, do you consider Captain Borman a hero?" Spring asked.

"Oh yes, he's a hero alright. He saved the White family and he saved himself. He would have saved his boat if that sea anchor hadn't broke," Jeannette replied.

"No more questions, Your Honor." The defense attorney headed for his seat.

Jack Farrington walked to the witness stand, appearing to be deep in thought. "Miss Thibeault, how is it that you know the defendant?"

"Oh, we met at Barney's," Jeannette answered.

"And what kind of a place is Barney's?" Farrington asked.

"It's a nice place where people drink and have fun," Jeannette said.

"It's a bar on the waterfront, is it not?" Farrington asked.

"Yes, it's on the waterfront, but it's a nice bar," Jeannette said.

"I'm sure it is, Miss Thibeault. You have been living with Borman since you first met him, is that not correct?" Farrington asked. The jury was well aware of Barney's reputation.

"Well, not the first night. I never sleep with a man on the first night, well almost never." Chuckles were heard from the spectators, whispers from the jury. Spring could see that his star witness was not doing that well.

"Now, Miss Thibeault, is it not true that your Mark Borman

purchased a very expensive house overlooking the sea on this island?" Farrington asked as he paced before the witness.

"Yes, I suppose so," Jeannette replied.

"You suppose so? Were you not living at Borman's house?" Farrington asked.

"Yes, but he didn't say he owned the house," Jeannette said.

"And did your Mark Borman have a house lady who cooked and cleaned the house? Did he not have a man to take care of the swimming pool, and the flower garden?"

"Yes," Jeannette said. She was not talkative.

"And where do you suppose all this money came from?" Farrington asked.

"I don't know," Jeannette said as she shrugged her shoulders.

"If it pleases the court, I would like to submit this photocopy as Exhibit 'A'. It's from the city records showing that the defendant is the owner of the house at 11 Hillside Drive, the house Mark Borman purchased shortly after arriving on this island. Your Honor, I have no more questions for this witness." The prosecutor headed for his table.

"You may step down, Miss Thibeault," the judge said, tapping his gavel. "This court will adjourn for today and resume tomorrow morning at 10:00 a.m. All rise."

Chapter Thirty-two

The courtroom filled early on the second day of the trial. In addition to the overhead fans a number of spectators brought hand-held fans. By the middle of the day the courtroom became stuffy. Jack Farrington was wearing his seersucker suit. His associate showed up at nine thirty to go over their notes from the first day of the trial. At ten sharp the judge's chamber door opened, and the sergeant of arms rang out with the now familiar, "All rise."

After the judge brought the courtroom to order, Bill Spring stood up and in a vigorous voice said, "At this time the defense will call Charles Vigneau to the stand." Charley Vee, as he was known around town, ambled to the witness chair. He was sworn in and seated. "Charley, may I call you 'Charley'?" Spring asked.

"Yeah, sure, everybody does," Vigneau said. He had lived on the island all of his life, and was known as one of the local characters.

"Charley, would you state, for the record, your occupation," Bill Spring was walking toward the jury when he asked this question. When he got to the jury box he turned around to hear Charley's reply. Bill Spring always looked a little disheveled. "I work for him, over there," Charley said, pointing to Mark Borman.

"Let the record show that the witness is pointing to Captain Mark Borman," Spring said as he walked along the jury box. "Charley, Captain Borman currently employed you as a gardener and handyman, is that not correct?"

"Yeah, sure, that's what I do," Charley said.

"Would you please tell the court what kind of a man Captain Borman is?" Spring asked from near the jury box.

"Well he's an okay guy with me." Charley was the laid-back type, sitting relaxed in the witness chair with his legs crossed.

"Charley, would you say that he is an aggressive person, a bossy man, or the type that would just let you do your job?" Spring asked.

"Oh, he'd never boss me around, I'd quit first. He's an easy-going fellow all right. Always ready with a smile and a slap on the back," Charley said. He had a ruddy complexion, with a nose that had seen too many shots of booze pass beneath it.

"Do you like working for Captain Borman?" Spring felt that this witness was working out well.

"Oh sure, he's a great guy. I'd just as soon work for him as anyone else on the island, and he pays good, too," Charley said.

"No more questions, Your Honor." Bill Spring returned to his table and whispered to his client.

Charley Vigneau grunted, crossed his legs, and refolded his arms. Jack Farrington approached the witness stand. He looked the gardener over and in a clear voice said, "Mr. Vigneau, you say that Mark Borman pays well. Just how well does he pay?"

"He pays good, five bucks an hour," Charley replied.

"And what is the going rate for a handyman on the island these days?"

"Oh I'd say about three fifty to four bucks an hour, that's what I usually get," Charley said.

"Now, Charley, if the going rate is three fifty to four dollars an hour, why is the defendant paying you five?" Farrington walked in front of his desk.

"Because he's a nice guy, that's why," Charley said.

"Charley, could it be that Borman has lots of money and that is why he is overpaying you?" Farrington asked.

"He ain't overpaying me, I'm worth five bucks an hour. He sure is a nice guy," Charley said as he nodded his head.

"No more questions, Your Honor," Jack Farrington said. He returned to his desk while Charley ambled to the back of the courtroom.

Bill Spring stood up and in a confident voice said, "Your Honor, the defense calls Letty Belanger to the witness stand." The witness took quick, short steps to the witness stand. After being sworn in she sat down, and placed her purse in her lap. Bill Spring approached her in a friendly manner. "Now, Letty, may I call you Letty?" Belanger nodded her head. "Fine, now you're the housekeeper for the defendant, Captain Borman, is that correct?"

"Yes . . ., yes, I clean the house, cook the meals and wash the dishes," Belanger said in a nervous voice.

"What kind of a man is Captain Borman, Letty?" Spring asked.

"He is just the nicest man I've ever met," Belanger replied.

"Well, Letty, working in his house day in and day out you certainly would be in a position to know. Have you ever seen the captain get angry?" Spring asked.

"On no, Captain Mark never gets angry; he's just the nicest man anyone would want to work for."

"Would you say, Letty, that the captain is a moody man or a man with an even disposition?" Spring asked.

"Oh, the captain has a very even disposition, always pleasant, never gets angry."

"Thank you, Letty. Your Honor, I have no more questions for this witness." Spring was pleased with this witness. His face showed a faint smile when he looked at the prosecution on his return to his table.

Jack Farrington rose and announced, "Your Honor, I have no questions for this witness."

Judge Larry McLean looked at his watch, picked up his gavel and announced a lunch break. The judge closed the door to his chamber behind him as the standing spectators filed out of the courtroom.

Jack Farrington sat down, after the judge left, with his associate, Phil Sealy. "Phil, I wish we had more than Bobby's word to go on. The captain has a strong history of being a respectable sea captain."

"I'm working on the leads you gave me. I have the feeling something will turn up," Sealy said.

"I certainly hope so. I'm counting on it, Phil," Farrington said.

Chief Inspector Dupree was not present for the morning session of the second day of the trial. Carlos, chief cook and bottle washer for the Water Front Café, was brought in for questioning. Joseph, upon hearing the news that Bobby had escaped her freight box, figured Carlos might be called in for questioning. He had been in trouble with the law before. Joseph felt Carlos could be his *Titanic*. He rehearsed him repeatedly on what to expect from the inspector. Joseph told him not to answer questions, no matter how many times they ask. Just tell them that you want your lawyer. He also made it very clear that if he talked his next home would be a pine box.

"Carlos, welcome to the police station, and our interrogation room. I am Chief Inspector Dupree, the one man that can save your ass." The inspector stood tall in his full uniform. Some unknown person had left behind a riding crop at the station; Dupree used it as a tool of intimidation. He had a feeling that Carlos would talk if enough pressure were applied. The interrogation room was a little larger than a walk-in closet, without windows or ventilation. It was painted the same pea green as the conference room.

"I know who you are." Carlos answered with apprehension, determined not to give anything away. He knew the threat on his life was real.

"I'm sure you do, Carlos," the inspector said as he walked around the table, slapping the riding crop against his leg. "You may also know that I always get my man. In this case, it's Joseph I'm after, not you. Now, how is it he talked you into this wacky idea of kidnapping a young girl?" the inspector said, guessing about Carlos's involvement.

"I don't know nothing about no kidnapping," Carlos said.

"Let's see, Joseph had you hire the truck so if anything went wrong it could be traced right back to you, and not to him. This was his way of setting you up to take the fall. All he had to do is make sure you kept your mouth shut, right?" the inspector said.

"If I knew something, Inspector, I'd tell ya. Honest, on my mother's grave," Carlos pleaded.

"You're very lucky we got a hold of you first, before Joseph had a chance to bump you off," the inspector said. He walked around the table, slapping his leg again and again with the riding crop. The room was dark with the exception of one overhead light that hung low over the interrogation chair.

"I'd tell you everything, if I knew something," Carlos said, following orders.

"You don't have to talk, Carlos. We know Joseph was behind the kidnapping, and we know he set you up to take the rap," the inspector said.

"You got Joseph all wrong, he's a nice guy. He always spoke kindly of you. Said you were the world's best police officer. Also, the people on this island were lucky to have you," Carlos said with an expression of innocence. Carlos had left his dirty apron back at the restaurant, but his shirt carried on the marks of his trade.

"Carlos, I think you got the shitty end of the stick. Joseph will just hire your cousin to run the restaurant and business will go on as usual. All he has to do is to make sure you keep your mouth shut, he's off the hook," Dupree said.

"I ain't talking, and that's all I've got to say." Carlos was looking around to see if anyone in the room smoked. The inspector picked up on this. He left the room to return to his office. On his desk, in an ivory-inlaid box, was a cigar that had been there for a half year. Returning to the interrogation room, he lit the cigar, blew smoke in Carlos's face.

"Now, Carlos, suppose you save yourself a lot of trouble and tell us what happened?" Dupree suggested.

"I ain't talking cause I don't know nothing about no kidnapping," Carlos said.

"No, you don't have to talk, and we don't have to hold you here in protective custody. All we have to do is spread the word on the street that you talked your head off, and then set you loose. How long do you think you will live once you leave here, Carlos?" Dupree was pretending to enjoy the cigar. Carlos was beginning to sweat, looking around to see if the sergeant had a cigarette. "Here's what we've got so far, Carlos. You're the guy that hired the truck, and you're the one who drove it into my car.

Joseph's hired people grabbed the girl, and nailed her into the shipping crate. That's all we need to know to put you away for the rest of your life," the inspector said.

Carlos, looking directly at the inspector, said, "You're making this all up, Inspector. I've gone straight ever since the last time I was in here."

"Kidnapping is a very serious offense, you'll be lucky if you get life in jail. The jury has the right to put you to death. Do you know how we put people to death on this island?" The inspector had the feeling that Carlos was smart enough to save his own skin. "Which do you think we should do, Carlos? Put you away for the rest of your life or send you back out on the street so Joseph can do you in? Did you ever hear the expression 'Dead men tell no tales'? Well, what's it going to be, Carlos?" The inspector was tapping his riding crop on the table, as he sat across from Carlos. Dupree blew smoke in Carlos's face as he watched him sweat.

"Ah, look, Inspector, maybe I should talk to a lawyer," Carlos said. His left eye began to twitch.

"Sure, you can talk to a lawyer if you like, however there's not a lawyer on this island that's going to take your case. First, you have no money to hire a lawyer. Secondly, your association with Joseph is so close that no lawyer would work for you if you did have the money. Next, there's the little item of the government wanting to know where you got money to hire a lawyer. Here's what I think I'll do with you, Carlos. I'm going to let you be our guest for tonight, and then put the word out on the street that you have been very cooperative. This way, not only do we get Joseph for kidnapping, we also get him for murder, your murder. How's that sound?" the inspector said with a smirk on his face and a slap on the table with his riding crop.

"Look, Inspector, I need a cigarette," Carlos said.

"Sure, you can smoke, just as soon as you talk," Dupree said.

"I don't know nothing. Joseph doesn't tell me his plans. Why don't you go talk to him," Carlos said as his left hand shook.

"Carlos, I don't believe you. Sergeant, lock him up," Dupree said. He had enough. Carlos needed some time to think about his situation.

"How about my supper, I haven't had my supper yet," Carlos asked.

"Sorry, Carlos, but this is not the Hilton. We feed our guests once a day, mostly soup, weekends we upgrade it to stew. Sometimes, on special days, we even add some meat to the stew. Take him away, Sergeant," the inspector said.

The judge's chamber door opened and the now familiar 'All rise' rang out. The afternoon session of the second day of the trial was about to begin. Judge Larry McLean tapped his gavel several times to settle the room down, "Counselor Spring, you may begin."

Bill Spring stood next to his client, put his hand on his shoulder and said, "I call Captain Borman to the stand." A buzz went through the courtroom. Borman stood up, threw his shoulders back, walked with authority. After being sworn in he sat straight up in the witness chair. Borman projected the dignity of his position as a ship's captain. He had grown a salt-and-pepper beard that covered his face. The trimmed beard fit his round face. He was dressed in his old Navy dress-blue jacket that had the gold braid removed. With his white shirt he wore a blue striped tie and khaki pants.

"Captain Borman, I would like you to tell the members of the jury, in your own words, what happened that dreadful night.

The night you lost your ship and almost lost your life," Spring said.

"Well, sir, we knew the hurricane was coming and we were well prepared for it. We had a few days to get ready. I watched the storm's progress very closely," Borman said.

"What exactly did you do, Captain, to prepare your ship for the storm?" Spring asked as he moved over by the jury. He wanted to make sure that the jurors heard every word.

"We battened down the hatches, that's what we did. We stored everything down below, got the sea anchor ready, and secured all gear," Borman said. His voice was deep, and agreeable, it was heard throughout the courtroom.

"And, Captain Borman, would you please tell the jury how your ship handled the storm," Spring asked.

"Yeah, sure, well when things got rough, and the seas were getting high, we lowered all sails and set the sea anchor. This settled the boat down nicely," Borman said.

"And for how long did the sea anchor hold?" Spring asked.

"She held very well, all day long, and most of the night," answered Borman.

"And then what happened, Captain?" Spring asked.

"She let go, that's what happened. My beautiful schooner got into the trough of the waves and was rolled over. Turned turtle she did, and then started filling with water."

"Why do you suppose the boat was filling with water, Captain?" Spring asked.

"A hatch was left open. The schooner righted herself after a while, but she had shipped a lot of water. If the hatch had been closed, like I told them, the boat wouldn't have filled with seawater," Borman said.

"Is this when you decided to abandon ship, Captain?" Spring

asked. He was pulling the story out of Borman much the way they had rehearsed it in the defense attorney's office.

"Nope, not then, first I turned the bilge pump on, but the batteries were shorted out. The water got into the engine room," Borman said.

"Then what did you do, Captain?" Bill Spring asked as he walked along the jury box.

"Then I went topside and tried to start the engine. I wanted to get the boat out of the trough of the waves," Borman replied.

"Did the engine start?" Spring asked.

"Nope, wouldn't start. The water got to those batteries too," Borman said. Spring felt the defendant was doing well. The jury was fascinated; they hung on every word.

"Captain Borman, you say the bilge pump won't work, the engine is out of commission, and the boat is in the trough of the waves. The ship is being rolled over by the huge waves and taking on water, is that correct?" Spring asked.

"Yes sir, that's exactly what happened," Borman answered.

"This seems like a very dangerous position to be in, is it not?" Spring asked.

"You bet, hurricanes are never fun to be in. I could've saved my boat if that sea anchor hadn't let go. Well with the schooner filling up fast, I figured the only thing to do was to take to the dinghies," Borman said.

"And how did you accomplish that, Captain?" Bill Spring walked over to the witness stand. The courtroom was quiet. Judge McLean was leaning toward the witness.

"I yelled to the people below, told them to prepare to abandon ship. 'Get your life jackets on,' I hollered, 'grab some water, get on deck right away'," Borman said. A few of the jurors sat with their mouths open.

"Now, if you would, Captain, please describe to the jury what happened next," Spring asked.

"Well, I got the emergency dinghy inflated and over the side. I tied it off to the stern of the schooner, and yelled for the people to get on board," Borman said.

"And did the White family get on board the dinghy?" Spring asked.

"Well, not easy, what with the storm tossing the dinghy around, the waves breaking over us, and the family having trouble getting overboard. The whole operation was one big struggle, I'll tell ya," Borman said.

Bill Spring walked up to his client and said, "I can well imagine the problems you were having, Captain Borman, please go on."

"Well, the parents were yelling at the kids. The kids were crying, afraid to get into the dinghy. We were all on the stern of the schooner and she was becoming very unstable. She had all the water she could handle and was about to go down. I was lucky to get everyone in the dinghy and set her free. Very lucky, before the schooner went under," the captain said.

"Was that the last you saw of the White family, Captain?" Spring asked, walking toward the jury box.

"Yep, that was it. I waved to them and got the hard dinghy off the cabin top. Turned her upright and got in, no time to launch her. The schooner went down under me, not a moment too soon, I'll tell ya," Borman said.

"Counselor Spring, we are out of time for today," Judge McLean said. He then addressed the court, "This court will resume at 10:00 tomorrow morning." Bang, the gavel came down.

"All rise."

Chapter Thirty-three

The people squeezed past one another to get to their seats. The sergeant at arms rang out with his "All rise," as Judge McLean tapped his gavel several times to quiet his court. He then informed the defendant that he was still under oath.

Bill Spring paced back and forth before the witness stand, holding his glasses in his right hand. He motioned with his glasses as he addressed the defendant, "Now, Captain Borman, you testified yesterday as to how you lost your ship and almost lost your life. Is that not correct?" Spring asked.

"Yep, that's right, almost lost my life," Borman said.

"And is it not a fact that you did everything in your power to save your ship and the White family?" Spring asked.

"That's what I did, sure as I'm sitting here," Borman said.

"Why is it then that the White family did not end up on the same island as you did? After all, both parties were in dinghies, both set adrift at the same time, is it not reasonable to assume that both dinghies would drift toward the same island?" Spring asked.

"A person might think so if he didn't know the sea. You see, we had different boats. One dinghy was heavy laden with four people in it, so it set deeper in the water. A rubber dinghy has little directional stability, you see. Also with four people in the dinghy it was more able to catch the wind." Borman stopped, asked for a drink of water.

"How would your dinghy handle the sea differently?" Bill Spring was pleased with the way Borman was presenting his story.

"I was in a hard dinghy, with good directional stability. I had less exposure to the wind cause I was lying down in the dinghy. You know, giving her a lower center of gravity, so I wouldn't get dumped. When you take in all these factors the two boats would drift at different speeds and in different directions," Borman said.

"And how did you find the island that saved your life?" Bill Spring asked as he walked back in front of the jury again.

"The fact that I reached an island was just the luck of the draw. Just the way things work out when you're on the sea," Borman answered.

"Captain Borman, would you please tell the members of the jury why you were making passage during the hurricane season?" Spring asked.

"I make this passage every year, taking my boat from Maine to the islands for winter chartering. Every year, I make this passage, every year I wait out the hurricane season somewhere on the East Coast. This year I was holed up in Newport, Rhode Island. I waited there until the season was over. I always wait till it's over, but this year, for some strange reason, we got a late one. Things just happen that way sometimes. Hurricanes are unpredictable, some years they're just unpredictable. Can't tell you why, cause that's Mother Nature, I guess," Borman said.

"Thank you, Captain. That's all the questions I have for now, Your Honor. I would like to be able to recall my client at a later time if needed." The judge nodded his head. The defense attorney returned to his table. The jury was abuzz with subtle excitement. Mark Borman turned out to be an excellent witness on his own behalf.

The prosecutor got up from his table, looked Borman straight in the eye for a long moment, then asked, "Is it not a fact that your chartering business was on the skids?"

"I've had better years," Borman said.

"Is it not a fact that you were behind on your boat mortgage payments?" Farrington asked.

"Like I said, I've had better years," Borman replied.

"Would you please answer the question," Farrington said.

"Yeah, I was behind one or two payments," Borman said.

"Your Honor, I would like to submit exhibit 'B' into the record. This is a statement from the mortgage company showing that Mark Borman was three months behind in his payments. The company had issued several notices," Farrington said as he handed the paper to the judge.

"Accepted, please continue with your questioning," the judge looked the document over.

"Is it not a fact, Mr. Borman, that the mortgage company was about to repossess your schooner?" the prosecutor said. He was speaking louder than necessary.

"Your Honor, I object to this line of questioning." Spring was on his feet, speaking stridently from his table in the courtroom. "Your Honor, I do not see what boat payments have to do with the captain's ability to save his schooner and the White family in a hurricane."

"Counselor, unless you are able to tie boat payments with the loss of the captain's schooner, I will direct the jury to discard these questions, they'll be stricken from the record," the judge said, giving Jack Farrington a stern look.

"Your Honor, it is my intent to show this court that the reason

Mark Borman deliberately pulled the plug on his schooner, after the hurricane was over, was to collect the insurance money. He would then be able to pay off the mortgage company and buy a house with the remainder of the insurance money," Farrington said.

"Objection overruled, you may continue, Counselor," the judge said.

"Is it not a fact, Mr. Borman, that you bought an expensive house and staffed it with a chef and a gardener? You also purchased a powerboat?" Farrington asked.

"Yeah," Borman said.

"Would you please tell the jury where all this money came from, Mr. Borman."

"From the insurance company," Borman said in a low voice.

"From the insurance company?" Farrington repeated, raising his voice.

"Yeah, from the insurance company," Borman said again in a soft voice.

"Have you ever before collected a large sum of money from an insurance company?" Farrington asked.

"Nope," Borman replied, still speaking in a low voice.

"Your Honor, I would like to submit exhibit 'C' that shows Mark Borman collected a sum of fifty thousand dollars from the Phoenix Insurance Company." The prosecutor handed the paper to the judge.

"The court will accept this document," the judge declared, reaching out to receive the paper.

"Now, Mr. Borman, you have just told this judge and the jury that you have never received a large sum of money from an insurance company. Do you know the penalty for perjury on this island?" Farrington asked.

"You asked me if I ever received a large sum of money. Fifty thousand is a drop in the bucket. I thought you were talking about a large sum of money." Borman was now covering his tracks, but it seemed that he was not fooling anyone.

"Mr. Borman, would you please tell the court why the Phoenix Insurance Company would give you fifty thousand dollars?" Farrington asked.

"My wife died," Borman answered, again speaking quietly.

"And under what circumstances did your wife die, and would you please speak up so the jury may hear your testimony?" Farrington asked.

"It was an automobile accident," Borman said.

"Is it not a fact, Mr. Borman, that you drove your car off the road while approaching a bridge? You then jumped clear while your wife, who could not swim, rode the car into the river and her death," Farrington said.

"It was not my fault. I fell asleep at the wheel. I woke up after the car went off the road." Borman was now speaking up.

"Would you explain to the court, if you were asleep, how was it you had time to wake up, and then jump clear of the car? How is it your wife, who was awake, had no time at all to save her life?" Farrington asked.

"I don't know. I guess men are just faster than women." The women of the jury looked at one another at this explanation.

"Would you please explain to the jury the reason you ran from the marketplace, here on St. Vincent, the day you first saw Bobby White. Why is it you dropped your shopping bundles and ran at the sight of Bobby White?" The prosecutor was close to Borman's face.

"I . . ., I thought I saw a ghost." Borman replied.

"And why would you think she was a ghost?" Farrington asked.

"The hurricane had been over for a couple of months, and no word of the White family. I thought that they were lost at sea," Borman said as he moved about in his chair.

"Did you make any inquires on behalf of the White family?" Farrington asked.

"No," Borman said.

"No? You lost four people at sea, and you made no inquires. You never called the Coast Guard nor stopped by the police station to see if there were any word, any word at all from the White family?"

"No," Borman said.

"Is this not unusual? Here you lost a schooner and four crew members, and you report it only to the insurance company? The only report you make was to the insurance company. Is this the action of a responsible person?" Farrington asked.

"Objection, Your Honor, the prosecution is badgering the witness," Spring said.

"Objection overruled. Please continue, counselor," Judge McLean said.

"Now, Mr. Borman, you would please . . .," Farrington was interrupted.

"It's Captain Borman."

"Fine, Captain Borman, would you please explain why it is that on the very day you saw a 'ghost' that you hurriedly packed your bags, grabbed your girlfriend, jumped into your powerboat and made an overnight trip to Barbados?" Farrington seemed to enjoy putting the pressure on the defendant.

"Yeah, it was a pleasure trip. We powered at night because it's romantic. The next day we decided to do some sightseeing by plane," Borman said.

"If it was a pleasure trip, why is it you told the dock boy at the marina that you were going fishing?" Farrington asked.

"It was just my way of telling him to mind his own business, that's all," Borman said.

"If it was an overnight pleasure trip, why is it you had packed two bags with enough clothing to last for several weeks?" Farrington asked.

"I like to travel in style," Borman replied.

"If you were taking a small plane to view the island why is it you told the office manager, of the charter flight business, that you needed a flight to Grenada?" Farrington asked.

"I wanted him to think that I was a big spender. I wanted to get his best plane, not just some small put-put," Borman said.

"That's all the questions I have for this witness, Your Honor." The prosecutor headed for his table as the courtroom buzzed with this new information.

Bobby leaned over and whispered in Murphy's ear, "Isn't he supposed to tell why he killed my mother and father?"

Murphy leaned down and said, "He'd never tell the truth." The judge brought his gavel down and announced that court would resume at 1:00 p.m. As he stood up from behind the bench the sergeant at arms bellowed, "All rise."

Dupree made his way to a pay phone as soon as the judge banged his gavel. "Good afternoon, Sheri, would you please call Sergeant Courtois to the phone." Dupree looked around to see Bobby and Murphy waiting for him on the courthouse steps. "Sergeant, how's our overnight guest doing? Well, give him some soup, then start the interrogation. Take shifts, I want him questioned all afternoon. Try the good cop/bad cop routine. I have a feeling that he'll talk sooner or later. Yes, I'm afraid Carlos will be with us for some time. We wouldn't want to lose our star witness," the inspector said. He then joined Bobby and Murphy for lunch.

After being seated in the restaurant the inspector excused himself and headed for the men's room. He stopped before entering and motioned his head at Murphy. It was a signal that he wanted to talk. Murphy stood next to Dupree, facing the front of the restaurant. He kept a watchful eye on Bobby.

"What did you find out about the people that are following me?" Dupree asked.

"Two men, they show up wherever you happen to be. I followed them to the boarding house, later spoke with the owner. They're from South America; he doubted that the address was correct. They don't look like very pleasant people," Murphy said as he watched his charge.

"Keep an eye on them. Let me know if they make contact with anyone here on the island. We may have to bring them in for questioning," the inspector said.

"Right you are, Chief. Does your office have a camera with a telephoto lens? I'd like to get some close-ups of these characters," Murphy said as he talked out of the side of his mouth.

"Sure, see Sheri, she'll get it for you," Dupree said as he entered the men's room. Standing in front of the urinal Dupree wondered, *Why the hell are South Americans following me? I could bring them in for questioning, but they wouldn't tell me anything. I've got that uneasy feeling again. Must put a stop to this second-income business, not good for my health. Somehow, got to put an end to it.*

Chapter Thirty-four

After the lunch break the courtroom began to fill as the judge hammered the courtroom to order. Jack Farrington stood up to address the court. "Your Honor, may counsel for both sides approach the bench?"

"Approach," the judge said.

Jack Farrington and Bill Spring stood in front of the bench. A low murmur could be heard from the spectators. Some were still pushing past the knees of others to get to their seats. People in the courtroom got to know their neighbors and made comments to each other upon filing in or out of the room. Farrington, in a low voice, said, "Your Honor, after reading the news about this trial, a person has come forward. He has a point of interest with direct bearing on this case. I would like to call him as a witness for the prosecution."

"Objection, Your Honor, the defense does not know this person or what he has to say," Spring said. He did not want any surprises, it was his client's word against Bobby's, and he wanted to leave it that way.

"Your Honor, this witness has a direct bearing on this case; he would have come forward sooner had he not been out to sea.

He's a sea captain who knows the defendant," Farrington pleaded his case.

"Very well, I will allow this witness to testify." The judge was giving the prosecution some slack. He signaled the sergeant at arms. The sergeant at arms walked down the center aisle with the new witness. When Mark Borman and Bill Spring turned around to see who this person may be, the entire courtroom did the same. Borman whispered to his attorney, something about the fact that this was bad news.

"Please state you name and your occupation," the bailiff said after he swore in the witness.

"My name is Paul Chivas. I'm the captain of the freighter *Louise*."

Farrington, his head high and a bounce to his step, seemed like a new man as he began to question the witness. "Captain Chivas, would you please tell the court your relationship with the accused, Captain Mark Borman."

"Well, sir, he came aboard my ship about three months ago when I was unloading supplies on the island of Mayreau," Captain Chivas said.

"Is that man here in this courtroom?"

"Yes sir, that's the man over there." Captain Chivas pointed to the defendant.

"Let the record show that the witness is pointing to Mark Borman. Now what was the conversation you had with Borman at that time?" Farrington asked.

"He told me that he was a shipwrecked sailor, and that he wanted passage to St. Vincent," Chivas said.

"Did he tell you why he was a shipwrecked sailor?" the prosecutor said as he moved closer to the jury.

"Yes, he did. He said that his fifty-foot schooner went down during the hurricane with all hands," Captain Chivas said. These words stunned the courtroom, created a buzz of conversation, followed by a lot of commotion. The reporters rushed from the room, and headed for the pay phones. The judge pounded his gavel.

"Quiet . . . quiet in the courtroom," the judge banged louder. It was ten minutes before order was restored, and the testimony of Captain Chivas was able to resume.

"Now, Captain, you have testified that Mark Borman said to you that he lost his schooner and all hands onboard. Is that not correct?" Farrington asked.

"Yes, that is correct, sir." Captain Chivas had a dignified look, with his gray, trimmed, Van Dyke mustache, and a dark blue jacket. His wrinkled khaki pants and dirty white sneakers did not show.

"Did you ask Mark Borman how he lost his schooner?" Farrington asked.

"Yes, sir, he said that the sea anchor let go while he was on deck. The boat got in the trough of the waves and rolled over. He said the boat got swamped and went down. I then asked him if he was wearing a life jacket," Chivas said.

"And what was his reply to that question?" Farrington asked.

"He said that he wasn't wearing one. When he came up for air the dinghy had broke loose and was close by. I said that he was one very lucky s.o.b. He agreed with me," Chivas said. All of the members of the jury had their eyes fixed on the captain.

"Was there more to the conversation?" Farrington asked.

"Well, that's about it. I was busy with getting the ship unloaded, keeping on schedule, so I did not have a lot of time for chitchatting. I did ask him if he contacted the Coast Guard." the captain said.

"And what was his reply?"

"He told me that the island he was on had no phone," the captain spoke firmly.

"Your Honor, that's all the questions I have for this witness." Farrington smiled at the captain before heading for his table.

Spring was slow getting up from his table and seemed to be deep in thought. "Captain Chivas, did you know the defendant, Mark Borman?" Spring asked.

"Nope, never met him before, that is, until he came aboard my ship," Chivas answered.

"Are you quite positive that you had never met Captain Borman before?" Spring asked.

"To the best of my knowledge, I had not met him before," the captain replied.

"You have never met him before?" Spring asked again.

"That's correct," Chivas answered.

"No more questions, Your Honor. At this time I would like to recall my client to the witness stand." Spring's request created a buzz among the spectators. Borman got up from his chair slowly; his posture was not as erect was it was before Paul Chivas testified. The judge reminded Borman that he was still under oath.

"Captain Borman, in the fall of the year 1966, you and your schooner were in Newport, Rhode Island, waiting for the hurricane season to be over. Is that correct?"

"Yes, that's correct," Borman said in a dejected mood.

"And while you were in Newport, did you have a chance to frequent one or more of the waterfront bars in that town?" Spring asked.

"Yes, I did," Borman said as he brightened up.

"And while you were having a drink did you meet a person by the name of Captain Paul Chivas?" Spring asked.

"Yes I did." Borman was now nodding his head in agreement.

"Is that person here in this courtroom?" Spring asked.

"Yes he is, sir," Borman said.

"Would you please point to that person?" Spring asked.

"That's him sitting there. We had a few drinks together, and we talked about boats, his and mine," Borman said as Spring seemed to come to life.

"Captain Chivas has just testified that he never met you before; how do explain that?" Spring asked.

"Maybe the captain has a faulty memory," Borman said with a grin.

"That's all the questions I have, Your Honor," Spring said. He had a very slight smirk on his face as he headed for his table.

Farrington jumped up from his table for the cross-examination. He looked a little upset. "Captain Borman, in your conversation with Captain Chivas, on the bridge of the freighter *Louise*, did you not say that you recognized the captain?" Farrington asked.

"Yeah, I said he looked familiar, and that we had met before," Borman answered.

"And did Captain Chivas recall having met you?" Farrington spoke with force as he walked toward the jury.

"I told him that we met in a bar in Newport, Rhode Island, a couple of years ago," Borman said.

"That is not the answer to the question I asked. Let me ask you again. Did the captain recall ever having met you before?" Farrington said, louder the second time.

"Nope," Borman said quietly.

"Now, Captain Mark Borman, would you like to change your

story, and tell the court what really happened after the hurricane, and the sinking of your schooner?" Farrington asked. His body language showed that he was elated at the change of events.

"I told the truth," Borman said in a low voice.

Chief Inspector Dupree walked from the courthouse to the police station. Sheri greeted him from behind the sliding glass window. "Oh, Inspector, I have a bunch of phone messages for you. Is the trial over?" Sheri asked.

"Yes, just about, Sheri. The jury went into deliberation late today," Dupree answered.

"What do you think, Inspector, is Captain Borman going to get away with murder?" Sheri asked.

"Well, it sure looked like it for a while, that is until that captain from the freighter showed up. I think he saved the day," the inspector said. He moved into Sheri's office to look over his mail.

"I hope he gets life in prison. I think life in prison is more punishment than putting him to sleep, especially in your prison, Inspector," Sheri said with a smile.

"What do you know of my prison? We have a very nice prison, complete with bedbugs, cockroaches and rats. Rats are very tasty, I'm told." The inspector smiled as he walked to the interrogation room.

"Sergeant Courtois, do you have a minute?" Dupree asked.

"Sure, Inspector; Carlos, don't go anywhere. I've got to step out for a moment," Courtois said.

"Don't worry, Sarge, I'm not going anywhere, smartass," Carlos said. He looked as though he had had a rough night.

"He's a tough nut, Inspector, I'm not getting anywhere with him. I think he's scared stiff of Joseph. Maybe it's about time we tell him that he's going back out on the street," Sergeant Courtois said in a low voice.

"Good idea, Sergeant," said the inspector. Sergeant Courtois looked at Dupree and nodded. The two walked into the interrogation room.

"Okay, Carlos, you're free to go," the inspector said.

"I can, I'm free to go? Just like that, I walk outta here?" Carlos asked.

"Sure, Carlos, you're free to go. We put the word out on the street last night that you made a deal with us," the inspector said. Carlos looked at the inspector with his head cocked to one side. He did not know if he should believe him or not.

"That's a lie, goddamn it. I never made no deal with you, that's bullshit. Joseph's not going to believe that crap," Carlos said.

"Maybe not, Carlos, but then you'll never know, will you? If I were Joseph, I wouldn't take any chances. Maybe you can be trusted, maybe not. The safe thing for the fat man to do is to eliminate anyone who could tie him to the crime. How would you like it if your life depended on some lowlife bottle washer?" Dupree asked.

"I'm not a bottle washer. I'm the manager of that joint. And I'm not a low life, either. I've got my pride; I do a good job," Carlos said.

"Well, Carlos, that's not what my people on the street tell me. They tell me that when Joseph heard about your deal with my department he blew up. Called you a low life, and a number of other things too bad to mention," Dupree said.

"I don't believe you," Carlos said as he shook his head.

"He was so steamed up that everyone in the restaurant ran out the door. Don't let that stop you, go talk to him. Maybe he'll let you off the hook, or maybe when you're not looking, an accident or something, who knows? We pick bodies out of the bay all the time." Dupree lit up a new cigar. Carlos was feeling ill. The sweat was forming on his brow as his eyes darted around the room looking for a cigarette.

"Look, guys, maybe I should hang around here for a few days. You know, long enough for Joseph to cool down. Maybe I could clean the floors or something." Carlos had a pleading look that reminded the inspector of a hound dog.

"Here's what I can do for you, Carlos: you tell us everything you know and I will speak to the judge. He'll go easy on you if I plead your case. You can serve your time on another island, a place where you'll be safe. It's up to you, talk and you live. Keep telling us that you know nothing and we'll put you out on the street. Your life is in your own hands, and now if you will excuse me I have lots of work to do." The inspector rose from his chair and started toward the door.

"Wait . . . wait, okay, you guys win. I'll tell you the whole story, but first I want our deal in writing, no tricks, okay?" Carlos pulled out a dirty handkerchief and wiped his face. "Can I have a cigarette now?" he pleaded.

Chapter Thirty-five

The fourth day of the trial was about to begin. The time was a little after ten o'clock in the morning, the spectators were pushing to get to a seat. The jury had deliberated late into the evening and rumor had it that a decision would be coming shortly. Inspector Dupree, Murphy, and Bobby White were in the front row with their heads together. Bobby was asking questions about court procedures, the jury, and if Captain Mark would be going to jail. At 10:06 the door to the judge's chamber opened; Judge Larry McLean walked to the bench as he buttoned his black robe.

"All rise," called out the sergeant at arms. The judge gaveled the court to silence as the jury moved into place. Each juror looked at the defendant, Captain Mark Borman, sitting at the table with his lawyer. The courtroom was dead silent as the overhead fans whirled.

"Members of the jury, have you reached a verdict?" Judge McLean asked.

"Yes we have, Your Honor." The chairperson of the jury stood with a piece of paper in his hand. The paper was handed to the sergeant at arms, who in turn gave it to the judge. Judge McLean read it over and handed it back. He said in a commanding voice,

"The defendant will rise," then less forcefully, "The jury will please read the verdict."

The chairperson of the jury stood again, and reading from the paper, said, "We, the members of the jury, find the defendant, Captain Mark Borman, guilty of sinking the schooner, *Vagus*, guilty of the murder of Jason White, guilty of the murder of Helen White, and guilty of the murder of Bradford White."

The courtroom erupted in applause. The judge was able to get things under control long enough to excuse the jurors. "Thank you, members of the jury. You are hereby released from duty," the judge said as he brought down his gavel. A loud cheer went up from the spectators. Murphy threw up his arms, gave out a yell. The inspector grabbed Murphy's hand, shaking it repeatedly. He then looked down at Bobby, who appeared to be crying. Bobby jumped up, laughing and crying at the same time.

"We did it, Inspector, we did it," Bobby shouted. Standing on the bench, she hugged the inspector and Murphy next. Crying, laughing, crying again followed by another round of hugs. Murphy pulled out his oversize handkerchief, wiping Bobby's tears.

"I want my mother and father back. I miss them so much," Bobby said between sobs. Murphy and Dupree looked at each other with an expression of two young boys who knew not what to say.

"Your mother and father are very proud of you, Bobby. You were a very brave girl on the witness stand," the inspector said.

"Would you like some ice cream, Bobby?" Murphy asked. Bobby nodded her head as she wiped her tears. On the way out of the courthouse Bobby walked between her two friends, holding their hands.

The raid on the Water Front Café required all the cars in the department, red lights flashing, tires screeching, armed policemen taking up their positions. Leading the raid was Inspector Dupree. He entered the café, with his pistol in hand, waving it like a sword. "Joseph Biello, you are under arrest for the crime of kidnapping; up against the wall. Sergeant, put cuffs on him, pat him down," the inspector said. He was pleased that things were working out. Joseph wasn't saying a word, just thinking . . . thinking hard. Thinking about how the inspector was connected to the Kaiser and the drug trade. Also he was thinking that he needed a good lawyer, and how to get out of this mess.

"Take it easy with those cuffs. They're too tight, gimme some slack, will ya?" Joseph's complaint fell on deaf ears as he was stuffed into the rear seat of one of the patrol cars. The car sagged on one side as Sergeant Courtois pushed Joseph's head down. The newsmen took photographs. "INSPECTOR DUPREE SOLVES KIDNAPPING," the headlines read.

Later that evening at the Dupree residence Bobby was surrounded by her friends. A celebration was in progress. Ute had been cooking most of the afternoon. Murphy had taken charge of the bar. Sheri had turned the music up a bit. The pop from the champagne bottle interrupted the conversation.

"Oh, champagne, can I have some? Please, can I have a glass?" Bobby was trying to put on a good face, although her despondency over the events of the day lingered.

"I'd say why not, but first you must ask Madam Dupree," the inspector said. He had removed his uniform, and replaced it with a smoking jacket for the party.

"Oh Madam . . . Madam Dee, please, may I have a glass of champagne? Please. . . pretty please?" Bobby asked.

"I suppose one glass wouldn't hurt," Madam Dupree said with a smile.

"Oh, thank you, Madam Dee," Bobby said. With that Bobby was up off the couch, skipping over to Murphy at the bar.

"Here you are, young lady, and don't let the bubbles tickle your nose." Murphy held out a tall, thin glass half full.

"Oh, thank you, Murph, how do I keep the bubbles away from my nose?" Bobby asked as laughter came from everyone.

"I propose a toast," declared the inspector as he held up his glass. "A toast to the bravest, smartest girl on the island of St. Vincent. I raise my glass to the girl that has captured the hearts of all those who have come to know her, Bobby White."

"Three cheers for Bobby White," Murphy called from the bar. "Hip, hip, hurray! Hip, hip, hurray! Hip, hip, hurray!" Bobby blushed as she hid her face behind her glass of champagne.

"Today, my department arrested the man who was responsible for your kidnapping, Bobby. Not to worry, for when this man is brought to justice you will not have to testify. One of the conspirators has confessed to his part in the affair. We have all the details. He was the right-hand man of the mastermind of the plot. As a matter of fact he was the only one that Joseph trusted. We now have them both locked up." Loud applause came from all present. The inspector made a small bow in recognition as he lifted his glass. A satisfied look was evident as he sipped from his glass.

"Inspector, does this mean that I'll be going back to Maine?" Bobby asked.

"Only if you wish to, my dear," the inspector replied.

"I don't know. I talk to my grandparents every week, and they keep asking when I'm coming home. I hate to leave you and Madam. You two are my very best friends ever. It would be awful hard for me to leave. Could we talk about this some other time?" Bobby asked.

"Certainly, my big girl," answered the inspector. Madam

Dupree put her arm around Bobby and gave her a hug. Ute announced that dinner was ready. The group departed for the dinning room.

"Ute, this meal is delicious. You have outdone yourself this time," the inspector said.

"Thank you, Inspector, that's very kind of you," Ute said. She was seated next to Murphy. On the inspector's right side was Bobby, with Sheri next to her. At the other end of the table was Madam Dupree. The table setting was lavish, the centerpiece being the flowers from Madam Durpee's garden. All the guests were dressed in their Sunday best.

" Inspector, a little while ago you said that you were going to arrest the two men that grabbed me and put me into the black car," Bobby said.

"True, Bobby, you see, if their prints are on file, and if they have not fled the island, then we have a chance. Sergeant Courtois is working on the files and I am hoping for a phone call from him shortly. Time is of the essence, for the morning papers will announce the arrest of Joseph. This will put the culprits to flight," Dupree said.

"It sounds to me that we must get awfully lucky on this one, Inspector," Murphy stated.

"Please, please, gentlemen. No more police talk at the dinner table. Let us talk of the string quartet that is coming to town next week, or the museum committee that is trying to put together an art show by local artists. I offered my paintings, but the other members of the committee just paused for a moment before continuing to talk of other things. Do you suppose they are trying to tell me something?" Madam Dupree said as she broke into a smile.

The party petered out as Sheri followed Bobby up to her

room to show her something very special. Murphy helped Ute take the dishes out to the kitchen. The inspector, quite satisfied with the day's work, put his arm around Madam Dupree as they walked to the study.

The inspector was on the job early the following morning when Sergeant Courtois burst into his office. "Inspector . . . Inspector, excuse me for not knocking, I believe I have found the kidnappers. Here, look at these photos and the fingerprints. Now compare them with the fingerprints we lifted off the limo," the sergeant said as he handed Inspector Dupree the material.

"Very interesting, Sergeant, please hand me my magnifying glass from over there on the table. Hmm, hmm, very interesting, very interesting, indeed, I believe you have found the culprits. Get out an all-points bulletin at once. Include every island within a hundred miles. We need copies of these photos for every man on the beat. Have Sheri print them up, and make sure they get distributed. If we are to catch these hired sewer rats, we must work fast," Dupree said.

That evening after dinner the inspector filled his brandy snifter a fourth full. He reached into his library of long-playing records, and pulled out the opera *Martha* by Flotow. The inspector settled into his overstuffed leather chair. When the music started his wife and Bobby walked into the room.

"Inspector, can we talk now?" Madam Dupree asked.

"Why certainly, my ladies, what may I do for you?" Dupree asked.

"Inspector, it's about Maine," Bobby said as she sat down on the ottoman. "I feel that I should go back to Maine, back to school, and back to my grandparents. Except leaving you and

Madam is like leaving home. I don't want to ever leave home again." Madam Dupree stood beside her, while Bobby had her arm around Madam's legs.

"Yes, I see. Well, we do have a problem here. Perhaps you could split your time between Maine and St. Vincent. I know your grandparents are very anxious to see you, and also they are interested in your education. Maybe we could make arrangements to have you here on the island during your summer vacations. I understand that the summer vacations in your country are very generous, something like three months long."

"It's only ten weeks," Bobby replied.

"Ah yes, ten weeks. I should be so lucky to have a ten-week vacation. Do you suppose, Bobby, that we would be welcome in your hometown, maybe on your winter vacation?" the inspector asked.

"Oh yes, oh yes, that would be super. I could introduce you to all my friends and take you skiing. Oh would you, Inspector? Would you come to Maine?" Bobby begged.

"Well it's a possibility, although I am not sure about the skiing thing," the inspector smiled.

"I'm going to miss you two terribly, but I know that going back is what I have to do. Can I stay just a little bit longer?" Bobby asked.

"But, of course, my dear. What say I book your flight two weeks from now? Would that be about right for you, Bobby?"

"Yes, oh yes, two weeks would be cool. I could do some shopping for my grandparents and all my friends. Well a few of my closest friends anyway," Bobby said. She jumped up off the ottoman and gave the inspector a hug. The inspector leaned over to turn up the music just as the opera was playing his favorite, *M'appari.*

Chapter Thirty-Six

At the police station the following day Sheri greeted Dupree with a smile. "Good morning, Inspector, Sergeant Courtois is in the interrogation room with the oversize person. He said that he would like your help as soon as possible." Chief Inspector Dupree was in a good mood for all the pieces were starting to fall into place.

"Yes, good morning, Sheri, you are looking lovely this morning. What does the mail look like?

"Thank you, Inspector, but the sergeant did sound anxious."

"Tell the sergeant I'll be there in a few minutes. It's a beautiful day, is it not?" Sheri smiled as the inspector thought of the ordeal of putting Joseph through some mental torture. He thought better of using the riding crop, for he felt that Joseph would not be easily intimidated, or maybe not. *Let's try the riding crop, it worked on Carlos.*

"Good morning, Sergeant, do you have a minute?" the inspector asked as he poked his head in the interrogation room. The sergeant stepped out of the room.

"What do we have so far, Sergeant?" the inspector asked.

"Nothing, he just keeps asking to see his lawyer," the sergeant answered.

"Well, to keep things legal, I suppose we'll have to comply, but first let's see what we can wring out of him," Dupree said. He walked into the room with his 'I'm in charge' stride. He did bring along his intimidation stick, the riding crop. After walking around the prisoner a few times, and bending the crop held with both hands, he said:

"Good morning, Joseph. It looks as though you've got yourself in a lot of trouble this time. What in God's name were you thinking when you decided to kidnap a dear friend of mine?" the inspector said. He had known Joseph for a long time.

"Look, Inspector, all you got is a confession from some dimwitted bottle washer. Who knows what you offered him for that confession? My lawyer will put so many holes in that piece of paper it will look like it's been used for dart practice. Now, get me my lawyer," Joseph said.

"Sure, Joseph, you can speak to a lawyer, but first let me explain how the system works. If you insist on your innocence the Commonwealth will have to take you to trial, which is very costly. Subsequently to pay for your lawyer you will be forced to sell everything you own: your house, your business, everything. The government, because you forced it to spend all that money on a trial, will be pissed off, and give you a heavy sentence. Therefore to keep yourself from going broke, and to avoid a heavy sentence, it would be in your best interest to sign a confession. So, you do some time for your greed. Look on the bright side, when you've done your time you'll have your home and your business to come back to. You will have something to return to. That's a lot better than doing twenty years, then have nothing to look forward to but being a street bum," the inspector said.

"Yeah that all sounds peachy but let's leave the legal stuff to my lawyer," Joseph said. "Ya got any coffee and a doughnut, make it two doughnuts?"

"Look, you'll get your lawyer, but first, before you decide to spend a lot of money, let me give you another piece of information. The two men you hired to grab the girl are in cuffs, on a plane back to St. Vincent. It won't take much for them to make a deal with us. Also, if you decide to cop a plea, I will be able to get you into the prison with excellent food. This prison is known up and down the West Indies for their gourmet cuisine. Oh yeah, a prison where the chef's only crime is stealing recipes. Or, if you decide on the difficult route, I will see to it that you go to the prison where the food is so bad that the rats won't eat it. Sergeant, get this slob a phone," the inspector walked out of the room.

"Bobby, put on your best dress. We are going shopping, and then we will have lunch at the best restaurant in town, that just happens to be in the best hotel in town," Madam Dupree said.

"Oh, a dress, Madam Dee, you know I hate dresses. Do I have to?" Bobby asked.

"I'm afraid you do, Bobby, because without a dress we won't be allowed into the restaurant. The men must wear jackets and ties," Madam Dupree said.

"Well, if you say so, Madam. I suppose that I'll have to use my best table manners too," Bobby said.

"That's right, Bobby, nothing but the best for us today. We'll buy the best meat, fish, and vegetables for Ute, and the best lunch for ourselves, now get a move on."

Murphy drove the ladies in the rented limo. The family car was still being repaired. The excuse for the slow progress, at the auto-body shop, was that parts from the States take forever. As the girls made their way through the market, Murphy was close by. He vowed never to get caught off guard again. Everyone Murphy looked at became a suspect. The shopping list was light.

Murphy carried the bundles back to the car. The trio walked to their next stop, The Cobbestone Inn. Built in 1813, it harbored a library full of history.

"What a beautiful restaurant. This place is super, just like in the movies. Look, the waiter's wearing a tuxedo," Bobby said, wide-eyed, as she looked around.

"That's not a waiter, Bobby, that's the maitre d'. He's like a head waiter. Shhh, he's coming," Madam Dupree said.

"Luncheon for three, ladies?" the maitre d' asked.

"Yes please, a table by the window, if you will," Madam Dupree asked.

Before the Dupree party had a chance to look at the menu a distinguished gentleman appeared.

"Madam Dupree, I have come to pay my respects, and to wish Bobby a very pleasant trip back to the States. Inspector Dupree tells me she'll be returning to the States shortly," the gentleman said.

"Why, Governor, how sweet of you, and who is the young gentleman with you?" Madam Dupree asked. Today the governor had left his wrinkled seersucker suit behind. He looked quite presentable.

"Oh yes, please let me introduce my grandson, Alessandro. Alessandro, I would like you to meet Madam Dupree and Miss Bobby White." The governor pushed forward his grandson, who shook hands with Madam Dupree and gave a slight bow.

"Pleased to meet you, Madam Dupree." He then turned to Bobby and said, "I have heard so much about you, Bobby. Could you, ah . . . ah . . . would you, your autograph?" Alessandro asked as he held out a newspaper clipping with Bobby's picture. His face flushed.

"Madam Dee, what shall I do?" Bobby whispered.

"Just write 'to Alessandro from Bobby', that's all," Madam whispered back. Bobby reached out for the material from Alessandro. She set the clipping on the table and signed her name. "Thank you, Bobby. Pleasure meeting you, Madam Dupree," Alessandro, said nodding his head again.

"Ladies, we must get back to our table. I am entertaining some people who think they're very important," the governor said as he smiled, nodding his head.

"Madam Dee, he's gorgeous. He's gorgeous." Bobby said.

"I didn't know you were interested in boys, my dear. You are growing up right under my eyes. When did you start taking notice of boys?" Madam Dupree asked.

"Just now, Madam," Bobby replied with a smile.

"Well forget about boys for now, you are much too young." Madam's attempt at a stern face was not convincing.

"But he's gorgeous," Bobby repeated.

"Yes I know, and you are a very good-looking girl yourself. I must watch you very carefully, at least until we get you on the plane. After that my responsibilities are over," Madam Dupree said.

"Oh, Madam Dee, you make it sound as if I were sixteen or something."

Murphy was grinning from ear to ear, but he dared not say a word.

"The waiter is here and we have not looked at the menu." Madam handed Bobby a menu and then opened hers. After the ladies had ordered, it was Murphy's turn.

"I'll have a beer and a hamburger," Murphy said. "Make that rare with a slice of onion." Anyone looking at the waiter may have seen his nose turn up.

"Good morning, Inspector, here is your mail. Sergeant Courtois is in a hurry to speak to you," Sheri smiled.

"Good morning, Sheri. You are looking lovely as always. Don't tell me you have a luncheon date with someone special?" the inspector asked.

"No, no one special today, I'm afraid. The sergeant does seem anxious to speak with you. I believe it has something to do with the extra-large person you are keeping out back," Sheri said.

"Okay, I'll see him right away. I hope it's good news." The inspector walked down to the interrogation room. He looked inside and motioned for Sergeant Courtois to come out in the hall. "Sergeant, good morning, what's the word this morning?" the inspector asked in a low voice.

"Inspector, I think Joseph is about to strike a deal. He spoke to his lawyer yesterday and he's not happy," the sergeant said.

"That's good news, Sergeant, let's go in and have a talk." The two men entered the room, and for a few minutes said nothing. "Joseph, I understand you would like to talk to me. I must tell you that I have a full calendar today. I don't have a lot of time for idle talk. What's on your mind?" the inspector said. He sat down on a chair opposite Joseph, with Sergeant Courtois standing by the door.

"Look, Inspector, I was talking to my lawyer and, well, the guy's expensive. I had no idea that lawyers get that kind of money," Joseph said.

"You should have thought of that before you started your adventure in crime," Dupree replied.

"Yeah, yeah, he wants seventy-five bucks an hour. At that rate, I'd be broke in no time. Fucking lawyers just love to see a guy get in trouble and then suck 'em dry. The first thing he asked me was, 'How much money you got in the bank?' Can you believe that?"

"You don't have to go that route, Joseph. Just give us a confession and I'll go to bat for you. Quite frankly, you don't have much of a case. The lawyer will defend you, take your money, and you go to jail. That's the way it goes. He ends up with your money, and you end up in the same place if you had a lawyer or not. So, if you are ready to confess, I'll have the sergeant here take care of the paperwork." The inspector got up and started for the door.

"Suppose, Inspector, if someone was guilty of kidnapping, and they signed a confession, what kind of time would he be looking at, theoretically speaking of course?"

"Think of it this way, Joseph, the Commonwealth would save a bundle of money on a trial. The judge could spend more time playing golf, and the only people losing out would be the lawyers. If I talked to the judge and told him that you were very cooperative, he'd take that into consideration. I'd say ten to twelve, with time off for good behavior you'd be out in eight, that's not bad. Now, on the other hand, without a confession you'd be looking at twenty years, hard time. You'd be an old man by the time you get out; a broke, old man," Dupree said.

"Okay . . . okay, you've got your confession. Now tell me about the prison with the gourmet cuisine. Is that for real or you just putting me on?" Joseph looked like a kid who wanted to believe in the tooth fairy.

"I've been known to stretch the truth now and then, Joseph, although that happens to be the truth, or close to it," Dupree said.

"How close to it?" Joseph was more interested in the food than in the fact that he would be spending the next eight years in jail.

Chapter Thirty-seven

Murphy walked into Ute's spotless kitchen at ten in the morning. Madam Dupree was pulling weeds in her flower garden, and Bobby was in her room writing to her grandparents. Murphy sat on one of the stools that dotted the island bar surrounding the kitchen stove.

"I had a wonderful time Saturday night, Murphy, a perfect date," Ute said as she poured Murphy's coffee.

"You did? That's great, would you like to do it again sometime? Maybe we could have dinner before the movie. That is, if you can get the night off," Murphy said.

"Sunday is my day off. The Duprees generally eat out on Sundays. They go to one of the hotels and have a large brunch after church. After that they just grab a snack for the evening meal," Ute said.

"Perfect, let's go out to dinner and maybe a movie after. Would next Sunday be too soon?" Murphy asked.

"That sounds delightful, Murphy. I'd love that. I've been meaning to ask you, uh . . . uh . . . how's your coffee?"

"The coffee is delicious, as always. What was it you wanted to ask?" Murphy, with his big hands clutching his coffee mug, looked at Ute.

"Well, I want you to know you don't have to answer if it's embarrassing. You don't have to tell me. You know that, Murphy, right?" Ute said as she cleaned lettuce under the faucet.

"Sure, but what's this all about? I've got nothing to hide. Tell you what, Ute?"

Ute came back to the stove. "Murph, do you have a first name?" Ute asked.

"Oh sure, but everyone calls me Murphy."

"I know that. You don't have to tell me, but what's your first name?"

"Oh, it's no big deal," Murphy said.

"Well then, what is it?" Ute asked with a smile on her face.

"Clarence," Murphy mumbled.

"Clarence." Ute's smile didn't change. "That's a beautiful name. Why don't you use it?"

"Look, I've always been a cop. Now, how would it sound if the bad guys went around calling me Clarence? Come on, Ute, tough cops have names like Sam or Mike."

"Clarence sounds tough to me, a little," Ute said, holding back her laughter.

"Can you imagine some dude saying to his partner in crime, 'Clarence wants me to put my hands up.'? How would that sound?" The corners of Murphy's mouth turned up.

"I think it would sound wonderful." Ute turned her head to suppress her laughter with a cough.

Murphy, in a playful mood, said, "You're laughing at me, aren't you?"

"No really, I had to cough. Forgive me, I'm in a silly mood." Ute said.

"Ute, you're beautiful when you laugh. I like your silly mood," Murphy said as he looked down into his mug.

The following morning Murphy was driving the inspector to work. The inspector enjoyed his ride to the office because it gave him a chance to read the paper. He felt important sitting in the back seat of his limo.

"Inspector," Murphy interrupted Dupree's reading.

"Yes, Murphy?"

"Inspector, I've asked Ute out to dinner and a movie this coming Sunday, if it's all right with you?"

"Certainly, Murphy, what you do with the best chef in the world, on your own time, is none of my business," the inspector said.

"Oh thanks, Boss, this means a lot to me. I think she is just, just . . ."

"I know what you mean, Murphy, but don't get any ideas about sweeping her off her feet, and leaving us with someone like Carlos for a cook."

"Don't worry, Inspector, I think she's going out with me cause there's no one else around. If I thought I had a chance with her I'd be on cloud nine," Murphy said.

Sunday evening after the movie, Murphy with Ute on this arm were walking down Bedford Street on the way to the family car. Murphy had borrowed the limo for their date. An occasional shooting star ran across a star-filled sky. Ute noted that the stars were especially vivid this evening. "That was a delightful dinner and the show was better than I expected. Just a charming evening, Murph," Ute said.

"Glad you enjoyed yourself. I think we lucked out on the movie," Murphy said as they passed a boutique shop with several paintings in the window. They stopped to look at them.

"I've heard that you paint in your spare time," Ute said.

"Who told you that?" Murphy had been unaware that Ute knew of his hobby.

"Oh, word gets around," Ute said. Her hand was still around Murphy's arm.

"Yeah, I do a little, watercolors mostly," Murphy admitted.

"Watercolors, that's my favorite medium."

"It is? Mine too, especially Winslow Homer," Murphy said.

"Oh, I love Winslow Homer. His watercolors grab the spirit of the moment. You get the feeling that you are right there," Ute said as she held onto Murphy's arm.

"Yeah, Homer is great. I like his loose style." Murphy held his chest out, head high. He looked like a new man with Ute on his arm.

"Are you going to show me your paintings sometime?" Ute asked.

"Sure, Ute, but you gotta understand, I'm just an amateur."

"How about tonight?" Ute asked.

"Tonight?" Murphy was taken by surprise. "Now? Tonight?"

"Why not? It's still early," Ute said, smiling.

Murphy was stunned. *She wants to go to my place. It's a mess. What am I going to do? I can't say no, this is embarrassing.* "Tonight . . . yeah sure, Ute, but I wasn't expecting anyone. You'll have to overlook the mess," Murphy said.

"It's been a long time since I've been in a bachelor's apartment. I'm sure things haven't changed. Don't worry if the dishes aren't washed, or the bed's not made," Ute laughed.

Murphy turned on a few lights as they entered his apartment. He picked up a few books that were lying on the floor, tried to kick a magazine under the couch. He lived over the garage of a large Victorian home that was converted to apartments. He preferred being apart from the others in the main house. He liked his privacy. The Victorian house was located away from the city. It had been part of a large plantation.

"This is a charming place, Murphy. Don't bother with picking up. I know you weren't expecting anyone," Ute said.

"Would you like a glass of wine? I have some Riesling," Murphy asked as he poked around the refrigerator.

"Yes, Riesling is fine. Do you mind if I turn the stereo on?"

"No, good idea, I have some jazz tapes on top," Murphy called from the small kitchen.

"Stan Getz, Shelly Manne, Johnny Hodges, Lester Young, you've got them all here," Ute said as she looked through Murphy's collection.

"See if you can find something by the 'Brute,' Big Ben Webster, or Flip Phillips, maybe Dexter Gordon," Murphy called from the midget kitchen.

"Here's one I haven't heard in a long time," Ute said as she inserted a tape. "I caught Ben Webster in Germany a number of years ago at a nightclub in Frankfurt. He was a big hit in Germany. I thought he was great, loved him," Ute said.

Murphy felt a little awkward as he sat down opposite from Ute. He had put on a few pounds since his retirement. He tried to pull in his stomach when he noticed it hanging over his belt. He put the wine down on the coffee table. Ute sat on the couch across from Murphy.

"How can I get to know you, Murph, if you sit over there?" Ute lifted the wine glass to her lips.

"Oh, yeah, sure, over there." Murphy had the feeling that he was weighed down by past events. *God, how long has it been? Wife's been gone five years now, and then my nervous breakdown.*

That took two years to recover. I haven't been with a woman in god knows how long.

"Take your jacket off and relax," Ute said as she kicked off her shoes. The low, sexy notes of Ben Webster set the mood. "Oh, he is so good. He gets a lot of feeling out of that sax. What got you into police work, Murph?" Ute asked.

"My father, he was a cop. It just seemed natural to follow in his footsteps. He got me on the force in Brooklyn. That's in New York," Murphy said.

"I know. You seem too young to be retired. I always thought of retired people as being, you know . . .," Ute did not finish the sentence.

"Old?" Murphy questioned.

"Not old, but older. You're not old at all," Ute said.

"I took early retirement. Less money but I needed out."

"Out of police work? I was under the impression that you loved police work," Ute said.

"I do, but that's another story. Someday, I'll tell you about it. How about you, what brought you to St. Vincent?"

"I got married at a young age. We were too young, it didn't work out. I worked at the blood lab for a number of years, and then got the bug to see the world. This is as far as I got," Ute said.

"Well, lucky for us. The Duprees think the world of you," Murphy said as he sipped his wine.

"I didn't realize that traveling costs so much. I thought that I would work a little to build up my reserve. Time just flew by, so here I am." Ute closed her eyes and suddenly remembered why she was there. "Your paintings, you were going to show me your paintings, Murph."

"The good ones I've framed and hung," Murphy said.

"Where?" Ute asked.

"In the bedroom. I'll get them for you."

"You don't have to do that. Where's the bedroom?" Ute was up off the couch, and headed in the direction Murphy was pointing. The bedroom was large with a cathedral ceiling. A tree looked through the sliding glass doors.

"Bed's not made," Murphy said apologetically.

"Mine's not either. Oh, is this your painting? I love it," Ute said.

"Yeah, I got lucky on that one." Murphy noted that Ute was his height with her shoes off.

"That sunset, you've captured it perfectly. I feel that I'm right there in the painting. It's beautiful, Murph."

"Thanks," Murphy said. He was a little embarrassed. Ute had caught him off guard.

"And this one, is this yours also?" Ute asked.

"Yeah, that one too," Murphy replied.

"You've got a real talent, Murphy. I love those old wooden boats. You should have been an artist," Ute said.

"Naw, it's just a hobby."

"You're too modest, Murph. If I had your talent I'd paint every day. What style would you call it?" Ute asked.

"I'm not sure. I take lessons from Laura DaRos. She has a place on the north side of the island. She comes here in the winter months," Murphy said.

"I've heard that she is very attractive?" With that remark Ute sat her drink down on the night table, and stretched out on the bed. Murphy sat down on the edge of the bed, leaned over and kissed Ute lightly. Ute reciprocated with passion.

"Not half as attractive as you," Murphy said as he tried to catch his breath. Ute, noting how uncomfortable Murphy was, felt she should end this right now.

"I don't know what came over me, Murph. I guess it was the wine. Let's go back to the living room, shall we?" Ute asked.

"Sorry, Ute, I guess I got a little overexcited. I haven't been with a woman for a long time," Murphy said as he followed Ute back into the living room. Big Ben Webster was still blowing softly.

"Maybe you should get out more often," Ute said. Realizing it was an inappropriate comment, she tried to think of a cover.

"I would if this island had more girls by the name of Ute." Murphy's little joke didn't go over that well. Ute finished her wine, and walked into the kitchen. She placed the glass on the counter.

"I think it's time I went home. Thank you for a lovely evening, Murphy. I enjoyed myself entirely, and you were a perfect gentleman."

"Yeah, too perfect, I'm afraid." Murphy's facial expression was one of sadness, mixed with bewilderment. Ute found her shoes and was hopping across the floor trying to put them on without sitting down.

"Ute, I'm sorry if I was out of line," Murphy said as Ute laughed and started to fall. Murphy grabbed her before she went down. Her left shoe would not go on. Ute looked up into his eyes. With his masculinity coming back from wherever it had gone, Murphy held Ute tightly. He kissed Ute with fervor, his passion welling up from deep down inside. Ute, now feeling better about the situation, returned his kiss.

"It's late, Murph, I really must go." Ute grabbed her purse and headed for the door. Murphy, with a grin on his face, followed.

On the ride back to the villa on the hill Murphy's smile didn't leave his face. The car radio was on high volume as Murphy kept time with his left foot. *So this is what cloud nine is like. Wow!*

Chapter Thirty-eight

Chief Inspector Dupree was told to meet the Kaiser late that evening. It seemed that whenever they met the weather was dark and damp. Fog had rolled in, which was not unusual for this time of the year. The inspector had an uneasy feeling about this meeting. He thought that the Kaiser may have had something to do with the two men that had been following him. Dupree sat in his car alone, his mind racing to find the reason for this meeting. It was an unusual request coming from the Kaiser. In all the years of doing business with these people there was always a go-between. He never dealt with the Kaiser directly, except on the one occasion, when a leak had developed. Now that the leak had been found, and plugged, the ship was sailing fine.

Not like the Kaiser to be this late, I wish he'd hurry up, and get here. I wonder what's on his mind? There, car lights, must be him.

Dupree was relieved to see that the Kaiser was alone as he pulled into the parking area. Dupree was out of his car, walking toward the Kaiser. Shaking hands, Dupree motioned toward the beach.

"Inspector, pleased you could make it. I have some news for you, not very pleasant news, I'm afraid. On the other hand if it were good news we'd not be meeting like this," the Kaiser said.

"When things are going along fine, I worry," the inspector said. He had brought along his riding crop. He was slapping his leg as they walked along the beach. The waves were high this evening, rolling in from far away and washing up onto the black sand. Dupree was not relaxed; he felt something was in the air.

"I'm retiring, Inspector, moving off the island. I've sold the business to some people from down south," the Kaiser said.

"From down south?" The inspector knew it, terrible news. He could smell it a mile away. "How far down south?" he asked.

"Colombia, to be precise," the Kaiser did not look up.

"You can't do that," the inspector said. "Those people are bad news. They'll move in and take over the island. I'll have no control." Panic laced the inspector's words.

"Sorry, Inspector, but you're part of the deal, you and the governor."

"No . . . no . . . no . . . we can't have a drug cartel here on this island. I won't permit it," the inspector said with anxiety.

"You should have thought of that before you got into the drug business, my friend," the Kaiser said. He was pleasant, but all business.

"But I'm not in the drug business," the inspector spoke louder than he wanted to, his face flushed.

"You and the governor have been on my payroll for years. Now it's time for me to move on. Perhaps you should think of moving on also. I must caution you, if you retire, it's best you disappear. The people from down south would not be pleased to hear that you're no longer part of the package; they play rough," the Kaiser said.

The inspector got that pre-diarrhea feeling in his stomach. He realized that the deal had been made, and if he did not go along with it, his life would be in grave danger.

"But. . . but," the inspector was at a loss for words. *How am I going to break this to Madam, she loves this island.* Dupree kept walking long after the Kaiser had left. *I might have known it wouldn't last, now look at the fucking mess I've got myself into. Talk about greed, I'm the greediest of them all. Perhaps we should get on the plane with Bobby. I hear that Maine is very pleasant in the summer months, yeah all three months of it, if you're lucky.*

The inspector walked the beach for several hours. He realized that his time on his beautiful island was indeed limited. The reality of the situation was beginning to sink in. He thought about his friends, and the fact that he would never be able to contact them, never be in touch again. His picture would never hang on the walls of the police station. *Why was I so eager for money? What good is that money going to do me now? Away from my home, my island, my friends. God, I wish I had not been greedy. The governor, how will I tell the governor? If I tell him what's going on, he'll also have to leave. That will really upset the drug lords. They'll certainly come after us. But, if they have the governor in their pocket, then maybe they'll leave me alone. I hate to leave the governor hanging, but what choice do I have? Now, everything I've worked for is gone, my life's work down the toilet. What a fool I've been. Madam is not going to leave this island, Christ, what a mess.*

As Inspector Dupree walked along the beach his riding crop slapped his leg harder and harder with each step. *What a fool I've been, Christ, what a fool.*

On the same evening that Dupree was meeting with the Kaiser, Bobby was getting ready for her plane flight back to the States. Madam Dupree had bought Bobby two pieces of luggage.

The youngster was trying to stuff everything she owned into her suitcases.

"Oh, Madam, I can't get it all in. What can I do?"

"Why not leave some of your things behind? After all, they'll be here when you come back. It's not as if you are throwing them away," Madam Dupree said.

"Do you suppose I could leave some of the dresses behind? We don't wear dresses where I come from. Well, we do for special occasions, like graduation, or someone's wedding, and stuff like that," Bobby said.

"I don't see why not. I'll hang them in your closet. They will be here when you come back. Maybe we will go to that restaurant in the hotel, maybe you will run into Alessandro again," Madam Dupree said.

"Oh, Madam, do you think so? But that will be a long time from now. Do I have to wait that long before seeing him again?" Bobby asked.

"I'm afraid so, Bobby. You are leaving tomorrow, and tonight we are having a 'going away' dinner in your honor. You see there is little time left for romance."

"Romance . . . romance, who said anything about romance? I just think he's cute, that's all." Bobby's face had turned crimson.

"Okay, Bobby, I'll stop teasing if you will get your bags packed. I've got to check on Ute and get Murphy out of the kitchen. If not, there'll be nothing ready for dinner," Madam Dupree said.

The following morning, on the way to the airport, Bobby asked to be driven through Kingstown. She wanted to see Bay and Bedford's cobblestone streets for the last time. She wanted to see the stone-block colonial buildings and the crowds at the marketplace.

"I have your tickets, Bobby," the inspector said. "You'll have to change planes at St. Lucia." Bobby sat between the Duprees in the backseat, and Murphy was at the wheel.

"Why can't I just fly right to Miami? I don't like changing planes. What if I get on the wrong plane or something?" Bobby said with concern.

"Not to worry, Bobby, the inspector and I will be flying with you as far as St. Lucia," Madam Dupree said.

"You will, Inspector? You and Madam are going to help me change planes?" Bobby's concern turned to excitement.

"Why certainly, Bobby, you see here on St. Vincent, we don't have an international airport. We'll take a smaller plane to St. Lucia. There we'll put you on a jet plane that will take you to Miami."

"Super," Bobby said.

When the four entered the airport terminal a steel band was playing calypso music. Much to Bobby's surprise, all of her friends were there. Ute, Sheri, and Sergeant Courtois all stood in a group, waving.

"Oh, Madam Dee, look, the whole gang is here," Bobby said as she ran up to them. She stopped before Ute, who gave her a big hug. It was Murphy's turn next.

Sheri said, "Here, Bobby, I bought you something for your trip." She handed Bobby a small, gift-wrapped package.

"Oh thank you, Sheri." Bobby gave Sheri a hug.

"Bobby, I have your tickets, I'll check you in along with your luggage," the inspector said. With the crowd of people around Bobby, she did not notice the governor standing at the edge. When the inspector returned, he saw the governor and said, "Governor, how nice to see you. What brings you to the airport today?" With that the crowd opened up and Bobby saw the governor.

"Well, to tell the truth, Inspector, it's my grandson who dragged me down here. He wanted to say goodbye to Bobby." Alessandro came forward with a rose and gave it to Bobby. The crowd drew back and not a word was spoken. Bobby reached out and accepted the rose without a word.

"Bobby, aren't you going to say 'thank you' to Alessandro?" Madam Dupree asked.

"Thank you, Alessandro," Bobby said softly. Alessandro bowed without speaking and backed away. With the calypso band playing nearby, conversation was drowned out. Bobby gave everyone a hug and a kiss. Madam Dupree held her hand and walked to the loading gate. Inspector Dupree excused himself for a quick trip to the men's room.

Two men followed Dupree into the men's room. The inspector did not notice them until one of the men gave Dupree a shove while he was in front of the urinal.

"I beg your pardon," the inspector said.

"The boss wants to see you, now," the man who did the shoving said.

Dupree now recognized the two men. The same two he saw on the boat to Bequia. His heart jumped. "I'm sorry, gentlemen, for I'm taking a flight to St. Lucia. Perhaps when I get back," Dupree said. He was then thrown up against the wall and relieved of his gun. Both men were large and muscular.

The larger of the two men grabbed the inspector's necktie and twisted it. The inspector's face turned red. "You're coming with us now. The boss said to club you near death if we have to. I don't care for blood, but my friend here loves it. What's it going to be, dumb ass," the large man said.

"If it's that important, I'll see your boss now," Dupree said as his face returned to something close to normal.

Chapter Thirty-nine

The villa was the most extravagant, luxurious complex on the hill. Chief Inspector Dupree, sandwiched between two large men, was escorted through the house, down a few steps to a beautiful pool that overlooked the ocean. The water sparkled as the gentle, sea breeze skipped along the swimming pool. Dupree could not help but admire the elegance of the setting. *Whoever the boss is, he certainly knows how to live.*

"Come in and sit down, Inspector, I've been meaning to talk to you for some time. Have some tea," said the man who appeared to be in charge. The man was dressed in clean, pressed, white pants. He wore a colorful shirt and sunglasses. He sat in white lawn furniture with a large sun umbrella.

"No, thank you," the inspector replied as he sat down on the edge of a lounge chair, across from his new host.

"Let me introduce myself. I am Senor Fernando Fuerzas Alvaro Araujo, better known as the 'Boss'. Now let's get down to business." The inspector nodded. "I have purchased this island from the Kaiser. You now work for me," the boss said.

"I believe you're mistaken, my friend. I work for the government," the inspector said. The words were no sooner out of his mouth when *wham.* The inspector saw stars as his body flew into the pool. He had been hit on the side of his head by one of the bodyguards who were standing behind him. His head came above the water with blood running from his nose. Stunned and dizzy, the inspector started to climb up the pool ladder. Without warning, the man whom the inspector thought was going to help him kicked him in the face. The inspector fell back into the water. He came up coughing and spitting blood. He moved to the low end of the pool, waited for his head to clear. His ears were ringing, his sight was blurred.

"You're right, you're the boss," Dupree mumbled.

"I beg your pardon, Inspector, I can't hear you," the Boss said.

"You're the boss," Dupree raised his voice.

"Are you sure, Inspector? You don't seem convinced."

Dupree looked around for an escape route. "I am convinced, you're the boss."

"Now, that's more like it, Inspector." Dupree walked out of the low end of the pool. "Here, take this towel, wipe your face, I hate to see blood. Now as I was saying, Dub . . ."

"It's Dupree," the inspector said, holding the towel to his face.

"The Kaiser tells me that you and the governor worked well together, and that he never had a problem with you two. Now that's the way I like it." The Boss sipped his tea. The inspector sat down again, this time not so close to the pool. Again he looked for a way out. His eyes darted from one bodyguard to the next.

"What do you want from me?" Dupree asked.

"I'm not changing a thing; business will go along as usual. Your job will be to make sure that the operation is not interrupted. If there is a hint that you are not protecting us from outside interference you may as well dig yourself a grave. That way your family will know where you are buried," the Boss smiled.

"But I can't stop the CIA from coming here and investigating," the inspector protested.

"That's your problem, Dupree, that's what I'm paying you for. I'm sure that you and your friend, the governor, will find a way, if you value your life."

The inspector, still dripping with pool water, wiped his face again with the towel he was handed. He looked at the Boss, who seemed as evil as one could be. A chill ran through his body. "My department will do whatever it can to protect your business," Dupree said.

"Your department will do everything to protect my business? For you failure is not an option. I will have two of my best men working with you at the police station. You will hire them as plainclothes detectives. They will be your bodyguards," the boss said. The inspector nodded his head as he held the towel to his lips. "The people that work for me work for next to nothing. That is what I'll be paying you, next to nothing. Do you have a problem with that, Dupree?" The inspector shook his head. "Good, now that we understand each other, I'm sure you'll enjoy our new arrangement." Dupree did not answer. "Oh, and one more thing, my men will be with you twenty-four hours a day. I would not want you to get any ideas about leaving the island," the boss said.

Dupree looked around at the surrounding area, the access road, the house, and the location of the guards. He saw no possible escape route, and too many thugs with Heckler & Koch MP7s. The MP7 is a submachine gun known in some circles as a personal defense weapon, or PDW. *Where the hell would I run to, we're on an island for Christ's sake! I'm out to sea in a kayak and a hurricane is coming.*

"Gentlemen," the boss said to his men, "take the inspector back to the police station and have him sign you up as his new detectives, and make sure he pays you well. Good day, Dupree," the boss said. The inspector nodded his head as one of the sumo wrestlers grabbed him under the armpit and hoisted him up off his feet. The trio moved through the house and out the two large, oak, front doors. No more than twenty feet from the house the men stopped, froze in place. In front of them, a dozen automobiles were lined up on the street. Several of the vehicles were marked as police cars. Behind each vehicle were three or four men with weapons pointed at Dupree.

A bullhorn broke the silence. "Drop your weapons, now. Drop them or we'll open fire." The Boss's two men ran for the house as Dupree fell flat on his face. "Fire!" The voice over the bullhorn bellowed. Too late, the men made it back into the house. Bullets whizzed over the inspector's head as he hugged the pavement. From the house came a counter attack, as small arms popped, larger weapons cracked and machine guns rattled. Dupree covered both ears while lying as flat as possible, not daring to move. Flying bullets flattened tires on the automobiles one after the other. Every car had a dozen holes in its side. Over the top of the hill, two helicopters appeared and circled the villa. The helicopters returned fire from the ground with rockets.

Helicopters, we don't have helicopters on this island. Where the hell did the helicopters come from? Dupree made himself as flat as possible as he spit dirt from his mouth.

Three or four loud explosions shook the ground as the rockets exploded in the villa. Fire broke out and spread rapidly as the sea breeze fanned the blaze. Billows of smoke set up a cover for the men behind the cars. It gave them a chance to run for the house. Five men were stopped by the large, oak doors. The man in charge of the commandos waved and hollered. He wanted a car to crash the doors down. He could not make the men behind the cars understand.

"You, go tell the captain to drive a damn car into the doors, now run," the lead man said. Run he did, as if a bullet were chasing him. The engine roared on one of Dupree's police cars as screeching tires laid down its own layer of smoke. For some reason the driver did not see, or perhaps was overexcited, for he drove directly at the inspector.

That crazy bastard, he's going to kill me. Dupree was wide-eyed. The police car raced over the pavement. Dupree made himself as small as possible. He closed his eyes, and held his breath. *This is it, God have mercy on my soul.* The car did not slow down until it hit the solid oak doors. The doors fell into the house with a crash. Dupree heard the impact; he looked up to see what had happened. The police car had driven over Dupree, missing him completely. He thought about the pilot having a heart attack while flying to Barbados, and the numerous gun battles he had been in. *Jesus Christ, I must have nine lives, and just used up five of them.* Someone was pulling on his arm. "You alright, Inspector?" the policeman asked.

"Get me outta here," cried the inspector, as a second person grabbed his other arm. The inspector was dragged to cover behind one of the autos. They sat him down and leaned him against a car wheel, out of harm's way. The amount of firing had slowed down. The helicopters circled a few more times and then disappeared behind the hills. Sheri was wiping the inspector's face with a damp cloth. "What the hell are you doing here?" the inspector asked.

"Your wife called from St. Lucia. She wants you to call her right away. She sounded very upset. She said that it doesn't take that long to go to the men's room."

"Give her a call and tell her not to put Bobby on the plane. I'm taking the next flight out of here. The three of us are going to Maine for a vacation," Dupree said.

"Right away, Inspector, but first I want to tell you that there are two men here, from the States, who want to talk to you," Sheri said.

"Okay, go make my phone call and thank you, Sheri. Tell Madam Dupree that I was called away, it was an emergency. You're a sweetheart, Sheri," the inspector said. As the two men approached Dupree rubbed his eyes. He thought he was seeing things. *What the hell, I must be dreaming or that kick in the face really scrambled my brains.*

"Well, Inspector, you beat us to it again," Mike Doyle said. "We've been after this guy for over a year, and you're the one who tracked him down. Congratulations. I underestimated you right from the start. I'm sorry we got off on the wrong foot."

"Not a problem, Mike, I certainly appreciate you and your boys showing up when you did. For a moment I thought that they had the upper hand," Dupree said.

"Good work, Inspector, we're proud of you," George Greenier echoed. "You sure know how to deal with these guys. They play rough you know."

Inspector Dupree Breaks Up Drug Ring, the headlines read. Inspector Dupree was not on the island to read the newspaper. In the past he had always enjoyed positive publicity from the newspaper. This time he just wanted to get away as fast as possible. He was with Madam Dupree and Bobby White on a flight headed for Maine. He had told Sheri that he would give her a full report upon his arrival in that faraway place. The inspector slid back his seat, put on the headphones and listened to the music. In his hand was a glass of the airline's finest cognac.

The End

Nautical Glossary

Aft – Toward the rear or stern of a boat.

Aloft – Up in the mast or rigging.

Anchor Light – An electric or kerosene light placed in the rigging during overnight anchoring to advice other boats of your location. The light is white.

Anchor Roller – A stainless steel or bronze roller over which the anchor-chain rides.

Anchor Windlass – A mechanical winch, manual or electric, which aids in hauling anchors and chains.

Anemometer – An instrument used to measure wind speed.

Avon – The Avon Manufacturing Company makes inflatable dinghies. Large, hard-bottom, inflatable dinghies with outboard motors are used on many ships as workboats.

Backstay – The wire rope giving aft support to the mast.

Back-up Plates – Reinforcing plates, usually steel or brass, used when bolting through material such as wood or fiberglass.

Baffles – Structural partitions in fuel and water tanks that restrain liquids from gaining momentum during violent boat movement.

Baggywrinkle – Fluffed short rope ends fabricated to prevent sails from chafing on the shrouds.

Ballast – High density weight carried in the lower part of the vessel to give her stability and enable her to right herself. Generally lead, steel, brick, boulders or concrete.

Barograph – A barometer equipped with a moving graph that records barometric changes.

Battens – Flexible fiberglass or wood strips utilized in a pocket in the leech of a sail to give the sail shape. Also used to set the sail with a roach.

Battens Pockets – Reinforced sheath on the leech of the sail that houses the battens.

Beam – The widest dimension of the vessel.

Bedlog – A set of raised tracks upon which the main hatch slides.

Belaying Pin – A short removable wood or metal pin, fitted in a rail of a boat for the use of securing running rigging.

Berth – A bunk or any sleeping accommodations of a vessel.

Berth Rail – A trim piece that keeps berth cushions in place.

Bilge – The area of the boat below the cabin sole sometimes used for storage of fuel and water tanks.

Bilge Pump – A high capacity manual or electric pump used to pump water out of the bilge.

Bilge Pump Strainer – A strainer or sieve attached to the intake of the bilge pump.

Binnacle – A housing for compasses.

Bobstay – The stay from the tip of the bowsprit to a fitting at the waterline, counteracting the pull of the forestay.

Bolt Rope – Rope around the edge of a sail needed to take the strain off the sailcloth.

Boom Bail – A "U" shaped bracket screwed to the boom through which blocks and lines can be led.

Boomgallows – A standard support upon which the boom rests when the sails are stored.

Boomkin – A horizontal extension of the bow of the boat used to accommodate the headstay.

Boomvang – A block and tackle used to control the upward movement of the boom.

Bowsprit – A horizontal extension off the bow of the boat used to accommodate the headstay.

Bos'ns Chair – A canvas or wood chair used for hoisting one up the mast.

Boot Stripe – A painted stripe above the yacht's waterline to catch oil or dirt. Also used for asthetic purposes.

Bridge Deck – A narrow part of the deck between the cockpit and the companionway or cabin.

Bulkheads – A structural partition dividing the interior of the boat.

Bull Nose – The rounded edge of decorative wood.

Bullseye – A high strength eyelet that can be secured to the deck to aid in fairleading lines.

Bulwarks – Raised portion of the deck that follows the sheer line.

Bung – A wood dowel glued to a sunken screw head to give the wood a finished look.

Butt Connector – A metal press fitting that unites two wires end to end without complex splicing.

Cam Cleat – A piece of deck hardware consisting of two cogs between which a line will pass in only one direction.

Cap Nut – A finishing nut with one side sealed off.

Car – A moving fitting attached to a traveler to which a block may be attached.

Cat Rig – A large main sail on a single mast, located at the bow of the sailboat.

Caulk – The material used in the seam of two planks on a wood boat.

Caulking – The act of driving caulk into a seam.

Ceiling – The finish material lining the inside of the hull.

Center Board – A retractable keel used in sailboats.

Charley Noble – A through deck fitting for a stove pipe.

Cheek Block – A fixed pulley that is attached to the side of the boom.

Chicken Head – A metal fitting at the top of a mast to which are secured the shrouds, stays and sheaves.

Chocks – Block of wood or metal on the deck that act as pads for deck equipment such as a dinghy, spinnaker pole, etc.

Chronometer – A very accurate clock used for navigation.

Clam Cleat – Similar to a cam cleat but without moving parts.

Clamping – Two parts held together mechanically.

Cleat – A piece of hardware used for securing a line.

Clevis Pin – A round piece of metal used to secure joint in the rigging.

Clew – The lower aft corner of the sail.

Clipper Bow – A bow that has a forward curve.

Club Footed Jib – A self-tending jib whose foot is attached to a boom at the clew rather that running free.

Coaming – The side of the cabin or cockpit.

Cockpit – The sunken area of a deck in which the helmsman and crew sit.

Cockpit sole – The floor of the cockpit.

Companionway – The entrance by which you pass through when going below from topsides.

Companionway Ladder – The steps or ladder in the companionway.

Cunningham Hole – A hole and cringle in a sail used to tighten the luff.

Cutter – A single mast vessel with two headsails.

Davit – An overhanging fixture from which a dinghy is supported for lowering or lifting the dinghy.

Deadeye – A method of rigging adjustment used in combination with lanyards.

Dead Light – A non-opening piece of glass in deck for letting light into the cabin.

Deck Beams – Beams that are athwartship for supporting the deck.

Deck Bridge – The piece of decking between the cockpit and companionway entrance.

Deck Fill – A metal deck fitting with screwdriver top through which water and fuel can be let to the tanks below.

Deck Pipe – A metal deck fitting through which chain is fed below.

Displacement – A very close estimate of the vessel's weight.

Dolfinite – A very oily bedding compound.

Downhaul – A line used to pull down sails. Commonly used in reference to a moveable gooseneck on tracks.

Draft – The vertical distance from the waterline to the lowest point of the keel.

Drops – General wood doors below bench cushions as access to stowage below.

D-Shackle – A "D" shaped shackle with threaded pin.

Echo Sounder – A fathometer.

Elbow Catch – A spring loaded catch for cabinet doors, usually hidden and accessible through a finger hole.

Engine Pan – A fiberglass molding bonded to the hull that catches engine oil.

Eye – A closed loop in wire rope or line.

Eyeband – A fitting on the tip of the bowsprit to which the forestay, bobstay and whiskerstays are attached.

Eyebolt – A bolt with an open loop for a head.

Eyelets – Brass loops sewn into sails for reef points.

Fairlead – A fitting that alters the direction of a line to keep it from fouling.

Fathom – Six feet of measure.

Feather – The art of bring a board of plank to a fine edge.

Fender – A bumper or rubber guard hung from the boat's sides.

Fiddles – Wood or metal guardrails along the counters, stove, or table.

Flare – The out curve of a vessel's side. To widen or ream the end of a pipe for coupling purposes.

Foot – The bottom edge of a sail.

Footpump – A water pump operated by foot.

Forecastle – The forward-most compartment where the crew is berth.

Forestay – The forward most stay supporting the rigging.

Freeboard – The vertical distance from the waterline to the sheer or gunwale.

Galley – The boat's kitchen.

Gallows – Holds the boom in place when not in use.

Gel coat – A very hard outer coating of a fiberglass boat.

Genoa – A headsail that is much larger than a jib.

Gimbals – A swivel arrangement by which stoves, tables and compasses are allowed to remain level.

Gooseneck – A swivel fitting that holds the boom onto the mast.

Grabrail – A handrail on the deck or inside the boat.

Grommet – A brass eye sewn into a sail.

Gudgeon – A hull fitting into which the pintle of the rudder fits.

Gypsy – A windlass notched for chain.

Halyard – Lines used for hoisting sails.

Halyard Winches – Winches with a drum for wire rope or standard rope used to hoist a sail.

Hank – The attaching clip of a sail that holds it to the stay but allows it to slide up and down.

Hatch – An opening in the deck for passage of cargo or people.

Hatch Coming – The built up area around a hatch to keep the water out.

Hatch Cover – A cover for the hatch.

Head – The toilet of a boat.

Headsail – A sail forward of the mast such as a jib, genoa, or staysail.

Helm – The tiller or steering wheel.

Hobby Horse – The pitching of the bow and stern about the center of the boat.

Inboard – Toward the centerline of the boat.

Inermediates – Stays that support the mast at a point between the spreaders and the masthead.

Jack Stays – Spreaders at the upper most of the mast.

Jam Cleats – A small cleat with that will jam the lines.

Jib – The foremost headsail.

Jib – flying – A jib set high on the forestay.

Jib – yankee – A jib with a high foot cut.

Jiffy Reefing – A method that quickly hauls the sail down for reefing.

Keel – The lowest part of a boat that runs fore and aft or sten to stern.

Ketch – A twin-mast sailboat with the mizzen mast forward of the stern post or rudder.

King Plank – The central plank of a deck.

Knot – A speed rating in knots per hours. One knot equals 6,080 feet.

Knotmeter – A boat's speedometer.

Lazarette – A stowage compartment in the aftmost section of a boat.

Lead-Fish – Lead in the shape of a fish hung over the side on steel line used as a sacrificial metal to prevent electrolysis.

Lead Pig – Small lead castings used for ballast.

Leeboard – Canvas or plywood board used to keep a person in his bunk in rough weather.

Leech – The aft edge of the sail.

Leeway – The sideway movement of the boat.

Lifelines – The lines attached to stanchions along the toe rail of a boat, generally in the area of 36 inches high.

Limber Holes – Holes in the bulkhead that allow drainage from on compartment to the next.

LOA – Length Over All from stem to stern, overhangs from the stem or stern not included.

Locker – A storage compartment.

Log – A mechanical device that records the distance the ship has moved relative to the water.

Log Book – A book kept by the captain to record weather, position and distance traveled.

Lubber Line – The mark on the compass corresponding to the center line of the boat.

Luff – The forward most edge of the sail.

LWL – The length at the water line.

Mainsail – The sail attached to the main mast, generally the largest of the working sails.

Make Fast – To secure or attach a line.

Mast Head – The top of the mast.

Mast Step – A fitting on the deck or below onto which the foot of the mast if fitted.

Mizzen – A sail attached to the mizzen mast.

Mizzen Mast – The aft mast on a yawl or ketch rig.

Mooring Cleat – A large deck cleat to which mooring lines are attached.

Negative Roach – A mainsail with no battens and a straight cut leech.

Non-Skid – A high friction surface for deck and cockpit sole.

Out Board – Away from the center line of the boat.

Outhaul – The gear used to tighten the foot of the sail along the boom.

Overhang – The bow or stern that hangs over the water line of the boat.

Pad Eye – A through bolted deck fitting to accommodate blocks, lines, etc.

Pennant – A short length of wire to which headsails are attached.

Pet Cock – A small ninety degree turn off-on valve.

Pilot Berth – A small elevated berth above a standard berth.

Pinrail – A rack that houses belaying pins.

Pitch – A sticky wood resin.

Plug – A wood dowel used to plug a thru hull fitting.

Poop – An overtaking sea swamping the aft deck and/or the cockpit.

Port – The left side of the boat facing forward.

Portlight – A small cabin side lite or window.

Preventer – A block and tackle rigged to prevent the boom from moving.

Pull Ring – Flush fitting swivel ring used to lift a hatch.

Purchase – Lines and block used to gain a mechanical advantage.

Quarter Berth – An aft berth located near the navigation station.

Quarters – An area reserved for a crew member.

Railstripe – A color line along the sheer.

Rake – Fore and aft inclination of the mast or stern post.

Ratlines – Horizontal ropes or strips of wood between shrouds forming a ladder.

Rat Tail – Faired or feathered rope end.

Reef – To shorten sail.

Reef Points – Grommets or ties for shortening sail.

Roach – The outward curve of the leech, added to increase sail area.

Rope Tail – The rope end of a wire halyard.

Rubrail – A bumper rail along the rise following the sheer.

Run – To sail before the wind or sailing with the wind.

Running Rigging – All moveable rigging such as sheets, lines and halyards.

Sail Track – A track on the mast or boom into which the sail slides are fitted.

Salon – The main living area in the vessel.

Samson Post – A strong post in the foredeck used as a hitch post for the anchor line or mooring line.

Schooner – A sailboat with the main mast taller and aft of the foremast.

Scupper – An opening in the toerail or gunwale allowing drainage.

Seacock – A through hull fitting in the bilge.

Seakindly – A vessel having characteristics that respond well to any sea.

Set Sail – To hoist a sail

Single Side Band – A short wave radio used for long distance communication by vessels.

Shaft Log – A bearing supporting a fitting guiding the screw shaft through the hull.

Shank – The shaft of the anchor.

Sheer – The curve of the gunwale from stem to stern.

Sheet – A rope or line for trimming the sail.

Shroud – Wire or solid rod rigging holding up the mast for athwartship support.

Slab Reefing – A reefing system that takes in slabs of sail.

Slides – Metal fittings on a sail that slides into the sail track.

Sloop – A single mast sailboat with a single head sail.

Snap Shackle – A shackle with a sliding closer.

Sole – The cabin floor.

Sole Timber – Sole supporting beams.

Spinnaker Car – A moveable fitting that attaches to the spinnaker pole and the spinnaker track that is on the mast.

Spinnaker Pole – A light spar that keeps the clew of the spinnaker outboard.

Spinnaker Track – A track attached to the mast over which the spinnaker car will slide.

Spreader – A strut on the mast attached to the shroud giving rigidity to the rigging.

Stanchions – Stainless steel posts attached to the deck or toe-rail supporting the lifelines.

Standing Rigging – Rigging supporting the mast that is not moveable.

Starboard – The right side of a vessel facing forward.

Stay – Wire rigging supporting the mast fore and aft.

Staysail – A jib like sail hanked onto one of the forestays.

Staysail Pedestal – A deck mounted fitting to support the staysail boom.

Steamer – A ship run on steam. Still used today regardless of means of propulsion.

Stops – Moveable fittings on a track the keep a block in place.

Storm Jib – A very small jib made of heavy material for heavy weather sailing.

Storm Trysail – A very small mainsail of heavy material for heavy weather sailing.

Stuffing Box – A fitting where the shaft goes through the hull to prevent water from entering.

Sump – The lowest point in the boat where water collects.

Swedge – The method of pressure fitting hardware to the end of a wire rope.

Tabernacle – A large deck bracket that houses the foot of the mast and the pin that allows it to be lowered onto the deck.

Tack – The lower forward corner of a sail.

Taffrail – A rail around the stern.

Tang – A metal fitting on a mast or hull to which rigging is attached.

Tender – A sailboat that does not stand up well to heavy weather.

Tender – A power launch used on large vessels.

Tiller – A steering handle attached to the rudder.

Toggle – A swivel fork uniting the turnbuckle to the chainplate.

Topping Lift – A line from the masthead supporting the aft end of the boom.

Transducer – A fathometer through hull fitting.

Transom – The flat stern of a boat from the waterline to the toe-rail.

Traveller – A moveable attachment that allows control over movement of the boom.

Tumble-Home -The inward curve along the sheer line of some vessels at midships to aft.

Turnbuckle – An adjustable fitting with threads to take up on rigging.

Upper Shroud – A shroud that is attached to the masthead to give athwartships (sideways) support to the masthead.

Vang – A block and tackle or solid metal hardware to keep the boom from lifting.

Vented Loop – A bronze fitting with a valve that prevents siphoning of water into appliances below the waterline.

VHF – Very High Frequency, a type of radio use by boaters for short range communication.

Waterline – A painted stripe from stem to stern located at the designed displacement.

Whiskerstay – Standing rigging which prevents athwartships movement of bowsprit or boomkin.

Wench – A mechanical aid made up of a drum and gears to aid in hoisting and trimming the sails.

Winch Pad – A wood or metal pad serving as a base for the wench.

Windlass – A winch to haul up the anchor rode, chain and anchor.

Yankee Jib – A high cut jib between the size of a working jib and a genoa.

Yaw – Falling off the wind or changing course from side to side.

Yawl – A double mast rig with the mizzen mast being stepped aft of the sternpost.